a340116

Praise for

The Sca...

"A potboiler of homicide, blac... sex—but one that St. James ... verve. *The Scarlet Pepper* ful... series debut, *Flowerbed of State*... then some."

—*Richmond Times-Dispatch*

"I'd been eagerly awaiting this sequel to *Flowerbed of State*, and am happy to report that it was well worth the wait. Casey is a smart character, and the setting of the White House and grounds is exciting. In fact, my heart was beating a little fast during the action-packed prologue; and the book got better from there."

—*MyShelf.com*

"The second White House Gardener Mystery . . . is a fabulous amateur sleuth starring a likable woman with commitment issues except when it comes to her passion, plants . . . Fans will enjoy this entertaining whodunit enhanced by the eccentric people who diligently work at the White House."

—*Genre Go Round Reviews*

Flowerbed of State

"This spunky new romantic suspense series is an obvious pick for readers who enjoy Julie Hyzy's White House Chef series (*Buffalo West Wing*), but also think of gardening mystery series such as Rosemary Harris's (*Slugfest*)."

—*Library Journal*

"Credible characters, a fast-paced plot, and a light look at political life in Washington, D.C., will delight cozy fans."

—*Publishers Weekly*

"[A] delightful debut mystery . . . Just the ticket for all us flustered and withered gardeners . . . Fans of cozy mysteries will adore this new series, and are sure to find themselves anxious for the next installment!"

—*Fresh Fiction*

Oak and Dagger

DOROTHY ST. JAMES

BERKLEY PRIME CRIME, NEW YORK

THE BERKLEY PUBLISHING GROUP
Published by the Penguin Group
Penguin Group (USA) Inc.
375 Hudson Street, New York, New York 10014, USA

USA / Canada / UK / Ireland / Australia / New Zealand / India / South Africa / China

Penguin Books Ltd., Registered Offices: 80 Strand, London WC2R 0RL, England
For more information about the Penguin Group, visit penguin.com.

OAK AND DAGGER

A Berkley Prime Crime Book / published by arrangement with Tekno Books

Berkley Prime Crime Books are published by The Berkley Publishing Group.
BERKLEY® PRIME CRIME and the PRIME CRIME logo
are trademarks of Penguin Group (USA) Inc.

For information, address: The Berkley Publishing Group,
a division of Penguin Group (USA) Inc.,
375 Hudson Street, New York, New York 10014.

ISBN: 978-0-425-25203-1

PUBLISHING HISTORY
Berkley Prime Crime mass-market edition / April 2013

PRINTED IN THE UNITED STATES OF AMERICA

10 9 8 7 6 5 4 3 2 1

Cover illustration by Mary Ann Lasher.
Cover design by Olivia Andreas.
Interior design by Kristin del Rosario.

For Jim . . . the love of my life and my partner in crime.

Acknowledgments

One day last spring my eight-year-old niece, Katie, turned to me and asked, "Can I be a character in your book?" I told her I'd have to think about it and then asked her if she wanted to be a good character or a bad character. She said—well, I'll let you find out how she answered that question yourself. Thank you, Katie, and the rest of my family, for your support and inspiration. If not for you, I wouldn't spend so much time thinking about ways to kill off characters. (Kidding!)

While writing this series, I always have tons of gardening questions. Most of the time, I can find the answers in one of my many research books. But from time to time I get stuck. That happened in this book. Luckily, Amy Dabbs, the Tri-County Master Gardener Coordinator, and Master Gardener Marcia Rosenberg helped me figure out over lunch one day what the heck Casey was doing in the fall gardens and how her work could relate back to my plot.

As always, enormous thanks go to Brittiany Koren for offering me the chance to bring Casey Calhoun to the pages of this book. Brittiany kept me going and made sure I didn't let the plot go too far astray. A big thank-you goes to Michael Koren for his understanding and patience for all those times Brittiany locked herself away in her office in order to help me hash out all the details.

Last but not least, I must thank the incredible authors in

the Lowcountry Chapter of Romance Writers of America, Sisters in Crime, and Mystery Writers of America, who patiently listened to me whine, patted my head, and told me to keep writing. Once again, I couldn't have done it without you!

Prologue

*And now, dear sister, I must leave this house or the
retreating army will make me a prisoner in it by
filling up the road I am directed to take.*

—DOLLEY TODD MADISON, FIRST LADY
OF THE UNITED STATES (1809–1817)

August 24, 1814

THUNDER rumbled in the distance. Or had the roar
of cannon fire started up again? Thomas McGraw,
White House gardener, told himself it was thunder. The
resumption of cannon fire would mean the British were
already practically on the city's doorstep.

His heart beat hard in his chest as he took the narrow
staircase two steps at a time. He'd been told to hurry. Time
had run out. Soon, the danger would be inescapable. Upon
reaching the top landing, he threw open a heavy wooden
door and rushed out onto the roof of the grand house.

Many in the city called this home simply the White
House. But not Thomas. To him, it was the Presidential Palace, as elegant as any grand palace in Europe. Although
Thomas had never traveled across the Atlantic, he knew his
fledgling country needed this house—an impressive mansion to stand as a symbol for the nation, to prove the

American people were capable of governing and providing for themselves.

This was especially true now. An unmistakable explosion of cannon fire shook the building, knocking him off balance.

Every day the British Redcoats marched ever closer. Now they were on the verge of taking not only the city, but also the country's seat of power. What would happen to the gardens and the grounds then? It had been difficult enough to keep the flowerbeds lush and healthy with all this heat and three weeks with no rain. Thomas had spent hours hauling buckets of water up from the Potomac just to keep the roses alive. And for what purpose? To have the President's garden trampled under the heavy boots of British soldiers?

His jaw tightened as he charged across the roof. The acrid scent of gunpowder hung heavy in the city's air. Its bitter flavor filled his mouth.

Through a red cloud of dust kicked up from the mass exodus from the city, Thomas spotted the lady he'd been sent to find. Dolley Madison's pale blue silk skirts rustled in the dusty breeze. She was leaning farther over the roof's parapet wall than Thomas thought wise.

The White House's very proper, very *French*, majordomo stood silently at Mrs. Madison's side as she peered through a copper spyglass. "French John" Sioussat ran his gloved hand along the rim of his top hat, which was nearly as shiny as his tall boots. Thomas called out to the two of them, but a sharp percussion of cannon fire completely drowned out his words.

"After you leave, I could spike a cannon at the gate," French John's voice boomed in the sudden silence. John's affection showed for the Lady Presidentress in the way his sober expression softened whenever he spoke with her.

Dolley didn't seem to notice. Her gaze remained fixed as she scanned the crowds of fleeing Washingtonians, watching for her husband's return.

"The cannon will blow the British clear out of the city should they dare step foot into your home," French John continued.

"Good gracious, no, Mr. Sioussat." Dolley lowered the spyglass. "We have already spoken of this."

"This is war," the Frenchman pointed out.

"Even more reason we mustn't forget that we're a civilized people. Besides, I'm not going anywhere before James returns."

For a second time, Thomas called out to the President's wife and the White House's doorkeeper. This time they heard him. He dragged his tweed cap off his head as they both turned toward him.

"M-Mrs. Madison," Thomas stammered. He hated being the bearer of bad news, but the situation had turned dire indeed. "Mr. Madison has sent a messenger." He swallowed another mouthful of foul air. "The British forces are on the verge of overtaking the capital. Everyone is being told to flee."

He watched the Lady Presidentress closely for signs she would break down or, worse, argue. Throughout the day she'd ignored her friends' and government officials' pleadings that she needed to make her escape.

But she was determined to wait for her husband's return.

However strongly she felt about the matter, though, Dolley must have realized for herself the time to abandon the capital city had come. She nodded and stiffened her spine as she slid the spyglass closed.

"Who brought this message?" she asked.

"James Smith," Thomas replied. Two days ago, Mr. Smith, a free Black man whom Thomas trusted with his life, had accompanied the President to the battlefield at Bladensburg. "He is downstairs, if you wish to question him."

With a nod, Dolley hastened toward the door that led back into the house. "We must hurry," she said. "There is still much to be done."

French John, with his long stride, followed closely

behind her. Thomas remained on the roof wringing his
hands, staring down at the lawn, and worrying about the
future of his garden, and of the nation he loved.

"Come along, Thomas," French John called as he poked
his head back through the door. He clapped just as cannon
fire made the building jump. "There's no time to dawdle."

Thomas joined Dolley in the State Dining Room just as
Mr. Smith, the President's messenger, concluded his report,
"Our army has failed in Bladensburg. Washington is next
to fall."

The news reenergized Dolley's acquaintances as they
urged her to go. A carriage was already waiting outside to
whisk her to safety.

Earlier in the day Dolley had emptied the government
offices, packing state treasures and important documents
in trunks meant for her own personal belongings. But as
she'd packed, she remained steadfast in her faith that her
husband would succeed. Even going as far as to push forward with preparations for a dinner to feed and entertain
over forty guests that evening.

Thomas watched in amazement as the determined lady
now scurried around the already set tables. She scooped up
the expensive silverware and stuffed it into her large reticule. Before she'd completed the task, she paused at the portrait of George Washington and frowned. "Save that picture!
Save that picture if possible. If not, destroy it!" she ordered.

French John snapped to action. "Fetch us a ladder,
Thomas."

Thomas did as he was told. The two men worked together,
while Dolley watched and her husband's friend, Charles
Carroll, paced as he grew more and more impatient.

The nearby cannon fire made the walls tremble as if the
building feared its grim future. The chandelier above their
heads tinkled like a wind chime as plaster rained down on
their heads.

Dolley needed to get as far away from this cursed place
as possible. She was running out of time. They all were.

"The frame is screwed to the wall." Thomas tugged,

desperate to rip the screws from the plaster. But no matter what he did, the frame would not budge.

French John and Thomas exchanged dark glances before cracking the gilded frame open and prying the canvas free.

"Now, please God, let me take you to safety," Charles Carroll implored. He sounded like a man on the verge of tossing the Lady Presidentress over his shoulder and hauling her, kicking and screaming, to safety.

Dolley's gaze traveled over the room as if memorizing its details before nodding. "I'm ready," she whispered.

The war rumbled ever louder and weighted the air within the room with its heavy smoke. Thomas wiped his eyes as he followed the brave lady down the steps and out to her waiting carriage. He prayed she hadn't waited too long.

She accepted French John's proffered hand and put her foot on the carriage step. The silverware in her reticule clanked when she suddenly pulled away from her doorman's grasp.

"Mr. Jefferson's treasure! Where is it? I didn't see it being loaded onto any of the carriages." She started back toward the house.

A burst of cannon fire roared. The ground quaked beneath their feet.

"We must go," Charles Carroll shouted. He grabbed her arm. "If you don't leave now, you'll fall into the hands of the enemy. You would make a better prize than anything Jefferson could have stashed within those walls."

"It's irreplaceable." Dolley tugged at the arm holding her.

Thomas rushed to her side. "I won't let the British bastards touch it." They might trample his plants, but by God, he wasn't going to let them have anything else. "I'll guard Mr. Jefferson's treasure with my life."

"Do you know where to find it, Thomas?" she asked.

"Aye, I know."

"We must go, Dolley," Charles Carroll urged.

Another cannon blast punched through the air.

"Very well." She climbed into the carriage. "Carry out

this task with the greatest of care, Thomas. The nation's future could very well rest in your hands."

Thomas, true to his word, hurried back inside and found Jefferson's polished wooden casket. It had been half-buried under a stack of crates that hadn't fit on any of the carriages.

It was too late to escape Washington on foot. And too dangerous. Hugging the heavy box to his chest, Thomas hurried away from the house and into the gardens he'd come to love so dearly.

With his expression set in a grave line, he took a shovel and started to dig.

Chapter One

*If life were predictable it would cease to be life,
and be without flavor.*
—ELEANOR ROOSEVELT, FIRST LADY OF
THE UNITED STATES (1933–1945)

Present Day

A dozen inky black starlings in the nearby oak trees craned forward as they twisted their heads left then right in that jerky motion birds make when trying to unscramble some unfathomable puzzle. I agreed with the birds. I might only be an assistant gardener with less than a year's experience working at the White House, but even I knew this wasn't how an official tree planting should happen. That's why the activity unfolding on the lawn in front of me made me shake my head with consternation.

"*Casey Calhoun*"—Grandmother Faye Calhoun would scold and wag her gnarled finger if she could see me now—"*I didn't raise you to stand around like a lazy peach.*" I still had no earthly idea why my grandmother thought peaches are lazy, but she was right—I'd been raised to work, not stand idle while others did my job. So why was the shovel in the President's hands, when the entire gardening staff was standing on the sidelines with our more than capable hands stuffed in our pockets?

President Bradley, a tall handsome man with a charismatic presence and a full head of brown hair, posed as he flashed his trademark smile for the cameras before thrusting his shovel into the South Lawn's rich soil.

Let me repeat that last part in case you missed it. The *President of the United States* had thrust a shovel into the ground!

Don't get me wrong. It's no skin off my nose if the President wanted a pair of commemorative trees planted. What had me quaking in my leather loafers was the fact that the President had *insisted* on *planting* the trees *himself.*

From digging the holes to dropping the root balls into the ground, President Bradley had insisted on doing it all. Well, not exactly all of it. I'd ordered the trees from our preapproved nursery and had selected the planting site. But when it came to the grunt work, he had insisted on taking over.

The President's large, farm-bred hands wrapped around the red handle of the slightly rusty shovel he'd personally selected from the gardener's shed. No golden commemorative shovel would be used today.

"In honor of dedicated fathers across the country, I plant a pair of little-leaf lindens. I plant these trees in thanksgiving for my twin sons." President Bradley's voice boomed across the South Lawn while a small army of photographers snapped pictures from behind a roped-off partition line.

"Speaking of Thanksgiving, Casey," Gordon Sims, the silver-haired White House chief horticulturist, standing beside me, whispered as if nothing odd were happening on the lawn in front of us, "Deloris and I would love for you to join us at our Thanksgiving feast this year."

"Hm? Thanksgiving?" I whispered back, unable to tear my gaze off the President. "Oh, you know I'd love to, Gordon, but I need to go home to Rosebrook. My grandmother and aunts have been calling daily about it."

The early morning sun was rising above the White

House's iconic round South Portico. With the grand home's stately columns in the background reflecting a soft pearly white, and President Bradley dressed in jeans and a flannel shirt with the sleeves rolled up to his elbows, the photos would probably become a defining picture of his presidency . . . as long as President Bradley managed to dig the pair of holes without any trouble.

A prickle of unease worried the back of my neck.

"I should have predug the holes," I whispered to Gordon.

"If you had, Bradley would have noticed. The press would have noticed," Gordon whispered back.

I don't know how Gordon could stand there looking so calm. So many things could go wrong. The President could hit a root. He could pull a muscle. It could start raining.

I studied a particularly worrisome line of dark clouds on the horizon. The weather reports had called for an afternoon storm. A chilly fall breeze swirled around us, signaling a cold front was threatening to move through the area several hours earlier than predicted.

"He should have at least let you serve as his right-hand man. It's tradition," I pointed out.

Gordon put a steadying hand on my shoulder. "It's okay, Casey. President Bradley wants to plant his children's trees, not just throw a shovel of dirt at them. It's our job to give him what he wants."

"Even so . . ." I dug my teeth into my bottom lip as the President removed his first chunk of soil.

"He needs to do this," Gordon said. "The poor man."

A month and a half ago, First Lady Margaret Bradley had given birth to a pair of tiny baby boys. Neither the pregnancy nor the birth had been very easy on her or the babies. Whispers on the backstairs continued to warn that the three of them were still frightfully weak.

And the new father, President Bradley . . .

His troubles were more numerous than ever. The economy was still struggling. Clashes in foreign lands had the military strained to the point of breaking. And gas prices were heading up again.

Bradley's advisors, all wearing black suits today, had lined up in the same way the starlings had on the branches in the tree. They tilted their heads in just about the same way, too, as they checked their cell phones. Only his press secretary, who was a new father himself, appeared content to watch the leader of the free world spend the morning digging a couple of holes in the South Lawn.

The President's strong features strained with each thrust of the shovel. An odd tightness squeezed my chest as I witnessed the grief of a man who clearly loved his wife and his children. Here was one of the most powerful of men, and he couldn't make his wife strong again. He couldn't make his newborn sons healthy. All he could do was dig that blasted hole.

Gordon was right. Who was I to take that away from him?

Even the press seemed to sense they were watching something extraordinary and remained unusually subdued.

"If anything goes wrong, Casey"—Lorenzo Parisi, Gordon's assistant for the past nine years, sent a sly look in my direction—"you'll get the blame for not talking Bradley out of this."

"I know. I know." I clutched my sweaty hands behind my back and bounced anxiously on the balls of my feet, praying for clear skies and easy digging.

Lorenzo was a tall man with dark Mediterranean looks. For the event he'd worn a modern-cut black Italian suit. Not real sensible if he was called on to help with the tree planting. But that was Lorenzo. He rarely wore anything sensible. Gordon and I looked like gardeners with our khaki pants, pullover shirts, and dark blue windbreakers with the White House logo stitched in white thread on the front.

Lorenzo pointed to the same ominous clouds I'd spotted earlier. "He could get struck by lightning."

Gordon shushed us.

"Should I tell Deloris you'll be joining us for Thanksgiving again this year?" Gordon asked Lorenzo. Lorenzo's family lived in California, and he rarely visited them. "She's baking your favorite sweet potato pie."

"Of course *I'll* be there," Lorenzo said. "I would never miss a family gathering."

While Lorenzo preened about how he'd attended many, many family events with Gordon, a movement at the far end of the East Wing caught Gordon's attention. "What is the Wicked Witch of the East doing out here?" Gordon grumbled.

"Who?" I squinted into the sunlight but only spotted bushes, trees, and a few staffers.

"Frida." Lorenzo nodded toward the squat woman lumbering in a crooked line toward us.

"The curator?" Frida Collinsworth was the White House's curator and seemed to keep to herself in the curator's office. She had a keen eye and a sharp mind for finding historical treasures in the White House storehouses. What she didn't have was sharp vision. The thick glasses perched at the edge of her nose seemed to tilt the plum-shaped woman slightly forward.

"She stopped by the grounds office this morning when you were out preparing for the planting," Lorenzo explained while Gordon continued to grumble underneath his breath. "Words were exchanged."

"Really? Gordon gets along with everyone," I said.

"I've never known *Frida* to get along with anyone," Lorenzo said. "But in the nine years I've worked here, I've never seen her as angry as I did this morning."

Gordon bared his teeth as Frida moved closer. The two had been working together on a Historic Plants of the White House exhibition with the National Arboretum. It was one of the First Lady's pet projects.

I'd been helping by researching the varieties of vegetable plants grown in the White House kitchen gardens during the office's early years so we could plant a founding fathers' kitchen garden in the spring.

"Frida accused Gordon of theft," Lorenzo whispered.

"Theft? Gordon? When?"

"She came in ranting and raving I'd stolen her research and notes she'd been compiling on Dolley Madison. Like

I'd be able to find anything in that office of hers. The place is as disorganized as your desk," Gordon said.

"My desk isn't *that* bad," I protested. Both Gordon and Lorenzo laughed, acting as if that were the funniest thing they'd ever heard.

I shushed them.

We were standing far enough away from the press and the President that there was no danger any of the reporters might accidentally overhear our conversation. Or might accidentally snap our picture. The first rule for White House staff was to keep out of the photos.

The second rule was to always act in a dignified manner.

While Gordon and Lorenzo wiped their goofy grins off their faces, Frida spotted the three of us. She wagged her finger at Gordon and then pointed to her watch.

"Look, the bat's trying to hex us," Gordon said.

"She's scheduled a meeting with the chief usher to discuss the so-called theft," Lorenzo clarified.

"Discuss, my foot." Gordon narrowed his gaze as he turned back to watch the President thrust the shovel into the ground again. "She wants to ruin me."

"Ambrose will put her in her place," I said. The chief usher had a firm rule against drama of any sort from the household staff.

"I don't know what will happen. This battle has been brewing for a long time," was all Gordon would say about it. After a few moments he added, "But if the Wicked Witch of the East thinks she can scare me, she can get on her broom and fly it up her—"

"*Gordon!*" I gasped.

He smiled.

It wasn't a friendly smile, and it seemed to warn even half-blind Frida to keep her distance.

I was still wondering about Frida's out-of-character behavior when President Bradley stopped digging. He leaned on his shovel. "The planting of commemorative trees has a long history," he said, "dating back to the 1830s when Andrew Jackson planted a pair of Southern magnolias in honor of his late wife, who tragically didn't survive long enough to see him take office."

"I know for a fact Andrew Jackson didn't personally plant those trees," I whispered to Gordon. Extra shovels were tucked discreetly behind some nearby boxwoods. Gordon, Lorenzo, and I were ready to lend a helping hand at a moment's notice.

When Gordon had suggested I take the lead in planning today's event, which had included picking out the planting site and coordinating with the Secret Service and the press secretary, I'd eagerly agreed and had pictured turning the event into a "teaching moment" for instructing the public on the correct way to plant a tree. So many people did it wrong.

Doing as much prep work as the President would allow, I'd removed the thick carpet of tall fescue grass and had marked how wide the two holes needed to be dug. I'd explained to him the holes needed to be deep enough to just cover the root ball.

To save President Bradley's back, we'd selected tree specimens that were barely six feet tall. Even so, the proper size of the holes for the trees was as deep as the root balls, and at least twice their width. A wider hole would have been better, but since the President was personally doing the digging, I went for the minimum recommended size.

It was the *depth* of the hole that was critical.

If the holes were too shallow, the roots would dry out and die. If the holes were too deep, the roots would be smothered.

Digging the holes was a task the gardening staff should have been allowed to perform. It was, after all, our job. If the trees died, we would be the ones to take the blame.

"I suppose I could sneak in at night and replant the trees if I need to," I mumbled to myself.

"Margaret carried my sons at no small cost to her health," President Bradley stopped digging to tell the reporters. "I told her and everyone else, 'I'm going to plant these trees.'" He drew a ragged breath. "It's the least I can do."

His gaze traveled over to me as he added, "And we're going to care for these trees without the use of chemical fertilizers or pesticides."

I nodded. The First Lady had personally hired me last year to implement the White House's first all-organic gardening program. She'd been pregnant at the time and had been looking to make the White House as safe a place for her new babies as possible.

President Bradley thrust the shovel into the ground again. "If you get bored, feel free to leave at any time. This might take a while."

"It will if he continues to give a speech between each shovelful of dirt removed," Lorenzo whispered in my ear.

I'd started to bat Lorenzo and his unhelpful comments away when the President's shovel hit something that clanked.

Frowning, I took a step forward. Gordon and Lorenzo followed.

"Nothing should clank there," I said. I'd studied the plans for the grounds well enough to know that.

Gordon took another step forward as he grimaced. "Mr. President," he called, "John, don't—"

With a determined look, President Bradley thrust his shovel back into the hole with greater force than before.

A low rumble shook the ground.

The three of us started to run toward the hole just as it exploded in the President's face.

Chapter Two

※ 🏛 ※

*Learning is not attained by chance, it must
be sought for with ardor and diligence.*
—ABIGAIL ADAMS, FIRST LADY OF
THE UNITED STATES (1797–1801)

MUD and water shot at least ten feet into the air from
the hole. I hooked my arm with President Bradley's
and pulled him away from the gushing geyser. Bradley's
Secret Service detail grabbed for him as well. One burly
agent knocked me to the ground and stepped on my hand
as the protective team converged like a tight cocoon around
the President. Moving as one undulating mass, they ushered him into a sleek black van and sped away.

Taking their cue from the President, Bradley's staffers
herded the soaked press back up the hill toward the White
House.

Nearly everybody who'd come out to watch the show
was slowly returning to their duties, but not Frida. She
stood at the edge of the lawn and squinted at us from behind
her thick glasses. Her lips were pulled into a grin that took
up most of her round face. She looked happier than a puppy
with two tails.

Gordon had noticed her, too. His fingers curled into a
pair of tight fists. He ground his jaw as he glared at her.

Her behavior was intolerable.

Every member of the White House staff was on the same team. We were supposed to do our jobs with pride and help one another. I had a mind to march over and wipe that oversized smirk off Frida's thin lips.

But I didn't have time. Lorenzo had already set to work moving the young little-leaf linden trees out of the damaging water spray. Gordon and I scrambled toward the nearest shutoff valve for the irrigation system as water rained down on our heads, soaking us with icy cold spray.

Gordon flipped the lid off the water box, but without the help of a wrench, neither of us could wrestle the corroded valve closed.

"Move over." A hard shoulder nudged me out of the way.

I looked up to find a warrior with short-cropped hair looming over me. Dressed in a black military uniform, dark sunglasses, and a menacing P-90 submachine gun slung across his chest, he looked like an assassin on a mission.

Good thing I knew he was one of the good guys. A member of the Secret Service's elite military Counter Assault Team—or CAT, as they liked to call themselves— he was one of the best of the best.

"*Jack*." My heart raced at the sight of him. Special Agent Jack Turner was my . . . my . . . Hell, I didn't know how to categorize our relationship. He made me nervous and happy and so very confused. I rarely knew what was going on in that head of his.

He grimaced at the stuck valve and then grabbed his P-90 submachine gun as if he were at a firing range and the valve was his target.

"W-What are you doing?" I demanded as I moved out of the way.

"Helping," he answered.

"Don't shoot it! That's not going to help."

One corner of his lips turned up. He shook his head as he spun the submachine gun around and used the butt of the P-90 as a lever to turn the valve.

The geyser sputtered and died.

"Shoot it? Oh, Casey . . ." He chuckled and slung his gun's strap over his shoulder again. His callused thumb gently brushed my cheek before he jogged back toward the rest of his team.

Gordon sat back on his heels and scratched his mud-splattered head. "I don't understand it. You checked for irrigation lines on the plans, didn't you?"

"Double-checked! Triple-checked!" I splashed through a puddle of water as I paced. "Out of all the things that could have gone wrong, this wasn't one of them, and this shouldn't have happened."

A few steps later, I tripped into a shallow hole and twisted my ankle. "Milo!" I cried. The President's overgrown puppy had recently taken to digging up the lawn.

Jack returned and watched me with a curious expression as I hopped on one foot and shook my throbbing ankle in frustration.

The rest of the team had joined him. "What's she doing?" Jack's buddy asked. "A rain dance?"

"I think so," Jack answered.

Jack and the other CAT agents offered to help us cordon off the President's muddy hole to keep anyone from stumbling into it. While they worked, we returned the tools and the trees to the utility shed that was hidden behind a canopy of trees on the west side of the South Lawn.

When we'd finished, I caught Jack's arm as we both shivered in the chilly fall air. Water dripped from my sodden bangs onto my nose. "Thank you for helping with the valve. What a disaster." I bit my lower lip and fitted my hand in his. "I'm glad you were here. I owe you."

An honest-to-God smile creased his lips. "Perhaps we can talk about payment later."

"Tonight?" I blushed like a schoolgirl. "What time?"

"Did I *say* tonight?" Jack's smile dropped as if it had never existed.

"You implied it." Although we saw each other several times a week at the White House, we'd only dated a hand-ful of times since I'd kissed him at the Fourth of July fireworks show. And he'd canceled our last two dates . . . at the last minute . . . and without a good explanation, which probably explained why everything about our relationship still felt new and uncertain and, well, terrifying.

"Casey?" Gordon called. "Are you coming? We need to figure out what happened here."

"Just a minute," I said, and then turned back to Jack. "Well, what's going on between us?"

"Go on." Jack gave me a little nudge with his shoulder. "We can talk about this later. I promise."

Since he always kept his promises, I relented. "Okay. Later."

Jack had played Watson to my Sherlock a couple of times this past year when I'd found myself in difficult situations. Although, if you were to ask him, he might say he was Ned Nickerson to my Nancy Drew, and then he'd make a remark about my perkiness just to get my blood boiling.

I am *not* perky.

Friendly? I'll admit I'm that. It's a Southern thing. My Southern-fried manners should never be mistaken for sugary perkiness, thank you very much.

Sure, I might have had a perky ringtone on my cell phone for a while this past summer. It was a mistake I had since remedied.

Kelly Clarkson's girl-power anthem, "Stronger," which celebrated Nietzsche's maxim "That which does not kill us makes us stronger," was my current ringtone of choice. Which reminded me . . . I pulled my phone from my pocket to switch the ringer back on. That's when I noticed that while the President had been digging his hole, a text message from a restricted number had come to my phone. The message was short and to the point.

Die.

THAT THREATENING TEXT MESSAGE ECHOED IN my mind like a bad special effect in a low-budget horror flick.

Die.

Die.

Die.

Who could have sent it?

I hadn't done anything recently, in several months actually, to merit a death threat. Even so, I rubbed my soggy arms to chase away the goose bumps that prickled my skin as Gordon, Lorenzo, and I sloshed back to the grounds offices.

Our offices were located underground, directly underneath the North Portico. Or as Lorenzo liked to say, in the bowels of the White House. Water dripped from our hair and the hems of our clothes onto the basement hallway's concrete floor. Our shoes squished with each step.

"This is your last chance, Gordon." Frida's shrill voice made me jump. She must have been lurking just inside the doorway, waiting for us.

Gordon passed her without a second glance. Undeterred, she followed. Her body swayed as her short legs struggled to keep up with Gordon's long stride.

Gordon picked up his pace.

Frida had to jog to keep up. "You won't like what I have to say to Ambrose."

"Why would you think Gordon would steal anything from you?" I asked.

"He wants to use my research to find Jefferson's treasure," she said, panting as she tried to catch up. "Isn't that it? You're hoping to upstage me. That's how you plan to get your revenge."

Gordon snorted at that.

"*Treasure?*" I asked.

Frida ignored me and instead wagged her finger at Gordon's back. "Don't you dare deny it, Gordon Sims. Just ask the First Lady's sister. She was the one who first noticed my research was missing. I bet you didn't realize how closely she's been working with *me* on the history project."

"She is? She's working with you?" I asked. That surprised me. Lettie Shaw had arrived two weeks ago to help

Margaret Bradley take care of the twins, only she'd spent most of that time in the grounds office. She'd rearranged my desk three times in an attempt to be helpful. Her attempts, unfortunately, hadn't been at all successful. Yesterday, it took me over an hour to find my to-do list. I'd finally found it filed under *D* for *Do*.

If Frida enjoyed working with her, the next time Lettie showed up, I planned to send her over to the curator's office.

"Of course Lettie prefers to work with me over Gordon," Frida crowed. "She's a university professor and is interested in the White House's history. We're kindred spirits, which makes Gordon jealous. He's always been jealous of the prestige the curator's office gets when all you get is"—her nose wrinkled as she looked us up and down—"muddy."

We'd reached the grounds office. Gordon grabbed my arm and yanked me inside.

"Go away, Frida," he snapped and slammed the office door in her face. He then stomped across the large room that served as storage space and office space that Lorenzo and I shared. With a huff, Gordon disappeared into his private office.

"Do we need to worry about her?" I asked Lorenzo since he'd been working for the White House for nearly nine years and knew the political landscape much better than I did.

Lorenzo looked at the closed grounds office door and then toward Gordon's office. "Frida's not someone you want as an enemy," Lorenzo said while I took a couple of towels out of my desk's bottom drawer. I tossed him one. "But Gordon knows what he's doing . . . I think."

"Of course I know what I'm doing," Gordon said as he emerged from his private office. He was using a small white terrycloth towel to dry his wet hair. "Now, let's figure out what happened out there with the irrigation line."

"What was she saying about a treasure?" I asked, unable to put the thought of digging up a box of glittering gold or jewels out of my mind. "Don't tell me she thinks Thomas Jefferson hid gold somewhere in the gardens."

Gordon stamped his wet shoes on the concrete floor, creating a small puddle underneath him. "I have no idea what she's talking about. She's always going on and on about finding so-called priceless artifacts here and there. She rarely makes any sense."

"I agree," Lorenzo said. "She's nuts."

"Exactly." Gordon draped the towel over his shoulder. "Now back to the matter at hand. Casey, what happened? How did you manage to locate the planting site over an irrigation line?"

"I don't know! I had selected the site because, according to my research, it was where Thomas Jefferson had originally planted an allée of little-leaf lindens along a carriage path." Gordon already knew this. He liked the idea of re-creating the historic planting one commemorative tree at a time. "I swear there wasn't anything on the schematic to indicate an irrigation line would be there." Even though I was wet and cold, I went straight to the large flat metal filing cabinet where the schematics and plans for the utilities in the gardens were kept and yanked open the drawer. The plans were right where I'd filed them.

Gordon took the schematic for the South Lawn and laid it out on Lorenzo's large wooden drafting table.

I pointed to the tiny pencil X-marks on the schematic I'd drawn to denote where, according to my research, Jefferson had planted the carriage path's allée of little-leaf lindens. "See. There are no irrigation lines indicated anywhere within the planting area."

"This schematic has to be thirty years old," Gordon said, studying the paper. "See here? And here? All of this predates the most recent upgrades to the irrigation system."

"It's the only schematic in the drawer," Lorenzo said after digging through the rest of the plans filed there.

"Are you sure you didn't misplace the current utility schematic?" Gordon asked. He glanced in the direction of my desk piled high with paperwork.

"Yes, I'm sure. I didn't lose anything." The large-scale and woefully out-of-date schematic seemed to be laughing at me from the drafting table. "That was the only one available."

"Are you sure?" Gordon asked again.

My heart quailed to see him frowning at me like that. My lovable supervisor had supported me time and again. Even when all the facts seemed to indicate I was wrong, he had stood up for me. I considered him more than a friend. He was fast becoming as dear to me as family. I loved him as a daughter should love her father. I didn't want to let him down. *But what could I say?*

I was disappointed in myself.

Not because I'd misfiled the schematic for the South Lawn, because I hadn't. It hadn't been there for my use. Perhaps Frida's rants weren't as crazy as we'd all thought.

What if there was a thief—or saboteur—in the White House?

Whoever had sent me that ominous "die" text message might have also taken the schematic in an effort to disrupt the President's commemorative tree planting.

"Yes, Gordon," I said, "you're looking at the only schematic I could find in that drawer."

"Ah, it's a mystery for you to solve." Gordon rubbed his hands together while an excited gleam brightened his blue eyes. "Perhaps I can join you on this caper."

I'd been a bad influence on him. He was starting to enjoy the trouble that seemed to find me. "I like my mysteries in fiction. Not in real life. I've turned over a new leaf, remember?"

"But we can call it the case of the missing paperwork," he said with a toothy grin. The grin faded as he observed my messy desk again.

I crossed the room and scooped up a pile of paperwork from my desk; not that it made a dent in the disorganization. It just made the papers in my arms as soggy as I was.

"With a little diligent work, I'm sure you'll figure out what happened." Gordon patted my arm. "You always do."

"I didn't lose it on my desk. I would have noticed a

large-scale plan in these piles when I was looking for my to-do list yesterday."

I dropped the soggy files and paced in front of the thirty-year-old schematic still spread out on Lorenzo's drafting table. What if there was a thief wandering the White House halls, and what if that thief had stolen the schematic for some nefarious purpose? If that was the case, then this was a matter for the professionals to be investigating, not the gardeners.

I reached for the grounds office's phone to report the possible theft. But just as I touched the phone's receiver, it pealed out an impatient ring.

I swallowed hard before picking up the receiver. "Hello?"

"Put Gordon Sims on," the man on the other end of the line barked without identifying himself or his office.

"It's for you." I held the phone out for Gordon.

After the short phone call ended, Gordon set the phone's receiver back into its cradle. He put his hand on my arm and gave a tender squeeze before announcing, "I'm wanted over at the West Wing."

He stared at the floor for a moment and then pulled off a shoe to wring water from one of his drenched socks into a small trash basket.

"Are you being blamed for Casey's mistake?" Lorenzo asked.

"Let's not start by placing blame." Gordon removed his other shoe and peeled off a second wet sock. "We'll get this straightened out."

"Don't you have time to change into dry clothes?" I asked. We all looked bedraggled and in dire need of a good blow dry.

"That irrigation line break will have already hit the national news cycle. Film footage of President Bradley getting thrown back by a spray of water must have made a spectacular video. The press would be foolish not to run with it, which means the press secretary will need to start answering questions like: What happened? Why did it happen?

Was it a breach in protocol? A security breach? Was the President at risk? They're important questions that need to be answered."

"Would you like me to go with you?" I asked. "It was my project. I should be the one to take the blame."

Gordon rubbed his damp hair with the towel again and seemed to consider my offer before he smiled. "Thank you, Casey, but no. Stay here and find that missing schematic."

"I didn't misplace it," I grumbled. "Someone must have walked off with it, stolen it even."

But Gordon didn't hear me. He'd already left.

"If Gordon loses his job"—Lorenzo jammed his finger in my face—"I will make sure everyone knows that you and your incompetence are to blame."

"Gee, thanks, Lorenzo, but I'm going to fix this." The back of my neck tightened. "Someone took that schematic. I feel it in my bones."

Lorenzo eyed my messy desk as if it were the proverbial smoking gun.

"I mean it. I only leave the unimportant paperwork in those piles."

"The purchase order for five tons of topsoil went missing for three weeks," he reminded me.

"Un-im-por-tant paper-work," I repeated, emphasizing each syllable. "The topsoil was delivered on time. I'm going to find out who took that schematic. You know *I* will."

"Not if I find it first." He started rifling through the papers scattered on my desk.

I didn't have the energy to stop him. Besides, maybe he'd make a few inroads in getting my desk organized. I picked up the phone and dialed the extension for the Secret Service's office.

The agent who'd answered couldn't understand why I was calling to report a missing schematic and had me repeat what I'd thought had happened several times. "I didn't misplace the schematic. It was stolen!" I finally shouted in exasperation.

She put me on hold.

A few minutes later two Secret Service agents, Steve Sallis and Janie Partners, appeared at the grounds office's doorway. I knew the two of them well. They often drew the short straw when it came to dealing with the gardeners. We seemed to have a reputation—*undeserved*—for being troublemakers.

Clashes between the grounds office and the Secret Service often occurred because the grounds office was required to coordinate all landscaping decisions with the Secret Service. If it were up to the Secret Service, all of the plantings would be mowed down. Bushes and trees provided hiding places and blocked an agent's line of sight.

Special Agent Steve Sallis stood at the door with his arms crossed. He was dressed in a black suit and had a black mood that matched, which was unusual for him. Not the suit, but the mood. I'd never known him to be stingy with his smiles.

Special Agent Janie Partners, who had a slight purple tinge to her chestnut-colored hair and wore a feminine black suit and a scarf with a batik golden oak leaf pattern, was also acting oddly subdued. She wrote fastidiously in a small notebook as I told them about Frida's claims of her research being stolen from her office. I then showed them where we kept the schematics and how the most recent one for the South Lawn was no longer there. While she seemed to be listening, I got the distinct feeling that neither Janie nor Steve really believed what I was telling them.

"Will everyone stop staring at my desk?"

"I understand your frustration," Janie said. She used the same tone the agents used with unruly tourists who wanted to jog across barricades or hang on the White House's iron fence to take silly pictures. "Why don't you look around a bit more and then call us back?" she advised with another nod toward my desk. "I'm sure the schematic will turn up."

For the first time in my life, I regretted my lack of interest in filing. And since Lorenzo had given up on digging through the piles of paperwork, after the agents left I changed into dry clothes and started the arduous task of organizing my desk myself.

I was halfway through the first stack when Gordon returned from the West Wing. Both Lorenzo and I jumped to our feet when we saw him. Our chief gardener looked positively ashen.

"What happened?" I asked with no small degree of alarm. I should have been the one to be raked across the coals. "What did they say to you? What did they do?"

Gordon shook his head. "Naturally, everyone on the President's staff is shouting right now. Images of the water exploding in Bradley's face are all over the news reports. Those news reports have spooked an envoy from the Republic of Turbekistan who was supposed to meet with the President this afternoon."

"Tur—where?" I asked.

"The Republic of Turbekistan. I know, Casey, I'd never heard of it, either. It's a small country in Eastern Europe that used to be part of the former Soviet Union." The lines on his face deepened. "The envoy has not only canceled this afternoon's meeting, he's gone into hiding. The West Wing is frantically trying to find and then reassure the envoy so they can reschedule."

"He went into hiding over a broken irrigation line? There must be something else going on," I said.

"Probably." Gordon crossed the room to study the out-of-date schematic.

"How important can talks be with a country no one has heard of?" I asked. "The meeting wasn't even listed on the President's schedule."

"Apparently, Turbekistan has recently discovered a large oil deposit, but they don't have the funds to build the infrastructure to extract the oil. And the leaders of Turbekistan don't trust the big oil corporations. So they're looking to partner with a country with deep pockets. In exchange for paying for the infrastructure, the U.S. will receive a sharp discount on the oil we purchase from them. I was told the negotiations with this envoy could make or break Bradley's presidency. The oil reserve is that large."

"The oil could be the boost to the economy this country desperately needs right now." Lorenzo glared at me again.

"That's true. And if the envoy doesn't feel safe, administration officials are worried he will take Turbekistan's oil and go negotiate with China," Gordon said.

"And if that happens?" I asked.

Gordon shrugged. When he wouldn't look in my direction, I suspected there was more to this story than what Gordon was telling us.

"If the envoy won't agree to reschedule the talks, what happens?" I asked again. "Will the grounds office be blamed? Will *you* be blamed?"

Gordon lifted his shoulders again in a shrug. "I'm sure it won't come to that."

"Hell no, it won't," Lorenzo said as he frowned at me.

"No, it won't," I agreed. "You're not going to lose your job because of a skittish envoy from some country out in the boondocks. I'm going to march over to the West Wing right now and tell President Bradley this was my fault." Sure, gardeners couldn't just waltz over to the Oval Office and chat with President Bradley, but I could try. "Or I could talk with the envoy, explain to him that what happened this morning was a mistake, an accident."

"No, Casey. You don't need to do anything. Let the West Wing handle the damage control. I'm sure, in time, it'll work out. I'm just tired." Gordon leaned his timeworn hands against Lorenzo's drafting table and lowered his head. "There's some pruning in the Children's Garden I've been putting off for too long already. I should try to get it done before I have to meet with Ambrose and explain to him that Frida's lost her freaking mind." He groaned. "I'm getting too old for this. I can only handle one fire at a time."

I wrapped my arms around him in a Southern-fried hug. "I'll make this right," I promised. "I swear I will."

"I'll make damn sure she does," Lorenzo added.

Chapter Three

*I've liked lots of people 'til I went on
a picnic jaunt with them.*
—BESS TRUMAN, FIRST LADY OF
THE UNITED STATES (1945–1953)

FEELING lower than a snake's belly, I vowed to myself I'd protect Gordon at all costs. He was not going to take the blame for my mistake.

If not for that darn missing schematic, I would have chosen a better location for the commemorative trees. The irrigation line wouldn't have broken. The envoy from Turbekistan wouldn't have canceled his meeting with the President. And Gordon wouldn't have looked so disappointed in me.

After a solid hour of sorting, filing, and tossing, the towers of mismatched paperwork on my desk were gone. Not only that, the stack of phone messages had also been handled. And as I'd suspected, there was still no sign of the missing schematic.

I called Special Agent Janie Partners to inform her that I'd cleaned my desk and the area around it. The plans weren't there.

She told me to keep looking.

"Wait," I said before she could hang up. "Has the Turbekistan envoy rescheduled his meeting with the President?"

There was a long pause before she said, "He hasn't."

Which meant Gordon's neck was still on the chopping block.

"Casey, are you willing to take some advice?" she asked.

"Of course. Always."

"I like you," she said. "And I don't want to see you get into more trouble. So please don't ask about Turbekistan again."

"Why?" I asked.

But she'd hung up.

Since the phone receiver was still in my hand, I dialed Jack's number.

As I waited for him to pick up, I practiced in my head what I would say. I'd be causal. I'd not say anything about the date he'd almost made, but canceled just this morning. Instead, I'd explain what happened with the schematic. Perhaps ask him if he could talk with Steve and Janie and convince them that I wasn't a nut. Someone had to have taken it. I'd tell Jack about the threatening text message, too.

Jack's cell phone flipped over to voice mail. I sighed. He was rarely able to take personal calls when on duty. I shouldn't have expected him to break the rules and take my call. But still, I was disappointed.

"Hi, Jack. It's Casey," I said after the beep. "I, um, I just wanted to talk through a few things and, you know, have you use some of your sidekick superpowers to help me put together the pieces of a puzzle in the grounds office."

I smiled to myself as I disconnected the call. Jack—a take-the-lead kind of guy—hated it when I called him my sidekick.

My gaze shifted to the to-do list sitting on the corner of my newly organized desk. As always, there were pages of tasks. Most would take me out into the gardens. And since I did my best thinking in the garden, I grabbed my wide-brim sweetgrass hat and gardening gloves. I dropped my clippers into the leather holster attached to my belt and headed outside to the gardens.

As I passed through the wide, arching hallways on the White House's ground floor, I noticed (not for the first time) how the arrival of tiny, twin baby boys had lightened the atmosphere. Despite the morning's fiasco, the butlers and maids had an extra spring in their step. I even heard the very proper chief usher making silly *goo-goo* noises.

Everyone moved with a new, happy purpose. We all wanted to make life as easy for the First Lady and her tiny new babies as we possibly could so they would grow strong and healthy.

I was doing my part by promoting organic, common-sense practices in the gardens. Much of my work was very similar to what happened in home gardens all across the country. The White House was, after all, a family household.

In the visitors' foyer near the East Wing, I pushed open the glass door that led out into the Jacqueline Kennedy Garden and hurried through. The geometrically planted garden was neatly tucked in a niche between the White House and the East Wing. In the past hour, more clouds had rolled in. The fall breeze stung my cheeks with its cool, damp slap.

I shivered as I surveyed the showy mix of deep orange chrysanthemums and flowering kale that needed to be tended and trimmed. Soon, we'd be pulling out all the annuals in these beds in preparation of the winter season. But until that happened, it was my responsibility to keep the fading plants looking as lush as possible.

I crouched down at the corner of the garden closest to the East Wing's entrance and started snipping off one spent chrysanthemum bloom after another. I dropped them into neat piles on the brick garden path.

I'd worked my way around one of the garden's many lollipop-shaped holly topiaries and had moved to the next one when the door leading out to the garden swung open.

I raised the brim of my hat to find the White House curator adjusting her thick glasses. She looked stouter, more wrinkled, as she stood there glaring down at me.

"Can I help you?" I asked, making no effort to hide my impatience with her.

"Tell your supervisor I've canceled the meeting with Ambrose," Frida Collingsworth said.

"You have? Does that mean you found your missing research?"

"I . . . I may have. And while you're at it, you can tell Gordon that my new assistant"—she turned to the handsome Arabic man who was hurrying to catch up with her—"Nadeem Barr, will be the liaison between my office and yours. I want nothing to do with any of you."

With a sigh, I rose from my crouched position beside a perfectly rounded chrysanthemum. Nadeem, her assistant, reached out a hand to help me. "Thanks," I said.

His cheeks darkened as he fought a smile. "I . . . um . . . It's nothing."

Nadeem was taller than my five feet six and looked considerably older than the last twenty-something assistant who had worked for Frida. Actually, he looked older than me, which wasn't very old at all. I wasn't forty. Not yet. I had a few months to go before my birthday. So on second thought, he didn't look that old at all.

And he was handsome, too, with dark brows that cloaked his deep chocolate eyes, and broad shoulders. He would make a convincing exotic prince, the kind who lounged with a beautiful woman on the cover of a romance novel. Not that I noticed things like broad shoulders or dark expressive gazes anymore. I only had eyes for Jack.

"It's good to meet you." I pulled off my gloves and wiped my hand on my pants before shaking his hand. "I'm sure we'll get along just fine. And forgive me, but Frida, you need to get that bee out of your bonnet. I don't know why you'd think Gordon would take anything from your office in the first place. And what were you saying earlier about a treasure?"

"Treasure?" She flashed a nervous glance at Nadeem and then back at me. "I—I—I have no idea what you're talking about," she sputtered. "Come along, Nadeem. I'll warn you now that the grounds office is famous for poking their noses where they don't belong."

I gritted my teeth and pulled my gardening gloves on again.

"It—It was, um, nice meeting you." Nadeem's voice was soft, halting, as if he carefully considered each word. "If, um, you know, if there's anything I can do to help—"

"Come along, Nadeem." Frida nearly ripped her shy assistant's arm out of his socket as she pulled him away from me. "There's no helping the grounds office. And don't get too used to any of them. I have a feeling there's going to be some major personnel changes coming down the pipeline soon."

Frida walked straight through my neat pile of dead flowers, scattering them.

"I, um, look forward to getting to know you better, Casey," Nadeem called as he let himself be dragged away.

I crouched down and swept the spent flowers back into their tidy piles before returning to work on the plants. As I snipped, I wondered about Frida's prediction that the grounds office was about to have personnel changes. She was obviously talking about Gordon.

And Gordon had said Frida was trying to ruin him.

But *why?*

And if she was trying to ruin Gordon's reputation, I couldn't help wondering if she would go as far as to sneak into our office to steal the South Lawn schematic.

It seemed like a stretch. I was still trying to piece together a plausible theory for what could have happened to the schematic when two ladies, both staffers from the East Wing, headed my way.

"Ever since she's come home with those babies, the First Lady has been unreasonable when it comes to her schedule," the older of the two ladies complained to her companion as they passed by on the garden path as if I were invisible.

"It's only been a little more than a month," her companion pointed out. "And the babies were born premature. Give it time. I'm sure things will improve."

I glanced up and watched the staffer, who I recognized as the First Lady's Chief of Staff, make an ugly face. That was interesting. This was the first I'd heard of unhappiness with the babies. Most of the East Wing staffers I'd spoken with were ecstatic with all the positive press the two bundles of joy were bringing to the White House.

"Things had *better* improve." The First Lady's Chief of Staff bit off the words as she yanked open the door to the East Wing. "I can't keep canceling events, especially those heavily attended by campaign donors. And Bradley needs help with that crazy Mr. Aziz. We need Margaret to play host."

"Who is Mr. Aziz anyhow? Is *he* a donor?"

"Oh, no. He's an envoy from some Eastern Bloc country. It's all hush-hush about why he's here. But from the briefing I was given, I got the distinct impression the President needs this visit to be a success or else we can forget about four more years of job security."

"But do you *really* think—"

The glass door closed behind them as they entered the enclosed breezeway that connected the East Wing with the main residence.

Not a moment later the same door the staffers had just passed through flew open. Lettie Shaw, the First Lady's sister, charged into the garden and hurried down the bricked garden path. Dressed in a smart pair of black pants and a black sweater, Lettie looked like an older, slightly chunkier copy of her famous younger sister. There was a bit of gray in her brown hair she kept slightly longer than Margaret's trademark pageboy cut.

She stopped a few feet away from me and, after adjusting the pea green raincoat she had draped over her arm, retrieved her buzzing cell phone from her pocket. A wide smile lit up her elegant features as she read the phone's caller ID. "Finally," she breathed.

I felt rather like Miss Marple hunched in the planting bed with my straw hat shading my face, quietly observing without anyone caring to notice.

Lettie answered the call with a brisk, "Hello." She then appeared to hold her breath as the person on the other line spoke.

The blush of pleasure drained from her cheeks as she listened. "Surely there is something I can do?"

Her smile completely faded away. "I've already lost my house and my car. I'm desperate. There has to be some way—"

After listening to whoever was on the other end of the call, she exploded with a violent burst of emotion. "No!" she shouted. "No, I can't ask her for help. She would never—" There was another long pause as she listened. "I see. Yes, yes. I know. I'll . . . I'll just have to . . . Yes, there is another way. Oh, I hate to do it, but . . . No, I can't talk about it now. Good-bye."

She glanced nervously around—her gaze floating over me as if I were invisible—before rushing down toward the South Lawn.

I raised my brow at that and made a note to work in this garden around lunchtime more often.

My hands barely had time to find a smooth rhythm again when Marcel Beauchamp, the well-respected interior designer who was busy redecorating the First Family's living quarters to accommodate the twins, lumbered out of the South Lawn and up the path toward the East Wing. Although he stood at least a foot taller than me, he had a wide barrel chest that swayed and heavy jowls that jiggled with each step. He passed by just as a fat raindrop hit the ground next to me.

Everyone called him a brilliant artist, and I'm sure he was. Yet he'd taken more time than I thought necessary to design the upstairs living space for the First Family. But what did I know about the temperament of an artist?

Because the First Lady was a lover of the outdoors, Marcel often visited the gardens for inspiration. Perhaps he got inspiration by rolling in the grass. At least it appeared that way as he brushed at a stain on the knee of his khaki trousers before he hurried inside.

A few minutes later Frida's assistant, Nadeem Barr, jogged up the bricked path from the South Lawn, his long legs covering quite a distance with each stride.

"Is everything okay?" I asked him.

He paused a moment. "Ms. Collinsworth, um, she sent me to get ready for our meeting with the garden historian from the National Arboretum. She was headed toward, you know, the Children's Garden. She—she was grumbling to herself about thievery and treachery. Is it always like this?"

"No, of course not," I answered, probably too quickly. In the short time I'd worked at the White House, there hadn't been a dull day. "Well," I amended, "we don't usually argue with each other so much, but I've noticed that one should expect the unexpected around here."

"Given your past experience, you should be well used to that."

My past? I drew back as if he'd struck me. "What do you mean by that?"

What did he know?

My past had been something I kept hidden from public view. And I certainly didn't appreciate hearing a near-stranger remark about a past that had torn my family to shreds and had nearly killed me.

"I—I just meant . . . um . . . in your line of work. Gardeners can't control Mother Nature and all." He held up his hands to the coming rain and flashed that disarming smile of his again. He did have a nice smile.

And he'd done a nice job of backtracking, but if he'd simply been talking about gardening, why did he say, *Given your past* . . . And why was he suddenly looking at me like that? Like I was a cracked porcelain figurine about to crumble at his feet?

What did he really know about my past? Who would have told him? Naturally, the Secret Service knew all about the tragedy, but they were professionals at keeping secrets.

At least one member of the press knew about my family's history, but she'd promised not to report on it.

My heart started to beat an uneven tattoo. I usually did a good job of keeping my past locked up, but on stressful days like today, it sometimes exploded in a blinding burst of emotions.

I had to fight to catch my breath if I was to have any hope of keeping the budding panic attack from hitting me with full force.

Breathe slowly.

In.

Out.

"Are . . . are you okay, Casey?" Nadeem lowered his voice and leaned in so close I could smell his sandalwood-scented aftershave. He lifted my hand into his.

I nodded as I concentrated on making sure a slow, steady stream of air filled my lungs. "I just need to breathe," I wheezed.

Focus on something safe. Like how there was an expertly trained Secret Service agent stationed in a tiny white hut at the edge of this garden.

"Nadeem." It was a struggle to catch my breath. If I could find out more about him, I might be able to calm the fear pulsing through my body as if I'd swallowed a sparking live wire. "That's an interesting name. Where are you from?"

"East Lansing," he said without blinking.

"Michigan?" I'd expected Pakistan or Iran.

"Yeah, Michigan. I know. That's not what anyone expects. My childhood . . . it wasn't anything exotic or exciting," he said with a shrug. "A simple, um, ranch house in the middle of the burbs."

The burbs. A normal guy. "So you really were just talking about gardening?"

"What—What did you think I was talking about?"

"Casey? Casey, there you are. You left a message you needed to talk with me?" Jack, my warrior in black, surged into the garden like an avenging angel.

He quickly zeroed in on Nadeem and how the new

assistant was holding my hand. He moved in with the same efficiency the agents had used when rescuing President Bradley from the broken irrigation line and got my hand out of Nadeem's grasp without even appearing he'd done it on purpose. But I knew better. Nearly every move Jack made was done with precision and forethought.

"Casey?" Jack's dark brows furrowed with concern. "Is everything okay here?"

"I . . ." I took a couple of deep breaths and was able to find my mental footing again. "Mm-hm, I'm good." I bit my lip to keep the anxiety out of my voice.

I briefly made introductions. The two men didn't look pleased to meet one another.

"You're new here," Jack said to Nadeem.

"Yes. This, um, past spring I graduated from the University of Washington's museology program."

"You *just* graduated?" Jack rubbed his jaw thoughtfully.

"It's, um, a second career." Nadeem tried out his disarming smile on Jack. It had no effect.

"And your first career?" Jack pressed.

"I was a fact-checker."

"A fact-checker?" Jack crossed his arms over his chest. "That's not a career."

"I, you know, worked for the federal government." Nadeem's smile never wavered. "I occasionally pushed papers around, too."

Jack kept his mouth pressed in a grim line as his gaze stayed locked with Nadeem's.

"My . . . my landlord"—Nadeem turned away from Jack—"told me that a young, beautiful gardener from the White House lived in the townhouse above me. And well, do you think he, um, meant you, Casey?"

We compared addresses while Jack's tough-guy grimace turned into a very real snarl.

"I'm glad someone from the White House rented that place," I said. "It's been vacant for as long as I've lived there."

"I'm glad I rented it, too. Well, um, I'd better go get ready for this afternoon's meeting. I'm already running late.

I look forward to working closely with you, Casey, and getting to know you better," he said. "Special Agent Turner," he added with a frosty nod.

"You're *glad* he rented the place?" Jack's brows rose after Nadeem had left.

"What? I was being friendly."

"I know the type. He was playing you." Jack folded his arms over his chest and looked delectably cranky. I don't know why, but I'd always thought a little jealousy was damn sexy on a man.

"Nadeem is too shy to play games. Besides, you heard him. We're neighbors. It might be nice to have someone to walk with to work."

Jack grabbed my hand. "I've told you this before, Casey. I'd be more than happy to walk with you to the White House, or pick you up and drive you."

"You don't live anywhere near me." I wiggled my hand free and gave his arm a teasing punch.

"I'd be more than happy to fix that."

"By going on a date with me tonight?" I asked.

"Tonight is . . . complicated." He rubbed the back of his neck. "I could—"

"I should go help Gordon," I blurted out in a desperate attempt to change the subject. Although we'd been dating for three months, he hadn't found the time to invite me over to his house. Not once. And yeah, that did bother me. It bothered me just as much as his canceling our dates without a good explanation lately.

"Wait," Jack said. "You're angry."

"No, well, maybe a little. But I do have to go. Nadeem said Frida was heading to the Children's Garden."

"So?" Jack asked. "Is that a problem?"

"Gordon is working in the Children's Garden. I should get there before the two of them kill each other." I'd never seen anyone get under Gordon's skin like Frida had this morning.

The intermittent raindrops were coming more often as I scooped up my trimmings and dropped them in a small bucket I carried with me. I then hurried diagonally across the South Lawn.

Jack followed along with me. "You'd said in your voice mail you needed to talk to me."

"Yes, I could use some of your sidekick superpowers."

"I'm not your—or anybody's—sidekick," he grumbled. "Wait . . . you haven't called me your sidekick since Parker was murdered. What have you gotten yourself into this time?"

"This morning was not an accident. Not exactly. Look, it's complicated and I don't have time to talk about it now. Gordon needs me. He's had a rough day already. That's part of the reason I needed to talk with you, but you're busy tonight. I get that. I'll figure this out on my own."

Jack grabbed my arm before we parted at the entrance to the Children's Garden, and he pulled me to his strong chest. "It's not that I don't want to be with you." Jack's voice turned all gruff and sexy.

"You don't need to—"

He pressed a possessive kiss against my lips that stole my breath.

I stumbled a few steps on wobbly legs when he released me. He crossed the lawn back toward the West Wing like a man on a mission. As soon as I caught my breath, I went the other way, darting down the narrow pathway that led to the Children's Garden on a mission of my own.

President Johnson had given the garden to the White House as a Christmas gift in 1968. Its secluded location, tucked between the tennis court and southwest gate, had been purposefully selected to provide a place for the children and grandchildren of the presidents to play away from the prying eyes of the press or the public.

"Gordon!" I called as I jogged down a narrow stone pathway that led into the garden. The pathway had been paved with handprints of the children and grandchildren of past presidents.

"Gordon?" I called again as I reached the garden's interior.

No answer.

At least no one was shouting.

Within the intimate space there was an apple tree for the children to climb and a small pond filled with yellow and white koi fish to amuse the children.

As I entered the heart of the garden, my heart stopped dead in my chest.

Gordon—my patient mother hen of a supervisor—was lying facedown in the koi pond.

He wasn't moving.

Chapter Four

"**G**ORDON!" I leapt into the shallow koi pond, grabbed both his arms, and lifted his head out of the water. His back, head, and arms were covered with water hyacinths. I brushed them away.

It took all of my strength to haul him out of the water. His body felt like dead weight.

No, no, no. Not dead.

"Please, Gordon." This couldn't be happening. Not to Gordon. Not to *my* Gordon.

I lowered him onto the garden's paved patio that surrounded the pond. And following first-aid training basics, I put my ear to his mouth. He wasn't breathing. I pressed my fingers to his neck, searching for a pulse.

"Gordon!" I shouted in his ear, trying desperately to get a response. "You won't die, you hear me? You can't die."

I couldn't feel his pulse.

A ghostly white squirrel scurried down to a low-hanging branch of the nearby Winesap apple tree. The squirrel sat up on its haunches and made a series of *chee-chee-chee* noises as it watched the drama unfolding in the Children's Garden beneath it.

"You don't need to scold me," I said as panic gripped my chest. "I'm hurrying. I'm hurrying."

My fingers shook as I ripped my cell phone out of my pocket and dialed the White House's emergency line. "This is Casey Calhoun," I said to the woman who'd answered. "I'm in the Children's Garden. Send a medical team. Gordon Sims isn't breathing. I can't find a pulse. Don't have time to provide more information. I'm starting CPR."

Not bothering to hang up, I tossed the phone, sending it skittering across the patio's paver stones. Saving Gordon's life was my main priority.

With the flats of my palms, I gave thirty quick chest compressions on the center of his chest. I then pinched his nose closed and tilted back his neck before giving two strong breaths into his mouth. His chest moved with each one. Good. I was doing it right.

As air entered his lungs, he threw up water and muck from the pond. Good. That needed to come out . . . I hoped. I tilted his head to the side and cleaned out his mouth before starting again with chest compressions.

I don't know how long I continued with the CPR. My arms were burning. My throat ached as if I'd been screaming.

Jack put his hand on my shoulder. Our eyes met. I had to blink mine to chase away the tears.

"He's dying," I whispered, terrified it was true.

"Not on my watch." Jack dropped to his knees beside me and took over the chest compressions, counting softly.

Jack looked like a holy mess. His face was flushed red from running. His short black hair needed to be combed. It looked as if he'd dredged his fingers through it as he'd charged down the hill to find me. He probably had. It was a habit of his, I'd noticed, to dredge his hands through his hair whenever he was worried.

But the concentration on his face paired with the steady

movement of his arms as he kept Gordon's heart beating was the most wonderful thing I'd ever seen.

"What happened?" he asked in that no-nonsense tone he used when things got hairy around the White House.

I sat back on my heels. In halting sentences I told Jack how I'd found Gordon. I rubbed the tired muscles in my arms. "I don't know what happened. Did he get into an argument with Frida? If so, where is she? Why didn't she help him? Perhaps he was so upset that he tripped and fell into the pond."

"Did he hit his head?" Jack asked.

"I don't see any blood." I ran my fingers through Gordon's silver hair. "There isn't a bump or a bruise." Would I see a bruise so soon after Gordon had hit his head?

There was what looked like smeared blood on the arms of his dark blue windbreaker. "Did he cut himself?" I asked just as the White House medical staff descended on the scene.

"We'll look him over for injuries," one of the medical technicians assured as he gently nudged me out of his way.

Time seemed to move in a halting motion, fast one moment and painfully slow the next. The medical staff had brought with them a metal gurney, defibrillator, and all sorts of other equipment.

An older doctor with kind crinkles around his eyes took over for Jack, placing his hands where Jack's had been while the rest of the staff set up their equipment. Jack rose to his feet and moved out of the medical staff's way. He then put his arm over my shoulder. With a tug, he pulled me snug against his side.

"Jack, tell me Gordon is going to be okay," I begged.

He pressed his lips together. Jack was straight as an arrow and had never—and would never—lie to me. "I don't know, Casey."

"But I *can't* lose him," I said, talking more to myself than to Jack. "I need him. He's more than the head gardener. He's . . ."

Through a steady veil of rain, I watched as the doctor ripped off Gordon's stained jacket and wet shirt, a shirt that was soaked for the second time that morning. Not able to watch anymore, I closed my eyes and focused on taking slow, steady breaths while I stood there twisting my hands together until they throbbed and burned.

Please, Gordon. Don't die.

"We're going to transfer him to George Washington University Hospital now," a soft female voice said after what felt like an eternity. A hand touched my arm. "They'll take good care of him."

I opened my eyes and watched the medical staff lift Gordon to the metal gurney. The nurse who had touched my arm hurriedly wiped her eyes with the back of her hand. She then jogged to catch up with the doctors and fellow nurses who carried Gordon up the narrow pathway that led out of the garden.

"I need to go with them. I need to make sure Gordon's okay." I tried to pull away from Jack.

"They don't need you in the ambulance." Jack tightened his hold on my shoulder. "Once things are settled here, I'll drive you to the hospital. Let's get you inside."

"Once things are settled here?" My voice broke. One minute Lorenzo, Gordon, and I were trying to figure out what had happened to cause this morning's irrigation line break. And now Gordon might not . . .

The ambulance's engine roared to life. Its siren cried out. "I need to be with Gordon. He shouldn't be alone."

"He's not alone." The special agent in charge of the Secret Service's Counter Assault Team, Mike Thatch, arrived with several other agents toting large black umbrellas.

Thatch met me head on. He squared his shoulders, which only made him seem taller than his already six-feet-plus height. "I've sent some of my men to go along with Gordon."

"You did?" I asked. My voice sounded thick from the tears that were threatening.

Jack seemed surprised as well. His dark, sexy brows had practically shot up to his hairline.

Thatch was Jack's supervisor and, from what I could tell, dedicated to his job. But he openly disliked me and disapproved of my past assistance in solving mysterious happenings at the White House. At the moment, though, Thatch didn't look at all irritated. His shoulders weren't hunched. (He tended to hunch his shoulders a lot when I was around.) And the unhappy curl to his lips had relaxed . . . a smidge.

"We all care about our head gardener." Thatch directed one of his men to come hold an umbrella over my head. I looked up at the umbrella's black canopy, not realizing it had started to rain so hard. "Until we understand what happened here, we're going to take every precaution available, especially considering how you're involved, Casey." He kicked a pebble with the toe of his polished black shoe. It clattered across the pavers to hit my leather loafer.

"Now that's unfair." I set my hands on my hips, ready to defend myself. "I have never intentionally set out to cause trouble."

"Tell that to our sopping wet President." Thatch seemed to fight the curl pulling at his upper lip.

"That wouldn't have happened," I shot back, "if the schematic hadn't been stolen from the grounds office!"

"It doesn't matter." He waved a hand in the air to silence me.

Doesn't matter? *Doesn't matter?* He thought my job performance, my reputation, didn't *matter?* I was so angry I sputtered a few meaningless sounds before giving up and shutting my mouth.

I set my hands on my hips as I glared at him.

"You're not going to cry, are you?" Thatch jerked away from me as if he feared I would grab his shirt and sob into his collar. His quick movement made the gray in his hair flinch like a startled carp in the koi pond.

He thought I was going to cry? Me?

I huffed a frustrated breath before realizing Thatch had

accomplished one thing I truly could feel grateful for. I hadn't cried. I surely would have given the pouring rain some good competition if he hadn't provoked me.

"Wait a minute. Did I hear you correctly? You said you sent agents to the hospital with Gordon? Why? You don't think someone attacked him, do you? I did see what looked like blood on his arms."

"No! Good Lord, I don't think that at all," Thatch said. "I sent my men to the hospital because I don't want our head gardener or his family to be overrun by the press." Thatch's gaze scanned the confines of the small garden. "But I do need to know what happened here."

As I explained how I'd found Gordon in the . . . in the . . . pond, tears burned in my eyes again. I blinked them away. "He is going to be okay?" I couldn't stop myself from asking.

"I'm sure he will be," Thatch was quick to say. "Do you know what Gordon was doing out here?"

I had to think back to what Gordon had said before he'd left the office. "He'd said something about pruning."

"I see," Thatch said. "And was he pruning in this garden?"

"He . . . he . . ." I couldn't think. I needed to get to the hospital. I needed to make sure someone had called Gordon's wife, Deloris. I should talk with her. She would want to know firsthand what had happened, what I'd seen.

But what could I tell her? What had happened here?

I glanced around the small space. The Children's Garden, a private refuge from the hubbub of politics, was nearly completely enclosed with walls made from a hedge of prickly holly bushes and a roof created by a canopy of American elms.

At the center of the space was the koi pond crowded with water hyacinths. That was where I'd found Gordon. I moved over to the pond. The agent holding the umbrella over my head followed.

Swallowing hard, I crouched down beside the pond and dipped my hand in the chilly water. A gold-and-white carp nipped the tip of my finger.

I quickly pulled my hand back. "What was he doing here?" I wondered aloud.

"That's what we'd like to know," Thatch said. "Hey, what's that?" he asked, pointing into the pond.

"Where?"

"In the water?" Thatch tugged on his suit pants before bending down beside me. He fished around in the pond and pulled out a cell phone. It was an older-style black flip phone.

"That's Gordon's," I said. "He must have dropped it."

"He might have been trying to call for help," Thatch said as he stood.

I craned my neck to glance up at Thatch and Jack, who were both frowning as they watched me. Thatch looked anxious to get away from me. His brows knitted tightly and he bit his lower lip as if keeping snide remarks from shooting out his mouth was causing him physical pain.

"We don't need to stand out here in the rain," he said.

I wasn't ready to go inside. I explained to them that Nadeem had seen Frida go into the Children's Garden, possibly to confront Gordon. "Frida had accused Gordon of stealing some historic papers from her office, which is insane. She must have realized how crazy she'd sounded because she'd backed off on her accusations. But she still seemed furious with him, which I don't understand. Where is she anyhow? I came down here to make sure they weren't arguing again. That's when I found him in the . . ."

I covered my mouth with my hand and, rising, walked out from under the protection of the umbrella and into the now driving rain.

Near the front of the garden, I spotted a freshly pruned elm tree. The cuts were the proper three-part cuts that a professional arborist would make. But . . . "I don't see any tools or branches on the ground."

Just then I did spot something out of place. At the base of the nearby Winesap apple tree, the same tree the white squirrel had perched in, I found a small mound of upturned soil.

I dropped to my knees and dug around the loose dirt in the shallow hole. Whatever Gordon had used to dig the hole had damaged some of the apple tree's roots. That didn't make sense. Gordon would never have been so careless, especially since there was no obvious reason why he'd have dug the hole in the first place.

"Do you see a shovel anywhere?" I asked. "No, not a shovel. Something smaller. A trowel. Do you see one?"

The small team of agents wandered around the intimate garden space, peeking in the colorful drifts of golden chrysanthemums and purple salvias that edged the open space.

Surrounding the koi pond was the oval patio made from paver stones. White metal chairs, a metal bench, and a small white metal table were where they were supposed to be on the patio. Behind the seating area was an expansive flowerbed. Seasonal flowers had been planted in front of a hedge of azalea and holly bushes. Taller shrubs and trees formed a living wall at the back of the garden. Behind them, a seven-foot fence covered in landscape fabric ensured complete privacy from the outside world.

"There's nothing here," Thatch said.

"I wonder if Frida took the trowel with her." Brushing off my damp pants as I stood, I spotted what looked like a garden tool's yellow handle sticking out of a pile of mulch near the back of the garden. "Wait a minute."

I pushed through a prickly hedge of hollies and reached under a bush to fetch the yellow-handled gardening tool. It wasn't a trowel but Gordon's pruning saw. What was it doing over here, so far away from the elms that had been pruned?

I had to stretch to pick up the saw—it shouldn't be left out in the rain to rust. The blade was already filthy with mud. As I lifted the saw, my arm brushed aside a pile of mulch that had partially hidden it.

And that's when I found Frida Collingsworth.

Chapter Five

Fatality seems connected with the occupants
of this office and Mansion.
—JANE PIERCE, FIRST LADY OF
THE UNITED STATES (1853–1857)

"**P**UT down the saw," Mike Thatch said. He held out both hands in front of him as he approached, taking each step as if he was afraid he'd trip a land mine. "Just set it on the ground."

"She's dead." I'd stated the obvious. Frida was lying half-buried in a pile of mulch. It wasn't a natural death. Her neck and the front of her blouse were soaked with blood.

"It must have been an accident. A horrible, horrible accident," I said because I couldn't believe she'd been murdered within one of the securest places in the world.

Thatch paled as he leaned over a holly bush and pressed his fingers to Frida's neck to check for a pulse. He sucked in a quick breath as our gazes met. His eyes widened with panic.

"Casey." With one blink, Thatch chased away any sign of emotion. "Put down the saw."

"Why?" I asked, still unwilling to believe what my eyes and instincts saw in front of me.

"It's bad enough that it's raining like the second flood is coming," Thatch said. "We don't need you tromping through the crime scene and getting your fingerprints all over the murder weapon, too. Put the damn thing down. Now."

"Murder weapon?"

"The saw in your hand smeared with blood."

"That's blood?" I tossed the pruning saw away from me and jumped over a small holly bush to land on a stone paver in the center of the garden. "The . . . that saw killed Frida? You think she was murdered?"

"The police will find that out for us." Jack gathered me into his arms. "They're on their way."

"Good," Thatch said. "We'll need to lock things down."

"Already under way," another agent said.

Thatch nodded. "Get everyone out of here. The police will want to erect tents. Get them ready. And post men at the garden's entrance. We've already had enough boots marching through the crime scene."

"The pruning saw . . . It couldn't have killed Frida," I said. The perfect cuts on the surrounding trees all had bore Gordon's signature touch. "It's Gordon's saw."

Gordon and Frida had been arguing earlier. I'd never seen Gordon so angry with anyone. But that didn't mean . . .

I hugged myself and shivered.

"I need to get to the hospital. I need to make sure Gordon is okay. Frida's death must have been an accident. Just an accident. Gordon couldn't have—"

"Let's get you out of the rain." Jack took a large black umbrella from one of the other Secret Service agents and held it over my head.

The rain was coming down with a punishing force now. I was soaked to the bone again, and hadn't even noticed. Mike Thatch and Jack were just as drenched. Neither of them had bothered with the umbrellas, either.

"It wasn't Gordon," I told Jack as he led me up the narrow trail and out of the garden. "He wouldn't do this."

"Let's get you inside, Casey," was all he'd say.

* * *

THUNDER RATTLED THE WINDOWS INSIDE THE
White House.

A maid draped a heavy wool blanket over my shoulders
as Jack and I, followed by the agents, entered the White
House. I pulled the blanket tightly about me to chase away
the chill.

One of the chefs handed me a piping hot mug of coffee
as we passed the kitchen.

Wide-eyed nurses came out of the physician's office.
Doctor Stan, the President's personal physician, even came
out of his office to watch the soggy procession down the
residence's main hallway. I could tell by their grim expres-
sions the medical staff already knew about Gordon and
Frida.

Of course they knew. Tucked into Dr. Stan's ear was an
earpiece that was tuned to the same frequency as the members of the Secret Service. He'd have listened in on the
frantic conversations taking place between the Secret Service agents as they'd reported in and made decisions on
how to proceed in the Children's Garden.

Everyone else who'd converged in the hallway from the
kitchens and housekeepers' offices looked as confused as I
felt. Their questions followed me down the hallway. "What
happened? Was there a security breach? Was Casey attacked
again?"

Soon everyone would know about Gordon and Frida.
Secrets didn't last long among the White House staff. Whispers spread like wildfires through these halls.

"Casey? There you are. What, um, is going on?" Nadeem
hurried out of the curator's corner office with a steep pile of
file folders in his arms and half-moon metal-rimmed reading glasses perched on his nose. "The meeting with Gordon
and Frida was . . . was supposed to have started ten minutes
ago, and I haven't been able to find them."

"They—they . . ." I swallowed around a lump in my
throat. "About that . . ."

Nadeem looked at the heavy blanket wrapped around my shoulders. Then at Jack, who was standing like an avenging angel at my shoulder. And then at the team of Secret Service agents filling the hallway.

His gaze narrowed. "What's going on?" he asked, his voice an octave deeper. He took a step toward me and straightened his shoulders. He no longer sounded like a befuddled researcher but like a man ready to take charge.

"Let the poor dove go get dried off. She's soaking wet," said an older woman as she emerged from the curator's office. She was wearing a black brocade dress belted high at the waist and sensible black shoes. Her long snowy white hair was piled on the top of her head in an elaborate bun.

She gestured toward me, her weathered hands moving like a woman used to holding knitting needles. Her faded blue eyes seemed to miss nothing as her gaze took in the drama unfolding around us.

If Miss Marple had stepped out of the pages of one of my favorite Agatha Christie novels, this would be exactly how I'd have expected the clever sleuth to look and act. This woman even had an English accent.

"Forgive me," Nadeem said to the Miss Marple doppel-gänger standing next to him. "Casey, this is Dr. Watson, the garden historian from the National Arboretum."

Not Marple, but a doctor . . . "Did you say Dr. Watson? As in Sherlock Holmes's sidekick?" A slightly hysterical giggle escaped before I clamped my lips closed.

"No, dear, not Watson. Everyone makes that mistake. It's Wadsin." She spelled it. "Joan Wadsin. I'm looking forward to working with the White House on developing the exhibition on the history of its gardens."

"It's a pleasure to meet you." My half-frozen hand snaked out from beneath the blanket to take hers in a polite greeting. My grandmother Faye had drilled good manners into me. *Child, when the world is falling down around our ears, we must make doubly sure we put our best foot forward. It takes the edge off the stress when everyone knows how to act*, she liked to say.

And sometimes, like when I was numb with shock, social rules did help.

"What has happened here? Where is Frida?" Nadeem demanded of Jack. "She should have returned by now."

Jack crossed his arms over his chest and didn't look open to providing any answers to Frida's new assistant. And I wasn't prepared to announce my grim findings to everyone standing in the hallway.

Gordon and Frida deserved better. Besides, the Secret Service might have reasons of their own for keeping a lid on that information for now. The staff would find out the horrible news soon enough.

"I'm sorry." I took a deep breath and patted Nadeem's arm. "Neither Gordon nor Frida will be available for the meeting. If you don't mind, could you take Dr. Wadsin to the grounds office and ask Lorenzo to show you Gordon's archived gardening notes?"

"Of course he can, dear," Miss Marple—I mean, Dr. Wadsin said. "And you need to get into some dry clothes before you catch a cold."

"Yes, I will," I said. "Thank you."

"Casey, they're waiting." Jack gestured down the hall and to the rest of the Secret Service team who had passed us as they headed toward the East Wing.

"Is there anything I can—" Nadeem started to ask.

"Just—Just get to work on the project," I said. "That's what Gordon would want us to do."

Chapter Six

He didn't get all of those injuries from a fall.
—MARTHA WASHINGTON, FIRST LADY OF
THE UNITED STATES (1789–1797)

D.C. Police Detective Manny Hernandez's pencil scratched nosily against the paper as he wrote in his small notebook. He huffed loudly. The quick exhale of breath made his salt-and-pepper mustache dance.

"Gordon must have been attacked by the same person who killed Frida," I said. "And that hole at the base of the apple tree. It's still bothering me. Why was it there?"

Manny and I were alone in the small office on the second floor of the East Wing. The room had been turned into a makeshift interview room for the police's use. The D.C. Police Department held jurisdiction over all investigations of suspicious deaths, even for deaths that occurred on the secure White House property. And everyone even remotely involved with Frida and Gordon was being questioned.

I'd first met the hard-boiled detective and his threadbare brown suits this past spring when he was assigned to investigate the death of a woman I'd found murdered in a nearby park. We'd "teamed up" again in the summer after one of the White House correspondents had been poisoned.

Manny was the D.C. police's go-to detective for high-profile and politically prickly cases. He knew how to get the job done without ruffling important feathers. But just because he could get along with the suspects and witnesses involved in a case didn't mean he wasn't capable . . . or dangerous.

At the first whiff of guilt, he'd clamp down with the same intensity with which my aunt Alba's old bulldog Beauregard would chomp on a butcher bone. And he sure as hell wouldn't let go until he got to the meat of the crime.

His tenacity was generally a good thing.

"So the head gardener and the curator had been arguing," Manny said as a prompt to redirect the conversation. He seemed determined to keep circling back to Gordon and Frida's disagreement and the blood on Gordon's sleeves.

"As I've already said, Frida had changed her mind," I told Manny. "She told me herself she was wrong to accuse Gordon of stealing her research."

"But Gordon didn't know that. And he was angry."

I don't know what he expected me to say to that. "I don't like the direction of your inquiry." I turned away from Manny and watched as a rivulet of rain rushed down the glass of a nearby window to form a small ocean on the windowsill. "I've told you what I saw. Now shouldn't you be asking me why someone might attack *both* Frida and Gordon?"

"Okay, Casey. Why would someone want to hurt both the gardener and the curator?"

"I don't know." I didn't know anything. I didn't even know if Gordon had survived the trip to the hospital. No one would tell me. The not-knowing clawed at my throat.

Manny's pencil scratched noisily against the paper in his small notebook as he made more notes.

"Are we done?" I asked.

He waved his hand toward the door. "For now."

Outside the small office, the hallways in the East Wing were crowded with uniformed police officers and Secret Service agents of every rank and uniform. Their voices were subdued as they spoke with one another.

I'd just started to descend the stairs to the first floor when I heard one voice boom out over the others. "Bryce!"

At the base of the stairs, a tall, broad-shouldered man with shimmering silver hair and dressed in a suit that looked as if it had been made especially for his larger-than-life frame paused and turned. I'd dealt with Special Agent in Charge of Protective Operations Bryce Williams a few times. He always treated the grounds staff with respect, even when he didn't agree with us.

"Bryce," Mike Thatch called again as he jogged to catch up with his supervisor.

The older man leaned against the stairway's railing. "What is it?"

Thatch had a cell phone pressed to his ear. "A representative for Lev Aziz contacted our switchboard."

"Aziz? Our switchboard? Or the White House's?"

"Ours, sir," Thatch said.

"Tell me they transferred him over to the Oval Office. Bradley needs to meet with Aziz. Immediately."

"I know, sir. But Aziz's man wasn't calling to talk about the meeting. He was calling about the curator's murder. I'm listening to the taped conversation now." Thatch paused. "That can't be right. Can you play back that last part again?" he said to whoever was on the other end of the phone call. "*What?*" After listening for a minute, he pocketed his phone. "Aziz's man said he would only talk with Calhoun."

"*Who?*" Bryce barked.

Thatch started to answer, but as his gaze lifted, he spotted me standing near the top of the stairs listening. He held up his hand. "We shouldn't talk about it here. We're not alone."

Bryce Williams stepped aside. "Forgive us. We didn't mean to hold you up," he said to me. His ice blue gaze chilled my bones as he watched me descend the steps. Thatch held the stairwell's door open for me.

"Aziz wanted to talk with *me?*" I asked them. That couldn't be right.

"I'm sure you misunderstood," Thatch said.

I itched to stay and find out what the two men were talking about. I also wanted to find out how the Turbekistan envoy could possibly be connected with Frida's death, but I was clearly not welcome.

I shuffled out of the stairwell and down the corridor. My head throbbed from worry and hunger and questions, lots and lots of questions.

"ARE YOU READY?" JACK INQUIRED, FALLING IN step beside me as I passed through the enclosed breezeway connecting the East Wing to the main residence.

"Ready for what?" I asked. The only thing I felt ready to do was collapse on the floor below me.

"I promised to take you to Gordon." He handed me his coat. "It's still pouring out there."

Jack drove to George Washington University Hospital.

"What do you know about Turbekistan?" I asked him as he steered his rusty old Jeep onto the ramp for George Washington University Hospital's parking garage.

"It's a country in Eastern Europe."

"Thanks for the geography lesson, but that's not what I was asking for." I told Jack about the conversation I'd overheard in the stairwell as he steered into a parking space.

Jack went still when I mentioned Lev Aziz's name. "You know about the envoy's visit?"

"Doesn't everybody? Do you have any idea why Aziz would want to talk with me?"

"I'm sure you misunderstood." Jack's shoulders tightened. This was clearly a conversation he wasn't comfortable having.

"What if I didn't? What if Aziz wants to be reassured the water line break was an accident and not sabotage?"

Jack flinched whenever I said the envoy's name. "I'm sure that's not it. Who told you about Aziz?"

"Someone in the West Wing told Gordon when he was getting grilled by the staff. Why?"

"Because the meeting with Turbekistan is classified.

Top-secret classified. Those big mouths in the West Wing shouldn't be talking about it. *We* shouldn't be talking about it."

"But—"

"I'm serious, Casey. Forget you heard anything. Forget I said anything, okay?"

"But what if I can help? Or what if this Aziz fellow is somehow connected to the thefts of my schematics and Frida's research and"—I swallowed around a lump in my throat—"what if he knows what happened to Frida and Gordon? What if Frida and Gordon saw something they shouldn't have? Something that involved these secret talks? Aziz wouldn't have been so skittish after the irrigation line break if he didn't think he was in danger."

"Whoa." He threw up his hands. "Those are several huge logic jumps you just made there, Casey."

"Are they? How can you be so sure?"

"Listen to me, there isn't a connection. Aziz has a reputation for being paranoid. Extremely paranoid. Anything he says is suspect." He opened the Jeep's door and got out. "And that's all I can say on that matter."

Not one to give up so easily, I told Jack the rest of the story about the stolen schematics and the missing research from Frida's office as we walked through the garage to the hospital. I hoped this new information would convince him to change his mind, and he'd tell me more about the President's secret meetings with Turbekistan and who might want to sabotage them.

Jack listened. Nodded sympathetically. But remained stubbornly silent on the matter.

My attention turned from Turbekistan's untapped oil and back to Gordon's health as I sidestepped out of the hospital's large revolving front door. I started to type a text message to Lorenzo to let him know where I was, what I was doing. Unlike the tech-savvy West Wing interns, I hadn't yet mastered the art of walking and texting. Before I'd finished typing the message to Lorenzo, I walked right into a post.

"Oomph," the post grunted.

My fingers stopped mid-text. "Oh! I'm so sorry." I quickly stepped back from the post, who wasn't a post at all, but a man with dark eyebrows and a little bit of gray in his black hair. Wait a minute, wasn't that . . . ? "Nadeem? Nadeem Barr?"

The tall man walked around me as if he hadn't heard me and slipped into the revolving door leading out of the hospital.

"What is he doing here?" I wondered aloud.

"What did you say?" Jack had been several feet ahead of me scanning the area, not because he thought there was some great threat, but because that's what he always did.

"I just saw Frida's new assistant." I pointed at the revolving doors, which were now empty. I turned a full circle, searching for Nadeem's tweed suit. "At least I think that was him."

What was he doing at the hospital?

Jack watched the empty revolving doors with the intensity of a sharpshooter on the White House roof. "Do you want me to follow him?"

No, I didn't want Jack to go. *I* wanted to follow the phantom White House assistant. For as badly as I wanted to get up to Gordon's room, I felt equal parts terror about what I might find once I got there. Gordon was my rock in this crazy city. I needed him to be alive and healthy.

"Casey?" Jack gently touched my arm. "Are you okay?"

"Yes, of course I am." I shook myself out of my thoughts and waved my hands in the air as if batting them away. "I'm sure I was seeing things. It's the stress. I'm hopelessly muddled whenever I'm stressed."

"You think you fall apart in stressful situations?" Jack's gaze flashed to the revolving doors where I'd last seen Nadeem. He started to frown again. "I don't seem to remember you falling apart last summer when—"

"I don't have time to stand here and reminisce." I grabbed his arm and gave him a little tug. "Let's go find Gordon's room."

The soft-spoken man at the visitors' desk directed us to

a private wing of the hospital. The elevator opened into an elegant wood-paneled foyer.

I'd heard of this area. It was reserved for the President and other important government officials. President Ronald Reagan had been treated here after he'd been shot outside the Washington Hilton Hotel. And just last month the vice president had stayed here after he'd torn an ACL during a charity tennis match.

At the double doors leading into the private wing, we found Secret Service Special Agent Janie Partners standing guard with a uniformed officer from the D.C. Police Department.

"Deloris is already here," Janie said, referring to Gordon's wife of more than thirty years.

"Have you heard anything about Gordon's condition?" Jack asked the question I'd been dreading.

Janie shook her head slowly. "I think in this case, that's a good thing."

I took several deep breaths, hoping to steel myself for the worst as we started to go in, when Janie called out to us, "Lorenzo Parisi blasted through about five minutes ago." She paused. "He's in with Deloris. He seemed quite shaken up."

"We all are," Jack said.

I reminded myself that the doctors here were the best, the facilities conducive to healing. Gordon was in good hands.

The best hands.

In the highly polished wood-paneled waiting area we spotted Deloris, Gordon's wife, a retired schoolteacher with a round face and red-rouged cheeks. She rose from the leather armchair as we approached. Though her curly permed hair looked as if she'd just stepped out of the hairdressers, not even a wave out of place, her eyes were red and puffy. I swiftly closed the distance between us.

Lorenzo had been crouched down beside her chair with his head nearly touching Deloris's perfectly coiffed hair. Whatever conversation they'd been having ended abruptly with our arrival. He straightened and crossed his arms over his chest as I pulled Deloris into a tight hug.

"How is he doing?" I asked, fighting back a lump in my throat.

"I—I don't really know. They got his heart going again, but . . . but . . . can the doctors keep it going?" She started to pace. "I've called our boys. They're both working on getting flights to Washington National." She continued to list everything she'd done since she'd arrived, including finding someone to feed their cat. "Can you think of anything else I need to do?"

"It sounds as if you have taken care of everything for now," I said and led her back to the leather armchair. She heaved a loud sigh and collapsed into its smooth cushion. "But if you do think of anything that needs to be done, we can help you."

Lorenzo nodded. "Of course we can."

"Do the doctors have any idea what happened?" I asked.

Deloris's hands shook as she dug around in her oversized floral-patterned pocketbook. "A cardiologist came out and talked with me just a little while ago. I told the doctor to write everything down for me. And I told him to write it legibly." She took her time unfolding a scrap of paper she'd retrieved from her purse.

"The cardiologist, he said that they believe Gordon suffered a cardiac arrest and collapsed." She glanced up at me. "You found him in a fish pond?"

"I did." My throat burned. My voice sounded raspy. "The koi pond in the Children's Garden."

She nodded. In the past thirty-five or so years that Gordon had worked the White House grounds, Deloris had visited many times and knew the gardens nearly as well as any member of the White House staff.

She nodded again before turning her attention back to the doctor's writing on the paper in her hands. "He must have inhaled some of the pond's water when he fell in. That, in addition to the heart failure, has caused . . . complications.

The cardiologist said—he wrote it here—that Gordon has aspirated lungs with pulmonary edema."

"What about the blood?" I asked. "He had blood on his arms. Do the doctors think someone attacked him? Cut him?"

She studied the paper in front of her. "No. He didn't say anything about cuts on his arms or signs of attack." She looked up from her paper. "He mostly talked about the near-drowning. Apparently his lungs aren't working . . . or they aren't working the way they're supposed to be working. It's all very confusing."

It bothered me that the doctor hadn't mentioned the cuts. Judging by the amount of blood I saw on his arms, they had to have been deep. "Are you sure he didn't say anything about an injury?" I pointed to the same place where I'd spotted blood on Gordon's arms on my own lower arms.

"Should he have? With everything that has happened, I can't keep it all straight. He didn't write it on my paper."

"I'm sure we'll find out everything soon enough," Jack said more to me than to Deloris.

"I'm sure you're right," Deloris answered. "I can't wait for my boys to get here. They'll know the right questions to ask."

"But . . . but Gordon's going to be okay?" I couldn't keep the warble from my voice.

"I don't know." Deloris took her time as she refolded the paper with the cardiologist's notes and tucked it back into her pocketbook. "The doctor, he said that it's a miracle Gordon's still alive." She pointed to a nearby door. "He's in there. They don't want me in there right now. That's why I'm out here. But even after they get him stabilized, the cardiologist said he'll be on a ventilator for at least several days. He'll be sedated the entire time. There's really nothing to do here but wait."

"If you don't mind," I said, "we'd like to stay with you for a while tonight. Do you need anything? Coffee, water, tea, a sandwich?"

Deloris leaned her head back in her chair and closed her eyes. "Coffee," she whispered.

After Jack went off in search of a cup, Lorenzo pulled me away from Gordon's wife. "What happened out there?" he demanded.

In halting sentences, I explained how I'd found Gordon and then Frida. "They both must have been attacked. But if that's the case, how did the intruder get past the Secret Service?"

"I'm not sure the police or the Secret Service will look beyond the iron fence for an answer," Lorenzo said.

"What makes you say that?"

"Think about it, Casey. You saw it yourself. Gordon and Frida had been arguing. And then you find them both in the Children's Garden. Frida is dead. Gordon may not survive the night."

My gut twisted. "*You're wrong.*"

Lorenzo lowered his voice. "What if I'm not? What if their argument turned—"

"*No!*" I couldn't believe what he was saying. I just couldn't. "Gordon isn't a violent man."

"I'm not saying he is violent. All I'm saying is that the situation looks pretty bad."

"You're wrong. Anyone who's ever met Gordon knows that he could never—"

"Casey?" Jack had returned. He was holding a tray of steaming cups. He motioned to Deloris, who had clearly overheard Lorenzo and me arguing. Her mouth had dropped open. Her eyes were wide with shock.

My face heated. I lowered my voice to a whisper. "Lorenzo, Gordon wouldn't attack anyone."

Deloris pulled herself out of the waiting room's armchair. "What are you whispering about?"

"Does she know about Frida?" I asked Lorenzo, who shrugged.

Deloris crossed the room like a woman on a mission. "Tell me," she demanded.

"It's nothing," I said.

"Nothing," Lorenzo quickly agreed, even though he'd wrinkled his nose as he said it.

Deloris turned her determined stare on Jack. He held out the tray for her. "Coffee?"

"No. I want the truth. What else has happened?"

"The curator—" Jack started to say.

"Frida Collingsworth?" Deloris interrupted. "What has that nasty old bat done this time?"

"She's—she's dead," I said.

"She's been murdered," Lorenzo added.

"Who did it?" Deloris asked coolly. "I'd like to shake that person's hand."

Chapter Seven

Every young girl should have the opportunity of learning out-of-doors by first-hand observation, the wonders and loveliness nature has spread so lavishly—and how it grows.
—LOU HENRY HOOVER, FIRST LADY OF
THE UNITED STATES (1929–1933)

JAMES Taylor crooned softly about traveling to Carolina, *my* Carolina, even if the trip was only taking place in his mind. A smile spread across my lips as the singer opined about the beauty and peace he was seeking in the Southern landscape, his soothing voice growing gradually louder.

Slowly coming awake, I eased my hand from the warmth of my bed's thick comforter. My fingers scrabbled along the surface of my bedside table before they curled around my singing phone.

"Hello?" I answered groggily.

"Gracious sakes, lamb, are you still asleep?" the woman on the other end drawled with a cultured Southern twang.

"Uh . . . no, Aunt Alba, if I was asleep, I wouldn't be holding a phone to my ear."

"Don't you sass me. Mama taught you better than that."

"That she did," I agreed. "I'm just disappointed to find out James Taylor hadn't snuck into my bedroom and wasn't singing sweetly in my ear."

"A man in your room!" my straightlaced aunt cried. "Now you're talking nonsense."

"I suppose I am, Aunt Alba." James Taylor's "Carolina in My Mind" was the ringtone I'd assigned to Rosebrook, the Calhoun estate in Charleston. My grandmother lived there with my aunts, Alba and Willow. "I was up late last night. I'm tired." I wiggled under the covers until I was sort of sitting up in bed. "What time is it?"

"Half past six."

I sat up straighter. "That late?"

"Yes, that late. The crows have been having a tea party on the power lines next door for more than an hour now. What are you doing staying up late to all hours of the night? Don't tell me you've let the big city corrupt you with their wicked ways."

"I—"

"It's unseemly for a young lady to be out past ten. Nine is preferable. You have a reputation to guard, especially given your post at the White House."

"Really, I—"

"I don't think the President would appreciate hearing you're gadding about town in the small hours of the morning."

"Aunt Alba. President Bradley doesn't—"

"Do I need to get on the next train—"

"Aunt Alba, please, listen to me." I loved the dear woman to pieces despite her antiquated notions of what women should and shouldn't do. "I was at the hospital last night. Gordon had a cardiac arrest. He's . . ." My voice cracked. "He's not doing all that well."

There was a long stretch of silence on the other end of the line. "Gordon? Oh, lamb, not the Gordon you garden with at the White House."

"Haven't you seen the news reports?" I hadn't, but that was only because I hadn't turned on the TV in the past twenty-four hours. I was sure all the news agencies were picking apart Frida's murder around the clock.

"Willow has been running me ragged with all this

planting and weeding. Ever since you've started work at the White House, Willow has been looking at our garden with a critical eye. Says she doesn't want you coming home and being disappointed with what we've been doing in our gardens."

"How could I ever be disappointed with anything at Rosebrook? It's home."

"I know that, silly goose. It's your aunt Willow who's keeping me from having any time to breathe . . . or watch TV. Are you okay? I know how much Gordon means to you. What happened?"

I explained to Aunt Alba about finding Frida and Gordon in the garden.

"Not another murder, sweet pea. It's that city. It's filled with nothing but evil."

"There's also a lot of good in D.C.," I tried to tell her, but as usual she didn't listen. In her mind, any city larger than Charleston was a gathering place for sin and vice. She'd been against my moving away from the beginning.

"Greed. Corruption. Crime. It's not a place for honest people like you and me. I'm only surprised you don't run into more trouble than you already have."

"Tell that to the Secret Service," I mumbled.

"What's that?" she said, but didn't give me a chance to answer before she launched into a recitation of crime rates of major cities. "I *am* sorry to hear about Gordon," she added, her voice softening again. "But you needn't worry about him. He's a gardener. We're hardy people. He'll recover."

I hoped she was right.

After getting off the phone with my aunt, I called the hospital. There'd been no change in Gordon's condition. He was still on the ventilator and unconscious. The nurse was quick to remind me that no change was actually a good sign. The doctors had emphasized several times yesterday it would take time for Gordon's body to heal. I needed to be patient.

I could do that. Patience was the cornerstone of gardening. Even Thomas Jefferson had once written, "Botany is

the school for patience." There was no rushing how fast a
plant would grow and flower. Sure, adding synthetic fertilizers might make the plant bigger, leafier. But that same
quick green-up could easily backfire and stop all flower
and fruit production.

Gordon's body needed time to heal. In order to do that,
he needed to know the grounds office was in good hands.
This was something I could do for him, something tangi-
ble. Part of that would involve continuing work on our
ongoing projects, as well as finding out what had happened
with those missing schematics.

After showering, I donned a pair of khaki pants and a
dark blue turtleneck shirt. Over it, I pulled on a light green
sweater embroidered with hundreds of tiny ladybugs, each
with their own unique expression. I brushed my hand over
a smiling ladybug on the sleeve. My grandmother Faye had
knitted the sweater for me. I wore it whenever I needed to
feel close to my family.

Thanksgiving was right around the corner. As if I could
already smell the rosemary-encrusted turkey and cornbread
dressing baking in the oven, I ached for a healthy heaping
of Grandmother Faye's, Aunt Willow's, and Aunt Alba's
embraces. I ached to go home to Rosebrook, the family estate
smack dab in the center of historic Charleston, South Carolina, and wrap all that was familiar and safe around me as if
it were one of my grandmother's crocheted blankets.

Gordon, with his soft-spoken manner and his steady
work-the-earth hands, was like a member of my family. He'd
flown under my iron-clad defenses, defenses that had taken
years to forge. Cheering my successes, offering advice, and
providing unflagging support when I felt as if I'd been
backed into a corner, he'd become more like a father to me
than my own father. Not a great feat. My own father was
never in the running for any "Dad of the Year" awards.

James Calhoun had led a shady life. My earliest memories were of fleeing one apartment after another in the dark
of night. We'd move locations, countries even, change our
names, change our language. For the longest time, I'd

thought he was, at worst, a con man or a thief. But this last summer, a memory had returned like a punch to the gut.

I'd been barely five years old as I'd watched my dad pull the trigger and kill a man in cold blood.

A year after the shooting, my father had abandoned my mom and me. Not even a week later, a group of men searching for my deadbeat dad attacked. When my mother had refused to tell them where he'd gone, the men shot us both. My mother had died.

I didn't.

Luckily, my grandmother and two maiden aunts had taken me into their home. They'd raised me as if I were the most precious child to walk the earth.

They'd also taught me to garden.

Families came in all shapes and sizes. I was blessed to have mine. But as Jack had pointed out last summer, I hadn't escaped my youth or James Calhoun without coming away with some very real scars. I was still punishing every man who took an interest in me for what my father had done.

But not Gordon.

I don't know why, but I'd never doubted his support. I'd never even tried to push him away. He had become my rock in this slippery, political microcosm also known as the nation's capital. I *couldn't* lose him.

I paused at my dresser and studied the sleep-deprived face staring back at me in the mirror. With a sigh, I poked the puffy skin under my eyes before quickly pulling my blond hair into a ponytail.

If I lost Gordon . . .

"Patience," I whispered.

Without even thinking about what I was doing, I stuck my hand in my top dresser drawer. After digging around in the drawer's rolled socks, I removed a creased and yellowed newspaper article I'd buried in the back of the drawer.

"Alyssa?" I called as I padded down the stairs of the old brownstone townhouse.

I stuck my head through the arched opening that led to

the kitchen. It was unusual for the kitchen to be so silent in the morning. My roommate tended to celebrate mornings with a symphony of grumblings and pot banging.

The brownstone's kitchen had been updated from its Victorian roots about thirty years ago. The large modern avocado green appliances looked out of place in the narrow room with tall ceilings that caused sounds to echo throughout the two-story apartment.

"Alyssa?" I called again.

No answer.

She must have left early for her job as a congressional aide to Senator Finnegan at the Capitol.

I was too worried about Gordon to eat, so I skipped my morning bowl of oatmeal and instead scooped the last of Alyssa's organic shade-grown hazelnut blend coffee grounds into the French press. After jotting down a note to myself to buy another bag of the nutty-flavored coffee, I settled at the small maple kitchen table and retrieved the yellowed newspaper article from my pocket. I carefully unfolded the brittle paper. This wasn't something I would have dared do if Alyssa had been around. Don't get me wrong; I liked Alyssa. I couldn't have asked for a better roommate. She did more than her fair share to keep the house clean, always paid her half of the rent on time, and had a wonderfully twisted sense of humor.

She also had an uncanny ability to read my emotions like the back of a cereal box, something she liked to do while she sipped her morning coffee.

My obsession with this old newspaper article was something I didn't want her to see.

She wouldn't understand.

I smoothed out the paper's creases with the flat of my thumb. Three months ago a White House correspondent had found the article and had given it to me. The newspaper was dated the same year my mother had been murdered.

The article detailed six murders my father had committed. I worried my lowered lip as I reread the damning article even though I'd read it enough times to have memorized every gory facet of his crimes.

Good old Dad had even killed a police officer to escape capture. The article went on to indicate the police believed he might also be responsible for my mother's death.

I closed my eyes against the images of that terrible night when I'd lost my mother. The memories flooded my mind with the force of a hurricane, threatening to sweep me away.

Picture a safe place. That's what a therapist had taught me to do when the memories overwhelmed me like this. Picture a safe place and go there.

My grandmother's attic.

I was safe up there.

It was a place where the past couldn't touch me.

I never really knew my father. Never really dwelled on his absence. But Gordon . . .

He'd filled a void in my life I hadn't fully realized existed.

Gordon didn't kill Frida.

I didn't care what Manny or Lorenzo or anyone else believed happened in the Children's Garden yesterday. Gordon *didn't* kill anyone.

He couldn't have.

So his wife had been happy to see Frida gone, bloodthirsty even. Gordon wasn't a violent man.

He was nothing like my father.

I fought off another dizzying wave of panic with a series of deep breathing exercises. I'd just completed the first set when Alyssa burst through the back door and swept into the kitchen with a blast of crisp fall air following in her wake. The heels of her designer leather boots clacked on the tile floor. Her dark blue silk fitted suit seemed to take on a life of its own as she hurried toward me. "Have you met the guy who's moved into the basement apartment? What a hunk! Too bad he's a—"

"Alyssa! I—I thought you'd left for work." I moved my

arm to cover the article. Too late. Alyssa stopped mid-step. Her manicured brows rose as her gaze shot first to the half-hidden article, then to my arm, and finally to my face.

"Casey Calhoun, I thought we'd agreed you'd throw that damned article out," she said.

"I was going to, but . . . I couldn't." I pursed my lips and, sitting up straighter, moved my arm out of the way.

Alyssa watched me for several uncomfortable seconds before sighing loudly. "Keeping that article isn't healthy. It makes you a slave to things you can't change." She spun toward the narrow counter behind her and poured the fresh-brewed coffee into *her* freakishly oversized mug.

I cried out a strained "No!" That was *my* coffee! Well, I had brewed it using her hazelnut beans, but I'd been the one who had scooped them into the French press.

"No? You think you can change things now?"

"No, of course I don't think that." I almost had to sit on my hands to keep from reaching out for her coffee mug.

Alyssa took a long sip. Her voice gentled as she asked about Gordon. I told her what the nurse had told me this morning, and I had to blink away tears as I spoke.

"Oh, Casey." She set her oversized coffee mug on the table in front of me, wrapped her arms around my shoulders, and pulled me into a tight bear hug. "He's going to be okay. I promise, honey. Ninety-one percent of men who experience a sudden cardiac arrest make a full recovery."

Alyssa had a habit of making up facts and figures to suit her purposes. I usually called her on it. But this was one lie I needed to believe.

"Thank you," I said, and hugged her back.

"Now, what was I saying?" Alyssa asked as she took her rich, fragrant coffee back to the kitchen counter and dosed it with far too much sugar. "Oh, right. It's such a shame he's a spy."

"Who? Gordon?" I couldn't think without my coffee.

"No. No. You're not listening to me. He. Is. A. Spy," she said, speaking slowly as if talking to a simpleton.

I glanced down at the ancient article on the table in front of me. I brushed my hand over its damning headline:

MURDERER ESCAPES POLICE

"You—You think my father is a spy?" That would explain a few things. God, I hoped he was a spy, unless . . . "You don't think he's spying for the enemy?"

"*Your father?*" Alyssa whirled toward me. She moved so quickly her long black hair slapped her in the face. "Get rid of that article already. Are you, or aren't you, the one who said you didn't want me to mention anything about *that man* ever . . . ever . . . *ever* again?"

"I did say that. And I don't." A wave of heat traveled up my neck. I'd also said that if I ever saw him on the street, I'd cross to the other side and then call the police.

He didn't deserve a daughter. And yet part of me cried out for him. What if he was a spy? The good kind like the ones who wore the white hats in the *Spy vs. Spy* cartoons?

I shook my head to put a quick stop to the thought.

Magical thinking. That's what the therapist had called it. Wishing for something that couldn't be true.

My father had never really been a part of my life, and I turned out about as normal as anyone else I knew. I wouldn't be thinking about him right now if Gordon wasn't in the hospital fighting for his life and unable to fight for his innocence.

"It's been three months since you were given that article, and you still can't throw it away? Have you at least talked to Jack about it? Have you even shown it to him?" Alyssa asked.

"Er . . . I haven't had the chance."

"Haven't had the chance? That's the excuse you're going to use?" Alyssa quirked her already arching brow. She'd graduated top of her class from Yale Law School and could outdebate the President. "And how long have the two of you been dating?"

"I wouldn't exactly call going on a couple of dinner dates with Jack as 'dating.' He hasn't even invited me to his house. Of course, he's been busy traveling with the President."

"But he was with you late into the night last night?"

"We were at the hospital with Gordon's wife. It wasn't the time or place to talk about murderous fathers."

"Are you going to see Jack today?"

"I don't know." Jack was scheduled to be on duty at the White House, although that didn't necessarily mean I'd get to see him.

"This thing with your dad is obviously eating at you, Casey." Alyssa waved her coffee mug like a magic wand. "*Talk* to Jack."

I wanted to talk to Jack about these things. Nothing reported in the newspaper article would surprise him. He'd already read the extensive background check required for my security clearance. My father's history must be in there.

But what if he knew something about my father I wasn't ready to hear? Wasn't it better to pretend James Calhoun didn't exist? That's what I'd done for a quarter century, and my life had been good. I'd been whole.

I barely remembered the life I'd lived before my grandmother Faye had rescued me. It wasn't until this past spring when I'd found a dead body in Lafayette Square that the door to those repressed memories had been blown wide open.

I started to fold the article back into a small square, but Alyssa snatched it out of my hands. She frowned as she read it for the first time.

A fresh wave of panic hit me. Although I'd told her about it, I hadn't let her read the article.

"This doesn't make sense." She stabbed the brittle paper with the tip of her painted nail. "Wasn't your family living under an assumed name at the time of your mother's murder?"

"Yes," came my strangled answer. I didn't want to go back to that time. Not with Alyssa. Not with anyone.

"And didn't it take several years for officials to figure out who you really were and get you to your grandmother?" she pressed.

I swallowed hard and then nodded. I'd spent nearly two years in foster care, being shuttled from home to home, never really given an opportunity to grieve or heal.

"So why in the world would the newspaper report that *James Calhoun* killed his wife? How did the reporter know his name or that he was even your mother's husband for that matter if the police didn't know it?"

"Perhaps the police—"

"No, something isn't right here. Something doesn't add up. You should have showed this to me sooner . . . or to Jack. Oh, I can tell by the look on your face you're not going to talk to Jack about this."

She whipped out her cell phone with dizzying speed and punched speed dial. "Barry, sweetie. Did I wake you?" A wicked smile spread across her lips. "Yeah, I liked that, too. But that's not why I called. I need a favor."

While Alyssa explained to what sounded like her current boy toy that she wanted him to run a trace on James Calhoun and how the police connected him to my mother's murder so many years ago, I protested. Not that it made any difference. Once Alyssa gets an idea in her head, there's very little anyone can do to change it.

I eased the article out from between her fingers, and after carefully folding the brittle paper, I tucked it into my backpack.

"There has to be another explanation. Perhaps he'd been living a double life and killed his other wife?" I dug my nails into my palms. "He didn't kill Mom. I was there. *He* wasn't."

If he had been there, my mother would still be alive. Those men who killed her had been searching for my dad, for *James Calhoun*. And the newspaper had mentioned James Calhoun's name. Not his false identity.

"If the police had known my parents' identities, why was I overlooked? Why did the officials allow a damaged child to bounce around in a foster system that wasn't equipped to help her?"

"I don't know, Casey," Alyssa said after she finished her call with Barry. "That's what we're going to find out."

I wasn't sure I wanted to. I certainly wasn't in a mood to travel back to that dark time. So I closed the door to those memories and took a page from Alyssa's playbook and bluntly redirected the conversation. "Who were you calling a spy?"

Alyssa, unable to contain her excitement, danced around the room. "The cute guy who's moved into the basement apartment. Man, he's got sex appeal dripping out his ears."

"Nadeem?"

"I've met plenty of spies since moving to D.C." Alyssa waggled her huge coffee mug at me again. "I know the look. And I also know they're always up to no good."

"Oh. He has a 'look'? That's not very convincing evidence," I said, eyeing Alyssa's coffee mug with envy.

"CIA or Special Forces or one of those divisions that has no 'official' name. Or perhaps he's working for a foreign government. It doesn't matter. He's a spy."

"For once your spider senses are wrong. Nadeem Barr is the new assistant for the White House curator's office. And believe me, the White House thoroughly screens its employees. No spies allowed."

"Have you met him?"

"Sure I have. And I'm glad he took the apartment." The basement apartment in our brownstone townhouse had remained vacant the entire time Alyssa and I had lived in the building's upper two stories. The basement was in need of a total renovation, vital repairs the owner seemed unwilling to make. Instead of paying to make the place habitable, the owner kept lowering and lowering the rent until I'd started to seriously worry about what kind of dangerous character might move in below us.

Not one to sit on my hands and fret, I did something about it and had told everyone at the White House that the apartment was available.

"He's been working on the History of the White House Gardens project with Frida and Gordon."

"Don't you find it curious that shortly after this assistant"—she used air quotes when she said "assistant"—"started working in the curator's office, the curator is found dead? Do you know anything about his past?"

"I think he said he was from Michigan."

"Well, *I* know something." Alyssa tapped the side of her slender nose. "Nadeem is not a researcher. He's nobody's assistant. He can't hide the truth from me. He's a spy."

Could that be true? Could he have been planted by a foreign country to thwart the White house talks with Turbekistan? If Frida had learned Nadeem was a fraud, she would have confronted him. But . . .

"Why would a spy want to work in the curator's office? I mean, they deal with historical documents and antique furniture. It's hardly a hotbed for espionage."

"I don't know why. To get inside the White House? Spies are clever. You never know what they are up to until it's too late."

I wasn't going to win this argument, and since there was no coffee to be found in the house because Alyssa had finished the pot I'd brewed, I scooped up my backpack. "I'll see you this evening, Alyssa. Try not to get into the middle of any international intrigues while I'm gone."

"Joke all you want, but mark my words. Something bad has already happened. Frida was murdered. And if that spy living in our basement is any indication, there's more trouble coming," Alyssa warned as I hustled out the back door. "Trouble spreads like weeds whenever there's a spy involved."

Chapter Eight

You've got to fight for what you believe in.
You have to finish what you start.
—JACQUELINE KENNEDY, FIRST LADY OF
THE UNITED STATES (1961–1963)

W HEN I stepped onto the townhouse's back landing, I spotted a man scurrying down our apartment's back steps. He was dressed in a camel-colored trench coat. His lapels were pulled up around the ears, and a camouflage hat was jammed low on his head. I only glimpsed the backside of him as he jumped down the last few steps and stumbled.

"Nadeem?" I called. The man limped to the basement apartment's back door and yanked it open.

"Nadeem? What are you doing?"

He must have heard me, but he didn't even look up before stepping inside and slamming the door closed behind him.

Had Alyssa been right about our new downstairs neighbor? Was *Nadeem* a spy?

The man had been wearing a long trench coat, the kind spies wore in bad movies. But then again, it was raining.

I stepped back inside and grabbed my rain slicker and umbrella from the hook on the wall behind the door. Determined to find out why the new assistant curator was lurking at our back steps, I rushed back outside and down the steps to stand at the door the man had disappeared through.

"Nadeem!" I beat my fist against the door. "Nadeem! I know you're in there. I saw you."

When no one answered, I moved along the side of the brownstone building to a small window that I had to stand on my tiptoes to peek into. The window looked into the basement apartment's kitchen. The lights were off. A dish and cup had been neatly lined up on a drying towel laid out next to the sink. On the round linoleum kitchen table sat a fat file folder with a White House emblem on it.

What I didn't see in the apartment was Nadeem.

Had he run through his apartment to escape out the front door, or was he hiding?

Either way, I was getting no answers by standing there.

I shivered as I walked to work through the chilly rain, but it wasn't the rain that made me feel cold. It was the icy prickle of fear.

First, Frida's murder and Gordon's near-fatal attack. Then I overheard Bryce and Thatch talking about how Aziz had believed Frida's murder was somehow connected to the meetings with Turbekistan. And now Nadeem, a new member of the White House staff, was acting strangely. How could I not be worried?

Had Nadeem been listening at the back door to Alyssa's and my conversation? A conversation we'd been having about him?

I needed to find out what was going on.

And I knew exactly how to do it.

"JACK?" I WAS SURPRISED HE'D ANSWERED HIS cell phone. His shift at the White House had started an hour ago. I checked the readout of my cell phone, worried I'd misdialed.

"Casey?" he asked. "Is everything okay? Are *you* okay?"

He sounded genuinely concerned, which was sweet.

"I'm fine." I'd ducked into the Freedom of Espresso Café. The barista waved and started to make my regular mocha cappuccino as I shook off my umbrella. On my way to the checkout, I picked up a bag of organic shade-grown hazelnut blend coffee beans.

"And Gordon?" Jack asked. "How's he doing?"

"No change there." I paid for my coffee at the counter and took a deep sip. "Actually, I called to ask about Nadeem Barr. Remember him? He's Frida's assistant."

"I remember." I could have cut nails with his voice. "He's your new downstairs neighbor."

"Good memory. Alyssa has it in her head that Nadeem is a spy. I know, I know. I already told her she was crazy."

Jack remained silent on the other end.

"But here's the thing. I might have caught Nadeem with his ear pressed to my back door just now. Well, I didn't exactly see him at the back door. I saw someone—the back of someone—on the bottom steps that leads to the back door. I don't know if it was Nadeem, but he went into Nadeem's apartment. When I knocked, no one answered. If it was him, why would he do that?"

"I don't know," Jack said, his voice still hard. "With everything that happened yesterday, I don't like it."

The "I don't like him" remained unspoken.

"I'm not even sure it was Nadeem. The man didn't seem as tall as Frida's assistant. But he was wearing a trench coat. Does that mean he's a spy? Of course it doesn't. It's raining." I took another sip of my coffee. Caffeine zinged through my body like an electric current. "Oh, it's probably nothing. Forget I said anything. Alyssa is putting weird ideas in my head."

"Can't do that. Not when it comes to your instincts about people, Casey. Not when Frida was murdered yesterday."

"I've been wrong in the past."

"You've also been right. Let me see what I can find out about your new neighbor."

"Thanks, Jack. You're a good friend."

He didn't answer.

"Jack? Are you still there?"

"I hope by now, and after everything we've been through, you think of me as more than a friend," he finally said.

"Well . . . um . . . um . . . of course you are." I could feel my cheeks heat with a deep blush.

"What, no declarations of undying love for me? You wound me, Casey."

"I . . . um . . ."

His deep chuckle made me smile. "You're blushing, aren't you?"

"No, I'm not," I huffed.

He went silent again. I felt like a fish dangling on his hook.

"Okay, I might be blushing . . . a little."

"You're too easy to tease." His deep, playful voice made my entire body feel all tingly and happy inside. "Drat, I've got to go. How about this, I'll ask you how friendly you want me to be next time we're kissing?"

"Or I'll ask you."

"And Casey?"

"Yeah?"

"Be careful."

IN THE WAKE OF FRIDA'S MURDER, THE SECRET Service had tripled security patrols. As I approached the White House, I counted more Secret Service agents and park police officers than tourists. And that was saying something. Despite the persistent rain, crowds lined the iron fence surrounding the White House grounds. Cameras flashed like streaks of lightning.

Nothing like a murder at a national landmark to lure people off their sofas and into the miserable weather to gawk. Not that there was anything to see from the North Lawn. The Children's Garden, which had been designed to provide the maximum amount of privacy for the First Family, was located on the other side of the White House on the South Lawn.

"Vultures, all of them," a gruff voice growled behind me.

I spun around to see who had said that and found myself eye to eye with an elderly man dressed in camouflage fatigues and a floppy camouflage hat. He leaned heavily against his cane.

I knew him in passing only. He was one of the regular protesters who set up day after day in Lafayette Square, the park located directly in front of the White House's North Lawn. He'd sit in his faded old lawn chair—the kind with the colorful plastic webbing—while holding a sign on his lap that declared: "Everyone deserves a safe workplace."

None of the grounds crew knew his name. We all called him "the unfriendly guy," because unlike many of the regular protestors, who would engage in conversations even if it was just to sell us on what they were railing against, he rarely spoke to anyone.

I could count the number of times I'd spoken with him on one hand and with most of my fingers folded down.

"I suppose we shouldn't be surprised by the crowd. People are curious by nature," I said to him.

The unfriendly guy shrugged. "Still, it's a circus. Of course I haven't been here as long as Connie." He nodded to the nuclear weapons protester who had lived outside the White House for years now as she huddled in her tent. Several tourists were hunched down beside her, listening as she spoke with animated gestures. "So what do I know?"

He placed his timeworn hand on my rain slicker's sleeve. "I heard what happened. Are you okay?"

"It's upsetting," I admitted, my gaze lingering on where his hand was pressing down on my arm.

The old man seemed to sense my discomfort. He lifted his hand and backed up a few steps. "I like Gordon. He's a good man. He'd bring me coffee."

"He did?" I didn't know that.

The man nodded once, causing the rain that had puddled on the rim of his hat to drip down his nose. "We'd talk sometimes about gardening. I used to garden when I was younger. At my mother's knee, I tended plants before I learned to walk."

"She must have been an amazing lady," I said, thinking of my own grandmother, who had taught me how to escape my demons by losing myself in the garden.

"She still is," he said.

I handed him my umbrella. "You shouldn't be out here in this weather. It's going to be cold and wet all day."

"You are too thoughtful." He held the umbrella over the both of us and walked with me toward the security checkpoint at the northeast gate. His halting gait made it slow going. "I have something here for you," he said when we reached the gate. He dug around in his large coat pocket. "Here. You'll see it anyway." He pushed a soggy newspaper into my hands. "They'll print the worst kind of gossip to boost their sales. I don't believe it. Never will believe it."

"Thank you, sir." I dug out a few dollars and handed them to him as well as insisting he keep the umbrella. "Find somewhere warm to go. The tourists will be back tomorrow. They can see your sign then."

As I waited in the line to pass through the Secret Service security checkpoint, I unfolded the newspaper the man had handed me. It was the morning edition from the national paper *Media Today*. The headline printed in an extra large font shouted:

MURDER AT THE WHITE HOUSE! CHIEF GARDENER MAIN SUSPECT

Chapter Nine

*Sometimes I feel a little worried as I think of you all
alone and this press and annoyance going on but I keep
myself outwardly very quiet and calm—but inwardly
(sometimes) there is a burning venom and wrath . . .*

—LUCY HAYES, FIRST LADY OF
THE UNITED STATES (1877–1881)

I crumpled the newspaper into a tighter and tighter ball
until it wasn't going to get any smaller without altering
its molecular structure.

The article was wrong.

Wrong.

Wrong.

Wrong.

Gordon was as much a victim in this as Frida.

How could anyone, especially Detective Hernandez,
think otherwise? I'd always considered Manny a smart man.
He knew how to read people.

The newspaper had to be exaggerating. Like the
unfriendly guy had said, *Media Today* was only interested
in selling papers. Not the facts.

It's not as if this was the first time the media had gotten
the story wrong when it came to the grounds office, but this
wasn't a story we could blithely ignore. This story could
push Gordon out of a job. And for no good reason. He was
not a murderer.

Manny and the rest of the police investigators would figure that out soon enough. But by that time, the damage may have already been done.

Since moving to D.C., I'd learned it wasn't the crime that destroyed a reputation. Just the hint of wrongdoing could sink a career. I needed to do everything in my power to protect Gordon's good name while he was unable to defend himself.

Although I could have followed the front drive up to the basement entrance located right under the North Portico and disappeared into the grounds office without passing anyone, I detoured around to the side of the building and entered through the East Wing's main entrance in order to gauge the White House staff's reaction to the newspaper's claptrap.

The first thing I noticed was that the police had relinquished their makeshift offices back to the First Lady's staff who worked there. The uniformed Secret Service agent manning the front desk nodded briskly to me and quickly turned his attention back to the security screen in front of him.

In one day's time the tone of the White House had gone from bouncing strides and bubbly baby talk to grim silences.

The few East Wing staff members I passed in the hallway avoided eye contact. I got the distinct feeling they'd all read the news article and were distancing themselves from a department of the White House in profound trouble.

Worry rumbled deep in my gut.

Rain beat on the windows lining the length of the East Colonnade like tiny fists. Tiny *angry* fists. Just yesterday I was on the other side of those windows weeding, pruning, and deadheading flowers in the Jacqueline Kennedy Garden and pretending I was the clever Miss Marple listening in on private conversations. Just yesterday, the most pressing concern had been finding the South Lawn's missing schematic. And the soaking of President Bradley had felt like the worst sort of disaster. *How foolish I'd been.*

"You're late!" Seth Donahue, the First Lady's social secretary, charged toward me like a silver-haired raging bull.

Seth had left a lucrative party-planning business that catered exclusively to the rich and famous to work for the First Lady. I suspected he'd been expecting the job to be more glamorous or exciting than it really was. Many of the guests invited to the White House events were rich (but not famous) donors, Washington power players, and common citizens. Very few of the guests would ever merit mentioning on TMZ or *Access Hollywood*.

Perhaps a gnawing sense of disappointment kept him in a perpetually bad mood.

"Is *that* what you're wearing?" he said without offering me a good morning or a concerned word about Gordon's condition or Frida's death—you know, the kind of polite convention any decent human would follow.

I looked down at my khaki pants, sensible leather shoes, and colorful ladybug sweater. "What's wrong with my outfit?"

He rolled his eyes. "Don't tell me you forgot."

"Of course I didn't forget." What was he talking about? I scoured my memory for clues and came up with nothing. "What did I forget?"

"Breakfast with the First Lady. You're on the schedule to help host this week. The guests are already arriving."

"I forgot."

"Obviously. Follow me."

In an effort to help boost her husband's favorability ratings, every other Tuesday the First Lady hosted a breakfast for various regional and occasionally national women's groups. Staff members would act as co-hosts and give a brief presentation to the assembled group about their duties at the White House. Since giving birth to her twins a month ago, Margaret had skipped the breakfasts, relegating hosting duties to the White House staff.

In light of Frida's murder yesterday, I was surprised the breakfast hadn't been canceled. And, I suspected, the questions I'd have to field from the ladies at the breakfast would be . . . difficult.

"Do I have time to check my messages and drop my backpack in the office?" I asked in an attempt to buy myself some extra time to mentally prepare for the assault.

"No. I'll find an usher to take care of your backpack. By the way, the West Wing is anxious to reschedule the tree planting," Seth said as he hurried down the hallway as if nothing had happened yesterday. "How long will it take to relocate the planting site?"

"I, um . . ." His question caught me completely off guard when my main focus this morning had been on Gordon and how to help him. "I haven't thought about—"

He held up a finger and mouthed, "Wait," when his cell phone buzzed. Without altering his long-legged stride, he continued up the stairs to the first floor while answering his phone with a brusque, "Go." After listening for a minute he demanded, "What do you mean she was out all night? We can't let this happen. First there's the public anger over the skyrocketing gas prices and now this murder—we're already at a breaking point. I thought you had a handle on *this* situation."

His gaze narrowed as he listened. "I don't care. She has to be controlled," he said. "She will ruin us if—" He grunted as he listened.

"Yes, I know. Just—" He drew a deep breath. "Just tell me that the press didn't find her and take pictures."

He glared at me as if I was intruding in on his one-sided conversation.

I smiled back.

This caused him to lower his voice. "Listen, you keep her behind a locked door if you have to. She will not cause a problem for the First Lady or the President, do you understand me? Well? I can't—"

He slammed his phone against his hand and muttered, "I can't believe he hung up on me," before jamming the phone into his pocket and turning back to me. "Now then, where was I?"

"You were talking about the commemorative tree planting."

"Right. The West Wing asked me, in Gordon's absence, to take charge of its planning. As soon as you relocate the planting site, get that information to me for verification. We can't have any more irrigation lines blowing up."

My nails dug into the palms of my hands as I reminded myself Seth was right. The grounds office—*namely, me*—had royally messed up. I shouldn't feel as if he was stomping on my toes by stepping up and volunteering to plan the rescheduled event.

"And the lawn," he continued. "The grass has been looking shabby lately. Yellow spots. And mole holes. I'm trying to schedule an outside photo shoot of the First Family. I can't have the lawn looking like that."

"It's not moles. It's Milo. He's been busy," I explained. "But don't you worry. Lorenzo and I will patch the lawn once it stops raining. Although keeping up with the gardens will be more work without Gordon, it won't be forever. Gordon will be back."

"You really think so?" he asked, sounding genuinely surprised.

"Yes! He will!" I started to argue that we shouldn't give up on Gordon just because he was being falsely accused by a newspaper. A newspaper! But we'd reached the East Room.

Seth took my backpack, wished me luck, and pushed me into the room.

I WASN'T EXACTLY ON MY OWN AT THE BREAK-fast. Staffers from the East Wing and the West Wing as well as the super-efficient household staff attended to the needs of the women enjoying a gourmet breakfast buffet. And the Secret Service had doubled the number of agents that would be present at such an event.

The beautifully dressed ladies filling the gilded East Room hailed from various regional garden clubs, which was why I'd been asked to co-host. As I crossed the large room filled with golden chairs and round tables draped in white linens to the crowded buffet table on the far wall, the normal conversations in the room died as all eyes turned toward me.

Low murmurs filled the space until the room sounded eerily like the buzzing of a thick cloud of the annoying no-see-ums that congregate in Charleston's marshes.

"That's her." "She found the body." "Do you think it was murder?" "That's what the news reports say." "I wonder if it is a conspiracy. A cover-up." "I read online that the President ordered the curator killed to divert attention away from the skyrocketing gas prices and the plummeting economy."

"They're all idiots," a voice murmured near my ear. While the lady who'd said it spoke quite loudly, you could tell by her inflection it had been meant as a murmur.

"Pearle!" I hugged the older woman who had spoken to me. "It's good to see you."

"And it's good to see you, my dear Casey. Mable? Where did she go?"

"I'm right here." Pearle's dearest friend ambled toward us. Three East Wing staffers followed in her wake carrying plates piled with eggs, bacon, and delicious pastries.

The elderly Pearle Stone and Mable Bowls were social lionesses who presided over the D.C. area. Political power players served as their royal court. And the two ladies looked like royalty in their stylish fall-colored dresses with short-sleeved sweaters.

Rumor had it the two of them determined the success or failure of many political careers. Even First Lady Margaret Bradley treated both Pearle and Mable with great care and invited them to the White House often.

The two old dears were also expert gardeners and generously volunteered their time in the First Lady's kitchen garden, which was how they knew me.

"Come." Mable hooked her arm with mine. "Sit with us."

Not more than a few seconds after Pearle and Mable had embraced me, the questioning murmurs faded in the room and were replaced with the rumble of normal conversations again.

"How is the First Lady faring?" Mable asked once we were seated at a table near the podium in the center of the room.

"I don't know. I haven't seen her since the birth of the twins." I took a bite of a chocolate croissant. I smiled with delight as its rich, dark chocolate flavors teased my senses. "We are all praying for her and her sons."

The ladies nodded gravely.

"I heard she's been feeling stronger," Pearle said. "And that she might even make an appearance this morning."

"I don't think that will happen," I told my two favorite volunteers. Seth hadn't said anything about the First Lady. And he would have said something about it if she'd changed her mind about coming to the breakfast. He knew the First Lady's schedule better than anyone else in the White House. "Margaret hasn't made any public appearances."

"Well then, we'll be honored to be her first." Pearle patted my hand as she and Mable shared a knowing look. "Won't we?"

"Oh yes, it'll be such a thrill." Mable then leaned toward me. "But enough about that. How are you holding up, dear?"

"I haven't had much time to process any of it," I answered honestly. "I still can't believe what happened yesterday."

"We don't believe a word of what was in the newspapers today. Our Gordon is a lover, not a fighter," Pearle said.

Both Mable and Pearle treated Gordon like he was a teen rock star and they were his groupies. They pursued (and sometimes pinched) Gordon during the volunteer sessions in the kitchen garden. Gordon would grumble about it, but I could tell he loved every moment.

"And that curator," Mable added, "may she rest in peace, had enough enemies to fill a museum."

"Did you know Frida?" I asked.

"Hate to speak ill of the dead, but she was a nasty piece of work," Pearle confided. Mable nodded in agreement.

"What makes you say that?" Lorenzo, Gordon, and

Deloris all seemed to share that view as well. I was still in shock over how coldly Deloris had reacted when she'd learned about Frida's untimely demise.

"We had the misfortune of inviting her to one of our power teas," Pearle said as she sipped on a cup of tea one of the staff members had brought to the table.

"She had all the right credentials," Mable added. "A prestigious position at the White House. An Ivy League education. And the ability to talk to us about our lovely antiques. Who wouldn't want to invite someone like that into your home?"

"What did she do?" I asked.

"Oh, she had decent enough manners when it came to introducing her to everyone, but she desperately wanted to shoot up the social ladder," Pearle said as if ambition was a grave sin.

"Did she ever!" Mable cried.

"And that was wrong because . . ." I asked.

"Honey, you don't ever want to have someone around who's so hungry for power she tears down everyone around her to the point that they're left feeling like victims on a bloody battlefield," Pearle said.

"What do you mean? What did Frida do?" I asked again.

But before either could answer, several other women joined us at the table, bringing a swift end to that enlightening conversation.

Had Frida recently taunted and antagonized someone who not only held a grudge against her, but was also capable of murder? It was possible Gordon wasn't the only person who'd been the target of her vicious attacks.

A staff member cleared her throat into the microphone at the podium. After welcoming the women and thanking them for coming to the breakfast, she introduced me and the presentation I had promised months ago to give.

Pearle and Mable led the applause and beamed encouraging smiles when I walked up to the podium. I began the presentation about gardening at the White House by giving an overview of organic gardening and how the practice involves a holistic approach that takes the ecosystem into consideration. This wasn't a new idea.

The founding fathers worried about the farming practices of their day. Many of the techniques used up the soil instead of enhancing it. In 1818, James Madison had said in a speech that the protection of the environment was essential for the survival of the United States. He urged that we needed to find a place within the symmetry of nature. We needed to learn to work the land without destroying it.

This point segued nicely into the work I was doing with the History of the White House Gardens project. Gordon had put me in charge of identifying plants grown in the gardens during the White House during those early administrations.

I shared with the group how many of the plants grown in the White House gardens during those early administrations came from seeds collected from the wilderness of this new nation as well as favorite varieties grown in Europe.

"Without the hard work of these seed savers, the gardens wouldn't have been quite so diverse or as representative of the new nation. Seed harvesting is nothing new. Cultures from the beginning have harvested seeds and carried their most productive crops with them as human settlements spread across the world. In Iraq, scientists have discovered evidence of seed banks from as far back as 6750 BC.

"Here at the White House we will be continuing the tradition of saving and preserving heirloom varieties tomorrow when we harvest the seeds from the First Lady's kitchen garden. I hope you join with us in the effort and harvest and share the seeds from your own home gardens. Together we can continue the work our founding fathers thought was so important."

A noise at the back of the room caught my attention. I looked up from my hastily scrawled notes and watched First Lady Margaret Bradley walk slowly and stiffly into the room. Nearly every head turned to watch her entrance.

Margaret had lost weight. Of course she had—she'd just given birth to twin baby boys. But that wasn't what I meant.

Her cream-colored dress hung loosely on her body. Her cheeks had lost their fullness. She looked pale, sleep deprived, and in dire need of a hug.

Despite all that, it thrilled my heart to see her. We'd all been so worried about her health.

Margaret indicated with a graceful nod that I should finish my presentation. While her shocked staff hurried to assist her, I quickly wrapped up my talk and turned the microphone over to the First Lady.

Pearle and Mable had known from the beginning the First Lady would show up. *But how?*

I'd already suspected my favorite volunteers had better sources of information than most covert intelligence agencies, but this was *amazing*. Clearly, not even Margaret's own staff had known she'd intended to make this surprise visit.

"Thank you, Casey. You and *every* member of our gardening staff is valued and trusted here at the White House," the First Lady said as she took her place at the podium. "I am grateful for the tremendous job the gardeners do. Casey, for example, is working hard on developing a founding fathers' kitchen garden that will take a prominent position in our spring gardens. I invite you to return then to personally tour this new showpiece."

I winced, wishing Margaret hadn't mentioned that garden. It was still in the early planning stage. I wasn't sure if we'd be able to develop it in time. I hadn't yet identified all the plants we'd be using or even tried to locate the heirloom seeds. Too late, though. Members of the First Lady's press pool who had followed her into the room were furiously scribbling notes about the founding fathers' kitchen garden as if it were already a done deal.

"The gardeners are always giving me so much to look forward to," Margaret continued. "I hope all of you will join me in giving them, especially our head gardener who is fighting for his life in the hospital, your wholehearted support while the police conduct their investigation into yesterday's tragedy."

Ain't that the berries! My grandmother's expression of happiness popped into my mind. News that the First Lady supported Gordon and believed him innocent would definitely make the six o'clock news. Hearing her say it planted a huge smile on my face.

I tapped my fingers against my chin, wondering what I needed to do to get Manny and the rest of the police detectives to come around to the First Lady's way of thinking.

Chapter Ten

*The independent girl is a person before whose wrath
only the most rash dare stand, and, they, it must be
confessed, with much fear and trembling.*
—LOU HENRY HOOVER, FIRST LADY OF
THE UNITED STATES (1929–1933)

AFTER breakfast had ended, I descended the stairs two at a time. I was anxious to get back to the grounds office to work on a plan to support Gordon. As soon as my feet touched the carpet on the ground floor, ushers and maids appeared from, seemingly, out of the woodwork to express their concern for Gordon.

"Please tell him we're all praying for him," said a maid who had worked at the White House her entire adult life and had served six administrations.

"He's a good friend," said another maid. "He tended my mother's garden every other Saturday for several years when she was unable to look after it herself. I can't tell you what that meant for her in her last years."

"He's helped almost every one of us. If there's anything we can do," an usher said, "just say the word and we're there."

I thanked them all and promised I'd tell Gordon the next time I saw him about the generosity of the White House staff, which led to the tearful maids taking turns hugging me. Their sweet lemony scent clung to my clothes. It smelled like Rosebrook, like home. The memory wrapped around me like a warm embrace. I couldn't wait to tell Gordon about this morning's incredible show of support from nearly everyone, including the First Lady.

Even Milo, the First Family's goldendoodle mix, barked an excited greeting when he saw me. He bounded down the hallway with unfettered puppy exuberance. I held up my hands, worried he might knock me over. The overgrown puppy was now close to eighty pounds. His wavy golden fur was damp, his paws muddy. Someone must have already taken him on his morning walk.

He wagged his shaggy tail with such enthusiasm his back legs skidded around the marble floor like a car spinning on a patch of black ice as he closed the distance. Despite his nutty behavior, he was a pretty dog. A blaze of white on his chest highlighted his shimmering gold color. The white blaze swirled down his chest through his golden fur and extended down his right leg.

A touch of white on the tip of his tail waved at me as he lurched up on his hind legs and smeared his dirty front paws on my clean pants. Then, as trained, he plopped his rear on the floor. His tail still wagging like wild, he waited to be praised for spreading his muddy excitement and cheering me up.

I patted the silly puppy's head. Gordon always took Milo on his morning walk. But not this morning, and he wouldn't be able to walk Milo for a long time to come.

Milo nudged my leg with his big brown nose. His pink tongue hung out the side of his mouth, and his lips were pulled tight like he was smiling at me.

"You're a troublemaker, that's what you are. Digging holes in the lawn again, you naughty puppy," I said in a goofy voice—because how else did you talk to a dog? I petted his scruffy head again. "Is that why your paws are a mess? Whoever walked you should have cleaned you off before letting you inside. Yes, they should have, you silly puppy. Let's go get them cleaned off."

Milo groaned with delight. When I stopped petting him, he pranced happily behind me down the hallway toward the grounds office.

"What a charming sight," a heavily accented voice said, "a lady and her dog."

I nearly jumped out of my skin.

Marcel Beauchamp, the First Lady's decorator, watched as he leaned his large body against the wall near the closed door that led into the curator's office.

I swear I had just looked in that direction and hadn't seen anyone.

"Milo is the President's dog," I corrected.

"*Mais* the gardening staff looks after him, *non?*" he asked. He reached down and patted the pup's head. Milo licked Marcel's fingers as if the interior designer had slathered his digits in steak broth.

"Enough. It tickles." Marcel wiped his soggy hand on a stained linen handkerchief he'd produced from his pants pocket. If I were Miss Marple, I'd be thinking about how Marcel must be a bachelor and didn't have a wife to watch after him.

But I wasn't Miss Marple, and my instincts had been sorely lacking lately. Like now, a quick glance at Marcel's ring finger and the band of gold that I spotted there said he was married.

"I don't believe we've been formally introduced," Marcel said and launched into a history of his professional career, beginning on the mean streets of Paris. His big break came when he was discovered by an actress I'd never heard of. Then he moved to New York City. "I've been featured in all the best magazines. I'm sure you've heard of me."

I hadn't, but I nodded. I didn't doubt he was famous. To be fair, the only magazines I read featured flowers and vegetables and gardening tools, not tulle drapes and paint chips.

My elementary education, however, had included daily French lessons. I considered myself passably fluent.

"How is your redecorating proceeding?" I asked in my Southern-flavored schoolgirl French.

"Oh! You speak French! *Bon. Bon*." He switched to his native language. His words flowed together as if there were no spaces. It was fluid and beautiful. And I didn't understand a word.

"I suppose I should stick to *bonjour* and *merci*," I said, laughing at myself. "My French isn't as good as I thought it might be."

"I was telling you that the First Lady is quite pleased with the garden theme I'm weaving in the babies' room. And I also expressed my condolences for Frida and wished your Gordon a speedy recovery. What happened yesterday, a terrible shock for everyone, *non?*"

"Yes, it was quite a shock. Thank you," I said and then wondered what Marcel was doing hanging out near the curator's office. "Is there something I can help you with?"

"*Merci, oui*. I wished to see the marks left from the time of Madison when the White House burned. I was told I could find evidence of that time somewhere around here, but I have yet been able to find it. Perhaps you may aid me in my treasure hunt?"

"I sure can. Follow me." I led him down the hallway and through a pair of heavy metal doors that opened into the basement hallway located underneath the North Portico. Down here was where the carpenter's shop, florist shop, chocolate shop, cold storage, bowling alley, and the grounds offices were housed. I turned around and pointed to the stone archway above the double doors we'd just passed through.

The edges of the brown stone wall still bore the black marks from the time back in 1814 when British soldiers had marched into Washington, D.C., and had burned the White House to a smoldering shell.

"Ah." Marcel reached up and ran his hand over the scorched stone. "These colors will be perfect for the sofa in the rooftop solarium."

"I thought you were supposed to be decorating a space for the nursery."

"I was. I am. But the babies, they need a place to relax . . . to play. Do you not agree?"

I nodded and left him to his contemplation of the stone. I had more important things to do, like cleaning off Milo's paws and getting rid of this newspaper containing such a slanderous article against Gordon. Then I needed to check my to-do list and decide what needed to be done in the gardens today. With Milo still following my every step, I dropped the newspaper's crumpled pages in an oversized recycle bin at the far end of the basement hallway.

"Any luck finding the missing grounds schematic?" Special Agent Janie Partners asked as she rounded the corner. Today she was dressed in a gray suit with a sedate silk blue scarf around her neck. Milo greeted her as if he'd found a long-lost friend, his tail wagging in large circles.

"No, and I've looked everywhere." I leaned in closer to her so Marcel couldn't overhear us. "Does the Secret Service suspect the schematic's disappearance is related to Frida's death? She was angry about the misplaced research from her office. The schematic went missing, too. It could be connected."

"It . . . could . . . be . . ." Janie said slowly.

"I've looked for the schematic everywhere." Janie and Milo followed me down the hall and into the grounds office. "It was not on my—"

That's when I spotted . . . "*My desk!*"

Had someone ransacked the office and tossed all of our papers onto my desk? Lorenzo's drafting table looked pristine. So did every other surface.

"I thought you'd said you'd cleaned up," Janie said.

Milo woofed.

"I did!"

"It looks worse than it did yesterday." She wrinkled her nose. "If that's possible."

Janie was right. My desk looked as if a filing cabinet had gotten sick on it. File folders sporting the familiar White House stamp along with heaps of loose papers were everywhere.

"What happened here?" I cried. "Lorenzo? Are you here? Do you know why my desk looks like this?"

Lorenzo emerged from Gordon's private office. "What's the matter this time?" he asked as if I constantly complained, which I didn't.

"My desk." I gestured to the offending piece of office furniture.

"Oh. That." He scratched the back of his neck. "My meeting with Nadeem and Dr. Wadsin ended abruptly yesterday when we heard about Gordon and Frida."

"Why were you using my desk when you have a huge drafting table sitting just over there?"

Lorenzo shrugged. "You were the one that sent Nadeem and Dr. Wadsin to the grounds office. I assumed you wanted them to use your desk."

I opened my mouth. And then closed it.

Lorenzo shrugged and returned to Gordon's office as if he belonged there.

"It was cleared off," I grumbled to Janie while I cleaned Milo's muddy paws with one of the towels I kept in my desk's bottom drawer.

Janie patted my back. "I'm sure it was. Hey, look at the bright side. There's a good chance you'll find the lost Ark of the Covenant under that mess. I'll leave you to it."

Milo followed Janie, jumping up and nipping at her hands with every step. When I tried to call him back—his paws still needed a good washing—Janie volunteered to take care of the task herself. With that settled, I started the arduous task of straightening my desk again.

I felt like an excavator in search of a treasure. Still there was no sign of the lost Ark of the Covenant or the missing schematic—not that I'd expected to find either.

I did locate my to-do list under a series of letters between Thomas Jefferson and Benjamin Latrobe, a land surveyor, which I couldn't stop myself from reading. After some discussion back and forth, the two men had concluded the White House grounds should be divided into two sections. The northern section was designated as public grounds, and the southern section, which overlooked the Potomac River, was designated as private grounds for the President's family.

Tucked in another pile, I found an interesting letter Dolley Madison had penned to her friend Eliza Collins Lee that could help me in researching my founding fathers' kitchen garden. In it, Dolley detailed the building of hotbeds for cucumbers, how they'd grown a giant variety of beets that her husband had received from France, and had transplanted some of Madison's hautboy strawberries from Montpelier.

Another find in the pile was a copy of a journal entry written by James Madison that listed the Latin names for the plants grown in their kitchen garden their first year at the White House.

I jotted down the plant list on my notepad and then went searching on the Internet to check on the availability of the plants through our approved vendors. The hautboy strawberry, also known as a musk strawberry, was available. A hardy native of France, the small fruit boasted a mix of strawberry, raspberry, and pineapple flavors.

The other plants on Madison's list, however, didn't come up in any of the vendors' databases.

I was puzzling over this problem when Nadeem Barr barged into the office. His white shirt was half-untucked from his neatly pressed suit pants and his silver tie was more than a little askew.

"Frida was right. The research she'd compiled on the gardens during the Madison administration is gone." He dredged a hand through his dark hair. "And now Frida is gone. I—I don't know what to do."

Chapter Eleven

I feel as if I'm on stage for a part I never rehearsed.
—CLAUDIA "LADY BIRD" JOHNSON, FIRST LADY OF
THE UNITED STATES (1963–1969)

"**Y**OU mean *this* research?" I pointed to the towers of folders I'd stacked neatly on my desk.

"Are—are you kidding me?" Nadeem sputtered in that shy way of his. "Those papers didn't belong to Frida. That's my personal research. They, um, came from various outside sources. Most of it came from the National Arboretum and Dr. Wadsin. Only Frida had access to the curator's papers, although, you know, I think Frida had showed her work to Gordon at their last meeting."

"Don't tell me you think Gordon actually took her stupid research?" I said. The skin on the back of my neck started to prickle.

"Of . . . of course not." Nadeem backed up several paces.

"What about the First Lady's sister?" I asked. "Didn't Frida say Lettie was working with her on the project?" And Lettie was in the gardens at the time of her murder. Not that I suspected the First Lady's sister of anything sinister . . . yet.

Nadeem nodded. "Yes. Yes. Lettie was helping some."

"Well then, perhaps you should ask her where Frida's research went. Perhaps she borrowed it."

"Oh, no. I mean, Frida didn't let anyone close to her special files and notes. She didn't even trust me with the keys to the filing cabinets. In the time I've worked here, I've only been allowed to read her notes just a handful of times."

"If you don't have access, how do you know what is missing and what isn't?"

"Considering"—he cleared his throat—"how Frida died, um, I thought I should look through her things. See if I couldn't find her notes on Dolley Madison. So . . . so I came in early this morning and jimmied the top drawer of her desk to get to her keys. And when I opened the filing cabinet that held her research for the Madison administration, all the folders marked *Gardens* were empty."

"What would someone want with those moldy old papers? They're not even originals, are they?" I asked.

"They're not. But she had more than just documents in her folders." He started to pace. "The value of her files was her personal notes. She could see things and put together facts in a way that just boggled my mind. And those notes are gone. Vanished. Poof!"

"Listen, Nadeem, there's no reason to panic over this. Not yet. We don't know why anyone might want to steal Frida's work. We don't even know the papers are truly missing."

Had Frida stumbled across a map to a forgotten treasure, the same treasure she'd accused Gordon of wanting to find? I doubted it. "The most likely explanation is Frida misplaced her work and wrongly accused Gordon of theft. Not a good explanation, however, since it does nothing to help clear Gordon of Frida's murder. What other projects was Frida working on?"

Nadeem listed several projects. Most involved the restoration of important pieces of furniture or the documentation of various pieces of work held in one of the White House's many storehouses.

"She didn't happen to be involved with planning President Bradley's meeting with Turbekistan's envoy?" The question popped out of my mouth even before I remembered that I wasn't supposed to know about the meeting.

"Tur—What are you talking about?" His dark brows flattened as he frowned.

"Nothing. Forget I mentioned it."

"If you know something about . . ." His voice lowered. He took a step toward me.

I backed up. My leg bumped against my desk. "I'm simply trying to figure out why someone would want to hurt Frida, and who at the White House had a motive."

According to Pearle and Mable, Frida had more enemies than friends, thanks to her out-of-control ambition. I looked at the piles of meticulously detailed research Nadeem had left on my desk yesterday. What if he'd made an important discovery? And what if Frida had stolen from him the proof of that discovery? What if she'd been getting ready to claim Nadeem's research as her own?

That would explain why Nadeem had been so anxious to dig through Frida's locked filing cabinets the morning after her death. It would also explain why he'd be so upset to discover her research was actually missing.

Or was Nadeem a spy, planted by a foreign government to disrupt the oil negotiations with Turbekistan?

Had I bumped into him at the hospital?

Had he been lurking at my back door?

That sounded like spy behavior to me.

I grabbed Nadeem's arm and pulled him away from Gordon's private office, where I suspected Lorenzo was sitting near the door, listening to our every word.

"What were you doing outside my apartment this morning?" I demanded in a harsh whisper.

Nadeem jerked back. "I—I don't know what you're talking about."

"Come on, Nadeem. I saw you running down the back stairs," I said, still keeping my voice low. "When I knocked on your apartment door, why didn't you answer? What's going on?"

"I—I—" he stammered.

I folded my arms over my chest and raised my brows, waiting for him to give me an answer. He glanced at the door to the hallway as if calculating an escape route.

"The person you saw, it—it wasn't me," he said at last.

"I suppose I also didn't bump into you at the hospital yesterday afternoon, either?"

He held up his trembling hands in surrender. "I swear. Ask your roommate. I met, um, Alyssa this . . . this morning as I left for the White House. She nearly tackled me as I walked out of the backyard."

That sounded like Alyssa. She had a habit of coming on too strong the first time she met a man. Any man.

"Then who did I see at my back door?"

Nadeem's top lip started to tremble. "I don't know. It wasn't me. I—I was anxious to get into the office to look for the research Frida had claimed was stolen. I want to impress the East Wing by taking charge. I, you know, I was hoping they might consider me for the head curator position."

"That is something I can believe." Everyone who worked at the White House possessed some degree of ambition. Apparently Frida had more than her fair share. "Who else has a key to your apartment?"

His eyes darted uncertainly toward the door again. "I mean it, Casey. I wasn't there. I don't know who or what you saw."

I watched him. He was acting unsure, nervous . . . and exactly like I'd expect a brand-new White House staffer to act, especially one who was as sensitive and soft-spoken as Nadeem.

Alyssa was crazy. This guy wasn't a spy. Spies had to be cool under pressure. That wasn't Nadeem. The more I questioned him, the more his top lip trembled.

Besides, although Nadeem might have a motive—make that several possible motives—for killing Frida, he didn't have the opportunity. Frida had sent him back to the East Wing before she entered the Children's Garden to talk to Gordon. He'd told me that himself.

"Okay," I said, "I believe you." *Maybe.*

Unfortunately, believing him didn't get me any closer to helping clear Gordon's name.

"Cathy? Oh, Cathy, there you are. I've been looking everywhere for you," came a singsong voice from the open door behind me. I cringed.

Lettie Shaw, the First Lady's sister, clomped into the office and picked up a file folder from the stack I'd already sorted.

Lettie was dressed casually in a blue-and-white-striped blouse. Her deep blue wide-legged pants swirled around her legs as she came to an abrupt stop. The heavy makeup she wore didn't completely hide the dark circles under her eyes. "I see you have some filing for me to do, Cathy."

"It's Casey," I gently corrected her and retrieved the file folder before she could lose it in her unfathomable filing system. "These papers need to go back to the curator's office."

"Of course." She pressed her fingertips to her temples and winced.

"Can I help you?" I asked when she continued to stand there rubbing her head.

"You wouldn't happen to have a flask of something hidden away in your desk drawers? I could use a little eye-opener this morning." She waved that thought away before I could answer her. "Never mind. You wouldn't. Everyone is such goodie-goodies around here. Anyhow, Seth said you're in desperate need of help. So I'm here to work. I could organize your desk again."

"No!" I jumped in front of my desk before she could upset the organized piles. "I mean . . ." My face heated. Please tell me I hadn't just shouted at the First Lady's sister. If she wanted to make a mess of the neat piles on my desk, I should let her.

"Lettie!" Lorenzo called out with obvious glee, confirming I was correct he'd been listening from behind Gordon's office door. He bounced into the room, his voice booming.

Lettie winced and backed away from him.

"As *senior* assistant, I'll be taking over the History of the White House Gardens project and anything else Gordon happened to be working on. And we'd love any assistance you could provide."

"Of course you would," Lettie muttered. She dropped into my desk chair and rubbed her temples some more.

"Wait a minute, Lorenzo," I said. "Why should you take the lead? I've been working on the founding fathers' kitchen garden project, which will be part of the historical garden exhibition. So it only makes sense I step in and fill the void until Gordon returns." I'd initially volunteered to take the lead on the entire exhibition. "If Gordon hadn't insisted on acting as project leader, I would have taken that position. Come to think about it, why *did* Gordon volunteer to take charge of the project if he hated working with Frida?"

"Because he didn't want *you* to work with Frida," Lorenzo said as if I should have already known.

"What? Why? Did he think I'd believe her crazy stories about missing treasures?"

"Missing treasure?" Lettie lifted her head long enough to ask.

Lorenzo glanced over at Lettie slouched in my desk chair and then at Nadeem, who was leaning forward on the balls of his feet, watching with rapt interest.

"Well?" I pressed.

"No, he wasn't worried about what you'd do, okay?" Lorenzo huffed. "It was because Frida had a nasty reputation for getting people fired. No one in the White House wanted to work with Frida. No one."

"I did," Nadeem said softly.

"I thought I did, too," I said. "She had a solid reputation for knowing everything about White House history."

Nadeem nodded. "All of the professors I studied under called her a savant. Her focus was clearly on the White House."

"She knew her history inside and out," Lettie agreed.

Lorenzo huffed again. "Fine. She was a genius and a saint. But that doesn't change the situation at hand. In Gordon's absence, someone needs to take charge."

"And you assume it should be you?" I asked.

"I am the senior assistant."

"And I'm in charge of implementing the organic gardening program," I countered.

Lorenzo snorted. "What does that have to do with anything?"

"Casey, I need to have a word with you," Jack said from the doorway. He was dressed in his battle dress black fatigues that made him equal parts sexy and dangerous. My heart sped up at the sight of him. He entered the room and stood directly between me and Nadeem.

Nadeem widened his stance and seemed determined not to be pushed out of the conversation. "We're, um, in the middle of something right now."

"I see that." Jack turned to glare at Nadeem. "Casey, it's about that situation we discussed this morning."

"This morning? Oh! Forget what I said. I'm sure I was wrong."

"You weren't wrong." Jack linked his arm with mine, which made my arm feel all tingly and happy.

"I wasn't?"

"If we can go somewhere private?" Ah, if only he wanted to go somewhere private for another reason . . .

Alas, Jack was on duty. And we were at the White House with security cameras covering nearly every inch of the building.

And Nadeem was a spy? My cheeks heated as I sneaked a glance in Nadeem's direction. His dark gaze narrowed. He watched me as if he knew Jack and I were talking about him.

"Go on, Casey, I have everything under control here. I'll take good care of Lettie." Lorenzo's eyes sparkled with barely contained excitement. Rubbing elbows with the wealthy and the powerful in D.C. gave him endless joy. He snaked around me toward my desk and the tidy piles of research on it. "Of course Casey would like you to organize her desk, Lettie. Just the other day she was commenting on your unique filing system."

"Was she?" Lettie brightened when she heard that. She picked up a pile of Nadeem's folders. "I have to admit my system tends to confound *some* people."

Just those who need to find anything in their office. I couldn't let her wreck havoc with my filing system again. It was already chaotic enough. "Uh, uh, Lorenzo? Doesn't Gordon have an entire file drawer devoted to historical documents?" I said. "And shouldn't we use Lettie to organize those files and pull out anything that will help us with the History of—"

"Sheesh, Casey, you didn't let me finish," Lorenzo said. "What I was saying before Casey interrupted was that even though Casey needs help, she can straighten her own desk. Lettie, since you've already been working with Frida on the gardens project, wouldn't you rather go through Gordon's files in search of additional information that can help us?" He briefly explained what was involved.

Lettie readily agreed.

"Fantastic," I said. "Let me show you—"

"I'll do that," Lorenzo cut in. "I'll be taking over as project leader."

"Very well. You win. I need to talk with Jack anyhow. Nadeem, why don't you get these papers back to your office and then continue going through Frida's filing cabinets? Perhaps the papers she lost fell behind a cabinet or desk?"

"I suppose . . ." Nadeem sounded like a heartbroken schoolboy.

"Once I'm done here and while Lorenzo is busy working with Lettie, you can catch me up on everything Frida's been working on," I said and pushed him toward the door. My plan was simple. Lorenzo would take the lead on the project and keep Lettie busy and out of trouble, which was

a full-time job, while I worked with Nadeem to retrace
Frida's last days. I hoped to figure out who else at the White
House had a motive for wanting Frida dead.

"Jack," I said as I marched out the door, "aren't you
coming?"

ONCE EVERYONE WAS SETTLED, JACK DIRECTED
me toward a set of heavy double doors that opened out onto
a sunken courtyard beside the North Portico.

The rain was still coming down steadily. The deep rumble of thunder vibrated in the cool air.

Although there wasn't usually shelter anywhere in the
courtyard, the kitchen staff had erected a large tent just outside the double doors so they could unload incoming pro-
duce and canned goods from a large delivery truck that had
backed into the space.

"Rain, rain, and more rain. I hope the kitchen garden
isn't flooding. Volunteers are coming in tomorrow to harvest seeds. I'll need to send an e-mail telling them to be
ready for mud," I said as Jack put his arm over my shoulder
and led me to the far corner of the tent and out of the way
of the kitchen staff.

"Uh-huh," he said. "You and Nadeem looked chummy
back there. You aren't planning to ditch me in favor of letting Mr. Tall, Dark, and Creepy play sidekick?"

"Only if you don't spill what you know about him." I
playfully shoved his chest. "What did you learn?"

"Only that Nadeem's security clearance is well above
my pay grade," Jack said. "And that's saying something. It
also means I can't touch his file."

"But he's an assistant curator."

"Exactly. Why would he need a security clearance level
that rivals the Secretary of Defense's?" Jack said. "So I did a
little poking around. Made a few phone calls to some of my
buddies working covert ops. My mentioning Nadeem Barr's
name caused quite a stir in the intelligence community this
morning. Turns out, our new assistant curator worked dark

ops for both the military and the CIA. Apparently he implemented off-the-book espionage plots and assassinations. And these guys don't like anyone, not even the Secret Service, poking into their business."

My mind buzzed.

Someone had murdered Frida yesterday. And today, I learn that her new assistant was an assassin?

The buzzing in my head grew louder. The envoy from Turbekistan had been worried that Frida's murder had been an attack against his negotiations with President Bradley. What if he'd been right? What if Nadeem was now working for the other team and was a mole? What if Nadeem had preemptively sent me that threatening text message to confuse me?

Good gravy. I'd caught Nadeem lurking at my back door, yet I'd let him talk me out of believing what I'd seen with my own eyes.

"Casey, I want you to be careful around him. This guy scares me," Jack confessed.

And no one scared Jack.

Chapter Twelve

There is nothing more important than
a good, safe, secure home.
—ROSALYNN CARTER, FIRST LADY OF
THE UNITED STATES (1977–1981)

"**W**HAT did I miss?" Lorenzo asked. He squeezed between a member of the kitchen staff who was pushing a handcart loaded with crates of oranges and the wall. And didn't stop squeezing until he'd positioned himself between Jack and myself.

"Well?" Lorenzo asked impatiently. "What are we doing to find Frida's killer?"

"Doing?" I asked. "*We?*"

"Gordon is my friend, too. I've worked with both Gordon and Frida for the past nine years. Well, not Frida so much. I spent most of my time trying to *avoid* her. But I care about Gordon, and I want to join in on the investigation."

I glanced at Jack and shook my head. "There's nothing for you to join." As much as I liked to pretend otherwise, I was not an amateur sleuth tucked within the pages of a paperback novel. I was flesh and blood. And I liked to keep my blood in my body, where it belonged. "All I plan to do is provide Manny with a few alternative suspects. You might remember the last time I got all mixed up in a murder investigation, I ended up accusing several innocent people."

"Yeah, you ended up looking like an idiot," Lorenzo was quick to agree, "but this is Gordon."

"Yes, and Manny knows Gordon. The detective is a smart guy. I'm sure once he sees that Frida had a bucketful of enemies, he'll get to the bottom of what happened."

"But the newspaper said—" Lorenzo argued.

"When do the newspapers ever get anything right?" I countered.

"Casey." Jack moved to stand next to Lorenzo. "This time the article did report the correct facts. Manny is being careful, collecting all the evidence before making a move. But from what I've heard, the DA will be pressing charges against Gordon before the week's end."

"No." I couldn't believe it. "Manny wouldn't let that happen. Once he sees that there are others who—"

"Everyone from his superiors to my superiors, and political powerhouses, are pressuring Manny to close the investigation as quickly as possible."

"That's why we need to help," Lorenzo said.

"No, we don't—" I said.

Jack grimaced. "As much as I hate to say this, I agree. Casey, you and Lorenzo are in a better position than anyone else to find out what really happened between Frida and Gordon. On the surface, all the clues are leading to Gordon. And I'm afraid Manny isn't going to be given the time to look any deeper."

"Are you serious? You want *me* to investigate?" Jack hated it when I stuck my nose where he thought it didn't belong.

Jack jammed his hands in his pockets and gave me a hard look. "Yeah, I'm serious. This time."

"So what do we do?" Lorenzo asked a little too enthusiastically.

I didn't have an answer for him. And I still wasn't ready to include Lorenzo in the "we" of our investigative team. Heck, I wasn't ready to include *me* in it.

The rain was letting up, and since I did my best thinking in the garden, I shook my head and walked out from under the busy tent into the cool drizzle.

Both Jack and Lorenzo followed as I wandered across the North Lawn, past the East Wing, and through a gate that led to the South Lawn.

"Wouldn't it have been faster, not to mention drier, to have cut through the White House?" Lorenzo groused when he saw where I was headed.

I slogged diagonally across the soggy lawn, down the steep hill. If Jack or Lorenzo (or anyone else for that matter) had chosen this path that sent us trampling on the grass after such a heavy rainstorm, I would have scolded them for it.

But I was determined as I made a beeline to the spot where Frida had died.

Yards of yellow police tape still marked the perimeter of the Children's Garden. At the periphery, I spotted two shallow holes in the grass that hadn't been there yesterday. "Who was watching Milo on his morning walk?" I asked.

"I don't know," Jack was quick to answer. "It wasn't me."

"Whoever it was, he did a horrible job. Milo has been out of control lately."

"Why are we looking for holes in the grass when there's a murder to solve?" Lorenzo asked.

"I'm not looking for holes. I'm looking for clues," I said.

"The police aren't going to let you anywhere near the crime scene," Lorenzo grumbled.

Maybe, I thought to myself as I walked up to the police officer who was huddled underneath an umbrella at a break in the yellow tape.

Jack lifted his brows, but didn't offer any advice.

Two paths led into the garden. For the privacy of the first families, both paths faced the White House. They were narrow and curved so that anyone who wandered down the footpath into the Children's Garden disappeared completely from view.

It was the farthest path, the one on the west side of the yard, that the police were using as a controlled entrance point. Although I didn't recognize the beefy officer standing guard at the break in the yellow tape, I read his name off the name tag pinned to his shiny black windbreaker.

"Lieutenant Brinks." I thrust out my hand. "I'm Casey Calhoun. I, um, found Frida yesterday."

"Sorry to hear that, ma'am," Lieutenant Brinks said in a deep baritone voice. His cautious gaze shifted to beyond my shoulder, where Jack and Lorenzo were standing a few feet behind me.

"I was wondering if—" I started to say.

"Ma'am," he interrupted. "I can't help you."

"But I didn't—"

"As I said, this is a waste of time." Lorenzo started to walk back up to the White House.

I flashed Jack an imploring look. With a few words, I was sure he could help talk our way into the crime scene. He smiled and shrugged and hung back, letting me do all the heavy lifting.

"Is Detective Hernandez—" I asked.

"He's the one who warned me about you, ma'am. Turn around." The lieutenant wagged his meaty finger at me. "And come back when we're done."

"We're done here." It wasn't Manny who'd made that announcement, as I'd hoped, but Mike Thatch, the special agent in charge of Jack's team.

Jack moved to stand beside me as Thatch emerged from the garden's narrow path.

"Of course the rain couldn't have stopped a few hours ago when the CSI guys were knee-deep in mud, trying to—" Thatch stopped when he spotted us.

"What are *you* doing here?" he demanded. His gaze was fixed solely on me.

"Funny thing about gardeners, you often find us lurking in—I don't know—in the gardens. We're like beetles— turn over a leaf, and look, there's another one."

"Ha. Ha." Thatch didn't sound amused.

"Wait! There's another one now." I pointed to Lorenzo's retreating back.

"What do you want?" Thatch rubbed his shoulder and stretched his neck to the right until it popped.

"Gordon didn't do it," I said.

He sighed and then stretched his neck to the left.

"I mean it. You've known Gordon longer than I have. You know he wouldn't hurt anybody. Since Gordon can't talk for himself right now, I'm going to speak up for him. I need to talk with Detective Hernandez. I need to make sure he understands that Gordon didn't do it."

Thatch rotated his hunched shoulders.

"Follow me," he said with a hint of resignation.

After directing Lieutenant Brinks to take down the police tape, he led Jack and me into the Children's Garden and to the grouping of trampled azalea bushes where I'd found Frida's body. A canvas tent had been erected over the area.

"The tent was set up to preserve what was left of the crime scene from the rain," Thatch explained before I had the chance to ask. "The CSI guys spent the past twelve hours sifting through the leaves looking for . . . anything."

He put his hand on my shoulder. I nearly jumped clear out of my skin in shock at the gesture. It was so out of character for him to offer anyone comfort, especially *me*.

"Gordon and I started our service at the White House the same year. He'd sometimes join me and some of the other agents after work to grab a beer at The Underground. I consider him a friend," Thatch explained.

"Then you should understand why I'm upset. I can't stand silently by when Manny is pushing to charge Gordon for a murder you and I both know he didn't commit."

His hand tightened on my shoulder. "You might change your mind about that after you hear what we know."

"I won't ever change my mind about Gordon."

Thatch turned me around so I was standing with my back to him. He then made a slashing motion at my neck. "This was how Frida was killed with the pruning saw. A quick, but deadly, slash."

I pushed Thatch away from me and rubbed my neck even though he hadn't touched me there.

"The surveillance video from the lawn shows Gordon entering the garden using the same path we took. He was holding the saw. Frida came down the path about an hour later. No one else came down this path. It was just the two of them in here." Anger—or perhaps frustration—strangled Thatch's voice. "The police lab found your fingerprints and Gordon's on the pruning saw's handle. And no one else's. What more evidence do you need?"

"What about the hole I found at the base of the apple tree?" I asked. "Why was it there?"

"The CSI techs dug through every inch of this space. They enlarged the hole. Why is it there? I don't know. Milo probably dug it."

"No, the edges were too smooth. It had to have been dug out with a trowel. Or something similar."

"It's just another hole in the ground, Casey. Forget about it." Thatch rolled his eyes as he said it.

I turned my gaze up to the canopy of oaks and elms above us. A fat raindrop fell from an oak leaf and hit me in the eye. "The Secret Service doesn't have any hidden cameras in here?"

"No, why would we? This garden is a retreat from the constant scrutiny for the First Family. President Bradley is adamant about keeping it that way," Thatch explained as if I should have already known that. "Besides, why would we need cameras in here? We keep vigilant watch over the perimeter of the White House and the perimeter of the fence. No one gets in or out of this garden without us knowing."

"And yet you don't know who killed Frida."

"I do know." Thatch gestured toward the path. "No one else came into the garden."

"I saw Nadeem Barr, Lettie Shaw, and Marcel Beauchamp heading either in or out of the gardens around that time. Is Manny talking with them?"

"You think the First Lady's sister should be a suspect?"

"It makes just as much sense as blaming Gordon," I shot back.

"I think what Casey is trying to say," Jack jumped in to say before I could jam my foot any farther into my mouth. Accusing any member of the First Family of wrongdoing was serious business. The kind of serious business that could end a career. "Was Ms. Shaw—or any of the others wandering on the South Lawn at the time—questioned? Did one of them see or hear anything suspicious, for example?"

"We're all doing our jobs. I'll thank you not to question that," Thatch snapped. "Manny has questioned everyone. And the cameras recorded what happened out here. No one else came into this garden."

Which was bad news for Gordon. Jack was right. The police and Secret Service had apparently already decided on Gordon's guilt. Motive, means, and opportunity were the cornerstones of building a conviction against a suspect. Did the police have those three pieces of the puzzle? Could they build a case against Gordon? I forced myself to see the investigation from Manny's perspective in order to try and answer those questions.

Motive? (Gordon and Frida were in the middle of a bitter argument. Gordon had claimed that Frida was trying to destroy him. Frida had hinted that she would get Gordon fired.)

Means? (Gordon's fingerprints were on the murder weapon.)

Opportunity? (Gordon and Frida were alone in the garden.)

"But Gordon didn't do it," I said more to myself than to either Thatch or Jack.

I suddenly felt trapped. The thick wall of bushes and canopy of trees that created the walls in the Children's Garden seemed to push in on me.

Other than one of the two winding pathways, there was no other entrance or exit to the garden. Chain-link fencing covered with thick curtains of black landscape fabric was sandwiched between tall hedges to ensure the garden's privacy. The fencing spanned the length of the western and southern ends of the garden. On the eastern side, the tennis court's chain-link fence blocked a hasty exit.

So Gordon and Frida were alone in the garden.

I frowned as I studied the fresh pruning cuts Gordon had made to the garden's privets and elms. He'd removed two sizable branches and several smaller branches from at least ten plants.

"Casey?" Jack asked. "Are you okay?"

"Of course I am. Why wouldn't I be?"

"You're spinning in circles," Jack pointed out.

"I'm thinking."

Thatch made a rude noise.

"The branches," I said. "Gordon was in the garden for over an hour while he pruned?"

"Obviously," Thatch said, pointing to the trimmed privets.

"He was in the garden the entire time? He never left?"

"It's all on the surveillance video," Thatch said.

"Then tell me this. If Gordon had never left the garden, and if he was busy trimming the trees and bushes in here, where are all the branches?"

Chapter Thirteen

*. . . steady as a clock, busy as a bee,
and cheerful as a cricket . . .*
—MARTHA WASHINGTON, FIRST LADY OF
THE UNITED STATES (1789–1797)

LETTIE Shaw hummed.

She'd settled into Gordon's office for the afternoon as she sorted through the historical documents that had been stored in a bottom file drawer. And she continued to hum, off tune, like a scratched CD, repeating the same short refrain over and over and over.

I crossed the room to where Lorenzo sat hunched at his drafting table.

"Why is she humming so much?" I whispered.

"Don't know. The hangover is wearing off, I suppose."

"Hangover?" Were First Ladies' sisters allowed to have hangovers? Was Lettie the problem Seth had been moaning about during that conversation I'd overheard? "Is there anything we can do to make her stop humming?" I whispered.

"Does it bother you?" Lorenzo lifted his head long enough to ask.

"I'm about to go mad. That, or cut off my ears. Or both," I said.

"Now you know how I feel."

"What? I—"

"Whenever we work at the greenhouse, you hum. The entire time, you hum. It's torture."

"I don't hum. Well, not much."

He glared at me.

"I sound like *that?*"

He nodded.

"Well, won't you say something to her?" I asked. "I can't think."

I'd even tried screwing my fingers in my ears, but the droning sound seemed to defy all barriers. I needed to concentrate.

The only thing I'd written on the yellow pad of paper since I'd returned from talking with Thatch was, "Where are the branches?"

Thatch had concluded that the CSI guys must have bagged and tagged the branches. I told him I hadn't seen the branches yesterday, either.

"I wouldn't have expected your untrained eyes to have noticed such a small detail," he'd countered, adding that the shock of finding Gordon *and* Frida would have blinded me to seeing anything important.

When Jack agreed with me, saying he also hadn't seen the branches, Thatch's face turned a funny shade of puce. He grumbled something about looking into the matter and then ordered Jack back to work.

Not willing to give up, I'd called Detective Hernandez. Manny's phone went straight to voice mail. I left a message telling him about the missing branches and asking him to check to see if the CSI team had collected them. That had been nearly an hour ago, and he still hadn't called me back.

And Lettie had hummed the entire time.

"What are you doing?" I asked Lorenzo as I peered over his shoulder to study the large-scale schematic he was currently marking up.

"I'm re-creating the schematic you lost the other day."

The quick movements of his pen made a *scratch-scratch* sound as he worked.

"I didn't lose it." Not that defending myself mattered. Lorenzo enjoyed believing the worst of me. I'd long given up on forging a friendly working relationship with him. He clearly resented that the First Lady had brought me in to develop an organic gardening program for the gardens last year.

Even though I didn't agree with how he vented his frustration, I was beginning to understand it. He'd spent the past nine years trying to catch the notice of the various first families who called the White House home, only to be ignored. Finally when a true gardening enthusiast had moved into the White House, he must have expected he'd get the recognition he'd long deserved. But that didn't happen. Margaret Bradley had, instead, hired me.

"Aren't you going to ask what I found out in the Children's Garden?" I said.

"Why should I? It was a crime scene. Off-limits."

"Actually, it's no longer a crime scene. We're free to send our crew in there to clean up at any time."

Lorenzo looked up from the schematic. "And?"

I explained to him about the missing branches. "The surveillance video shows Gordon entering the Children's Garden and not leaving. So where did those branches go?"

"Gordon must have taken them out through a gap near the gardening sheds," Lorenzo answered without even having to think about it.

I'd known there were *narrow* gaps in the Children's Garden's fencing and landscape fabric. I'd torn my way through one of them when pursuing a killer this past spring. I'd *torn* my way through. "I don't understand. He would have had to cut through the fabric."

"No, he wouldn't. He could pin back the landscaping fabric and pass through an opening next to the gardening shed." Lorenzo pushed back from the drafting table. "We use it all the time."

"An opening in the fencing? Does the Secret Service know about this?"

"I don't know. I don't see why they should. It's not a security matter. The fencing is there as a visual barrier. It has nothing to do with fencing someone in or keeping someone out."

"And there's an opening, a gap in the fencing?" I said again as the idea took root. "You mean I didn't have to maneuver the wheelbarrow down that winding path this past spring when planting all those thousands of bulbs? Why didn't anyone tell me?"

"Why should I have told you?"

"Right. You wouldn't have. But why didn't Gordon—"

"I told him you already knew about it, but you didn't care to use it." Lorenzo smiled. It was a teeth-flashing, not particularly friendly, expression.

"Gee, thanks, Lorenzo. Okay, there's a gap in the fence. So . . ." I wished Lettie would stop that infernal humming. I needed to think. I hurried back to my desk and grabbed my yellow pad. "So anyone on the South Lawn at the time—"

Lettie broke out singing. The loud tuneless song she belted out made me completely lose my train of thought.

"Do you know who else was in the gardens at that time?" Lorenzo asked.

I closed my eyes and tried to block out Lettie's off-key tune. "What is that song?" I asked.

"I don't know. Focus, Casey." Lorenzo snapped his fingers. "You were on the South Lawn. Who else did you see?"

"I saw some East Wing staffers, but they went in before Frida came out." I lowered my voice. "Lettie Shaw was out there." I'd overheard her odd phone conversation. It sounded as if someone had been pressuring her. "Marcel Beauchamp was outside, again, getting inspiration for his designs. And Nadeem Barr, but Frida had sent Nadeem back inside before she went into the Children's Garden. And I'm pretty sure Marcel went back inside a few minutes before Nadeem did."

"We'll need to find out if anyone else was out there. Perhaps your boyfriend can help out with that."

"Okay, I'll ask Jack."

"Ask Nadeem, too."

"Ah . . . not him."

"Why not? He might have seen someone."

"Because . . ." Should I tell Lorenzo what I knew about Nadeem? Knowing Lorenzo, he wouldn't believe me. "We shouldn't talk with him yet. He might still be a suspect. And if he isn't, he might insist on helping our investigation."

That last part convinced Lorenzo. "Good point. We don't need anyone taking credit for the work we're doing."

"Right. When Gordon was carrying away the pruned branches, anyone could have slipped through the gap in the fence—"

"Or through the second one where the Children's Garden backs up to the kitchen garden."

"There's more than one?" I asked.

Lorenzo nodded.

"Okay. Someone slipped through one of the many gaps and killed Frida," I said as I started to put some of the pieces together. "Gordon returned and found Frida."

"The shock of it caused his heart failure, and he fell forward into the pond," Lorenzo added as I wrote this all down on my yellow notepad.

Lorenzo snatched the notepad out of my hands. "What are you waiting for? Let's go look for evidence that this is what happened so we can show it to that detective friend of yours."

He didn't make it more than a step when Lettie stopped singing. "Lorenzo," she called from inside Gordon's office, "you have to see this—

"Oh, Cathy, you're here, too," she said as she poked her head out of Gordon's office.

"Casey," I corrected.

"Right," she said. She waved a file folder in the air. "I found this in Gordon's cabinet. Look! It's Frida's missing research. How do you think it got into Gordon's office?"

"It can't be the same research." Even Frida had admitted Gordon couldn't have taken it.

But Lettie was shaking her head. "No. Frida had let me look through her papers and notes from the Madison administration one afternoon. I remember seeing this." She flipped through the pages. "And this. What could it mean?"

"It means nothing," I said. And yet I needed to be sure. I took the file and carried it to the curator's office. Lettie and Lorenzo jogged behind me to catch up.

The curator's offices were located on the same floor as the grounds office, but in the main part of the White House off the north hall. The office was created in 1961 after the White House was officially declared a museum, a move that had been spearheaded by First Lady Jacqueline Kennedy.

The oddly shaped space had first served as a kitchen. It later became a furnace room, a servants' dining room, and an upholstery shop before becoming the curator's office. Bookshelves crammed with documents lined every available wall space in the windowless room.

That's where I found Nadeem . . . *the killer spy.*

Half-moon glasses perched on the end of his nose as he read from the pages of a three-ring binder stuffed full of papers. On the top of the page he was reading was written *HMS Fantome.*

The spectacles made him look scholarly, and harmless. Were they props or did he really have bad eyesight? I watched him for a moment, trying to imagine this handsome, dark-skinned man with his beguiling smile traveling the world to kill enemies of the state. He looked more like a researcher, someone who preferred to spend his days in a library rather than dodging bullets or installing bombs in world leaders' cigars.

I tentatively knocked on the door. I didn't want to startle someone who might kill first and ask questions later. "Nadeem? Are you busy?"

The way he flipped his notebook closed and jumped up from his chair made him look suspicious. "Yes? Has—has something happened?"

Either that or his nerves were shot. If he were a spy, wouldn't Frida's murder just be another day at the office for him? Wouldn't he be trained to hide his nerves?

I handed Nadeem the file folder. "Tell me this isn't part of the research that is missing from Frida's files," I said, "and we'll get out of your way."

He flipped the folder open and thumbed through a few of the pages.

"Where did you get this?" He flipped through some more pages.

"I found it in Gordon's office," Lettie announced.

Nadeem swallowed hard and slowly turned to the next page. "Let me check something." He sat down at his desk and punched some keys on his computer. A table popped up on his screen. "Yes. Yes. It's all there. This is the missing research. All except for Frida's personal notes."

"How can you be sure?" I asked.

"They've been indexed in this database. This is the research Frida had accused Gordon of stealing."

I could have kicked Nadeem for saying that in front of Lettie.

"Ow!" Nadeem cried and grabbed his shin.

"Sorry," Lorenzo said. "My foot slipped."

I bit back a smile, but Lorenzo's kick had come too late. Lettie pushed her way in front of me and leaned over the desk to look at the computer screen. "I knew it! This is the stolen folder," Lettie crowed, sounding even more excited.

"Missing," I corrected.

"I found it in Gordon's file cabinet. You don't think . . ." Lettie's voice trembled with excitement. "It has to be . . . Gordon killed Frida because he wanted Jefferson's lost treasure for himself. I can picture what happened now. Frida caught Gordon trying to steal the treasure, and when she confronted him—" She made a slicing motion over her throat. "We have to take this to the police."

"No, we don't need to involve the police." Lorenzo grabbed the folder. A photocopied letter fell out and fluttered to the floor.

I snatched up the paper before Nadeem could. The assistant curator shifted nervously in his chair as I studied what looked like a copy of a letter Dolley Madison had penned a few years after her husband's presidency. She was writing to a woman whose name I didn't recognize.

I read the part aloud that had immediately caught my attention. "I had entrusted Jefferson's treasure to the gardener, a Mr. McGraw, I believe he called himself. In the pandemonium following our return to Washington and having to contend with the near-destruction of the White House, I never had a chance to quiz him about the fate of the treasure. Did the British take it as part of their spoils? My attempts to contact Mr. McGraw have been for naught, but I am continuing my efforts to locate the man in question. I am steadfast in my determination to find the treasure my friend Mr. Jefferson had left to our proud nation. I would appreciate any assistance you might provide in my endeavor."

Lettie punctuated the air with her finger. "Oh, it's the treasure Cathy was talking about earlier!"

"Casey," I corrected.

"I'm going to take this to the police. I'm a very good sleuth, you see. Like a young Miss Marple." Lettie jabbed her finger in the air again. "I already know what happened."

Did I sound that silly when I claimed to be like Miss Marple? No, I'd never made that claim aloud. Well, maybe just once or twice . . .

"Gordon hasn't even looked at these files," Lorenzo said. "He was only working on the project with Frida because he had to. Casey, how in the world do you always manage to make things worse?"

"Me? I didn't do anything."

"Exactly! You haven't done anything to help Gordon."

"You were the one who suggested I should play amateur sleuth."

"Well, stop. You're not helping."

"You were trying to solve the case, too? We should pool

our mental resources, Cathy. But then again, I don't really need help, do I?" Lettie said as she picked up the phone receiver on Nadeem's desk. "I'm sorry to have to do this to your supervisor. I'm sure you were fond of him," she said as she dialed. "But guilt is guilt. It would be wrong to try and cover up evidence." She stood up straighter. "Hello? This is Lettie Shaw, the First Lady's sister. No, I'm not in trouble. Why do you people always ask that? Listen to me. I'm in the curator's office. And I have proof the head gardener is a murderer."

While Lorenzo sputtered, clearly fighting the urge to tell the First Lady's sister she was nuts, Nadeem leaned back in his desk chair and crossed his arms over his chest. He looked oddly pleased with himself.

Chapter Fourteen

> *It's odd that you can get so anesthetized by your own pain or your own problem that you don't quite fully share the hell of someone close to you.*
> —CLAUDIA "LADY BIRD" JOHNSON, FIRST
> LADY OF THE UNITED STATES (1963–1969)

WHILE we waited for the Secret Service to come take a look at the folder and listen to Lettie's wild theory, I pulled out Frida's desk chair. I sat down with my elbows propped on my knees and my chin in my hands.

Everything was going wrong, so wrong. I knew in my heart Gordon was innocent. Why couldn't everyone else see it that way, too? Everyone who knew Gordon liked him. Except Frida, apparently. Was it a case of professional jealousy? Or had something else happened?

Had that *something else* involved Gordon's wife, Deloris? I hadn't expected her cold-blooded reaction to Frida's murder.

My thoughts whirled while Lettie chattered excitedly, carelessly forgetting that the three people in the room with her had personally worked with and, for the most part, liked the two players in what she was now calling a "fascinating drama."

Nadeem watched her with a look of amusement,

although he'd flinch whenever Lettie mentioned Frida's name.

Lorenzo, who'd never been able to hide his emotions, cursed under his breath and then stomped out into the hallway.

Lettie just kept on talking.

Trying my best to ignore her, I swiveled Frida's desk chair around. Frida's desk was clear of any papers. Was that Nadeem's doing, or the police's? The only thing on her normally messy desk was a small notepad.

Although the top page was blank, I could see a faint imprint of writing, which was presumably from the last sheet that had been torn off. Was I looking at the last note Frida had written before her death? I picked up the notepad, turning it this way and that. I couldn't make out the words.

I grabbed a pencil from a White House coffee mug Frida had used as a pen holder and, like any junior spy knows, rubbed the lead lightly over the paper to reveal the imprint from the previous page.

I know who you are. I know what you're doing, appeared on the paper. I glanced over at Nadeem. He was no longer listening to Lettie but was now watching me. His brows furrowed deeply as I ripped off the page with the ominous message and stuffed it into my pocket.

"What was that?" he asked me.

Lettie stopped her monologue about how she was such an asset to her sister. "What was what?"

"Nothing," I said. "Just a scrap piece of paper."

"Oh," Lettie said and launched back into how she was saving the taxpayers thousands of dollars by bringing the investigation to a quick close. She wondered if there would be a reward.

Nadeem didn't say anything. But the assessing look he gave me made the hair on the back of my neck take attention.

Nadeem had admitted it himself. He wanted Frida's job. And now Frida was dead. Jack was right. I needed to be careful around this ex-assassin.

* * *

"IF THE POLICE REFUSED TO LISTEN TO HER, what are you so worried about?" Alyssa asked later that evening as she chopped carrots. She had kicked off her high-heeled leather boots and was cooking, which meant trouble was brewing up on the Hill. I reached for the tops of the carrots before she could toss them into the trash, but Alyssa slapped my hand away.

"Well?" she said, holding the leafy carrot tops hostage. "Tell me what happened after Lettie handed the papers to the police. What has you so worried?"

"I'm worried because Manny didn't listen to *me*, either. I told him about the gap in the Children's Garden's fencing and the missing branches from the garden. But he brushed me off. I gave him the paper from Frida's notepad, and he barely looked at it before stuffing it into a file folder. Worse, he wouldn't even look at me. It was as if Manny had already made up his mind that Gordon is guilty."

"If they've already sent Gordon down the figurative river, why would both the Secret Service and the police ignore Lettie's new evidence?" Alyssa dropped the carrot tops into my hand and started chopping onions. "Why would they dismiss anything the First Lady's sister tells them? That seems politically"—she paused, searching for the right word—"hazardous."

Alyssa was right. The Secret Service agents should have treated Lettie with the same consideration they gave any other member of the First Family—equal measures of friendliness and caution. But they'd acted as if they'd wanted to get away from Lettie as fast as possible. Had they heard her singing? The agents had handed both Lettie's and Frida's research over to Detective Manny Hernandez with a head-spinning speed.

"She imagines herself a young Miss Marple," I said.

"Is that so?" Alyssa peered at me speculatively.

"I bet she's been keeping the Secret Service busy with her so-called sleuthing. I'll have to ask Jack about it."

"You do that," Alyssa sniffed when I scooped the discarded root ends of the onions from the counter and set them on the windowsill above the sink. "Where is that hunky Secret Service agent of yours anyhow?"

"Still on duty at the White House. I left early to visit Gordon at the hospital, plus I needed to look something up at the library." I carried the bright green carrot tops back to the kitchen table, where I had a history book open to a section that talked about the 1814 burning of the White House. "Did you know the British carried off a cache of silver flatware and china from the White House, and a wealth of gold coins from the Treasury Building?" I asked Alyssa as I read the account of the siege. As I read, I plucked all but a few small leaves from the discarded carrot tops. "The Brittish then shipped the treasures back to England on the *HMS Fantome*."

"I do remember something about that in history class," she said as she dumped the chopped carrots and onions into a sizzling frying pan. She started working on the next set of vegetables that she planned to add to her vegetable stir-fry. "Didn't the *Fantome* sink shortly after leaving port?"

"I don't know. It doesn't say." I made a note to find out. The *HMS Fantome* was written on the document Nadeem had been so quick to hide when we'd brought him the missing Dolley Madison research.

What if Nadeem had applied for the assistant curator position not because of a burning desire to learn from Frida, or to sabotage the talks with Turbekistan, but because he was searching for lost treasure? His arrival at the White House had marked the start of trouble between Frida and Gordon.

But if D.C.'s treasures from that time period ended up on a sunken ship, why would Nadeem be searching for Thomas Jefferson's treasure at the White House?

"Oh, well. It doesn't matter anyhow. He wasn't in the garden at the time of Frida's death," I said. "He told me that he'd left her before she entered the Children's Garden."

"What's that?" Alyssa asked as she dumped the last of her vegetables into the frying pan.

"Nothing. Just thinking something through." There was no way I was going to tell Alyssa she'd been right about Nadeem. Encouraging her generally led to trouble.

So I closed the book and then pulled several wineglasses from the kitchen cabinet's top shelf. "Have you heard from Barry about . . . this morning?"

"You mean about the article you refuse to pitch into the trash? Yeah, he called back. He got all prickly about it, too. Wanted to know why I was asking about James Calhoun's whereabouts and then put his supervisor on. The jerk. I asked him to do me a simple favor, and he turned it into some big federal case."

Ah. That was why she was cooking tonight. Guy trouble.

"So he had no answers for you?" I asked as I filled each wineglass with a little water before setting a carrot top in the water.

"No. What in the world are you doing?" Alyssa asked as she stirred our dinner.

"I'm gardening." She should have known that about me by now. When I had a problem to work through, I needed to keep my hands busy with gardening . . . even if it meant making do with the materials at hand.

"Gardening in wineglasses? That's a new one."

I lined up the glasses on the plant shelves I'd built in front of the kitchen window. "I'm rooting the carrot tops. When I plant them outside in the spring, the swallowtail butterflies will love their leafy greens."

"Okay. And the bottoms of the onions?"

"Once they dry out a bit, I'll plant them. They'll eventually grow new onions."

"Only *you'd* think of that." Alyssa shook her head. "How's Gordon?"

"The same, I'm afraid. The nurse promised that no change was still good news at this point," I was quick to add. "Is dinner ready yet?"

"The rice still needs five minutes," she answered.

I'd started setting the table when the doorbell buzzed.

"It's your turn," Alyssa said from the stove.

I wasn't sure whose turn it was to answer the door; not that it mattered. She was cooking. I wasn't. My stomach grumbled with every step through the living room and to the front foyer. I peeked out the window and smiled.

My hunger forgotten, I eagerly swung the door open.

Jack, dressed in jeans and a black leather coat, leaned against the door frame.

"Just the guy I was hoping to see," I said. "Would you like to come inside? I could split my dinner with you."

The way he backed away, you'd have thought I'd told him that I'd just armed a bomb. "You—you cooked?"

"No, Alyssa is cooking. Thai, I think."

"Oh." The corners of his lips hitched up just a smidge. "You had me worried there for a moment. After the last time you tried to cook for me, I now have the fire department on speed dial."

I gave him a playful push. "Very funny. Are you coming in?"

"Alyssa's in the kitchen?"

I nodded.

"Let's keep what I've learned this afternoon between the two of us for right now. Besides, I could use a little alone time with you." His gaze brushed against me like a tender caress before zeroing in on the entrance to the basement apartment. His shoulders dropped. "So that's where he lives."

"It is," I said.

"Is he home?"

"I don't know."

Jack gave a single stiff nod. Clearly he didn't like my new living arrangements. And I didn't like an unhappy Jack.

I grabbed his hand. "Since you're not interested in coming inside, let's go for a walk around the block." The storm had passed, leaving in its wake a brisk evening and a large harvest moon hanging low in the sky. A cold wind gusted down the street.

"I've been thinking about what happened today with Lettie." I tucked my arm around his and snuggled against his warmth. We fit together nicely. "What's going on with her?"

"You know I can't discuss the First Family," Jack said.

"I know, but this is me. I'm not going to run to the press. Is Lettie giving the agents a hard time? They acted as if she had the plague this afternoon."

"There have been a few . . ." He shook his head. "I can't talk about it."

"She's irritating, isn't she? I get that. Don't forget that Seth sent her to help in the grounds office. Barely an hour into her task, she stumbles across the missing Dolley Madison research—purely by chance—and she thinks she's the greatest sleuth ever."

Jack stopped and glanced over at me. "Can't take the competition?"

"As if," I huffed. "She thinks Gordon is guilty. Anyone with half a brain can see he's not."

"Detective Hernandez would disagree with you, and he's a smart guy."

"He's being rushed. He'll change his mind once he looks at all the pieces."

"Unfortunately, no one can seem to find those pieces. That's why we need to gather them together for him."

"I handed over the imprint of that threatening note Frida had written, and Manny barely looked at it. Frida wouldn't have written 'I know who you are' to Gordon. She'd just go and yell at him. It has to be someone she didn't know well."

"Or someone she was afraid of," Jack suggested. "It's almost as if she didn't want the recipient of the note to know she wrote it."

He had a point. Frida hadn't signed the note.

"Neither of us knows all the details of the investigation," Jack continued. "Manny's keeping his mouth shut. He might already have the original note. Or he can't use what you found because you removed it from where you found it. Anyone could have written that note you discovered. If you find evidence, tell someone about it, but leave it for the professionals to pick up. It's important to their job and may help Gordon."

"You're right. I should have already known that," I said. I'd read enough mystery novels to have picked up a thing or two about police procedure. "It's just Nadeem was watching me, and I got nervous and shoved it in my pocket."

Jack drew a slow, controlled breath. "Nadeem. I'm worried about your working with him. The information on his background is locked up tighter than . . . than . . . the White House." He shook his head. "I don't know how he got clearance for the assistant curator position. I sure as hell wouldn't have given it to him."

"Most of the time Nadeem acts like a nervous assistant. Are you certain your sources are right about his past? He's not at all suave and smooth like an international spy."

"Believe me, Casey, the movies don't always get it right. Most of the spies I've met act like bumbling idiots. Who would you suspect of espionage—the sophisticated, cool-under-pressure playboy or the dimwitted, jump-at-his-shadow tourist?"

"The playboy. Oh, I see what you're saying. Well, it doesn't matter because I know Nadeem isn't our guy. After all, he came over and talked with me before Frida entered the Children's Garden. So he couldn't have murdered her."

Jack was shaking his head as if he knew something.

"Why? What have you learned?" I asked.

"That's what I came over to tell you. This afternoon I watched the surveillance videos of the South Lawn that were recorded the day Frida died. I saw Nadeem leave Frida and then circle around toward the kitchen garden."

"But he told me that he—"

"He lied. That's what guys like him do. They lie."

"But why would he—" I started to ask when Jack's cell phone buzzed.

He glanced at his phone's readout and groaned. "I've got to go."

"Will you be back?" This was the third time Jack had left abruptly in the past couple of weeks. It was becoming as worrying as never getting invited to his house.

"Probably not," he said, offering no explanation about where he was headed, or why it was so urgent.

"You're not actually married with a wife at home, are you?" I laughed as I said it.

He didn't laugh with me. Instead he wrapped me in a hug, rubbing his strong hands up and down my back. For all his faults, he was an expert at hugs. "I'm sorry," he said.

"Sorry?" I wiggled out of his embrace. "Sorry that you're married?"

"What? No!" He dredged his hands through his hair. "I'm sorry you think I'm trying to hide something from you. It's nothing. Really. Nothing. There's just something I need to work out. It's not—" He closed his eyes and huffed. "I just have to do this."

I wanted to press him to explain himself, but it wasn't as if I was being completely honest with him. I was still holding on to that article about my father like a child holds on to a security blanket. I don't know why I couldn't talk to Jack about it, or about my father's crimes. I just couldn't. But keeping Jack out of that part of my life felt dishonest. I needed to trust him. I needed to trust I would be strong enough to hear what Jack might know about my murderous dad. Even so, my heart clenched at the thought of telling him.

"Are you going to be okay?" he asked after he'd walked me back to my front door.

I nodded.

"I'll let you know what happens with the note you found in Frida's office. Hopefully Manny will take it seriously." He brushed a quick kiss across my lips and was gone.

I was still standing on the front stoop when my cell phone sang the first few notes of Kelly Clarkson's "Stronger." At first I thought Jack was texting to remind me to lock the front door. I pulled my phone from my pocket and hit a few buttons.

My smile faded as I read the incoming message. Like the odd text I'd received shortly before Frida's death, this one had come from a restricted number. This time I didn't dismiss the threatening message as a wrong number. The same word as before glowed ominously on my phone's screen.

DIE.

Chapter Fifteen

*I want minimum information given
with maximum politeness.*
—JACQUELINE KENNEDY, FIRST LADY OF
THE UNITED STATES (1961–1963)

ON Wednesday morning, the ground was still satu-
rated from the previous days' heavy rains, but the
skies were clear save for a few high wispy clouds. The roar
of jets from the nearby Ronald Reagan National Airport
filled the air as I herded five eager garden volunteers through
the security checkpoint at the southeast gate and across the
lawn toward the First Lady's legendary kitchen garden.

One of my proudest achievements, the kitchen garden
was located at the bottom of the South Lawn next to the
fountain. The garden was in a spot where it could be viewed
by the public but was far enough away from the iron fence
that the Secret Service didn't have to worry about food
tampering.

Just a few weeks ago, a class of schoolchildren helped
harvest over four hundred pounds of leafy green vegetables,
broccoli, radishes, pumpkins, potatoes, sweet potatoes,
peppers, and tomatoes from the fifteen-hundred-square-
foot space.

"Casey." Special Agent Janie Partners jogged across the

lawn to catch up to me. Today she was wearing a dark blue suit with an unusually tame, matching blue scarf. Her short hair was now ebony black. Her eyes were hidden behind the Secret Service's standard-issue dark sunglasses. "I heard about the threatening text messages."

"News travels fast around here," I said as I continued walking toward the kitchen garden. "Jack insisted on driving me to work this morning. Not that I minded." Last night I'd contacted both Jack and Detective Manny Hernandez about the texts and had left both of them detailed messages. Manny never called me back but had sent over a uniformed officer to take my statement and look at the phone.

Quite honestly, I didn't think much of the threat; not when there was work to be done in the garden.

Janie disagreed. She stepped in front of me and crossed her arms over her chest like she was blocking an overenthusiastic voter from mobbing the President. "You need to stop."

"Go on ahead to the garden," I called when my volunteers noticed I was being waylaid and had turned their curious gazes onto me. "I'll catch up in a minute." I shifted the large sweetgrass basket, filled with gardening gloves, trowels, and hand trimmers, from one hip to the other. "What do I need to stop? The first text message arrived before Frida's murder. It's not connected."

Janie shook her head. "That's not what I'm worried about, Casey. You need to stop investigating Frida's murder. Let the police handle this one."

"I can't. While everyone is rushing to judgment and calling Gordon guilty, he needs someone to prove his innocence."

Janie looked decidedly uncomfortable. She tugged on her dark blue suit coat as if it had suddenly shrunk two sizes. "Have you thought about what you might find?"

"Yes. I'm going to prove that Gordon wasn't in the garden at the time of Frida's death."

Janie lifted her dark sunglasses. "What if you don't? What if you learn something you don't want to hear, Casey?"

"I won't." Slowly, I realized what she was saying. "You think he's guilty."

She bit her lower lip and started shaking her head. "I like Gordon, but some people snap. I don't know why. No one does. Just take my advice. I know how much you care for Gordon. I don't want to see this destroy you."

"It won't, because he's innocent," I said too loudly.

The volunteers, who had already started to work weeding in the nearby rows of vegetables, stood up to watch me.

"He's innocent," I repeated. Let the world hear me say it. My voice started to shake. "Manny is wrong. Gordon would never hurt anyone. He couldn't."

"I've seen the evidence, Casey. Manny hasn't missed anything. You were there. You saw it. Gordon had Frida's blood splattered all over his clothes. He was the last person to see Frida alive. And once Manny dots all of his *i*'s and crosses all of his *t*'s, he's going to charge Gordon for the crime."

"You're wrong. And Manny's making a huge mistake. If you'll excuse me, I have work to do. Gordon wouldn't appreciate it if I neglected his gardens. For the past thirty-plus years, this place has been his life. I won't have him coming back and finding it in shambles. And he will be coming back. As soon as he's well, *he's coming back.*"

"I hope you're right. And Casey?"

"*What?*"

"Milo has been digging holes again." She pointed to a line of upturned earth near the tennis court.

I groaned.

MY TWO FAVORITE VOLUNTEERS, THE ELDERLY Pearle Stone and Mable Bowls, ambled over to meet me. Pearle, dressed in a velour lavender running suit, led the way with her arms held wide. "Casey, Casey, how are you holding up, my dear?"

Mable, who liked to prove that because she was six months younger than her eighty-year-old friend, she was that much more nimble, pumped her arms and reached me first. She, too, was dressed in a comfortable velour track suit. But hers was powder pink with glittering white racing stripes down the legs.

Anyone who'd ever met either woman outside the garden would want to copy their flawless fashion sense. But the two women also had a wicked sense of humor and enjoyed finding the most outrageous outfits for their volunteer time in the kitchen garden. Mable wiggled her skinny hips and smacked her bright red lips.

"Honey, we've got to find a way to bust our hunky Gordon free," she shouted. I doubted she realized it was a shout. The two ladies were both in denial that they needed hearing aids.

Pearle, huffing, caught up with Mable, and threw her soft velour-coated arms around me. "Sweetie, anyone who says anything bad about Gordon will be immediately sent to the lowest circle of social hell."

"*Junior League*," both of them said at the same time.

I laughed even though I was a longtime member of the Junior League.

"The poor dear, even her titters are weighted down with melancholy," Pearle said to Mable.

"I don't know what you're talking about. Her titters look perky enough to me," Mable replied.

I laughed again at the pure joy Pearle and Mable brought me.

Mable leaned close to me and shouted, "I heard that Frida's shifty new assistant—what's-his-name—and the First Lady's sister were both in the gardens when the incident occurred."

"Don't forget, the overpriced blowhard Marcel Beauchamp might have been there, too," Pearle added.

Mable nodded. "I hadn't forgotten. Clearly, one of them saw something."

"Or perpetrated the crime," Pearle finished.

"I thought Detective Hernandez was keeping a tight lid on that kind of information," I said, truly amazed by how many details the two knew about the investigation. It sounded as if they knew more about the investigation than some of the members of the Secret Service.

Mable touched the side of her nose and smiled slyly, which only made me wonder what else they knew.

I hooked my arm with Pearle's and led the pair of living, breathing national treasures back to the kitchen garden, where the other three volunteers were waiting. "You wouldn't happen to know who killed Frida?" I asked.

"Now, honey, if we knew that, Gordon wouldn't be in such a fix." Pearle patted my hand. "But we have faith you'll come through for him."

"I'll do my best."

"That's all anyone can ask," Mable said.

When we reached the other volunteers, I started to pass out paper envelopes and pencils to the five ladies. "Today, we're going to gather seeds from the bolted lettuce, broccoli, and spinach, but not the radishes. We're going to plant a couple of different varieties of radishes next year. This one didn't perform as well as I would have liked," I said and gave instructions on how to harvest the seeds and mark the date and variety on the envelope.

On Thursday, which was tomorrow, the grounds crew was scheduled to pull out the fall crops and prepare the soil for the winter garden. That's right, even in D.C., where snow falls every year, we were going to attempt a winter garden. It was Gordon's idea. His buddies from the United States Department of Agriculture were coming to assist in installing hoop houses for the winter garden on Friday, the same day Gordon was going to be charged with murder . . . if you believed the rumors.

Which meant I was running out of time.

After I finished answering questions and handing out the gardening tools and gloves, I maneuvered over to where Pearle and Mable were collecting seed pods from the tennis ball lettuce. The lettuce was an heirloom variety that had been one of Thomas Jefferson's favorites. As I helped collect seeds, my gaze traveled to the stand of hardwood trees that lined the northern border of the kitchen garden. The trees acted as a buffer to the Children's Garden and weren't many yards away from where Frida was killed. Had someone walked through this garden, past the bolting broccoli, on their way to murder Frida?

"Helloo!" a high-pitched voice carried across the lawn.

"Oh dear, not her." Pearle pulled her straw hat lower on her head.

"I like her," Mable said. She rose from the lettuce plot, pulled off her gloves, and smoothed out her velour track suit. "She has a sense of humor."

"Since when do you think desperate is funny?" Pearle asked. "Poor Margaret, she's got her hands full already with her newborn twins. She doesn't need another baby to nurse."

"I thought Lettie was here to help her sister with the twins," I said. Not that I'd seen much evidence that Lettie was spending any time with her sister and nephews.

Both Mable and Pearle shook their heads. "From what I've heard, she lost her job and her husband in the same week. That's why she's here."

"There has to be a reason why her life collapsed all at once, a trigger," I said. And if that was the case, why would a woman whose life was in shambles be so interested in Frida's work in the bowels of the White House? Unless . . . unless she'd heard about a missing treasure and had a desperate reason to get her hands on it.

"I hear she drinks," Mable said.

"The Secret Service can't keep up with her," Pearle said as she snipped off the tops of the bolted lettuce. Her hands moved with the steady grace that could have only been developed through years of experience in the garden.

"That's not necessarily a bad thing," Mable said with a twinkle in her eye. "And she's not afraid to say what she thinks."

"That would be fine if she had a thought in that bubble she calls a head," Pearle replied.

I shushed them both as Lettie Shaw half stumbled, half

trotted down the hill toward the garden. "Good morning, Cathy," she called.

"It's Casey," I corrected.

"Bubblehead," Pearle murmured.

"Margaret told me that the volunteers come on Wednesdays. She suggested I lend a helping hand. She just loves this garden. When she's not talking about her twins, she's going on and on about the garden and what to plant in it next. So"—she set her hands on her hips—"what are we doing today?"

She grimaced as I explained to her how we were collecting seeds from select plants in the garden. "Wouldn't it be easier to buy fresh seeds and seedlings next year?"

Lorenzo had asked me the same question about a month ago. Even though I knew he was just giving me a hard time about my organic program, I'd given him the same answer I gave Lettie now. "There are many good reasons to save seeds. Perhaps the best reason for the White House, besides setting a good example, is that we can harvest seeds from the plants that thrived in this specific location. We'll then propagate those seeds next year. At the end of the season, we'll save the seeds from those plants. Over time, we will be planting seeds that are best suited for this location. Your sister has also requested that I collect seeds so she can include White House seed packets in the gift baskets she gives out to visiting dignitaries."

"Gifts, yes. Good idea," Lettie said as if she hadn't listened to a word I'd said. I'm not sure she had. Her gaze had been locked on the back of the Children's Garden the entire time. "Yes. I'd like to help."

"I, too, would wish to assist in this," Marcel said as he trotted down the hill to join us. He was dressed in gray trousers, a white shirt, and a bulky dark red winter jacket.

"Of course," I said. What else could I have said? Members of the administration and the staff were encouraged to spend time working in the kitchen garden. The chefs and kitchen staff were the most active. Even the President's press secretary, who had grown up in New York City and had absolutely no idea what he was doing, had spent several hours pulling out newly planted peas in the spring and newly planted carrots in the fall. He had mistaken them for weeds.

Pulling weeds was a good stress reliever for a staff that was constantly under tremendous pressure to perform. Knowing that, I tried not to complain too loudly when the staff mistakenly pulled out the plants and left the weeds.

I welcomed all willing hands, even Lettie's and Marcel's, into the gardens on Wednesdays. After showing the two of them the plants we were harvesting seeds from, I gave them a pile of envelopes and turned them loose.

After about an hour, most of the volunteers had completed their work, while I'd managed to plug the holes Milo had dug. In the same hour, neither Marcel nor Lettie had filled any seed packets. Marcel seemed enamored of the color of the soil. He'd spent the entire time wandering aimlessly through the garden, randomly pushing his hands in the dirt. He lifted a handful up to the light as he murmured to himself, probably contemplating rug or drapery colors.

Lettie, on the other hand, had wandered over to the edge of the kitchen garden. She was standing under a cluster of oaks and little-leaf lindens that created one of the many visual barriers for the Children's Garden. She seemed keenly interested in one particular area. She kept looking back at the rest of us, as if gauging if she was being watched.

She was being watched. I made sure of it.

I hadn't forgotten the curious phone call I'd overheard shortly before Frida's murder. It had sounded as if Lettie was in trouble and in need of quick cash. I wondered if her loss of fortune caused her to lose her job and her husband. Or was it the other way around? Had she lost her job and her husband and now, as a consequence, found herself strapped for cash?

She'd said to whoever had been on the other end of that mysterious call that she had a plan to get it, whatever "it" was.

While Nadeem was still my number one suspect—a

retired trained assassin with an obvious interest in hidden treasures, plus he'd lied to me about leaving the gardens before Frida had entered the Children's Garden—I couldn't discount that Lettie had been working with Frida at the time the Dolley Madison research had gone missing. If Frida was as anxious to shoot up the social ladder as Pearle and Mable had claimed, I would imagine Frida would have been more open with her special files with the First Lady's sister than she'd have been with her brand-new assistant.

And if Lettie's reason to go searching for a missing treasure was so strong that she'd kill for it, wouldn't she also want to cover her tracks? What better way to cover those tracks than to "play sleuth" and discover "evidence" that made Gordon look as if he wanted Frida dead?

I stood with my hands on my hips, making doubly sure I didn't allow Lettie out of my sight as she poked around in the bushes. When she disappeared from view, I followed her.

I took the path that led through the canopy of trees and connected the kitchen garden with the nearby grounds shed. And as I'd suspected all along, in a wheelbarrow that had been left out in the weather were the missing branches from the Children's Garden.

This was it! Proof that Gordon had left the Children's Garden through one of the gaps in the fencing. Proof that anyone else could have entered the garden the same way.

I quickly typed a text to Manny, Thatch, and Jack, telling them what I'd found and where I'd found it. I also included pictures of the branches stacked up in the wheelbarrow.

"What are you doing?" Lorenzo shouted. I jumped. Lorenzo was dressed more casually than usual. He wasn't wearing a suit coat. His dress shirt sleeves were rolled up to his elbows. And he wasn't wearing a tie. He also had dark circles under his eyes as if he'd worked through the night.

"Look!" I pointed to the wheelbarrow. "The missing branches!"

"Took you long enough to go looking for those things," he grumbled.

"I kept getting distracted with other things, like, oh I

don't know, Lettie and her efforts to prove Gordon's guilt.
I'm sending pictures of them to Manny. If that doesn't convince him that Gordon didn't kill Frida, I don't know what
will."

"This will." He thrust a file folder into my hands.

I looked up at Lettie. She was still in the same place.
Good. Then I looked down at the folder in my hands. My
brows creased as I read what was inside. "I don't understand. This is a spreadsheet."

"It's not *just* a spreadsheet. It's a listing of the files that
are in the grounds office's filing cabinets."

"Is the missing South Lawn schematic on the list?"

"The missing . . . Why are you still harping about that
stupid schematic? You misplaced it. Finding it won't help
Gordon."

I didn't agree. I had a feeling that it was as connected to
Frida's murder as the stolen Dolley Madison research.
"Well?" I asked as I scanned the spreadsheet.

"The schematic's on the list," he said grudgingly.

"I knew it!" I clapped my hands.

"But that doesn't mean you didn't lose it."

"I didn't lose it. The schematic was stolen just like—"

"Focus, Casey." Lorenzo snapped his fingers in front of
my nose. "I'm not working long hours trying to cover your
mistakes. This is about Gordon and keeping him from
going straight from the hospital to jail."

"I'm focused on Gordon, too. Don't you see the connection? The murderer stole both the Dolley Madison research
papers and the schematic. He's using the schematic like a
treasure map to help him look for the missing treasure."

"I suppose that could be one explanation. But look
here." Lorenzo had highlighted an entry near the bottom of
the spreadsheet. I read it. Startled, I read it again.

"I don't understand. Why are Frida's research files listed
on the grounds office's inventory?"

"It happened this past summer," Lorenzo said with a
sigh as if I should have already known. "Assistant Usher

Wilson Fisher digitized many of the files and recorded everything else."

"This is what he was doing? He nearly drove me out of my mind with requests for this and that. But if he recorded that the Dolley Madison folder was in Gordon's office, how did Frida get her hands on it?"

"I doubt she did. This is the government, Casey. Anytime someone touches a piece of paper, it duplicates itself. See here. There's an asterisk and a number after the description."

"So?"

"So the asterisk denotes that the pages are all copies. The number notes the office where the originals are kept."

"Oh! So what Lettie handed over to the police was a copy, which explains why Frida's notes were missing from the folder. The original is—don't tell me—in the curator's office. Thank goodness for Fisher and his love of paperwork. This proves Gordon didn't take Frida's folder."

Lorenzo smiled proudly as he tapped the highlighted line in the spreadsheet. "This spreadsheet proves the folder Lettie found yesterday has been in that drawer since at least this past summer."

"Unfortunately, we still need to find out what happened to Frida's copy of Dolley Madison's garden notes and letters. I bet someone desperate to find the treasure took Frida's notes." I chewed the inside of my cheek as I thought about it a little longer. "Someone in desperate need of money."

Lettie was in need of money. Desperately.

I looked back at the thick stand of trees that separated the kitchen garden from the Children's Garden, where the First Lady's sister had been poking around. She was gone.

That's when I made a decision.

"If we're going to find out who killed Frida, we're going to have to find that treasure."

Chapter Sixteen

*I live a very dull life here . . . indeed I think I am
more like a state prisoner than anything else.*
—MARTHA WASHINGTON, FIRST LADY OF
THE UNITED STATES (1789–1797)

*C*RASH.

Lorenzo and I exchanged glances.

After completing everything we'd needed to do in the gardens, and seeing the volunteers on their way, we'd gathered around Lorenzo's drafting table and started work on a master list of everything we'd learned so far. We knew about the well-hidden gap in the Children's Garden fencing and the location of the branches. We knew Gordon had a *copy* of Frida's research, which proved he had no reason to steal *her* copy. And we knew who else had been in the gardens at the time of Frida's murder.

Despite knowing all that, we couldn't figure out what Lettie had been doing in the gardens this morning. When we'd looked for her, she wasn't in the kitchen garden or the Children's Garden. We later learned she'd left the White House to meet a friend. Nor did we have any idea of how to hunt for a treasure that had been lost for nearly two hundred years.

"I still think the missing schematic is being used as a treasure map," I said as I added it to our list of stray bits of evidence that still needed to be sorted.

"You're just trying to cover your—" Lorenzo started to say as he struck through what I'd just written.

Smash.

"What in the world is going on out there?" I asked, rising.

I hurried down the basement hallway, through a set of double doors, and out onto the East Courtyard. In the sunken area between the North Portico and the White House residence, another series of crashes tore through the space. Lorenzo lagged behind, peeking around my shoulder as if he was using my body as a shield.

Ambrose Jones, the efficient and utterly proper chief usher who presided over the entire White House staff, tossed a White House plate at the wall. It exploded into several hundred pieces. He picked up another plate. I recognized it as one of Ulysses Grant's official china platters with a beautiful hand-painted flowering hosta decorating the center. Ambrose didn't even look down at it before he gave the work of art a toss.

"Wait! What are you doing? What's going on?" I cried with no small measure of alarm. Had the pressure of his job finally made Ambrose snap? And why was no one stopping him from destroying the historic plates with immeasurable value?

"They're chipped," he said. "Unusable."

"But—but they're priceless!" I rushed over and saved a delicate dessert plate from his hand.

"Not anymore," Lorenzo said. He snatched the dessert plate away from me and handed it back to Ambrose. "To keep chipped presidential china from becoming collectibles or sold on online auction sites like eBay, any piece of china that is no longer usable is destroyed. Smashed," he explained.

"The kitchen staff saves up the cracked and chipped

bowls, cups, and plates. When someone needs to work off a little stress, the retired china is taken outside and rendered completely unsalable," Ambrose added.

I'd heard of the plate smashing, but even now had trouble picturing a man as proper and, well, as uptight as Ambrose taking part in the tradition.

"Have you heard the latest?" Ambrose asked as he weighed the elegant green and white dessert plate from Truman's china collection in his hand. "The police are on a witch hunt. It doesn't even seem like they're looking at alternatives. Gordon could never." He threw the plate at the wall with a surprising burst of anger. "Would never." He bent down and picked up a bowl with a large chip on the rim out of the plastic storage container beside him.

"We know," Lorenzo said, gritting his teeth.

Ambrose handed him the bowl.

Lorenzo gave it a toss. The fine china hit the stone wall with a satisfying shatter. "Thank you. That helped."

Ambrose nodded gravely. "I wish we could do more than toss the china at a wall."

"What did you think about the ongoing tensions between Frida and Gordon?" I asked. "You don't think Frida could have pushed him over the edge?"

Ambrose didn't have to think about my question before answering, "If that were the case, he would have killed her years ago. She'd given him ample reason to stop turning the other cheek, but he never did. He put his job before his ego. Anyone who doesn't know that doesn't know Gordon," he said as he smashed another plate against the wall.

"We have new information that might help Gordon— Lorenzo discovered it—but we haven't been able to talk to Detective Hernandez." Manny even ignored the calls that Lorenzo had placed to him. "He's clearly avoiding us."

Ambrose lowered the plate he was about to toss. His dark brown eyes widened. "You have information?"

I nodded. "It won't clear Gordon, but it should undo some of the damage that's been done so far. He didn't steal Frida's files."

"Hurry, then! The detective is meeting with the First Lady in her third-floor office, but he won't be there for long."

"THIS ISN'T GOING TO WORK." LORENZO dragged his feet like a petulant child. "The Secret Service won't just let us walk up to the First Family's private quarters."

"No, they won't." That's why I had a heavy bag of topsoil slung over my shoulder. Lorenzo was carrying the spreadsheet printout that we needed to show Manny.

The bag of topsoil was our ticket to the third floor . . . I hoped. I wasn't sure how I'd let Lorenzo talk me into doing the heavy lifting. Why wasn't I carrying the paperwork while he had this heavy bag pressing down on his shoulder?

"Surely they'll realize no one starts seeds this time of year." Lorenzo slowed his step as our destination grew closer.

"Even if one of them does know better, they won't question us. We're the gardening experts," I mumbled out the side of my mouth. "Oh, hi there!" I called to the pair of uniformed Secret Service guards stationed at the elevator that led up to the White House's third floor. "We need to get this up to the greenhouse ASAP. With everything that's happened in the past several days, we're behind schedule on all our projects. I'm sure you understand."

Neither of the burly guards looked the least bit sympathetic. "Let me see if it's on the schedule," the larger of the two grumbled and disappeared into the adjacent office.

"Schedule?" Well, that blew a giant hole in my plan to get upstairs and ambush Manny.

Lorenzo snorted in my ear as if to say, "I told you."

"I didn't know we needed to be on a schedule," I told the guard who'd remained behind. "We'll just be a few minutes. It's important that we get the potting soil up there."

"We can't bend the rules, ma'am," he said.

"I don't have any record of anything happening in the

greenhouse," the second guard said when he returned. "If it's not on the schedule, it's not happening."

Lorenzo snorted and danced from foot to foot like a nervous racehorse getting ready to bolt.

"This bag is getting heavy," I said to buy us time while I tried to think of something, anything we could say or do to convince the Secret Service guards that we needed to get upstairs. "Isn't there anything you can do?"

"No." The first guard seemed to draw an impenetrable wall with that one word. "Come back when you're on the schedule."

I was about to admit defeat, something I didn't want to do since that would give Lorenzo an endless supply of I-told-you-so's for years to come. But what else could we do? The Secret Service guards looked as if they'd put down deep roots smack dab in front of the elevator doors. There'd be no budging them.

Think. Think, I told myself. There had to be a way to get the spreadsheet printout to Manny.

"Lorenzo! And . . . and Cathy! Just the duo I was hoping to find," Lettie called as she bounded down the hallway toward us.

The Secret Service guards shrank away from the First Lady's sister like she was poison ivy.

"What do you have there, Cathy?" she asked, poking the bag of potting soil with such force that I had to do a sidestep dance to keep from tipping over.

"It's Casey," I corrected, wondering if Lettie was mangling my name on purpose.

"Right." She stuck her finger in the air as if to say she'd make a point to remember that. She glanced at the Secret Service guards. Her toothy smile faded. "I'm ready to get back to work on the historical gardening notes, especially Dolley Madison's. I did tell you that I'm a university professor of American history, didn't I?"

"Yes, I think you might have mentioned that. And we do appreciate your help." I added the last part when Lorenzo, who had claimed to be in charge of the project, snorted again. "We're not dealing with research papers today. We had hoped to prepare the seed flats in the greenhouse so they'd be ready once the seeds arrive for the founding fathers' kitchen garden, but apparently there's some trouble with that. Our name's not on the schedule. So we can't get upstairs."

"The seeds?" she asked.

"Yes," I said. The seeds I hadn't been able to order because, apparently, they no longer existed. "While the National Arboretum will have the bulk of the display, your sister has been excited about the founding fathers' vegetable garden we'll be planting this spring. It's all ready to go. We just need to get upstairs to start the seeds."

A little white lie. If I didn't have my hands full holding this heavy bag of potting soil, I would have crossed my fingers.

Child, lies are lies. The devil doesn't own a ruler, so he can't measure the size of your sin, Grandmother Faye liked to tell me. *And hellfires burn just as hot for the little white lies as they do for a humdinger.*

She was usually right about these things, but with Gordon's reputation—not to mention his freedom—on the line, I was prepared to risk a little cosmic retribution in exchange for helping him.

"You can't get upstairs to the greenhouse?" Lettie muttered. Her gaze shifted slowly to the Secret Service guards, who backed farther away from her. "I can't see why that's a problem."

The second guard cleared his throat. "I'm sorry, ma'am, but they aren't on the schedule. It's the policy. There's nothing we can do."

"Come on, Casey," Lorenzo said as he glanced up and down the center hallway. "Let's not make a scene."

I was about to agree with Lorenzo and follow him back to the grounds office, but then Lettie blurted out, "They're my guests!" She latched on to Lorenzo's arm before he could make a clean escape. A crowbar wouldn't pry her loose. "I want them to accompany me upstairs to show me around the greenhouse. Do you have a problem with that?"

The guards exchanged wary glances.

I held my breath.

The guard who'd been adamant about us not getting to the third floor gave a stiff nod. "Of course not, ma'am," he said as he hit the elevator's call button and stepped out of the way.

The third floor of the White House was a later addition built on the roof of the original structure. The space started out as a storage area accessible only by a ladder. Then, a sleeping porch was added. By 1952, the third floor had been transformed into a large living space that included several guest bedrooms and additional offices for the First Lady and her staff. There was also a game room, a solarium that doubled as a family room where the First Family could escape and relax, and tucked against the northwest side of the roof was a greenhouse.

The elevator doors slid smoothly open. Lettie nodded to the Secret Service guard who was sitting in an old desk chair near the lift. He nodded back and returned his attention to his newspaper as we walked down the hallway toward the glass door that opened out to the rooftop deck.

Did I happen to mention that the door to the rooftop deck and the greenhouse was located right next to the entrance to the offices the First Lady had started using since giving birth to her sons? This was the part of the plan that neither Lorenzo nor I had really thought through. We couldn't just stumble through the wrong door, especially not with Lettie following us around. After all, she was the one who was dead set on proving Gordon's guilt.

So close. And still, we were going to fail.

I glanced longingly at the First Lady's office door as we walked past. There was nothing we could do but head out to the greenhouse and prepare the planting trays for seeds that didn't exist.

Lettie opened the door to the rooftop deck. At the same

time, Lorenzo gave me a hard shove in the center of my back with his shoulder. I would have been able to catch myself if not for the huge bag of potting soil slung over my left shoulder. Not that I didn't try. I trip-skipped several steps before stumbling over Lettie's foot. My face hit the tan Berber carpeting. The bag of potting soil landed with a dull thud. The thin plastic split open to send a dark cloud of soil billowing into the air.

In the stunned silence that followed, the door to the First Lady's office swung open. The First Lady, dressed in a tailored lavender suit with matching flats, stepped out into the hallway with Detective Manny Hernandez at her elbow.

"Margaret!" I said, so happy to see her.

Her delicate brows furrowed as she frowned down at me and the spilled bag of potting soil. "What's going on here?" She'd addressed the question not to me or Lorenzo or even her sister, but to Manny. Her voice was filled with suspicion.

"Sorry," I said as I scrambled to my feet and brushed off the black soil as best I could. "I seem to have lost my footing," I said, and grudgingly nodded to Lorenzo. This was the opening we'd been hoping for. "I had meant to tell you yesterday how so sorry I was about the broken irrigation line on Monday. It was an inexcusable mistake. And my fault. Not Gordon's."

I stepped over the broken bag of potting soil and wrapped my arms around the First Lady. Impulsive, yes. And terribly inappropriate. But in my defense, her cheeks were drawn. Her eyes were bloodshot. And she looked in dire need of a hug.

"Thank you," she whispered when I released her from the caring embrace. "Your cheek is bleeding."

She dug around in her pocket for a clean tissue. She smoothed it out before handing it to me. I pressed the tissue to my cheek for a second before taking a look. Small spots of blood flecked the white tissue.

"Thank you," I said and pressed the tissue to my cheek again. "I guess I hit the floor pretty hard, darn my clumsy feet. I apologize about the mess."

Manny, dressed in a freshly pressed brown suit, glared daggers at me. His salt-and-pepper mustache flared. "What are you doing here? As if I can't figure it out."

"They're my guests," Lettie proclaimed. "We're working on your garden project, Mags. Cathy was worried—"

"You mean Casey," Margaret gently corrected.

"Yes, of course. She was worried that with everything that had happened in the past few days, she hadn't started the seeds for the founding fathers' garden. And if she doesn't start them now, they won't be ready to be planted in the spring."

Lorenzo groaned as Lettie repeated my little white lie.

"I personally helped select many of the plants," Lettie continued. "We're going to grow the historic heirloom plants in the greenhouse, just like you wanted." I winced at the embellishments Lettie had added. "In fact, Mags, I've been taking a leading role in the project."

I could feel the heat of hell's fires nipping at my heels. I should have listened to my sainted grandmother. Even if it had been for a good cause, I shouldn't have lied. I held my breath and fully expected the First Lady to call me out and chastise me for making up stories. Margaret, a first-rate gardener, knew darn well that it would be months before we needed to start the spring seeds.

The First Lady, however, didn't even blink. "Thank goodness," she said with her usual grace. "With everything that's been going on, I was worried the planting would be delayed. I hope you haven't had trouble finding sources for the seeds."

Lorenzo looked like he was trying to tell me how to answer the First Lady with his bouncing eyebrows.

"We're still working a plant list," I said and then had to dodge Lorenzo's attempts to kick me. Apparently, that wasn't what he'd wanted me to say. But it was the truth. "Some"—make that most—"of the plants might not be available."

"Send me a copy of the planting list when you finish," she said and then turned to the detective. "You must know

I support the grounds office in all their projects. Especially Gordon's."

Manny's lips twisted, which caused his mustache to do a little hula dance. "Yes . . . um . . . I need to get back to the station. If you have any other questions about the investigation, please don't hesitate to give me a call."

"Yes, thank you for taking the time to meet with me. I feel in the end you'll do the right thing." Margaret patted Manny's hand.

Manny stepped over the broken bag of potting soil with as much dignity as he could muster and headed toward the elevator.

"Well, that's done. Let's get this mess cleaned up and out to the greenhouse," Lettie said.

"What do we do?" Lorenzo mumbled without moving his lips.

"You'd better hurry. The detective is getting away," the First Lady whispered back.

"But I thought we were going to get the planters ready," Lettie said, looking around.

"We will. In a minute." I snatched the printout from Lorenzo's hands. "Won't be a minute."

With Lorenzo sputtering protests about my leaving him to deal with Lettie alone, I jogged down the hall and stepped into the elevator with Manny just as the doors slid closed.

"You've been avoiding me," I said.

Manny stared straight ahead.

"Gordon didn't do it," I said.

He continued to stare at the brass elevator doors as if they were the most interesting things he'd ever seen.

"I have evidence." I shook the printout.

Manny tapped an impatient finger against his leg.

"I thought we were friends, Manny. Why are you doing this?"

A bell dinged, announcing that we'd arrived on the ground floor. The doors slid open.

Manny stepped out of the elevator and gave a nod to one of the Secret Service guards.

"Where do you need to go now, sir?" the guard, clearly his assigned escort, asked.

"I'm ready to go back to headquarters," Manny replied.

Both men appeared content to pretend I didn't exist.

But I'd gone through too much trouble to give up now. So I dogged their heels as they headed toward the exit in the Palm Room. "You have to listen to me. I found the missing branches. They were next to the grounds shed. And Lorenzo found evidence that the papers Lettie gave you have always been in Gordon's office."

The sunny Palm Room connected the White House residence to the West Wing. The room, with doors on each of its four walls, served as a staging area for guests and a passageway to the Rose Garden on its south side. The door opposite it, which was the door Manny was currently exiting through, opened out onto the North Lawn.

Manny's quick stride carried him past a small exterior guard hut attached to the West Wing and down the curving driveway toward the northwest gatehouse.

I sprinted to catch up to him and thrust the printout against Manny's broad chest. "This spreadsheet proves that the papers you have are only a copy of the ones Frida claimed were stolen."

He stopped, looked at the paper, and nodded once.

"You can check its authenticity with the assistant usher. He's the one who cataloged the files this past summer," I said, pushing the spreadsheet into his hands.

"I never thought Gordon stole from Frida," Manny said.

"You didn't? Of course you didn't. Just like this past summer, you're working an angle. You're putting the pressure on Gordon so the real killer will make a mistake. Isn't that right?"

Manny didn't answer—not that I'd expected he would.

"So if the research Lettie gave you isn't relevant to the investigation, can we have it back? We need it for our—"

"No." Manny folded the printout in half and stuffed it into his suit jacket pocket.

"But if you're not going to use them, why are you holding on to them?"

"They might be important."

"But you said they weren't."

He stopped and turned toward me. "Look, I did say that. Missing papers or missing branches or missing schematics aren't going to make or break the case I'm building against Gordon. But thank you for all those texts and photos you've been sending me the past few days."

"Wait a minute, I'm confused. You just said you didn't think Gordon was guilty of stealing from Frida. So why are you still building a case against Gordon?"

"This is a murder I'm investigating, Casey, not some petty office theft."

"But Gordon couldn't have killed anyone."

His dark brown eyes met mine. "Do you think I enjoy this part of my job? Even the First Lady"—he gestured back at the White House—"is telling me to get off Gordon's back. Every single person I've met loves him. I get that, but at the same time I can't ignore the evidence."

"Evidence? Gordon was attacked. He's lucky to be alive."

Manny shook his head. "I've talked to his doctors. Hell, I've had my pathologist talk to his doctors. There's no sign of bruising or cuts or anything on him. No one pushed him into the pond."

"But the blood I saw—"

"Was Frida's. He killed her in a fit of anger, attacked her from behind. That same fit of anger triggered his cardiac arrest."

"No. That's not true. He wasn't in the garden. He left the Children's Garden. The branches—"

"Yes. We'd already found the branches. The police do have a little experience in conducting murder investigations. But branches or no branches, nothing changes. Even if Gordon left the Children's Garden, he obviously returned. You were there. You found him."

"But if he didn't steal Frida's research, if he wasn't

interested in finding some stupid treasure that probably doesn't exist in the first place, what is his motive?"

"I can't talk about the case."

"Come on, Manny, you were talking about it just a second ago."

"I was talking about the alleged theft, which isn't part of the murder investigation."

"Frida's murder has nothing to do with Gordon. If you'd just open your eyes long enough, you'd see that. Gordon would never hurt anyone. And he had no reason to hurt Frida. Sure, she'd gone all nutty on him, but he could handle a little nutty."

"Knowing that he worked with you for the past year, I believe that. You've pushed *me* to the edge often enough."

I let the dig slide because it only strengthened my argument. "Then you agree with me. Gordon is innocent. You need to tell that to the press before they put him on trial in the court of public opinion and completely ruin his reputation and his nearly thirty-five-year White House career."

Manny's mustache quivered as he closed his eyes and inhaled deeply. "I should have all the pieces together by Friday afternoon. That's when I'll take what I have to the DA's office. I'm sorry, Casey. I really am. I hate this part of my job. The people I take into custody leave behind friends and families who grieve for them. It tears me up inside to see it. But I'm not the one who forced them to break the law. And it's still my job to arrest them. I have to do it."

"You *can't* be serious. You're going to encourage the DA to pursue charges against Gordon even when there's clearly no motive?"

Manny started to walk away, but he stopped and turned back around. He mumbled something.

"What?" I asked.

"I said, there is a motive."

"Impossible."

"Talk with Deloris."

"Gordon's wife?" My stomach clenched as I remembered how pleased she'd seemed when she'd heard Frida had been murdered. Well, perhaps *pleased* was too strong a word. No, it wasn't. She *had* been pleased. "What does Deloris have to do with anything?"

"Ask Deloris," Manny said as he walked away. "I've got work to do."

Chapter Seventeen

If you want a friend in Washington, get a dog.
—BESS TRUMAN, FIRST LADY OF
THE UNITED STATES (1945–1953)

Ask Deloris. Manny was crazy if he believed I'd badger Gordon's wife with questions about her past when she had her hands full working with hospital staff and worrying if Gordon would even survive.

No, don't even look down that dark path. Gordon *was* going to survive.

I gazed out over the North Lawn. This was Gordon's domain, his love for the past thirty-five years.

Fall leaves flecked in shades of dark reds and gold floated on the wind, swirling over the White House's iron gates. The leaves didn't know or care that they were entering one of the securest residences on the planet.

Given what had happened on Monday, I was starting to wonder if all this high-priced security was simply an illusion. Frida was dead. Gordon was critically ill. Because someone had figured out how to fool the system? A stab of dread grabbed my neck as I looked around me. Someone inside this iron fence was a killer.

It was a horrible thought.

So horrible, the Secret Service and the police were willing to point a finger of guilt at the first person they could find. And they weren't alone.

On the other side of Pennsylvania Avenue, news crews had set up field studios in Lafayette Square as they reported twenty-four hours a day, spinning a story about how a head gardener could lose his mind and attack a colleague. Every day, every hour, every minute that passed edged the situation ever closer to the point of no return, the point where Gordon's fate would be sealed and no amount of evidence to the contrary could stop the justice system from steamrolling over him.

What did Deloris know?

Milo gave a deep-throated bark and bounded across the North Lawn toward me. His unruly mop of yellowish-gold fur danced and waved like a rock star's long mane.

I held up both my hands. "No. Milo, no."

His yellow eyes sparkled with wild, puppy excitement. No amount of admonishment would slow him or turn his course. With a leap, his muddy front paws hit me with a smack in the chest. I staggered backward several steps as I absorbed the impact of his nearly eighty pounds of muscle. His long tail kicked up a breeze as his pink tongue slipped out of his mouth and licked my face.

"Off," I ordered. I twisted to the side to dislodge the oversized puppy. Black mud smeared down the front and side of my dark blue shirt and khaki pants. "What have you been doing?" As if I needed to ask.

He'd been digging.

Again.

"You should know better," I scolded. He looked up at me with his adorable brown puppy dog eyes and wagged his tail. Gordon and I, not to mention the highly skilled dog trainer who'd been brought in, had worked long hours to train Milo to direct his boundless energy into less-destructive activities.

After wiping the dog slobber from my face, I reached for Milo's leather collar, but he took off running before I could grab hold of him.

"Milo! Come!" I clapped my hands.

The naughty puppy took off running toward "Pebble Beach," the flagstone area alongside the western end of the curved driveway where television correspondents reported from the White House. Milo stopped when he spotted a correspondent filming what looked like a live segment on Pebble Beach. The puppy looked . . . intrigued. He crouched low to the ground as he edged his way toward the fieldstones.

Wouldn't the reporter be surprised when a large puppy with a wild gleam in his eye crashed the interview?

"*Milo,*" I called in a whispery, but commanding, voice that I hoped wouldn't be picked up by the reporter's microphone. "*Milo, come here.*"

I moved as close as possible without risk of walking into the shot or upsetting the Secret Service agents who were keeping watch over the area. Actually, I waved my hands at the agents, hoping they'd spot Milo and grab his collar, but there was a ruckus going on at the gate as a black sedan followed by a couple of SUVs entered the property.

I prayed the envoy from Turbekistan was sitting in the backseat of the sedan.

Milo didn't notice the incoming motorcade. Crouched low with his butt in the air, he flapped his tail, making it look like a loose sail in a windstorm. He inched toward the reporter who was standing with his back to us so the camera would capture a dramatic shot with the reporter in the foreground and the White House rising up behind him.

"*Milo,*" I whispered as I dropped to one knee next to a wide white oak tree. Sometimes when I got down to his level, he'd run over to me. "*Over here.*"

The pup cocked his head in my direction. He then looked back at the reporter. His ears tilted forward as he seemed to consider what he should do, although I suspected I already knew the choice he was going to make. His muscles quivered with delight.

With an excited yelp, Milo broke into a run with his ears plastered on the sides of his head. He raced past the Secret Service agents on duty, leapt over a low boxwood hedge, and landed on the fieldstones. With deliriously happy barks, he launched himself at the surprised reporter.

I had to give the man credit. After a moment of stunned silence, the reporter smiled at Milo and rubbed the pup's scruffy head. "Looks like I have a junior reporter joining me." After introducing Milo, not that the President's famous pooch needed an introduction, the reporter—now wearing a goofy grin—continued his report.

I was now close enough to hear the sandy-haired journalist. He wasn't reporting on the sky-high gas prices or the tensions in the Middle East. It was Frida's murder that had suddenly captured the nation's attention. "Special Agent in Charge of Protective Operations Bryce Williams was called to testify before a joint committee of Congress today," he said, his voice growing loud with excitement.

Milo, enjoying the attention, smiled for the camera with his big loopy grin and tongue hanging out the side of his mouth. He looked as if he was planning on staying put. He might as well stay. The damage had already been done.

"Security lapses have caused many to question President Bradley's safety. Is the Secret Service doing enough to secure the White House? I have to wonder myself if enough is being done. Take, for instance, the appearance of the President's dog just now. Where is his minder? Why isn't he being watched?"

I'm right here, I felt like shouting. And I would have spoken up if not for my disastrous track record for speaking with the press. Even President Bradley's press secretary, Frank Lispon, had begged me to just keep my lips sealed around the press and let the professionals—professionals like him—do their jobs.

So I did. I leaned against a white oak and, crossing my arms over my chest, waited for the reporter to conclude Milo's interview.

Since gardeners pretty much had free rein on the

grounds, the Secret Service agents jogged by without giving me a second glance once the mysterious town car had entered the property and the gates had closed.

The doors to the sedan were swept open. I held my breath, hoping that Lev Aziz would emerge . . . not that I knew what the skittish envoy looked like.

And I certainly didn't recognize the dark-haired man who stepped out of the sedan and was hurried into the West Wing.

"Was that Lev Aziz?" I asked a Secret Service agent who was heading back to the northwest gate. Getting those oil negotiations started would relieve some of the pressure Manny must be feeling to swiftly close Frida's murder investigation.

"Nope," the agent answered. "The Turbekistan guy said he wasn't coming out of hiding until his safety could be assured. Hey, wait, you aren't supposed to know about any of that."

"Well, I do," I said. After all, Aziz had said he'd wanted to talk with Calhoun . . . *me*. "I'm willing to help out any way I can, but no one seems interested in letting me."

The agent chuckled as he jogged past. "You're just a gardener. What can you do?"

"But—" I started to argue. Too late, the agent was too far away to hear me.

I'd started to inch my way back to Pebble Beach to see if I could lure Milo over to me when out of the corner of my eye I spotted Marcel, the First Lady's interior designer. He came lumbering around the corner of the West Wing. His shoulders were slightly hunched, and he was wearing his bulky dark red winter coat and matching mud boots. He appeared to be deep in thought as he kept his head down. He looked as if he was studying the ground or contemplating how to coordinate the colors in the nursery with the colors in the solarium. His thick arms swayed left-right-left-right with each step as if he needed their motion to help propel him forward.

Milo saw him, too. With his ears turned forward, a sure sign he was on high alert, his head jerked away from the camera as he tracked the interior designer's movement with the same intensity with which he watched the squirrels in the trees.

Special agents Janie Partners and Steve Sallis, both dressed in dark suits and matching dark sunglasses, moved to intercept *not* the puppy who was somewhere he shouldn't have been but the color-coordinated Marcel.

Milo, seeing that the Secret Service agents were going to get to his prey before him, gave chase as well. He jumped off Pebble Beach, over the boxwoods, barking as if it were dinnertime and the chef was bringing him a choice cut of steak.

The reporter, left alone on Pebble Beach, shook his head and chuckled before turning serious again. He reiterated that Milo's appearance only underscored why every loyal American should be concerned about White House security.

Half bent over to keep out of the camera shot, I darted after Milo before he caused even more trouble. I managed to snag hold of his collar at the same time Steve grabbed Marcel's arm.

"Where do you think you're going?" both Steve and I demanded.

"Sorry, I was talking to the dog," I said when Marcel howled a protest.

"I wasn't," Steve said.

Janie stepped back and hid a smirk while she let her partner handle the emotional French designer.

"Move out of the way, *monsieur*," Marcel said with an annoyed huff. "I am doing important work for the First Lady."

Steve stood his ground. "Sir, how did you get past the security guards posted at all the entrances?"

"I waved as I walked past."

"Impossible," Steve said.

"You call me a liar?" Marcel's accented voice rose with indignation. Milo barked and tugged at his collar, anxious to get to Marcel. His tail waved madly. And he was drooling. I'd never seen Milo act so excited to see anyone. Not even the First Family elicited such unbridled enthusiasm.

"It's true," I said. An intern had followed him around,

serving as an official escort the first several times he'd ventured out into the White House lawn. But recently Marcel had enjoyed free access to the grounds. "He's been out in the gardens every day."

"*Merci*, Casey," Marcel said, puffing out his chest. His French accent deepened. "I am here at the invitation of the First Lady. I must be allowed to do my work. I must be allowed to seek my inspiration." He'd pressed his thumb to his forefinger and lifted his hand in the air for emphasis.

"Sir, I understand that, but you have to follow protocol," Steve said evenly.

Marcel jerked his arm out of the agent's grasp. "Protocol? Protocol? What is this protocol to me? I am an artiste. I am—I am—" He stammered before switching to his native French. I caught a word here and there. Very few of the words I heard flow from his tongue were ones my grandmother would wish me to repeat in any shape or form.

"Cut the crap and speak English," Steve said with a sharp edge of impatience.

"I am upset. The words . . . they come . . . difficult."

"Yeah, right," Steve said as if he didn't care that Marcel was having trouble with his English. The friendly agent wasn't usually so harsh. I wondered if the stress of Frida's murder and the pressure the press and members of Congress were putting on the Secret Service were getting to him.

"You—you make English come more . . . difficult . . . by your harsh . . . tone."

"Well then, don't speak. Just listen. You do not wander the lawn without prior approval. If you do it again, you will be escorted from the premises. Do you understand?"

"*Oui, oui.*" Marcel sounded cowed like a scolded child. "I understand. May I go? I am late for a meeting with the florist."

"Not until a proper escort arrives," Steve said, which caused Marcel to huff and puff with annoyance again.

"I'm heading back to the grounds office. Since the florist shop is just down the hallway, I can see that he gets there," I said.

Steve hesitated. "I don't know. We have to follow—"

"She has oodles more security clearance than an intern," Janie stepped forward to point out. "She's more than quali-fied to serve as his escort."

Steve sighed. "Okay. Go on, *Frenchie*."

"*Merci*," Marcel said to me as we headed across the North Lawn and down the steps to the sunken West Court-yard tucked behind the North Portico. Milo threatened to pull me over as he yanked at his collar, whining and yip-ping with each step.

"Calm down," I said, but he refused to listen. It was as if the excitement of running amok on the North Lawn had made him forget all his training.

Marcel didn't seem to notice when I stumbled down the last several steps into the courtyard. "I will call you in the future when I need an escort, *non?*"

"No, I can't—" I started to explain. I had more than enough on my plate already with trying to save Gordon's reputation and keep him out of prison for a murder he didn't commit. But Marcel didn't give me a chance.

"*Bon*," he said as he hurried inside. "It will be good. We will discover the lawn's secrets, you and me. The green of the grass can shimmer in the morning. I wish to see it from all angles. The shiny shade will make a perfect trim for the nursery, do you not think?"

I was still in the courtyard cleaning Milo's paws with the garden hose that was there for just this purpose when Lorenzo located me. "Thanks for letting me clean up that bag of potting soil by myself. What happened with Manny?" he demanded.

I blushed for forgetting he had been stranded in the roof-top greenhouse with Lettie and the First Lady, then quickly summed up the frustrating conversation with the detective. "I don't want to upset Deloris with this. But we need to find out what he's talking about. I'll call Pearle or Mable and see if one of them would agree to—"

"Casey, stop! This is exactly what we need to talk about." He held open the door for Milo and me. It was a short walk down the hallway to the grounds office. "You can't just run off half-cocked and make the decisions. In Gordon's absence, I get to make the decisions. I'm the senior assistant."

"No, Lorenzo. It's true that you've been here longer, but our titles are the same. If you look at Wilson Fisher's organizational chart, you'll see we're on the same level."

That had been the wrong thing to say. Lorenzo's face darkened several shades. His voice was a low growl as he said, "We have *never* been on the same level."

"Fine. Let's just focus on Gordon."

"That's what I'm trying to do!" he shouted. "And you're running around, lying about your founding fathers' vegetable garden when both you and I know it's going to be an absolute failure."

"What do you want me to do, Lorenzo? We can't really back out now. Margaret has considered the project a done deal for quite a while now. She expects me to—"

"This is part of the problem with you! You refer to the First Lady as Margaret instead of Mrs. Bradley or the First Lady. You act as if she's your best buddy. You're disrespectful."

"I'm friendly."

"You're a *junior* assistant gardener. You're not supposed to be friendly with the First Family!" And *that* was the crux of the problem. My relationship with Margaret Bradley was eating Lorenzo from the inside out.

"What would you have me do? Should I turn the other way when she passes by? Should I ignore her when she speaks with me? Good gravy, Lorenzo, she personally asked me to work for the White House because she'd already met me; she knew my work."

A vein throbbed on his temple as he sent death threats in his heated glare. After a moment, he threw his hands in the air and marched out of the room. When he returned, the vein on his temple was still jumping.

"*Gordon*," he forced from behind clenched teeth. "Gordon should be our focus. Can you at least try to focus on helping him?"

"What do you suggest we do?" I asked, keeping my arms still folded defensively over my chest.

"I don't know. I'm not the super sleuth."

"Well, we could try and follow in the killer's footsteps. We could find out what was in Frida's missing file folder and try to re-create her notes. And we could go looking for Jefferson's lost treasure."

"I don't believe it exists."

"I'm not sure I do either, but someone seems to. I wish Manny hadn't been so adamant about keeping his hands on the 'evidence' Lettie had given him. I'm not sure how quickly we can rebuild that file. We have to get this done before Friday."

"And it's already Wednesday," Lorenzo said with a sigh. "There is someone who might be able to help us out, someone who has been studying the history of the gardens with a single-minded focus."

"Not Nadeem. We can't trust him. For all we know, he could be the killer." The more I thought about it, the more I suspected he was up to something nefarious.

Lorenzo shook his head with disbelief. "How can you suspect Nadeem? He's afraid of his own shadow. I thought you were good at this, at solving mysteries. But you're not, are you? How in the world did you crack those other murder cases?"

"Luck?" I took a towel out of my bottom drawer and started to dry Milo's paws. Enjoying the extra attention, the puppy thumped his tail loudly against the floor as he made happy grunting sounds.

Lorenzo huffed and grabbed his windbreaker off the coat tree behind the door. "There is someone else we can talk to. Someone almost as knowledgeable as Frida was about the gardens."

"Who?"

"Dr. Wadsin, the National Arboretum's garden historian. Remember I worked with her the other day? She's brilliant."

Chapter Eighteen

❧ 🏛 ❧

If we mean to have heroes, statesmen and
philosophers, we should have learned women.
—ABIGAIL ADAMS, FIRST LADY OF
THE UNITED STATES (1797–1801)

DR. Joan Wadsin was waiting for us at the nineteen-
sixties flat-roofed, modern-designed, concrete-and
pebble-sided Visitor Center of the National Arboretum.

Seeing her standing in front of the full-glass double
automatic doors, I had to blink. Twice. No matter how many
times I told myself that she wasn't, my mind still insisted I
was looking at my favorite fictional sleuth: Miss Marple.

She was dressed in a demure flowered print dress that
hung to her knees. Less than an inch of her slightly saggy
pantyhose was visible because she was also wearing bright
yellow rubber rain boots. Boots, I must add, that were
already caked with thick mud. In contrast, fresh orange and
white chrysanthemum blooms were tucked in the head-
band of her straw sun hat.

"I hope you don't mind if we walk and talk," she said
after Lorenzo and I had greeted her. "A visitor has reported
that one of our Franklin trees has been damaged."

I gave a start when I noticed she was holding a pruning
saw that was identical to the one that had killed Frida. Like

Miss Marple, she missed nothing. She raised her brows and tucked the pruning saw under her arm so it was practically out of sight.

"It must be a terrible strain on your nerves," she said as we followed her down the roadway to a dark green garden cart filled with gardening tools—shovels and trowels among the mix. I grabbed the cart's handle before she could and pulled it across a field toward one of the arboretum's many experimental forests. Her rubber rain boots made a soft slapping sound as she trudged across the damp grass. "Such wicked happenings."

Lorenzo grunted in agreement, his jaw still tense from our argument about the First Lady and who was in charge in Gordon's absence.

"We can't understand why it happened," I said. "That's why we're here."

"We're doing what the police refuse to do," Lorenzo grumbled. He slid me a disgruntled look. "At least one of us is."

"I see," Dr. Wadsin said.

We passed a circle of twenty-two sandstone Corinthian columns. Those columns were the same ones that had once supported the east portico of the Capitol Building. In times gone by, those stately columns had stood as silent witnesses to presidential inaugurations from Jefferson to Eisenhower. Now they watched over a small pond in the National Arboretum's experimental forests at the outskirts of the city.

The storm's passage had ushered in a damp winter wind that seemed to blow straight through me. Beyond the historic columns, a forest of orange and gold-tinged trees shimmered in the afternoon light.

The four-hundred-plus-acre Arboretum served educational, scientific, and conservation roles. If I hadn't been so worried about Gordon and how entangled he'd become in Frida's murder investigation, I would have happily trudged through the muddy paths to see the new cultivars of trees and shrubs the Arboretum was developing. In several years, many of their experimental varieties would show up for sale in garden centers all across the country.

I loved how the new and old mingled in these gardens with relative ease.

If only the same could be said about the White House gardens or the two gardeners butting heads. Gordon would know how to smooth over the prickly feelings and come to an agreement. He had a talent for bringing calm to any discussion . . . except when it came to Frida.

There had to be a history there.

I looked straight ahead and watched the golden leaves dance in the wind. "I want to talk with you about Gordon and Frida. I understand you worked with both of them on several projects."

"Casey"—Lorenzo's voice tightened with irritation— "this isn't why we fought heavy traffic. It's more important to ask her about the—"

"There's plenty of time to discuss whatever you both need to discuss," Dr. Wadsin said with a kind smile. "There's no rush here."

"Thank you," I said. "I'm glad we can talk out here where we don't have to worry about being overheard . . . and misunderstood."

"Yes." She nodded slowly. "No one could possibly sneak up on us out here in the middle of a field. I feel like a spy. Too bad I don't have secret information to hand to you."

The keen intelligence and good humor sparkling in her eyes helped to settle my nerves. "How well did you know Frida?" I asked.

"I've been garden historian for the Arboretum for the past twenty years. Frida was the one who had told me about the job opening. The fact that she lived in D.C. was the main reason I took the position. I was living in Manchester at the time and knew very few Yanks."

"Oh, I didn't realize you were close to Frida."

"We were roommates at university. But don't misunderstand me. I also consider Gordon a good friend. What the newspapers are saying cannot be true." She frowned as she said it. "While I cherish both of their friendships, I do know that they had trouble working together. It wasn't always that way. It wasn't until . . ."

"Until what? What happened?" I pressed.

"Oh dear, dear me." She struggled in her haste to step across a shallow puddle and ended up splashing at the edge of it. "Looks like kids have been trying to climb the poor thing."

She stood in front of a small tree. Its leaves were a brilliant, almost iridescent red. Large white flowers that reminded me of camellia blooms decorated the tree like Southern Christmas ornaments. Several branches had snapped on one side of the tree. "Do you know about the Franklin tree?" she asked as she began to saw off the closest damaged branch.

"Not well," I said, dismayed that she had left us hanging about Gordon and Frida's relationship. "What happened between Frida and Gordon?"

"The Franklin is related to the camellia," Dr. Wadsin said.

"That would explain the flowers," I said.

"It's a bear to transplant," Lorenzo said with a scowl.

Dr. Wadsin chuckled at that. "It is a finicky devil. Thank you," she said when Lorenzo took the pruning saw from her and took over the task of removing the damaged branches. "Did you know that the tree has an interesting history? It was discovered in the late seventeen hundreds by the botanist John Bartram. His friendship with Benjamin Franklin is how the tree got its name. Sadly, by 1803, the tree was extinct in the wild. The only reason the tree still exists at all is because of arboretums like this one."

"Is that so?" I said. "It's like the arboretum is a zoo of sorts, keeping endangered species going until they can be reintroduced into the wild."

"Exactly. Climate changes over time, habitats change. If the change is too rapid, trees and other plants won't have time to migrate or adapt. Oh! Listen to me prattle on. I do beg your pardon."

I was about to ask her about Frida and Gordon again

when she spotted a smilax vine snaking up a slightly larger specimen of the Franklin tree. "I really ought to take care of this." She grabbed a shovel from the garden cart.

"Please, let me help." I took the shovel from her. With my foot on the shovel's rim, I thrust it into the ground.

The soil was soft from the day and a half of heavy rain. Even so, it was work getting down to the vine's thick tubers and wiry roots that clung to the ground with what seemed like the tensile strength of steel.

"You had started to tell us why Frida and Gordon were so angry with each other," I prompted.

She'd propped her hands on her hips as she watched me work. "It was years ago, but some people have long memories."

"What happened?" I asked as I reached down and plucked a fat tuber from the turned-up black soil. I gave it a toss. It landed in the garden cart with a thunk.

"Deloris happened." One gray brow rose. "She's Gordon's wife."

"Yes, we know," Lorenzo said.

"Of course you know Deloris. Lovely woman, isn't she?"

I told her what Manny had told me, which didn't take long since he really hadn't told me anything at all. "Why didn't Frida and Deloris get along? Before Monday night, I didn't realize the two women even knew each other."

"So, you don't know? I would have thought the White House would have been awash with gossip about the horrid affair. Perhaps it is, and the staff is keeping the unpleasant discussion away from the two of you. I can only imagine how painful it must be to hear people think the worst about a friend."

"They are all lies," Lorenzo said as he removed a second broken branch.

"Not all of it. Did you know that Deloris used to be the White House curator? Frida was her assistant."

"Really?" Lorenzo said.

"Deloris's career was taking off. She was writing articles for several newspapers and magazines about the treasures in the White House. And then a priceless silver soup tureen and mahogany card table that dated back to James Madison's administration both went missing. Guess who reported those important items were gone?"

"Frida?" I guessed.

Dr. Wadsin nodded slowly. "And guess who took the blame?"

"Deloris?" I couldn't believe Gordon's wife could do anything wrong. "She didn't steal anything, though?"

"No, the missing items were eventually located, but that was months after Deloris had been dismissed under a cloud of guilt."

The image of a power-hungry assistant curator didn't mesh with the thick-glasses-wearing woman who seemed to have a singular focus on her research. "Are you sure?"

"Sure as rain."

"But that had to have been ages ago. Deloris has worked as a schoolteacher for the past fifteen years. Why would anyone think Gordon would act now?"

Lorenzo supplied the answer. "Dolley Madison's missing papers. Frida accused Gordon of theft in the same way she'd accused Deloris. What if she was trying to get him sacked?"

"That might explain why Deloris hadn't been surprised or upset when we'd told her someone had murdered Frida. But why would Frida fake another theft?" I asked. "Why now?"

Dr. Wadsin shook her head. "I don't know. She was happy in her position as curator. Plus she was at the top of her field. What did she think she'd gain from chasing Gordon from the White House?" She tapped her chin. "I'd like to see what was in the missing file."

"We found it," I said. "Well, the First Lady's sister found it . . . well, she found a copy of it. It was in Gordon's office."

"Really?" Her eyes sparkled with sudden interest. "In his office, you say? As if he had, in fact, stolen the papers? That's interesting. Now I really want to see that research."

"I'd love to show it to you, but the detective took it. 'It's evidence,' he said when I asked for it back." I did a fair imitation of Manny's deep, authoritative voice. "Of course, the First Lady's sister is now convinced Gordon killed Frida because they were both searching for a treasure that had been lost when the British burned the White House."

"A treasure?" Dr. Wadsin clapped her hands. "How intriguing!"

"Finally," Lorenzo said. He'd finished cleaning up the damaged Franklin tree. After he'd gathered the pruned branches and dropped them in the garden cart, he wiped his hands on a pressed cotton handkerchief he'd produced from his pocket. "We've wasted enough time talking about ancient history and rumors. Gordon didn't kill anyone. And we're going to prove it. At least *I* am. That's why we're here. I know it sounds crazy"—he nodded toward me as if he thought I was the root of all crazy—"but it looks as if the killer thinks there is a treasure, so that's where we need to start looking for clues. The police won't. To them, believing in hidden treasure is like believing in fairies."

"But what you do or do not believe doesn't matter," Dr. Wadsin was quick to say. "What matters is what the killer believes."

"Exactly," Lorenzo said. "Even if there isn't a treasure, we need to act as if there is one. We need to follow in the killer's footsteps."

"Find the treasure, find the murderer." Dr. Wadsin tapped her chin again. "It might work."

"But we don't have Dolley Madison's garden notes," Lorenzo said. "Or the notes that Frida made, which Nadeem seems to think are even more valuable. That's why we need your help."

"Have you heard anything about a lost treasure from the time period of the Madison administration?" I asked.

"Hm . . ." She took the shovel from me and returned it to her garden cart. I wrapped the spiny vines that I'd dug out from around the Franklin tree into a loose ball and tucked them underneath the shovel to keep them from falling out. "Rumors of treasures hidden within the White House walls or on the grounds have popped up again and

again over the years. Some think the Masons hid ancient
secrets and perhaps a cache of gold within the foundation
walls. But even if they had, Harry Truman's administration
would have found it when they started gutting the building
in the 1948 renovation. Other rumors claim there's money
buried in the Rose Garden. For what purpose? That's for
the conspiracy theorists to decide, I suppose."

"But what about Dolley Madison's notes?" Lorenzo
pressed. "Before the detective took them, we read a letter
she'd written talking about a treasure Thomas Jefferson
had left at the White House. The treasure was apparently
hidden by the gardener at the time when the British stormed
D.C. Have you seen that letter? Do you know what she's
talking about?"

"Curious," Dr. Wadsin said. "While I'm not an expert
on Dolley Madison, I've spent nearly half my life studying
Thomas Jefferson's notes and letters. His botany notes, you
must know, are atrocious. He calls plants by several names,
often by the wrong names. But he loved his plants nonethe-
less. Did you know that Jefferson even acted as a spy for
agribusiness? He smuggled premium rice varieties out of
Italy at the risk of death if caught. He wanted the rice to
help plantation owners in South Carolina compete in the
global marketplace. Oh dear, however have I managed to
stray so far from my point? What was I saying?"

"You were talking about Thomas Jefferson and if he left
a treasure at the White House," I prompted.

"Right. I've never heard or read about anything like
that. I doubt he would have had a reason to keep it secret."

"But what about the letter we read?" Lorenzo said.

"I'm not saying that it's not possible," Dr. Wadsin said,
"just that its existence hasn't shown up in any of Jefferson's
documents."

"We've hit another dead end, then?" Lorenzo scuffed
the ground with his toe and then winced when he noticed
his action had caused mud to splatter on his shiny leather
shoe. "Casey, I told you this was a waste of time. There is
no treasure or treasure hunter. It's a love triangle. Frida got

herself caught in bed with another woman's husband . . . or maybe even another man's wife."

"Frida? In a love triangle?" Dr. Wadsin chuckled softly. "Crikey, if it wasn't old and valuable, she wasn't interested."

"That value she sought was both monetary and power, isn't that right?" I asked.

"I'm afraid so. Frida had very few friends. Besides me, I can count on one hand the number of people who will truly grieve her passing."

"Nadeem Barr seemed fond of her," I said in a weak attempt to comfort.

She nodded sadly and changed the subject. "Besides losing Dolley Madison's garden notes, how is the work on the White House garden history progressing?"

"I've hit a wall with the founding fathers' vegetable garden. I can't find a vendor that carries the varieties of plants grown in the first kitchen gardens," I said.

"I was afraid that would happen," she said. "Many of our historic vegetables didn't survive the industrialization of the farms. There are far fewer varieties available today than there were at the turn of the century."

"But the First Lady is expecting it to be planted this spring. The press is expecting it, too. Tuesday morning she described what we were doing in great detail at one of her breakfasts in front of her entire press pool," I said. "This afternoon I sent a list of plants to the horticulturists out at Monticello. They've been helpful with providing seeds for the kitchen garden. I'm hoping they can help track down some of these plants as well."

"I'll talk with the Arboretum's directors and see if there's anything I can do on my end. Perhaps you can use alternative varieties."

The three of us started our trek back to the Visitor Center. Lorenzo insisted on pulling the garden cart. He hurried on ahead of us, grumbling about how he should have never let me butt my way into his investigation and his projects—as if I would force my way into anything he was doing.

"He's quite a pill," Dr. Wadsin said.

"He's good at what he does," I felt the need to say. Even if it rarely felt that way, Lorenzo and I were, after all, supposed to be on the same team.

"You don't have to explain. Despite all her faults, I considered Frida my friend."

Soon, we were back at the Visitor Center. I gave Dr. Wadsin a big hug and thanked her for her help.

"I'll ask a few colleagues about what you've told me. If I find anything out, I'll give you a call. We all want the same thing," she said. "Justice."

"Frida deserves at least that much," I promised.

"What we need are Dolley Madison's notes back," Lorenzo said. "There's a reason someone stole them. The key to why Frida is dead must be in those pages."

"That may be true," Dr. Wadsin said. "But it's just a file folder of old letters, such a small thing. You don't really need it."

Such a small thing.

I wanted to believe her. Truly, I did. But like the tiny but deadly rosary pea, I knew the smallest things could prove the most dangerous.

I agreed with Lorenzo. If we were to find out what had happened in the Children's Garden on Monday, we needed to walk in the killer's footsteps. We needed to find out why Frida had written "I know who you are and what you're doing" on a notepad. And more important, we needed to find out why that note proved to be a deadly threat to its mysterious recipient.

Lorenzo and I waved good-bye to the garden historian and took the path to the gravel parking lot where we'd left the White House grounds van. As we walked, a niggle of worry tickled the back of my neck.

I whirled around and spotted a tall man dressed in a putty-colored raincoat hurrying in the opposite direction. The mysterious man looked like Nadeem. I called his name and jogged after him. But he took off running and disappeared into the woods before either Lorenzo or I could get a good look at him.

Chapter Nineteen

I didn't make it home until close to nine o'clock that chilly Wednesday night. Outside, winter was nipping, anxious to rip the golden leaves from the trees. The weatherman on the radio had warned that temperatures might dip into record low territory. As a precaution, I'd carried my potted plants inside before collapsing on the sofa and tossing my arm over my eyes.

Alyssa, dressed in gray sweatpants and her favorite pink T-shirt that had been bead-dazzled with the word *Sexy* across the chest, had already staked out her favorite spot on the sofa. Her feet were propped on the coffee table. Her long legs were crossed at the ankles.

She'd taken her contacts out for the night. Oval-shaped glasses perched on her nose as she wrote notes on a stack of papers on her lap.

Playing on the TV was one of my favorite movies, a romantic comedy. The scene unfolding on the small screen was one that always made my heart clench. As I watched it, I felt nothing as the hero kissed the heroine after telling her he was leaving. No tingling on the back of my neck. No longing tug in my chest. Nothing. I was numb.

"What happened today?" Alyssa asked as she sipped a glass of wine. "You look worse than when you left this morning."

"I feel worse." After spinning my wheels all day, I felt no closer to finding out what had happened in the Children's Garden on Monday than I was yesterday. The only bright spot was that, after returning from the National Arboretum, Lorenzo and I set aside our differences for a few hours and made real progress listing what vegetables were grown during those first few administrations. Not that many of the seeds for those plants were commercially available. Or privately available.

"Where's your Secret Service man?" Alyssa asked as she marked a line through a sentence and scribbled some notes in the margin of some papers she'd brought home from the senator's office.

"I don't know," I said. And that was part—albeit a large part—of the reason I felt like my heart had taken a tumble over a rocky ledge.

Shortly after five o'clock, Lorenzo and I had headed through the security checkpoint and out the southeast gate. It closed behind us with a loud clank as we walked over to Sherman Park.

Located behind the Treasury Building, the small pocket park looked almost as if it were part of the White House lawn. More often than not, the park might as well be considered within the iron fence since the Secret Service used the area to line up groups prior to White House tours.

Because of its location, the care and management of the small, square park fell under the purview of the grounds office. Our fall plantings of flowering chrysanthemums in the flowerbeds created what looked like a bumpy carpet of orange. At the center of the park was a larger-than-life statue of General William Tecumseh Sherman as he sat astride a horse atop a tall granite pedestal. Apparently, this was the spot on which Sherman had stood when reviewing the troops who were returning from the Civil War in 1865.

I don't know if he stood in this exact spot or hundreds of yards away. It really didn't matter. What mattered to me was the dark-haired man dressed in jeans and a black leather jacket who was leaning against the granite base of the statue. My heart picked up a beat. I widened my stride.

"Jack," I called with a smile. As I closed the distance, I went to wrap my arms around him. But before I could, Lorenzo pushed his way in between us.

"Where is it?" Lorenzo demanded of my dark knight. He must have overheard me talking with Jack on the phone earlier. I was quickly learning Lorenzo's hearing was nearly as sharp as Frida's had been.

After talking with Dr. Wadsin and learning very little about how to find out more about this missing treasure, I'd contacted Jack to see if he could use his Secret Service cachet to get Manny to release Dolley Madison's papers to him.

"Tell me you succeeded where Casey has failed. Tell me you persuaded Manny to return the research papers," Lorenzo said.

"No can do." Jack reached around Lorenzo to clasp my hand. "Hi, Casey. Manny said he's holding on to everything until he's completed his investigation."

"I can't believe it. Casey, this is your fault, you know. You should have never let Lettie anywhere near Gordon's files."

"My fault? You were practically jumping up and down with excitement when I suggested you work with Lettie. Besides, I thought you were project manager and senior assistant gardener and all. So doesn't that mean this is your fault by default?"

Lorenzo answered with a not-safe-for-work word.

"Why is that one folder so important?" Jack inquired. Lorenzo let loose all of his pent-up frustrations with a string of creative gardening curses. There was one about a slug and a gardening glove that made Jack's mouth drop open. He shook his head and asked, "Didn't you say the file Manny found wasn't Frida's?"

"You're right. It's not important," I said. "Come on, Lorenzo. If you're done venting your spleen, let's get to the hospital."

"But—but," Lorenzo sputtered. "Those papers are the only clue we can find to Thomas Jefferson's lost treasure."

Jack raised a brow as he gave me an appraising look.

"I'm sure there isn't actually a lost treasure," I said before Jack could ask if I'd lost my mind. "But someone seems to believe strongly enough that there's gold—or *something*— buried in the South Lawn that he . . . or she . . . is willing to steal and kill for it. I was hoping that we could look for the treasure in an effort to trick the killer into acting. But without Dolley Madison's letters and notes, our boat is as sunk as the *HMS Fantome*."

"You know the *Fantome?*" Marcel appeared from behind General Sherman's statue like a magician stepping out of a sudden puff of smoke.

I jumped. Even Jack seemed to have been taken by surprise, which almost never happens.

"What were you doing back there?" I asked.

"I was studying the color contrast of the flowers with the statue in the evening light. It is complicated, do you not think so?"

"You have been warned to stop lurking around like this," Jack said.

"I am beyond the fence." He made a face. "Until I talk with the First Lady and change the inconvenient rules, I must make do how I can."

"You know about the *Fantome?*" Lorenzo asked, much to my chagrin. We had involved too many people with the investigation as it was.

Involving Lettie had only strengthened the police's case against Gordon. We didn't need another busybody working to pin Frida's murder on the wrong person.

But it was too late. Marcel sounded only too excited to talk about the infamous ship. "*Oui, oui.* I have read articles about the ship's sinking. So full of treasure, but lost at the bottom of the ocean. History is fascinating, is it not?"

"The *Fantome?* More treasure?" Jack sounded amused.

I was surprised to find out Jack already knew about the British ship that had been carrying American gold and treasures the troops had stolen from the White House in 1814.

"It's at the bottom of the Atlantic Ocean," I said.

"*Oui*, that is where I believe the First Lady's sister will also find *Monsieur* Jefferson's missing treasure, rotting away in its hull. She seems so adamant about looking for the treasure. But it will take years before anyone knows exactly what is on the *Fantome*. I believe I read somewhere that the English, they want to steal the treasure from the brave explorer who discovered the sunken ship. The matter . . . it is in the courts."

"Lettie?" I asked. "You've been talking to Lettie about the *HMS Fantome?*"

"*Oui*, the lady, she seemed most interested in *Monsieur* Jefferson's work. It is all she talks about. Please, *pardonnez-moi*. I have more to see before the darkness, it falls." With a brisk nod in my direction and a glare in Jack's, he shuffled out of the park and up the street toward the Treasury Building.

"Lettie?" I said again. "Why would she be talking to Marcel about Thomas Jefferson and sunken treasures?" She wouldn't be interested in such things unless she was . . .

Chapter Twenty

*I wish that my husband's friends had left him
where he is, happy and contented in retirement.*
—ANNA HARRISON, FIRST LADY OF
THE UNITED STATES (1841–1841)

NOT Lettie. Not the First Lady's sister. She wouldn't . . .
She couldn't . . . *Could she have . . .*

Those thoughts kept circling my mind as the three of us—
Lorenzo, Jack, and I—made our way to the surface parking
lot that looped through the Ellipse Park, a park directly adjacent to the White House's South Lawn. The parking lot was
reserved for White House employees and was where both
Lorenzo and Jack had parked that morning.

Neither Jack nor Lorenzo said a word as we crossed the
wide expanse of grass to where Jack had parked his Jeep. I
wondered if the men were pondering the same thing I was.
Was Lettie, flaky Lettie, guilty of murder? Why else would
she be researching the *HMS Fantome* if she wasn't searching for clues to where Jefferson's missing treasure had gone?

If Lettie was guilty, it would explain why Frida had
written the anonymous note I'd found. It would have been
political (and career) suicide to sign a note that baldly said,
"I know who you are, and I know what you're doing."

Pieces of the puzzle started to fall into place as I was

forced to look at Lettie's motivations in a new light. What if she'd been working to set Gordon up to take the blame? She'd been in the general area of the garden at the time of Frida's murder. And she'd been the one to find Gordon's copy of Dolley Madison's papers. But how could she have set up finding the papers? Wouldn't it have been easier to plant the stolen copy of the notes in Gordon's filing cabinet?

No, that part didn't fit. Also if Lettie needed money, why not simply ask her rich and powerful sister for help? That part didn't fit, either.

"No, it couldn't be her, could it?"

"What's that?" Lorenzo asked.

"Nothing," I mumbled. "Just thinking something through."

We'd reached Jack's Jeep. "Would you like to ride with us?" I asked Lorenzo.

"No, I . . . um . . . have a date tonight. I'll need to leave directly from the hospital to get there on time."

"A date?" I smirked as I asked. "With who?"

As expected, his complexion darkened with embarrassment. "I already told you that I—"

"Don't worry, I don't really want to know," I said. "I'm going to stop at the bakery and pick up something for Deloris and her sons. That is, if it's okay with you, Jack?"

"It's a good idea," Jack said.

"Good. We'll meet you at the hospital, then," I said to Lorenzo.

"If it's all the same to you, I'll follow along to make sure you don't get Deloris and her sons some kind of inedible girly food," Lorenzo said and then headed off to where he'd parked his car.

"He's really going to follow us to the bakery?" Jack asked as he backed out of the parking space and started driving toward my favorite bakery.

"Apparently."

Jack fell silent, which wasn't unusual for him. But in the silence, I could definitely feel tension building, which was unusual. "Did you talk to Nadeem this afternoon?" he asked.

"He was never in the office. However, I think—"

"Good," Jack said before I could tell him that I might have seen Nadeem at the National Arboretum.

"No, not good. How can I prove who killed Frida and set up Gordon if the suspects are never around?"

A muscle in Jack's jaw twitched. "I want you to stay away from him."

"Why? What have you heard?" I asked.

Jack didn't immediately answer. "Just stay away from him, Casey."

"Why?" I asked again. "What have you heard?"

"Nothing," he answered too quickly. He pulled a frustrated hand through his hair. "Even if Nadeem is innocent, I shudder to imagine how he'll react if he thought you were poking around in his business."

"Okay." I decided not to tell Jack about what had happened at the National Arboretum. After all, I'd probably startled an innocent tourist—not Nadeem—by charging the poor man like I had.

Sure, Nadeem was the one who'd been acting oddly and showing up in the most unexpected places. Nadeem was the one who I'd caught researching the *HMS Fantome*. And Nadeem was the one who was a trained killer.

But there were still too many questions that needed answering, like what was Lettie doing?

It was a stellar piece of lunacy—as Grandmother Faye would say—to doubt Nadeem's guilt and suspect the First Lady's sister, but . . . *why was Lettie so intent on proving Gordon guilty of Frida's murder?*

Was she playing sleuth or treasure thief?

If Frida had suspected Nadeem of being a treasure thief, she would have confronted him. In person. Not via an anonymous letter.

Despite the heavy traffic, by the time we'd finished at the bakery and arrived at the hospital, I was still chewing on my thumb and trying to work out the puzzle that just seemed to lead me to more questions.

Jack steered his old Jeep into a parking spot. Lorenzo parked his tan sedan next to the Jeep.

I had looked forward to visiting Gordon all day. Although I knew he was still on a respirator and in a medically induced coma, I wanted to tell him about our progress in the gardens and how we were fighting for him. I also needed to tell him how much he meant to me.

The Secret Service and D.C. Police still had guards posted at the entrance of the private suite at the hospital. Jack remained behind to chat with the agent on duty as Lorenzo and I hurried on through the double doors.

Deloris, her hair and makeup as perfect as ever, rose from a waiting room chair when she spotted us. A thirty-something version of Gordon was slumped in the chair beside hers. He looked as if he hadn't gotten a wink of sleep in days. Another man in his late twenties, who had Deloris's good looks, had been pacing. He turned to greet us.

"We brought chocolate croissants," I said, offering the bakery box. "I know they are Gordon's favorites. I hoped you'd enjoy them, too."

"Thank you. They are my favorite." Even though Deloris accepted the gift with a smile, she placed the box on a coffee table in the middle of the waiting area without even peeking inside.

Her son wasn't so shy. He tore into the box and took a huge bite of a croissant.

"They are good," he said with his mouth full.

"Swallow before you talk." Deloris nudged him with her elbow. "This is Kevin. And Junior is sitting over there." She then introduced Lorenzo and me to her children as Gordon's assistants. It was basically true—we were Gordon's assistants. Still, I bristled at the description. I considered Gordon as close to me as my grandmother or my aunts.

Kevin nodded since he'd stuffed the rest of the croissant into his mouth and was still chewing. He looked as if he didn't want to take another elbow to the ribs.

"It's been a tough night," Junior mumbled from where he was slumped in the chair.

"I can only imagine," Lorenzo said. "I'm so sorry about

what happened to your father. We're doing everything we can on our end to help him, but if you can think of anything you might need, we'll get it for you."

"You are helping Gordon?" Deloris asked as if no one had told her about the impending indictment. "Helping him how?"

When Lorenzo started to tell Deloris about Manny and his determination to bring murder charges, I stomped on his foot. "We're helping by keeping the gardens in good order, of course. We're working extra hard on all the projects." I paused. "Can—Can we see him?"

It felt as if my heart was in my throat. My voice sounded like it was, too.

"The doctors don't want too many people in the room at a time," Deloris said.

"Okay, we can go in one at a time." I moved toward Gordon's room.

Deloris stepped in front of me. Her smile looked brittle. "He's not awake. He won't even know you are there."

"I'll know," I said.

But Deloris refused to move. "The doctors say it's important that he rests so he can heal. Too many people have already been here today wanting to see him."

"Who else has been here?" Lorenzo asked before I could.

"Well, that detective. What's his name?"

"Manny Hernandez," I supplied.

"Yes, that's the man. He stopped by to talk to me for a while. And then there was that other man. He had dark skin. He looked Arabic. Kevin, do you remember his name?"

Kevin mumbled something unintelligible as he finished off the last of another croissant.

"Was it Nadeem?" I asked. A sick feeling twisted in my stomach as I waited for her answer. He seemed to be popping up everywhere. Everywhere he shouldn't be.

"I think it was."

"That was his name," Kevin answered as he grabbed another croissant. "Nice guy."

Junior, his eyes still closed, nodded in agreement. "Good guy."

"Did he visit with your husband?" I asked, feeling more than a little alarmed. He barely knew Gordon. And he might be a killer. Heck, according to Jack, Nadeem *was* a killer.

"Good gracious, no." Deloris held up her hands as if trying to hold me back. "No one but hospital staff and family have been in the room with Gordon. He needs his rest."

"So we can't see him?" Lorenzo asked.

"No, you can't," she answered.

"I don't know why not, Momma," Kevin said.

"When your father wakes up, it should be his family that he sees. Don't you agree?"

"Of—of course," I managed to say. If she didn't want the two people who spent the bulk of the day with Gordon to lend their support, who were we to stop her? She was part of his family. We weren't.

Lorenzo ground his jaw and flashed me a look that said this was my fault. "You know what's best, Deloris."

Why was Deloris sending us away? It suddenly felt like a repeat of history . . . ancient history. My fingers curled into a pair of tight fists.

Deep breath.

Don't panic.

Gordon wasn't my father walking out on me. And Deloris was only saying that Gordon needed his kids by him.

Not his co-workers.

We weren't as important.

No, that couldn't be what Deloris was saying to us. She was upset. We all were upset.

"If there's anything you need," Lorenzo said tightly, "we'd be more than happy to—"

"We have everything under control, don't we, boys?" She smiled at her sons. Junior still had his eyes closed. I hoped he was getting some needed sleep. Kevin, on the other hand, jammed his hands into his pockets and shrugged. "You know what's best," he said, clearly cowed by his strong-willed mother.

After wishing them well and asking Deloris to call if there was any change in Gordon's condition, Lorenzo and I headed out of the private wing.

Jack, who was still in deep conversation with his fellow Secret Service agent, gave a start when he saw us emerge through the double wooden doors.

"What happened? Is Gordon okay?" he asked.

"He's the same," Lorenzo grumbled.

"We didn't get to see him. S-She didn't want us to . . ." I started to explain. I desperately needed to feel Jack's arms around me. I also needed to tell Jack about Nadeem, but before I had a chance, his phone buzzed.

He glanced at his phone readout and cursed. "I'm sorry, Casey. I've got to go."

"Where?" His arms still hadn't reached out for me.

He brushed a quick kiss against my lips. Whatever had been on his phone's readout had clearly distracted him. "Lorenzo, would you mind driving Casey home?"

Lorenzo glanced at his watch and shrugged. "Why not? I have plenty of time before my date."

I grabbed Jack's hand. "Where do you have to go?"

"It's just something I need to take care of. Nothing for you to worry about." How could I not worry when *he* looked worried? "I'll see you tomorrow?"

Though my eyes burned, I nodded and released his hand. "Sure. Go. I'll be fine." *Eventually.*

It shouldn't have stung when Deloris had said I wasn't part of Gordon's family. But it had.

It stung as if Gordon had rejected me.

As if *my father* had rejected me all over again.

And now I watched with my hands curled in tight fists as Jack jogged down the hallway until he ducked around a corner and out of my view. I had no idea why he kept disappearing without an explanation.

I reminded myself he had his duties to the White House.

I shouldn't be jealous. I shouldn't ask too many questions since I already knew that much of what he did, saw, or heard was classified and couldn't be repeated. But that didn't make his leaving me when I needed him most sting any less.

So that was how I'd ended up slumped on the sofa next to Alyssa . . . feeling twice rejected.

Unconsciously, I reached into my pocket and touched the old newspaper article about my father and the crimes he'd committed. I don't know why I'd stuffed the article in my pocket or why I felt the need to keep the reminder of my father's abandonment and betrayal so close. Thinking about him only made the pain in my chest sharpen.

Not one to sit and stew about things I couldn't change, I jumped to my feet—upsetting Alyssa's paperwork. "Sorry." I helped her pick the papers I'd spilled up off the floor.

"What's wrong with you?" she asked.

"I can't just sit here. I need to . . . to . . . find out who the blazes is scratching at our front door."

I marched over to the front door and swung it open.

"You!" I shouted.

Nadeem gave a startled yelp and jumped to attention.

He'd been bending over, as if preparing to tape the piece of paper clutched in his hand to my front door.

"What are you doing?" I demanded.

The piece of paper he was trying to hide behind his back had one word written on it in bold block letters, DIE.

"It's not what you think." Nadeem backed down the brick steps.

"You're the one who's been sending me those threatening messages?" I followed him down the steps.

"No! I'm not."

"Then why is *that* in your hand?" I pointed at the paper he was trying to hide behind his back.

He glanced down the road and then back at me. "I don't have time to explain."

He took off running.

Chapter Twenty-one

*I once had a rose named after me and I was very flattered.
But I was not pleased to read the description in the
catalogue: no good in a bed, but fine up against a wall.*

—ELEANOR ROOSEVELT, FIRST LADY OF
THE UNITED STATES (1933–1945)

ALYSSA hugged my arm. I think it was to keep me from running the other way when she tossed open the door to the bar. A blast of loud music and stale air slapped my face.

"I don't know about this," I said, trying to pull away again.

After getting both Jack's and Manny's voice mail when I'd called to report Nadeem's threatening behavior, Alyssa suggested I call the White House to see if Jack had been called back on duty.

I did.

He hadn't.

I ended up speaking with Special Agent Steve Sallis, who'd told me that he thought Jack was at the Secret Service's favorite bar, The Underground.

When Alyssa had heard that, she'd insisted we change into party dresses and go looking for him. "If he's at a bar, he won't be able to hear his phone," she explained.

I wanted to believe her, but I knew Jack kept his phone on both ring and vibrate.

"He'll want to know Nadeem is behind the threats," she'd said as she tucked me into one of her bright pink dresses that was much too low in the chest. I tugged at the spaghetti straps to cover myself but ended up making the skirt obscenely short. So I ended up grabbing a white sweater as we hurried out the door and buttoned it up all the way.

"None of this makes any sense," I shouted over the loud music at the bar. "Why would Nadeem send me death threats even before he killed Frida?"

"What?" she shouted back.

"Never mind."

"Is that the First Lady's sister?" Alyssa shouted directly into my ear. "What's her name?"

"Lettie Shaw. Where?"

Alyssa pointed to a woman over near the band who looked like Lettie, only this woman was wearing heavy makeup. The skirt of her gold sequined dress was several inches shorter than mine. When she reached across a table for a shot glass, she flashed her bright red panties to the room. She looked—as Aunt Alba would say—like a twice-baked tart on a mission to be taste-tested.

I hoped I didn't look like her. Alyssa had insisted I apply more makeup than I was used to wearing, including a shimmery eye shadow she had called her special diamond dust, but was just sticky glitter. And she'd also insisted I wear my blond hair loose.

I pushed an unruly strand out of my eyes . . . again . . . as I watched Lettie—if that woman across the room was indeed Lettie. If it was, what was she doing out at The Underground dressed like *that?*

Holding my hair out of my face, I edged through the crowd toward her. Was she looking for more ways to frame Gordon for murder? Was she a killer in search of a lost treasure?

I didn't make it very far across the room when I was jostled by a rowdy group of agents and cops crowding into the bar. By the time I managed to squeeze past them, the woman was gone.

"She couldn't have been Lettie," I said.

"What?" Alyssa shouted.

"Nothing." I held on to Alyssa's shoulder and pulled her ear toward me. "This is a mistake," I shouted just as the music softened.

"You don't have to shout." She rubbed her ear. "Nadeem is acting weird. You need to report it."

"I could call the police department. Or better yet, I could leave another message with Manny. Let's go."

Alyssa caught hold of my arm again. "But what if Jack is here?"

What if he was? First, Deloris had coolly reminded me I wasn't part of Gordon's family, even though *I* loved Gordon like a father.

Was I about to find out that Jack was playing fast and loose with my feelings? Why else would he have left me at the hospital to rush to a bar? Was it because he'd made another date? Was I about to become his *ex*-girlfriend?

I wasn't ready to do this. I doubted I'd ever be ready. Although I'd never trusted a man enough to make an open declaration of my feelings, it didn't mean that I *didn't have* feelings. I'd fallen hard for Jack. Too hard.

And what a terrible time to realize it, but blooming hell, it was true.

I loved him. Had probably loved him since that embarrassing day I'd pepper sprayed him in the face.

Alyssa tightened her grip when I tried to bolt. "Even if he isn't here, we're going to have fun. You know, fun?"

My roommate was an even-if-it-kills-me kind of party girl. While she worked long hours for Senator Finnegan, she'd make up for it in a big way by going out and blowing off lots of steam once or twice a month.

"You need this more than I do," she shouted over a surge in the music as she resisted my tugging and guided me over to a pair of empty bar stools. "Look at you. The murder investigation and work have taken their toll."

I peered into the mirror hanging behind the bar and poked at the puffy skin under my eyes. "You're right. I do look terrible. I should be in bed. Let's go home."

She ignored me and ordered a Capitol staffer favorite—Red Bull and vodka. I ordered a low-calorie beer.

With drinks in hand, we both turned our bar stools so they faced the interior of the bar.

"Do you see him?" she asked.

"No." Although I spotted several groups of Secret Service agents, Jack wasn't party to any of them. My heart started pounding.

"Maybe he's not here yet."

"Maybe he's not coming."

"His loss. Those guys over there look cute." Alyssa pointed to a group of buff men with shaved heads and tattooed arms.

"They look like criminals, Alyssa."

"Yeah, they do." Alyssa's smile grew as she watched them. "Let's go see if they're guilty of anything wicked and in need of punishment."

"No! I'm not going over there!"

"What happened to your insatiable urge to play detective and unearth criminals?"

"I think I left it at home, where *I* should be."

Alyssa, sensing I was about to run off, hooked my arm with hers again. "Look," she shouted in my ear. "In that booth back there, isn't that Jack?"

In one of the booths lining the bar's dimly lit back wall, I spotted Jack. He wasn't alone. My heart dropped into the toes of my sensible shoes. The other occupant of the booth was a tall leggy blonde in a painted-on black dress. She looked like a fashion model.

Although they sat directly across from each other, they leaned in over the table so close that their foreheads were nearly touching. Smiling, the blonde reached her hand across the table and placed it on Jack's.

How could I compete with *her?* She had the kind of curvy body guys drooled over. Her breasts, two round perky globes, looked like they might pop out of her tight dress at any moment.

I gulped down half my beer.

"She could be his sister," Alyssa said.

"I don't think brothers and sisters kiss like that." Much to my horror, the blond cupcake had leaned even closer and had pressed her lips to Jack's.

Unable to watch any longer, I closed my eyes and turned my stool back toward the bar. I felt as if I was moving in slow motion as I set my beer down in front of me, pulled several dollars out of my wallet to leave as a tip, and jumped off the stool.

At least I hadn't made a fool of myself. I hadn't declared my love for him.

Jack—straight-as-an-arrow Jack—was apparently no different than any other guy I'd ever met. He didn't know how to be faithful.

Or perhaps this was my fault. I glanced at the haggard image of myself in the mirror behind the bar. What man would want me? Heck, my own father hadn't thought I was worth saving.

"I'm going home," I croaked.

"Forget Jack. He's a jerk." Alyssa swallowed the last of her drink and followed me toward the bar's exit. She was shaking her head. "None of this makes sense. Why would that other agent tell you to come here if this is where Jack meets his other women?"

"I don't know. I don't care."

The cool night air stung my eyes as I pushed through a crowd coming in the door. "Casey?" Special Agent Steve Sallis pulled away from the group and followed me. "It is you. Wow, you look great. Did you find Jack? Are . . . you . . . okay?"

"Peachy," I said without slowing down.

"We're changing locations," Alyssa said as she jogged to catch up to me. "This place fell far below our expectations."

"Casey?" Steve called after us. "What's happened? What's going on?"

I ignored him and marched toward home. Alyssa quickly caught up and started tugging on my arm again, promising to take me to a better place. "There's a club on

U Street where the spies like to hang out. Maybe we'll get lucky and bump into Nadeem. We can take turns interrogating him."

"He's probably a murderer."

He'd lied about how long he had spent in the garden the day Frida had been murdered. He was sending me threatening messages. But did that mean he'd killed Frida?

I'd wanted to talk to Jack about what I'd learned, but . . .

Oh, Jack. Why had I let myself feel safe with him? I was a fool. A stupid, stupid fool.

I twisted away from Alyssa. I wanted to go home.

"We don't know who Nadeem is, or what he's doing. But you should be careful around him," I warned her.

"Careful never had any fun. Come on, Casey. You can't let Jack do this to you. If you go home, you're going to spend the night crying in your bedroom, or eating ice cream."

That was exactly what I'd planned to do.

"I'll put my energy to better use than that," I lied. "I'll keep myself busy. I have those heirloom seeds to order." And I had tears to shed.

She'd opened her mouth to argue with me when her phone chirped. She pulled it out of her pocket. As she read the text message, a broad smile spread across her lips. "Barry is looking for me."

I liked how hearing from him had made her eyes sparkle. "Go on." I gave her a push. "Go have fun."

"I could ask him if he has a friend." Without waiting for an answer, she'd started typing on her phone.

"Don't. I wouldn't be good company."

She frowned as she gave me an assessing look. "Are you sure? I don't want to leave you."

I forced a smile. "I'm sure. The house is two blocks away, and it's early. I'll be fine."

After a few more minutes of indecision on Alyssa's part, she hugged me tightly before we parted company.

I wrapped my sweater tighter around me and braced myself against the harsh fall wind that howled down the cavern of buildings. The cold weather matched the icy feeling that was tightening like a vise around my heart.

Jack. I'd trusted him. I'd really trusted him. How many men had to hurt me before I learned my lesson?

I didn't need anything else. I didn't need Jack. It wasn't as if I'd moved to Washington in search of love. Gardening was my passion, my life.

A feeling of unease tiptoed down my back. Was I being watched? I looked around, but saw nothing out of the ordinary. Just a street crowded with couples enjoying the evening. Wait, was that Lettie?

I spotted just a glimmer of gold material. It could have been anyone.

Even so, I picked up my pace.

I turned the corner and entered a residential area where the streetlights were dimmer. The Victorian townhouses on the street, with their pulled drapes and locked doors, reminded me of secrets people kept. Everyone at the White House seemed to have secrets.

Lettie Shaw was desperately trying to keep something from her sister.

Nadeem Barr had lied about . . . everything.

Deloris was actively keeping everyone away from Gordon.

Marcel Beauchamp had delayed the design project for a reason, a reason he wouldn't admit to having.

Even Lorenzo was hiding the woman he had started dating.

Everyone had secrets.

Even Gordon.

And Jack . . .

Tonight Washington felt like a darker place. And this neighborhood, my neighborhood, seemed more dangerous than ever before. I shivered and focused on the light shining above the door at my brownstone apartment. It was just a few houses away.

Just a half block away and then I could lock myself inside the safety of my home.

And cry.

I was almost to the brownstone townhouse when a fig-ure moved in the shadows directly beside me. Before I could run, a hand shot out like a bullet and grabbed my shoulder.

Chapter Twenty-two

You've got to fight for what you believe in.
You have to finish what you start.
—JACQUELINE KENNEDY, FIRST LADY OF
THE UNITED STATES (1961–1963)

I screamed and spun toward my attacker. Using the force of my entire body, I slammed my elbow into the side of his head. It was an effective move I'd learned in a self-defense class Jack had encouraged me to take at the end of the summer.

It was a slam, slam, slam. Three quick blows.

Unlike the rubber dummy in the class, which just bounced back to take more, my attacker threw his hands up and fell backward, landing hard on the sidewalk.

"Casey . . . stop . . ." he wheezed.

I stumbled away from the man who'd grabbed me. I was already digging around in my purse for either my phone or my bottle of homemade pepper spray when I recognized him. "Jack?"

The lying, cheating creep! I pulled my arm back to hit him again.

He threw up his hands. "Casey! Casey! It's me!"

"I know." I started to swing.

"Please, let me explain."

I lowered my arm. "What do you want?"

"Damn, that's an effective move." He rubbed the side of his head. "Didn't you hear me calling your name?"

"No, I didn't. What do you want?"

"I should have remembered your ears turn off when you're upset. Steve told me that he saw you running out of The Underground." He paused to rub his head again. "What you saw—"

"You don't have to explain." I didn't want to hear his excuses. Or his lies.

Jack never lied, a voice in my head reminded me.

I huffed at that annoying voice.

Okay, so Jack didn't lie. That was even more reason I didn't want to hear what he had to say, especially if he was going to tell me how he'd met another woman. I certainly wasn't in the mood to hear him tell me *that*.

I offered my hand to help him to his feet.

"Where's your pepper spray?" he asked. "Not that I want to be dosed with that fire potion again." I made my own pepper spray from the habanera peppers I grew on my kitchen windowsill.

"It—It's in here somewhere." I dug around in my purse some more.

"That thing is large enough to hold a compact car."

I tested the weight of it in my hand. "It would have made a good weapon. I'll have to remember that next time."

He rubbed the side of his head and grimaced. "Hopefully I won't be on the receiving end. If you're walking the streets alone, it's a good idea to keep your pepper spray and cell phone in an outside pocket of your purse or, better yet, in your pocket."

He sounded as if he really did care.

"You don't have pockets in that dress, do you?" And a smile creased the corners of his lips as he looked at me in a way that made me feel all warm and tingly and . . . Ohhh, he shouldn't do that! I was still furious with him!

"You look good." His voice deepened. "*Really* good."

"What are you doing here?" I asked with an impatient tone. "You obviously had more important things to do than to worry about me. I've been trying to get in touch with you, but you ignored my calls."

He reached into his pocket and pulled out his phone. It had been so thoroughly smashed the screen had been reduced to a spiderweb of glass. Wires were sticking out of its side. "I've not been able to take calls."

"I saw you," I said. "I know you were at that bar with someone else."

"I know. Steve told me he saw you running out. And that you were upset. Did you really think I wouldn't come after you?"

Not able to bring myself to look at him, I studied the neighbor's flowering clematis vine. Small white flowers covered the iron fence lining the sidewalk. I spotted the beginnings of a powdery mildew infection on the deep green leaves closest to me. Cutting off the infected parts and spraying a solution of baking soda and water would probably do the trick of keeping the powdery mildew from spreading, especially so late in the season.

What was I doing? Was it really that much easier, and safer, to focus on my neighbor's gardening problems than to focus on the very real problem in my personal life?

Hadn't I always done that?

Was gardening a means to keep everyone in my life at arm's length? It was my grandmother who had encouraged me to join her and my aunts working in the garden. They had been worried about me after my father's abandonment and my mother's death.

After a chaotic childhood of being hustled from one place to the next, often in the middle of the night, I'd found solace in the regularity of the seasons and in the steady rhythm of my grandmother's and aunts' hands as their nimble fingers weeded and snipped. Working out in the garden had become both a safe haven and a lifeline to the only family left to me.

It still felt like a lifeline to my sanity. But what if I no longer used gardening as a bridge to humanity but as a wall?

If my interest in the clematis climbing my neighbor's fence was any indication, the answer to that question would be an unequivocal yes.

Even so, I kept staring at the clematis's white flowers because if I looked at Jack, if I gazed into his honest green eyes or saw how perfectly his arms would wrap around me and comfort me, I might convince myself to believe how he planned to explain away why I'd seen him kissing another woman. Lord love me, I wanted to believe he wanted me and no other. I wanted to believe I'd hallucinated the entire kissing episode at the bar.

"If you were at the bar, why didn't you come over and ask me to explain myself? Why did you run away?" he asked.

He expected me to say it, that I saw him kissing that extremely beautiful woman? Well, I couldn't. I just couldn't.

"Casey, please. Can we go to your place? I want to talk about this. Will you let me in?" he asked.

I hugged myself as if my sweater couldn't keep away the cold and shook my head. I feared if I spoke aloud, my voice would betray the storm of emotions whirling inside my chest.

"I know what you think you saw back at the bar," he said. "But it's not what you think."

What else could it have been? I pinched my lips even more tightly together.

"Simone is my ex-girlfriend."

He stepped closer.

Unable to trust myself, I stepped back.

He followed.

"Casey, she's not been part of my life for over a year now. I don't know why, but she refuses to accept that. I only agreed to meet with her because she found out about you and threatened to contact you. She . . . she's kind of unhinged. I don't trust her."

His nearness made me ache to reach out to him. I tightened my grip on my sweater's sleeves.

He touched my shoulder. "I told her that she needed to move on with her life."

"You kissed her." My voice cracked.

"She kissed *me*." His hand moved up to my neck. "I didn't want her to. If you had stayed a little longer, you would have seen me tell her in no uncertain terms that she was no longer welcome in my life. She knows about you. And she's"—he hesitated—"angry I've moved on. She smashed my phone."

"I can understand why you'd want to be with her. She's beautiful."

"Casey, *listen* to me." He caressed my cheek. His lips moved closer to mine. "You're the only woman I want in my life."

"But she's so—"

His lips covered mine in a long, sensual kiss that made me tingle all the way down to the tips of my toes and had the power to make me forget my name, the street I lived on, everything. "She's not you," he said. "You are the most beautiful woman I know. Inside and out. You are gorgeous. And kind. And smart." A smile teased the corners of his lips. "And you're dangerous to be around. You keep me guessing. You make me feel alive. If you haven't figured it out already, I love that about you."

I could have drowned in his kind green eyes. I drew a long breath. This was the Jack I knew . . . and trusted. He never lied. He would never try and hurt me.

If I kept holding back on him, I would lose him.

I wanted Jack in my life. I drew in another deep breath.

It should be like peeling off a bandage. I'd feel better once I got the words out. I just needed to do it. I needed to tell him how I felt.

"There is something that I want to tell you. I . . ." *Like removing a bandage*, I told myself and took a deep breath.

"Is that why you came to the bar looking for me?"

"W-Well, no. I came to the bar tonight because of Nadeem."

"*Nadeem?* What does he have to do with this?"

"You remember those threatening text messages I've been getting?"

"How could I forget?"

"It's Nadeem. He's been sending them. I caught him as he tried to stick a threatening note to my front door."

"I knew he couldn't be trusted. What did he say to explain what he was doing?"

"He didn't. He ran away." Jack seemed surprised by that. He started to question me about what exactly Nadeem had said, but I still wanted to peel that bandage off our relationship.

"Jack, wait. There's something else I need to tell you."

His brows rose. "Something else?"

"Yes." I screwed up all my courage. "I hope you are telling me the truth about your ex and about your feelings for me because I . . . um . . . I'm starting to—"

"*What the hell is Nadeem up to now?*" Jack grabbed my shoulder much like he had right before I'd sucker punched him, and he pulled me deeper into the shadows cast by a large oak street tree.

We both watched as Nadeem emerged from his basement apartment. Dressed from head to toe in black, he looked like a cat burglar on the prowl.

"Is that a gun?" I whispered. There was something cylindrical in Nadeem's hand. But it was too dark to tell exactly what it was.

Jack didn't answer. His body had gone rigid as he watched Nadeem make his way toward a sleek black Jaguar parked at the curb.

Nadeem looked left and then right, as if making sure no one was watching him. He unlocked the car, opened the driver's side door, and climbed in.

"We should follow him," I said, expecting Jack to argue it was too dangerous or that we should let the police handle the investigation.

He didn't. "My Jeep is parked around the corner. We need to hurry or we'll lose him."

My fingers linked with his. Jack flashed a heated smile in my direction as we took off running down the street. I couldn't help smiling back. My heart pounded in my chest from the excitement of the chase.

We were going to catch Nadeem in his nefarious web and clear Gordon's name. I could feel the certainty of it coursing through my veins.

Together, Jack and I could do anything. But I still needed to tell him how I felt . . .

JACK'S JAW TIGHTENED AS HE GUIDED THE JEEP around a corner and entered a quaint suburb about a half hour outside the downtown area. The heavy traffic coupled with Nadeem's flashy new Jaguar had made it easy to catch up to and follow him.

As soon as we'd entered an area with less traffic, Jack cut the lights and kept a fair distance between him and Nadeem's Jag.

The grid of streets led us past aging one-story bungalows, many with trucks parked on the lawn or a sedan rusting as it sat up on blocks in a short driveway.

A timeworn canopy of oaks created long shadows that seemed to swallow Nadeem's sleek black Jaguar as he pulled farther away from us.

With each street we'd turned down, Jack's expression darkened until he looked positively furious.

I sat in the passenger seat of Jack's old Jeep, feeling pretty grim myself. Jack took a corner too sharply, making the springs in the old seats squeal. We should have been home, exploring our relationship, working out this mess with his ex. Instead we were in the middle of the suburbs following a man who may or may not have killed Frida and who'd definitely been sending me threatening notes.

"He's probably driving out into the burbs to visit friends," I said.

"Unlikely. He's dangerous. And he's up to something."

"But is that *something* murder? Why would he send me threatening texts even before he killed Frida? Perhaps there's another reason he's trying to scare me?"

"As you'd pointed out, he was in the garden when Frida was murdered," Jack reminded me.

"Yes. So was Lettie. And she's researching the treasure, too."

"And he has the covert training."

"Well . . ." There was no arguing that. Lettie didn't have the same killer skills Nadeem was purported to possess. "And you think he killed Frida in order to be the first one to find Thomas Jefferson's missing treasure and steal it?"

"You're the one that came up with that idea. I don't know what he's up to, but whatever it is"—Jack pointed to a yellow bungalow on the corner as a shadow moved across the neatly mowed lawn—"I'm going to find out."

Nadeem's Jaguar was parked several houses away. Jack pulled to a stop behind it.

We surveyed the yellow house. I held my breath, half expecting Nadeem to jump out of the shadows and demand to know what we were doing. I knew then I wouldn't make a good private detective. I felt too antsy, too self-conscious. Every sound made me jerk with a guilty start.

There were no lights in the windows or illuminating a front porch that spanned nearly the entire front of the house. It was a small home, but cute with iconic Arts and Crafts–style trim. "No one's here," I said.

"Looks that way," Jack agreed, his jaw tightening even more. "The porch light should be on, though. I wonder if Nadeem cut the power."

"What do you mean?" I asked.

Jack held up his hand. "He's gone around to the back of the house."

I continued to hold my breath as we watched the shadows around the house. I don't know what I was expecting to see.

Jack sighed loudly.

"Do you think he's inside? I wonder what he's doing," I whispered.

"I'd like to know that, too."

"Should we call the police?"

"No," he said as he unbuckled his seat belt and clicked a button on the dome light so it wouldn't turn on when he opened the driver's side door.

"What are you doing?" I followed as Jack silently slid out of the Jeep.

"Stay here." He retrieved a handgun from a holster concealed in the waistband of his jeans as he made his way toward the house. "I'm going inside."

Inside?

"What do you mean you're going inside?" I hissed. "You mean inside the house?"

Straight-as-an-arrow Jack, who always wanted to let the police take control when things got hairy, was going to break into a stranger's house? Wasn't that a felony? If he got caught, it would spell the end of his career.

"Stay here," he whispered.

I stayed beside the Jeep for about a millisecond before following.

"What happened to staying at the car?" Jack asked when I caught up to him. We stood side by side at the front door. The white paint was just starting to peel on the door trim.

"Stop. I'm not going to let you break the law." I grabbed his arm. "This is serious. We can't break into someone's house."

"I'm not breaking in." He slipped a key in the door and turned.

"You have a key? Why do you have a key?"

He swallowed deeply. "This is my house."

Chapter Twenty-three

A politician ought to be born a foundling
and remain a bachelor.
—CLAUDIA "LADY BIRD" JOHNSON, FIRST LADY OF
THE UNITED STATES (1963–1969)

"**Y**OUR house?" My voice squeaked just a bit as I said it.
Jack turned to me and raised a brow as if expecting
me to make fun of where he lived.

But what could I say? It was a cute house with a tidy lawn
and not at all what I'd expected. It was so . . . domestic.

Besides, I was reeling from the shock that it took tailing
a suspicious White House assistant curator to get Jack to
invite me to his house in the first place. "Really? This is
your house?"

"Shhh . . . Not so loud." As Jack eased the door open, he
held his hand out in warning. "Stay here."

With his gun leading the way, he entered the house while
my feet stayed glued on the front stoop, my mouth gaping
open. My eyes grew wide as I took in the pile of mail, magazines, and bric-a-brac littering an ornate oak entryway
table just inside the small foyer. So this was Jack's house?
I'd imagined he'd be neater.

Jack moved with care as he skulked down a hallway and
disappeared around a corner. I held my breath, listening for

movements. I stayed there for a few seconds more before hurrying across the threshold.

He expected me to stay outside when all the good stuff was happening inside? Like that was going to happen.

A cloying musky stench hung thick in the entranceway's stale air. Holding my nose, I continued down the same short hallway Jack had taken and found myself in a small living room at the back of the house. That's where I found the source of the odor. A heaping pile of dirty laundry started on the hardwood floor in the living room and spread onto an end table and over the back of a brown leather sofa.

So Jack was a class-A slob. I could live with that . . . probably.

Before realizing what I was doing, I'd already gathered up a few dirty shirts and a scattering of magazines from the floor. A loud crash from the front of the house jolted me back to the dangerous situation at hand.

A man shouted. Glass shattered.

I dropped the dirty clothes as I charged toward the noise.

There was another shout.

And a vile curse.

I grabbed a large ceramic lamp, ripping it from its outlet. Nadeem was a highly trained killer. Not that Jack was lacking in those skills; those deadly skills were something about him that filled me with both fear and excitement. But I wasn't willing to take the chance Jack might get hurt.

I ran down the hallway, leapt over a half-empty laundry basket, and burst through a door that led into a small office.

By the light of the streetlamp shining into the room's lone window, I could make out the shadowy figures of two men as they fought. Fists flying. Heads ducking. They seemed evenly matched.

But that still didn't explain why Nadeem would want to break into Jack's house.

"Nadeem!" I held the lamp like it was a baseball bat that I was prepared to swing.

Both men looked up at me in surprise.

"What do you think you're doing?" I demanded.

Before I could get an answer, Jack's fist connected with Nadeem's jaw. The assistant curator dropped to the ground like a sack of topsoil.

"What did you do that for? I was trying to question him." I dropped the lamp on the floor and knelt down next to Nadeem.

Jack joined me. "He hit me first."

While I grabbed a pillow from a nearby chair to tuck under Nadeem's head, Jack unzipped Nadeem's black jacket and dug around in any pocket he could find.

"Plus he broke into my house."

"You have a point there."

Nadeem groaned.

"He's unarmed," Jack reported.

"Then what did I see in his hand back at the house? It looked like a gun."

"I don't know. Maybe this?" Jack handed me a heavy flashlight that was lying on the floor.

"That might be what I saw," I said, turning the flashlight over in my hand.

Jack sat back on his heels and rubbed the side of his head where I'd hit him earlier that evening.

"Are you okay?" I asked him, feeling kind of guilty for that.

"Hey! Who's in here?" a man's voice seemed to echo through the house. "Why is the door wide open? And the electricity, is it switched off? Jack? Dan?"

Jack muttered, "*I didn't want it to happen like this,*" under his breath as he helped me to my feet. He then called out, "Back here!"

A uniformed police officer came barreling into the room. He shined his flashlight in my face. I held up my hand to block its bright glare. "Oh! Sorry, Jack. I didn't know you had company." He rubbed the back of his neck. "You never have company." He had the same dark hair and general sculpted features as Jack's. "I'll . . . I'll just make a quick sandwich and get out of here."

Nadeem groaned and rolled around on the floor as he

started to regain consciousness. Jack pressed his foot on his chest and growled, "Don't move."

The flashlight's beam jerked to illuminate Nadeem's face as it twisted in pain. "Wait a minute. What's going on here?" The officer flicked his bright light over the room. Like the rest of the house, the office was a mess, with papers scattered all over an antique oak desk and on the hardwood floor. The top drawer of a file cabinet was open. A crystal trophy lay smashed next to the large oak desk. "What happened in here? It's a mess."

How can you tell? This room looks just like the rest of the house. I had to bite my tongue not to say it. But really, have some pride in where you live.

Jack toed Nadeem, who was now fully conscious but had (wisely) decided to stay put on his back. "This jerk broke in and tossed the place."

The officer pulled out his handcuffs. "Do you want me to arrest him?"

"Not yet." There was a wild gleam in Jack's eyes that made my heart pound, and not in a good way. He rested his booted foot squarely on Nadeem's chest again and pressed. "Why don't you take a walk around the block?" He paused a beat. "Take Casey with you."

Nadeem let out a cry of distress.

"I'm not going anywhere." With a wide stance, I planted myself like an invasive weed. I wasn't going to budge from the spot where I stood on the room's hardwood floor. I was determined to discover what Nadeem was doing firsthand.

"Oh, ho! So you're Casey?" The officer shined his flashlight in my face again. His grin widened as he looked me over from head to toe. He nodded his approval. "Nice."

"Shut up," Jack grumbled.

"And you are?" I asked at the same time.

"I'm Frank, of course. Jack's brother."

"His brother? Your brother is a cop?" I looked at Jack as I asked it.

"What? Jack hasn't mentioned me? Jack, I'm hurt." Not so hurt that he didn't chuckle and wink at me. "If you'll excuse me, I'm coming off a long shift and seriously need to get something to eat."

"While you're at it, could you get the lights back on?" Jack called as Frank left, leaving us in darkness again.

"Your brother works with the police?" I rounded on Jack to demand. "Why haven't you been using your contacts with him to get us information about the murder investigation?"

"Different jurisdiction. Frank is over in Arlington."

The lights flipped on. And we all seemed to breathe a sigh of relief, including Nadeem.

"Hello? I'm still down here." He waved his hand at me while completely avoiding Jack's glare.

"And you!" I said to Nadeem. "What were you thinking? Why in blazes would you break into Jack's house?"

"I didn't think he'd come home so early."

"We followed you here," Jack said.

"Ah." Nadeem shook his head slowly from side to side. "I'm getting too old for this. And rusty, apparently."

"You haven't answered my question. What are you doing here?" I asked.

"Isn't it obvious?"

"No, it's not!"

"I suppose it wouldn't be to you." With the back of his hand, he thumped the boot still holding him down. "Lover boy has you so wrapped around his little finger that you can't see the danger that's right there in front of your nose."

Jack huffed and lifted his boot. He then reluctantly helped Nadeem to his feet. "What danger?"

"You." Nadeem poked Jack in the chest. Nadeem's halting, nervous speech pattern was gone, replaced by an authoritative tone that demanded attention. "The danger you pose to Casey."

"Me?" Jack looked taken aback. "You're the one who's lying and skulking around."

"I didn't want to believe it, but really, Nadeem. Things don't look good for you. You're the one who had the best opportunity to kill Frida."

"You think I killed Frida? Casey? I'd never hurt anyone!"

"Really?" I said. "I heard you were a trained assassin."

"I'm retired."

"You don't deny it?" My hands started to shake. I clasped them behind my back to hide my sudden nervousness. "And you didn't step out of retirement even for a moment after Frida found out you were going behind her back to find Jefferson's lost treasure?"

"What? No! I'm not—"

"Then what were you doing here, in my house?" Jack demanded.

"I was searching for proof, a piece of evidence I could use to prove to Casey that you're trying to hurt her. Casey, hear me out," he quickly added when he saw I was going to step in to defend Jack. "Jack has been lying to you."

I crossed my arms over my chest. "Jack never lies."

Nadeem refused to back down. "Ask him. Why didn't he tell you that he was also in the gardens when Frida was killed? If he's so innocent, why didn't he tell you that?"

My confidence wavered. Jack might not lie to me, but he had a long-standing habit of not telling me everything he knew. His running off to meet with a crazy ex-girlfriend at the drop of a hat being a prime example.

"If that's the truth, why are you sending me threatening text messages? Why were you trying to post a threatening message on my front door tonight?"

"I'm not sending them." He said the words so smoothly, so calmly.

"I caught you in the act of posting that note on my door less than three hours ago."

"About that"—he had the good grace to look uncomfortable—"I wasn't posting the threat. I was removing it."

"If you were taking it off my door, why run?" No wonder Nadeem had retired from the spy business. He was a terrible liar.

"I wasn't running from you. I was following the woman who put it there. I followed her to a bar called The Underground. That's where she met up with *her* lover, who also happens to be *your* Jack."

After Nadeem had made that accusation, I'd expected I was going to have to fling myself between the two like a medieval maiden desperate to keep her rivals from killing each other. A small jolt of disappointment zinged through my chest when it didn't happen.

"*Simone.*" Jack said her name with a curl of disgust. "I should have suspected she was behind those hateful messages. As I already told Casey this evening, she's my ex-girlfriend who can't seem to accept that our relationship ended a year ago."

"I hope you're not going to believe him! He was meeting this woman in a bar, probably to plan new ways to manipulate you."

"And they kissed," I added. "I know. I was there."

"*She* kissed *me*," Jack insisted, with a rare note of panic in his voice. I didn't do anything to reassure him, not while the devil kept whispering in my ear, *Let him stew.*

"Think about it," Nadeem continued while Jack flexed his jaw muscles. "Jack has always been at the center of any trouble you've gotten into."

"Well, that's not exactly true," I said. "He's helped pull me out of trouble."

Nadeem shook his head in protest. "Answer me this, then. Before you met Jack, how much trouble did you get yourself into?"

That was easy. After my mom's death, I'd grown up and spent my adult life in the garden. It wasn't until I'd moved to D.C that I turned into a living magnet for murder.

But there had been a time long ago when danger and death were a part of my life. I closed my eyes. A flash of a gun burst through my memory. "I watched my father kill another man." My voice cracked. "A year later, my mother was murdered. I watched her die."

Jack put his arm around me. "Leave her alone."

"I'm sorry. I didn't mean to dredge up painful memories, Casey. I just wanted to point out that it wasn't until you met this guy that bad things started to happen . . . again. Why? Why is he dragging you into danger? I thought if I dug through his files, I might find something to explain what he's up to, something I could bring to you to prove that Jack's not good for you."

"And did you find anything?" I asked, knowing he hadn't. Jack had nothing to hide.

"I didn't find anything only because I didn't have time to look."

"Who asked you to come search my house? Don't tell me you were just being a protective neighbor, because we both know that's BS," Jack demanded. "Who made you Casey's protector?"

"No one." Nadeem raised his hands as if swearing he was telling the truth.

Jack raised a brow. "No one? You just happened to move into Casey's downstairs apartment. You just happened to get a job at the White House in the department right across from hers. And you just happened to start following her around and acting like her self-appointed protector."

"When he puts it that way, it does sound unbelievable," I agreed. The more I thought about how Nadeem had made himself part of my life, the angrier I got. "What's going on here? Who are you, Nadeem Barr? Why are you butting into things that have nothing to do with you?"

"I did it because he knew I'd gotten the White House position. He asked me to keep an eye on you and keep you safe!" he sputtered with frustration. "I would do anything for that man. He's saved my life more times than I could count. I'd walk through fire for him."

"Who?" Jack demanded before I could.

Nadeem thrust his finger toward me. "Her father."

Chapter Twenty-four

Turn a corner and meet your fate.
—EDITH WILSON, FIRST LADY OF
THE UNITED STATES (1915–1921)

"I wasn't supposed to say that," Nadeem said. He plopped down in the desk chair and propped his head up with his hands.

Had I heard Nadeem correctly? Did he really say *my father* had sent him? A man who had abandoned me? A man I never thought (or hoped) I'd ever see again?

"When did you last see him?" I had to know.

Nadeem shrugged. "This afternoon."

"*In D.C.?*" Everything that followed was a jumbled blur. "Call the police," I remember saying as Jack suggested we move this conversation to the stinky living room. "We need to call the police and report what's happened here."

"I'm more interested in getting to the bottom of things than in pressing charges." Jack turned to Nadeem. "Does her father think Casey is in danger?"

"We both do. For the past several days Casey's been getting those threatening notes tacked to her front and back doors."

"I have?" I shook my head, hoping to chase away the dizziness and growing panic pressing harder and harder on my chest. "If my dad is in town, I'd put my money on him putting the notes on my doors."

"It was Jack's girlfriend," Nadeem insisted.

"Why should I believe you?"

"I saw her do it."

"And I know my dad," I countered. "I know too much about his past. He should be in jail. Is he still in D.C.?"

Nadeem looked at me for several moments before answering. "Yes, he's in the area."

"What else?" Jack demanded as we walked down the hallway to the living room. "It can't just be the notes."

"I haven't seen any threatening notes," I said at the same time. "Just the text messages."

"I've been removing them before you see them, that's why," Nadeem said. "Your father noticed the first one and took it down."

I grabbed my throat. "He—he's been to my house?"

"That morning when you thought you saw me on your back stoop, you said the man you confronted ran into my apartment," Nadeem said. "The man you saw dressed in the trench coat was your father. He was taking down the threatening note."

"Why?" My throat felt like it was closing up. "Why was he at my house? What does he want from me?"

"Your father wants to protect you, Casey. After he found that first one, he started to worry. He asked me to keep an eye out and track down the perpetrator posting those notes." He turned to Jack and sneered. "And imagine my surprise when all this trouble gets tracked back to your not-so-*trust-worthy* lover and his leggy girlfriend."

"Tell me he's not talking about Simone," Frank said from the kitchen.

"The model? I thought you put an end to that relationship ages ago." A man dressed in a blue EMT uniform emerged from the kitchen and pushed a glass of water into my hand. "Hi, I'm Dan. We met several months ago, but I doubt you remember. I suppose you've already met that big lug hiding in the kitchen, Frank. Jack and Frank are my brothers. We all live here."

"Thank you," I said before I sipped the water.

"Sorry about the mess." He scooped up armfuls of living room detritus and carried it off to another room.

"You can't deny it," Nadeem said to Jack. "Because of you, Casey's life is in danger."

Jack, I noticed, was pacing. He looked . . . worried. "Does Mr. Calhoun agree with your assessment? Does he blame me for Simone's threats?"

"No, he's got this crazy idea that you're good for Casey. But how can that be when all you do is lead her into trouble?"

My father knew about Jack? He knew about Jack's crazy ex-girlfriend before I did? The room started to get fuzzy.

"Has someone called the police yet?" I asked. The buzzing in my ears grew louder.

"About Simone?" Nadeem asked.

"No. About my—my—"

"Casey?" a distant voice called to me. "*Casey*."

I opened my eyes to find Jack kneeling next to me on the floor. He was cradling my head in his lap. He brushed his hand through my hair.

"What . . ." I had started to ask what had happened, because I knew I couldn't have swooned like a weak-kneed romance novel heroine—someone must have hit me over the head—but what came out was, "What's that awful smell?"

Jack picked up a dirty sock that was lying near us and tossed it across the room. "This is why I never invited you over here." He cast a disgusted look at his brothers, who were watching from the kitchen. "They're pigs."

Dan oinked.

"Now that you know your father is in D.C."—Nadeem crouched down next to me and put his face into my line of vision—"he'll want to meet you. I can arrange it."

"No!" I stumbled to my feet and away from Nadeem.

"No! Keep him away from me! I want nothing to do with that lying, murdering bastard. We need to call the police. We need to tell them where they can find him. He needs to answer for getting my mother killed and for murdering all those innocent people."

"What are you talking about? He's never murdered anyone," Nadeem said.

Jack wrapped his strong hands around mine and held on tight when I tried to pull away. "I know you resisted talking about him before, Casey. I know this is hard for you, but it's time you know the truth about him. Your father, he's a hero."

A HERO.

My father?

"You have to be kidding," I said.

It had been nearly an hour since Jack had made that announcement, and I still didn't believe it. I doubted I ever would. Sure Jack never lied, but that didn't mean he was never wrong.

"I worked with him for years," Nadeem said. "He's a legend at the agency."

"The CIA?" I started to feel dizzy again.

"Sort of," Nadeem hedged. "The agency we worked for was a little less . . . restricted . . . in our activities. Because of your father's work and sacrifice—and your mother's when she was alive—wars were averted, the Berlin Wall came down, countless lives were saved."

"But at what cost?" I demanded, but held up my hand. I didn't want to hear the answer to that. I didn't want someone to tell me that my mother's life or my childhood wasn't as important as those nameless, faceless lives that hadn't been scarred by murder.

And besides, I had evidence that my father was a cold, heartless killer. While I dug around in my large purse for the damning newspaper article I carried everywhere with me lately, Frank brought out a tray filled with bottles of cold beer. He offered me a glass for my beer. After another glance around the filthy house, I politely declined the glass.

Dan, who I'd learned was the youngest in the family, blushed furiously as he picked up the dirty laundry, dumping armload after armload into another room. Jack intervened when Dan powered up a vacuum cleaner that roared like a jet engine.

I wished Jack hadn't stopped his brother. The tan carpet was coated with potato chip crumbs, cereal, and I was afraid to wonder what else.

Since Dan had cleared off the sofa, I sat down with my bottle of beer and continued my search for the newspaper clipping. Nadeem left the room without a word to anyone. Jack followed.

"Sorry about the mess." Dan rubbed the back of his neck much the same way his brother did when he was feeling regretful. "We don't get many visitors."

"I can see why," I said. "You could hire a maid."

"We tried that," Frank chimed in from the kitchen over the clanking of dishes and running water. "She quit after the first week."

"Can you blame her?" I said.

"Don't blame Jack for this mess," Dan said as he wiped off the sofa's seat cushion and sat down next to me. "You should see his bedroom."

"Excuse me?"

His blush returned. "I didn't mean it that way. I meant he keeps his room freakishly clean. His office, too. But don't go in there. Frank said it's a disaster area now."

"I saw it. It looks about as bad as the rest of the house," I said as I picked up a handheld cheese grater that was digging into my hip—how did that get tucked into the sofa cushion?—and moved it to the coffee table.

Dan nodded toward the hallway, where both Jack and Nadeem had gone. "Who is that other guy? If he broke into our house, why hasn't Jack kicked his—"

"Dan! Watch your language." Frank sauntered into the

room and whip-snapped his brother in the back of the head with a soapy dish towel.

"Hey!" Dan cried, rubbing his head.

"Casey is Jack's . . . er . . . guest." He flashed me a toothy smile that wasn't nearly as disarming as Jack's. "I have to apologize for this one. It's my fault he has the manners of an ape. And Jack's. We wore Mom down. By the time Dan came along, she'd given up."

"I see," I said, smiling. Despite the stress and the disgusting mess, Jack's brothers had an easygoing manner that made me feel welcome.

Frank plopped down next to me on the sofa, sandwiching me between him and Dan. He draped his arm over my shoulder and asked, "But really, Casey, tell us. Who is that guy? And why didn't Jack kick his . . . you know?"

I explained, very briefly, how Nadeem was the assistant curator at the White House and how he might have been involved with the murder investigation. Then I asked, "If Jack is so neat, why does he put up with this mess? He could pick up after you."

"He's never here," Frank answered.

"I'm looking for a place," Jack said as he came back into the living room. Nadeem was with him.

While Nadeem stayed at the entrance, Jack crossed the room to the sofa. He glared at his brothers crowding around me and gave Frank's foot a swift kick. Dan jumped up from the sofa as if he'd taken the blow. Frank remained pressed up against me. His smile grew a little wider, but after a moment he lifted his arm from my shoulder, which seemed to placate Jack.

"After our mother retired and moved to Boca," Jack explained, "we bought the house from her. At the time, it seemed like the perfect solution. The bottom had just dropped out of the housing market, so buying the house was helping Mom. And between travel and long shifts, it seemed wasteful to pay rent on an apartment I rarely visited."

"If you're still working long hours and traveling, why are you looking for a place?" I asked.

Jack's expression softened.

"Perhaps he's looking for a place for two." Frank nudged me in the arm.

"*Oh . . .*" Jack had been making hints lately that he wanted to move our relationship to the next level, but I'd never let him finish that thought because I didn't know if I was ready. "Are you sure he wants to move in with me, or just escape the garbage heap you call home?" I whispered to Frank.

"He was fine with his living arrangements here when he was dating crazy Simone," Frank answered.

Jack kicked his brother's foot again. "If you're done discussing things that are none of your business, could you two meddlers get out of here? Casey and I need to talk to Nadeem, in private."

After much grumbling and feet dragging, Dan and Frank headed out to a local bar.

Nadeem claimed the spot on the sofa where Frank had been sitting, which earned him the same hard glare Jack had given his brothers.

"Now that they're gone, we can finally talk about important matters," Nadeem said, seemingly oblivious to Jack's death glare. "What we need to discuss is classified."

"I don't know that it's classified," I countered. "It's important that we get to the bottom of what's going on and what you're up to. And I agree that including new players right now would just slow us down. But I don't think any of this would be considered classified."

"No, it *is* classified," Nadeem countered with absolute assurance.

"Really? Gordon's murder investigation? You should tell the newspapers that. They seem to be printing every minute detail. Or are you talking about Lev Aziz? Is he involved with the murder investigation?"

"The murder investigation? No, I meant your father's history."

"This history?" I handed him the newspaper clipping I'd finally located at the bottom of my purse.

Nadeem barely glanced at it before tossing it aside. "That? That was just a story the agency planted to help insert your dad into a deep-cover assignment."

"If that's true, why would they use his real name in the article? That doesn't sound very covert to me," I said.

Nadeem hesitated before saying, "His cover had already been blown. It's . . . it's a long story, and it's my understanding that things were chaotic at the time. Your mother had died just a few days before they inserted him into the assignment."

"Wait a minute. You're trying to tell me that my father was taking assignments *days* after my mother's murder? What kind of cold-hearted man does that?"

"The kind of man who is hungry for justice," Nadeem said.

"Justice?" The word tasted sour in my mouth.

"I don't understand how you can't know," Nadeem said. "James Calhoun is the bravest, smartest man I've ever met. He is most definitely a hero."

"I don't know why I'm listening to you, the one who has lied about his past."

"I didn't lie," Nadeem said.

"You said you were a fact-checker," I countered.

"I was . . . of sorts."

"And you've been stalking me."

He shrugged as if caught. "I have . . . but for good reason."

"What reason is that?" I looked to Jack to see if he'd help me. He had stepped back and was watching the exchange with a half smile as if he was enjoying watching me interrogate Nadeem.

"I did it to make sure the killer doesn't try to come after you."

"Bull. You were skulking around the hospital before I'd even arrived, before anyone really knew what had happened."

Nadeem was silent for a moment.

"Well?" Jack finally spoke up. "Do you have an answer for her?"

Nadeem turned toward Jack. "Not one she's going to like."

"Spit it out," I said.

"Your father knows how important Gordon is to you. He asked me to go to the hospital. He wanted me to check on security to make sure everything was being done to keep the head gardener safe."

"My father knows how I feel about Gordon? How does he know that? Has he been *watching* me?" I rubbed my arms and shivered. "What does he want from me?"

"That's a question you should be asking James. I've only been helping, not directing. He cares very deeply for you."

I snorted. "You can't be talking about the same man who ran away in the middle of the night like a coward. Because of him, my mom was murdered while I watched. Those same men shot me in the gut and left me to die. I was only six years old! Where was your hero then? Where was he when I was put into a broken foster system because no one knew my real name . . . *I* didn't even know it. We'd moved so many times, changed names so many times, and I'd been told to trust no one. I had shut down. I didn't speak for nearly a year. You're telling me that I should consider a man who could turn his back on his own family a loving dad and a hero? Are you *insane?*"

Nadeem looked to Jack for help again.

"She has a point," Jack said. "He owes her an explanation."

"He owes me nothing. I don't want to see him. Ever. Let's talk about something else, something important like saving Gordon's neck."

Nadeem opened his mouth to say something but, wisely, closed it again.

"Gordon," I said through clenched teeth. "We need to focus on Gordon and whether or not you played a role in Frida's murder."

"I agree. We have to be careful. The murderer could be in the room with us." Nadeem flicked a glance in Jack's direction.

"You're crazy," I said. "Jack's not involved with Frida's murder."

"Are you sure? If Jack or his *girlfriend*"—Nadeem added that last bit with an extra emphasis on *girlfriend*—"is behind the threats you've been getting, how do we know there's not a more sinister plot being hatched here?"

"This isn't about Jack. This is about you."

Nadeem's gaze narrowed as he watched Jack move across the room like a predator stalking his prey. "Where was Jack at the time of the murder? Has he told you?"

"Jack's not a suspect," I said. "You are."

"Isn't he? When there's the promise of riches and treasure involved, I've learned the hard way you can't trust anyone. Why are you so blind when it comes to him? I already told you I saw Jack in the garden around the same time that Frida was murdered. And yet you say nothing. If he cares so much for you, why does he keep lying to you?"

Chapter Twenty-five

*If I should be so fortunate to reach the White House,
I expect to live on twenty-five thousand dollars a year,
and I will neither keep house nor make butter.*

—SARA POLK, FIRST LADY OF
THE UNITED STATES (1845–1849)

JACK went still. Deadly still.

I held my breath, waiting for him to bite Nadeem's head off for tossing around false accusations.

"Yes, you saw me in the garden," Jack admitted. "I was doing my job, you moron. And I wish to hell that I had seen something, because we all know Gordon is innocent. I went back and watched the surveillance feeds several times because on Monday I was distracted by an unescorted assistant with the curator's office who had no business wandering all over the South Lawn. Instead of saving Frida, I was following you."

"You have some nerve blaming me for causing distractions. Your crazy girlfriend has done nothing but cause one commotion after another with her threats."

"Ex-girlfriend. But you're right." Jack rubbed a hand over his face. He sounded tired. I didn't blame him, I was tired, too. It was after midnight, and we all had to work in the morning. "I'll make sure Simone's family and the police know that she's been sending you threats. I won't take the risk that she might actually hurt you. I'm also going to make damn sure she understands I want her completely out of my life."

He knelt down in front of me and took my hands in his. "I never dreamed she'd go this far and frighten you."

"I haven't been scared. I haven't had the time," I said. "I've been too busy wondering why Nadeem keeps popping up where he shouldn't be. He's the one who's been scaring me."

"I already explained that," Nadeem protested.

"Did you?" I demanded, still angry with him for breaking into Jack's house. Jack could have been hurt in the scuffle. And I was still angry with Jack, for that matter. I released my hands from his and tucked them under my arms. He should have told me about his ex-girlfriend, especially if she was causing him trouble. I was sick of secrets and lies. "All we have, Nadeem, is your word and your constant attempts to push the spotlight of suspicion off you and over to Jack. To me, that in itself is suspicious behavior."

Nadeem slouched on the sofa and crossed his arms over his chest like a pouting child. "I didn't do anything wrong."

"Then why were you researching the *HMS Fantome* and trying to hide it when I came into your office?" I asked.

"I wanted to help. I wanted to find Frida's killer and . . ." He sank a little deeper into the sofa cushions. "You wouldn't understand."

"Try us," Jack said. When Nadeem kept silent, Jack added, "If you don't, I'll get my brother to come back here and arrest you for breaking and entering."

"If you're arrested, you'll lose your job. That is, if you're really at the White House to work in the curator's office," I added.

"It's true! It's been my lifelong dream to work with such a historic collection."

"But you're also part of the spy business," I said.

"I'm *retired* from what you call the spy business. When I got out, I went back to college and pursued a joint master's degree in art history and museum studies. The opportunity to work with Frida was a dream come true for me.

And no, I didn't pull any strings to get the position. My grades and performance spoke for themselves."

"And what about moving into the basement apartment where I live?" I asked, still not convinced he was telling us the complete truth.

"It was available. Frida handed me your flyer about the apartment."

"But you had the money and could afford a nicer place," Jack was quick to point out. "You expect us to believe you didn't know James Calhoun's daughter lived one flight above you?"

He didn't answer right away. "I knew she lived there," he finally admitted, but quickly added, "How can you blame me for wanting to get close to her? I've heard about James's amazing daughter, the daughter who was beautiful and talented, for the past fifteen years that I've worked with the man. And now she's become quite a legend in D.C. for saving the President. Who wouldn't have wanted to live near her?" He looked at me as he said it and smiled that dazzling smile of his. "Your father wasn't exaggerating. You are the first person to notice that I was keeping surveillance on you. Not even the super spies in the Middle East who live on the edge of paranoia and see enemies even in the eyes of their most trusted friends and family ever suspected I was watching them. But you did. You're pretty amazing."

What could I do but smile back?

"Okay, okay," Jack said. "Let's say for the sake of argument that you're telling us the truth—"

"You know I am," Nadeem insisted. "You talked to James just now. Didn't he tell you all this?"

"He did," Jack agreed, much to my surprise.

"What?" I couldn't believe it. "You *talked* to my father? When was this? Why didn't you tell me? Have you been in contact with him all this time, too?"

"No, I haven't. Honest, Casey, I haven't," Jack said. "When Nadeem left the room a few minutes ago, it was to contact your father to tell him what had happened and what you now knew. Nadeem then handed the phone to me. I promise you, Casey, this was the first time I'd ever had the privilege of talking with the esteemed James Calhoun."

"*Esteemed?*" I sighed. My father was not the hero everyone seemed to think he was. And his intrusion into my life was an unwelcome distraction. Time was running out. If we didn't find any evidence to the contrary, Gordon would be charged with murder.

"Your dad told me that he trusted Nadeem with his life and that we should, too." Jack grimaced. I couldn't tell if his unhappiness was at his reluctance to trust Nadeem or his discomfort because I wouldn't jump on my father's hero bandwagon with him.

"So you'll believe me when I say that I was researching the lost treasure because I wanted to find the killer as badly as you did?" Nadeem asked. When neither Jack nor I answered right away, he quietly added, "Frida was my friend. Why wouldn't I want to find the bastard who killed her?"

"So if you're working toward the same goal as us, what have you learned that we don't already know?" Jack inquired.

"I found something before Frida's death. If you have a computer, I can pull up the copy I made."

"My laptop is in my office," Jack said, "unless you smashed it. In that case, you're buying me a new one."

We had to climb over the piles of laundry still in the hallway on our way back to his office.

"What did my brothers say to you?" Jack couldn't stop himself from asking as we entered his office.

"Dan tried to get me into your bedroom," I said, which caused his dark brows to disappear into his hairline. "You know, you could pick up after your brothers."

"I used to, but I was curious to see how long it would take before they started cleaning up after themselves."

"I wouldn't have done that," Nadeem said as he stepped over the spilled paperwork in Jack's office. "This isn't a healthy living environment."

"I didn't ask for your opinion," Jack snapped. He pushed Nadeem out of his way and powered up his laptop computer.

Nadeem righted the office chair and set it at the desk in

front of the laptop. Once the computer was up and running, he sat down and navigated through several secure networks with the ease of a hacker. "Here it is."

He offered me his place at the desk chair so I could see what he'd found without having to crane my neck over his shoulder. An image of a crinkled newspaper article that was very similar to the one I'd been carrying in my pocket flashed onto the screen. Instead of a tragic tale of murder and loss, the article detailed how the treasure hunter, Cowboy Baker, found the sunken *HMS Fantome* and how he had been fighting the English government for the right to the treasure he planned to bring up from the ship's watery grave.

In the margin had been scribbled, "Jefferson. It exists! It's still here. It never left the grounds."

"Still *here?*" I looked up to find Nadeem watching me closely. "You mean Thomas Jefferson's missing treasure? Frida thought it was still hidden somewhere on the grounds?"

Nadeem grinned like a kid at Christmas. His eyes sparkled with excitement. "That's Frida's handwriting. I told you her notes were more valuable than the documents. I believe she'd been on the verge of finding Thomas Jefferson's lost treasure. That was why she was being so cautious with her research. She wanted to make sure she got all the credit for the discovery. I have a feeling that there's something in Frida's missing files, something that *isn't* in Gordon's copy, something Frida added that was helping lead her to the missing treasure. It must also be the same something that got her killed."

"If Frida knew where the treasure was hidden," I said, "then why haven't we seen evidence she was searching for it? And why hasn't her killer been actively looking for it, too? Why the wait?"

It seemed as if only Milo—the overgrown puppy with a sudden obsession for digging up the South Lawn—was searching for the treasure.

And then it hit me.

Oh, Milo . . .

Chapter Twenty-six

Well, Warren Harding, I have got you the presidency. What are you going to do with it?

—FLORENCE HARDING, FIRST LADY OF
THE UNITED STATES (1921–1923)

*D*IE. The text message from Jack's jealous ex-girlfriend glared up from my cell phone's readout early the next morning. I deleted it and stuffed the phone back into my pocket. I didn't have time to play her childish games.

Still, the threatening message did give me pause. I stopped my work in the kitchen garden long enough to scan the empty Ellipse Park beyond the White House's iron fence. Was Simone out there somewhere watching me?

Was *my father?*

No, don't think about either of them. I couldn't let myself be distracted by what my father was doing in the area. Or why Jack hadn't called off Simone yet.

We had one day to clear Gordon's name before the DA accused him of killing Frida. Which meant we had one day to find Jefferson's lost treasure in an effort to force the killer's hand.

On top of that, the garden projects couldn't be ignored.

I didn't have time to fall apart just because my father, a

father I hadn't seen in decades, decided to pop up at this inopportune time of my life.

If not for Nadeem, I wouldn't be worrying about dear old dad. But if not for Nadeem and yesterday's late-night confrontation, I wouldn't have figured some things out. Thanks to him, I now had plan.

As long as I stayed focused.

"I'm going to turn her in," Lorenzo announced out of the blue. I didn't even know he'd come down to the kitchen garden.

"Turn who in?" I asked from where I was crouched down next to a raised bed filled with broccoli plants.

"Lettie, that's who," Lorenzo said.

"For what?" I grabbed the base of the closest broccoli plant. The plant had grown so big during the fall months that it now resembled a small tree. But the season was coming to an end, and the plant's leaves already had large yellow splotches. With a quick twist, I tugged the broccoli from its bed.

After giving it a good shake to dislodge the dark, nutrient-rich soil from its thick roots, I inhaled the rich scent of earth and tossed the plant into the pile of other plants that were coming out of the garden.

Milo woofed and chased after the plant. He picked it up, gave it a shake just like I had, and trotted back over to me with the broccoli in his mouth. His tail wagged like a flag on a battleship returning home from war. He dropped his prize at my feet.

In all the time he'd been out here helping me, he hadn't tried to dig a hole in the yard. Not once.

And I was pretty sure I knew why.

"How can you *not* know what I'm talking about?" Lorenzo demanded. "Haven't you been paying attention? Lettie. Killed. Frida."

"She may have," I agreed. I picked up the plant Milo had dropped and tossed it into the pile again.

"*May have?* You heard Marcel in the park yesterday. Lettie has focused all her energies on getting her hands on

Jefferson's treasure. She needs it to solve whatever money troubles she's gotten herself into. She's obviously willing to kill to do it. And frame Gordon for her crime."

"That might be true." I pulled out another large broccoli plant by the roots and gave it a toss into the pile. Milo promptly grabbed it and carried it back.

"I overheard her talking in the hallway. She's setting up an interview with a reporter," Lorenzo said.

I lifted the rim of my sweetgrass gardening hat and turned my head in Lorenzo's direction. "A reporter? What does the East Wing think about that?"

Milo dropped the plant I was trying to put in the discard pile at my feet again and woofed.

"I don't think they know. But from what I heard, she's going to meet with a reporter. I bet she wants to make a public case against Gordon." Lorenzo started pacing. "She's going to go to the press to make sure he's convicted in the court of public opinion even before the DA makes a move."

Lorenzo stomped through my pile of discarded plants. Dirt and bits of stems stained the upturned cuffs of his expensive suit pants. He didn't seem to notice, which only proved how upset he was. "Casey, we need to stop her."

"I agree." I picked up the broccoli plant Milo had carried back to me and sat back on my heels. "Her going to the press does complicate things."

With a violent twist, Lorenzo snatched the broccoli plant from my grasp before I could toss it back onto the pile. "What's wrong with you? Gordon's life hangs in the balance, and you're playing fetch with the dog." He shook the plant at me.

"I'm not playing with the dog, I'm testing a theory."

Lorenzo glared.

"Look at him." I pulled out yet another spent plant and tossed it. Milo bounded into action and carried the broccoli back to me. "He's always trying to help in the garden. Not that he's ever that much help. But he's always been interested in what we're doing and has always tried to turn our work into a game."

"What a smart dog," Lorenzo said dryly. "So what are you planning? Train Milo to copy you with the hopes he'll have better luck sniffing out the killer?"

"No. I don't think we can get him to point his paw to our culprit, although that would be an interesting idea . . . No, it wouldn't work."

"Then what are you planning?" It was obvious Lorenzo was losing his patience, if he'd had any to begin with.

"Look at the holes Milo has dug. He digs in just a couple of areas. Why?"

Lorenzo shrugged. "Those are his favorite spots. Dogs have favorite spots. Perhaps the ground there smells like a squirrel. Who knows what goes through that mutt's mind."

"I don't think that's it. Watch." I retrieved a trowel from the sweetgrass basket I'd carried down to the garden with me and dug a small hole. Milo woofed excitedly and started to dig as well. His front paws scraped at the ground, sending soil flying everywhere.

"So? How does that help Gordon? The DA is going to press charges tomorrow."

"I know."

Lorenzo pulled at his hair. "If he does, Gordon's career will be over. O. V. E. R. I don't know why I'm surprised that you're not helping him. You never help. You go off on these tangents and just end up getting in the way. I bet you couldn't investigate your way through an open door if your life depended upon it."

"You might be right about that last part," I grumbled. I should have connected Milo's strange behavior with the murder (and the robberies) sooner. But I now knew what was happening. I simply needed to figure out how to prove it.

Lorenzo stomped back up the hill toward the White House. "I'm going to report Lettie."

Milo must have thought Lorenzo's quick movements looked like an invitation to play. He gave an excited woof and loped after him.

I stood up and pulled off my gardening gloves. "Lorenzo, wait. Don't you see? Our treasure hunter has been searching for the treasure all along and has been using Milo to cover up the evidence."

"I'm going to stop Lettie!" Lorenzo yelled back as he continued up the hill. "I'm taking over. If not for you and your carelessness, Gordon wouldn't be in this position in the first place. Frida might even still be alive!"

My mouth dropped open. Lorenzo really believed that? He really blamed me for Frida's death?

Of course he did. He was constantly finding fault with my work. He cheered my mistakes. And he would be happy to see me gone.

So why should I run after him? Why should I stop him from accusing the First Lady's sister of murder? After all, he might be right. Now that Nadeem had made a strong case for his innocence, Lettie was the only suspect left.

But Lorenzo didn't have iron-clad evidence to back up his accusation. He didn't have *any* evidence.

Not my problem.

He'd said it himself. He didn't want my help.

Child, doing the right thing only when it's easy won't win you a seat on the bus to Heaven, my grandmother Faye had scolded many, many times. And she was right.

If I didn't stop Lorenzo, he'd unwittingly destroy his White House career. I knew that. And it would be wrong not to try and stop him.

"Lorenzo!" I ran to catch up with him.

Chapter Twenty-seven

I've always felt that a person's intelligence is directly reflected by the number of conflicting points of view he can entertain simultaneously on the same topic.

—ABIGAIL ADAMS, FIRST LADY OF
THE UNITED STATES (1797–1801)

"CASEY!" Marcel exclaimed as I hurried into the Diplomatic Reception Room from the outside. I bounced off the designer's round chest.

"So sorry," I said. "I'm in a hurry. Did you see Lorenzo come through the center hallway?"

"*Non*, he is not here."

"He must have gone another way. But where is he headed?" I wondered aloud.

"I cannot tell you." Marcel latched on to my arm. "But I must go outside. And as you remember, the Secret Service requires you to escort me."

I tried to wiggle out of his hold. "The Secret Service said you need an escort. They didn't say it had to be *me*. You need to find someone in the East Wing who can help you."

The Diplomatic Reception Room, located on the ground floor under the iconic half-round South Portico, was one of the many oval rooms in the residence. Its walls were covered with a modern reproduction of an 1830s wallpaper depicting dramatic, larger-than-life landscapes such as the Natural Bridge in Virginia, Niagara Falls, and Boston Harbor. I barely saw the beautiful walls before Marcel pushed me back outside.

"We are in a hurry, *non?*"

I was about to break away from him and charge back into the Diplomatic Reception Room to search for Lorenzo when I spotted him outside. He was with Special Agent in Charge of the Counter Assault Team, Mike Thatch. Milo did a little dance as he followed along with the men.

As luck would have it, the two men and dog were heading the same direction in which Marcel was dragging me . . . right into the Rose Garden.

The Rose Garden, tucked between the West Wing and the main residence, was in full fall bloom, with baskets of bronze-colored "Denise" chrysanthemums hanging from the Jackson magnolia tree. The garden consisted of a central lawn bordered by flowerbeds. Saucer magnolias and crabapples provided height. Geometric boxwood hedges provided visual rhythm. And grandiflora and tea roses stood alongside annuals such as chrysanthemums, asters, salvias, and flowering kale, providing a range of textures and bright colors to the space.

I watched with dismay as Lorenzo and Thatch, several yards ahead of me, traversed the garden and took a direct path to the colonnade that led to the West Wing. There, they met up with several other Secret Service agents . . . and Manny.

Well, doesn't that just take the biscuit. I'd been bending myself into a pretzel just to get a few minutes, conversation with Manny, and all Lorenzo had to do was walk up to him.

Pulling Marcel along with me, I followed the same path Lorenzo had taken, but was sidetracked by Seth Donahue, the First Lady's high-strung social secretary. Unfortunately, no matter how I tried, there was no sidestepping a determined Seth.

"You've been ignoring my texts," Seth said.

"I've been busy," I replied.

He pointed to the grassy area in the center of the garden where three White House workers dressed in navy blue jumpsuits were positioning a familiar-looking sofa.

Nadeem scurried behind the workers, placing little plastic discs under the sofa's legs so that the antique wouldn't be sitting directly on the grass.

"Oh!" Marcel exclaimed and lumbered over to chat with Nadeem and study the sofa's blue silk upholstery with a decorative eagle medallion motif stitched in golden thread.

"What is that?" Seth demanded as he pointed toward them.

"A sofa?" I guessed. "I'm in a hurry. I need to talk to—"

"No!" Seth marched over to a small patch of crabgrass in the fescue lawn and stomped on it. "This is what I don't understand."

"It's a sprig of crabgrass. As I said, I'm in a hurry."

"*Crabgrass?*" The way his voice squeaked, you'd think I'd identified a nuclear warhead instead of a common weed.

"They pop up occasionally," I said.

"It can't be there. I have a photo shoot scheduled to start in ten minutes. And I need per-fec-tion. That—that thing is ugly. It'll ruin everything."

"Okay." I reached down and plucked the sprig of grass from the ground. "See you around."

"Wait." He blocked my path again. "Aren't you going to check for more weeds? This is an important photo shoot." He lowered his voice. "The President, First Lady, and her twins will be having an official portrait made this afternoon. The First Lady insisted on staging the photos in the garden. Brilliant idea. If only the gardens weren't in shambles. I miss Gordon. He knew how to keep the grounds in tip-top shape."

"I miss Gordon, too." More than Seth could imagine. I also missed how Gordon could handle Seth with more tact than I ever could. "Now if you'll excuse me, I need to stop Lorenzo from—"

"Don't forget about the commemorative tree planting,"

Seth said and dodged in front of me again. "I need those revised planting plans from you."

"Honestly, with everything that's been going on, I haven't had a chance to work on it."

"Well, *start* working on it. I've rescheduled the tree planting for Monday."

"Monday?"

He nodded. "And as I've already told you, I need to approve the planting location. I need the new planting site in my hands today."

I suspected Seth was the only one who felt a burning need to reschedule the commemorative tree planting, but since he'd put himself in charge of coordinating the details for the grounds office, I didn't have much choice but to agree.

"I'll get right on it," I said.

"No, Casey, you'll work on it now. I want it on my desk in an hour."

Since I didn't have time to argue, I gritted my teeth and nodded.

"Seth, this is not right," Nadeem called from the grassy area of the garden. "Frida would never have approved of us taking a Bellangé sofa out of the Blue Room."

"She's not here," Seth said coldly.

"This sofa is one of the oldest in the collection. It's part of the original pieces the Monroe administration had purchased after the 1814 fire," Nadeem pointed out to no effect.

"It is most lovely." Marcel nodded as he ran his hand over the silk fabric.

"You." Seth rounded on Marcel while I rushed to catch up to Lorenzo. "Monday. Whether the rooms are done or not, you are leaving on Monday. So stop wasting time and get your work done."

"Wasting time?" Marcel cried.

"Monday," Seth countered.

"Impossible." Marcel slashed his hand with an angry

swipe through the air. But he seemed to back down almost immediately. "*S'il vous plaît*, Seth, you cannot expect me to work a miracle. There is still too much to be done."

"The sofa shouldn't be sitting in the damp grass. We shouldn't be moving the furniture around," Nadeem groused. But he was only an assistant, a new one at that, and Seth clearly had no plans to listen to him.

As much as I wanted to hear the end of both of those arguments, I didn't have time.

"Lorenzo." I waved my hands as I closed the distance between us. "Lorenzo."

"Casey, did you put him up to this?" Manny asked, his salt-and-pepper mustache quivering.

"No, I . . ." I furrowed my brows. "Lorenzo, what have you said?"

"I told him what he needed to hear. I know who killed Frida. It wasn't Gordon."

His loud declaration of knowing the killer's identity caused Seth and Nadeem to look our way. Marcel continued to *oh* and *ah* over the sofa.

"He didn't mean it," I announced to everyone within earshot. "I mean, yes, Gordon is innocent. And I suppose in a way, Manny, I put him up to it."

"That's not true," Lorenzo protested. He would have said more, but the Palm Room's double doors swung open at that very moment. Several Secret Service agents, half a dozen East Wing staff members, and the First Lady's official photographer preceded First Lady Margaret Bradley into the Rose Garden.

Margaret didn't notice the commotion going on around the historic sofa in the garden. Her full attention was on the pair of babies I assumed were nestled in the basinet she was carrying.

Lettie hurried out the door after her sister. She had a baby's blanket draped over her shoulder and was snapping pictures with a cheap digital camera.

"You don't need to do that," Margaret said.

"I'm capturing these precious moments," Lettie said.

"We have a professional photographer to do that."

"It's not the same thing." Lettie lifted the camera and snapped pictures of the First Lady crossing the Rose Garden to the antique sofa.

The First Lady was dressed in a stunning almond-colored dress with a wide sash tied high on her waist. Her sister, in contrast, wore old jeans and the same blouse as yesterday.

"Lorenzo! Cathy!" Lettie waved when she spotted us, indicating that she wanted us to join her.

"*Casey*," her sister muttered with a note of exasperation.

"We're not through here," Manny warned.

"Certainly not," Lorenzo said. "I haven't had a chance to tell you what's going on."

But Lettie was still waving us over. And the Secret Service agents who had acted as a blockade to the First Family stepped aside to let us enter into their protection zone.

"Oh! The babies!" I cried with delight and hurried over to meet them.

Lorenzo, torn between doing what he thought was necessary to help Gordon and his desire to make friends with the First Family, reluctantly followed.

A pair of red-faced cherubs peered out from a soft blue blanket nest in the basinet. "Hello, Bradley boys." I wiggled my fingers at them in greeting.

"Shh . . ." Seth hissed.

"They'd been crying all morning," Margaret explained. "They're so tuckered out I don't think a marching band would disturb them."

"But they're doing well?" I asked and then puffed out my cheeks and pursed my lips, opening and closing my mouth like a fish might. I was hoping to entertain the babes, but I think they were still too young to get the humor.

"Oh, yes." The relief in Margaret's voice was wonderful to hear. Her face lit up with joy. "The doctors have given my two little sirens a clean bill of health, especially their lungs. That's one reason why John suggested we take the publicity photos. That, and to head off the controversy

with . . ." She trailed off. "Forgive me." She then quickly
corrected herself. "How is Gordon doing?"

"There's no change in his condition, which we're told is
a good thing," Lorenzo said. "But we're worried about
what the police might do to hurt him."

"I'm worried, too," she said.

"Worried about what?" Lettie asked as she snapped pictures of us.

"About Gordon," Margaret said.

"You don't have to worry about him. The DA will be
pressing murder charges tomorrow. Once that's out of the
way, Lev Aziz will come out of hiding, and everything will
work out."

"You aren't supposed to be talking about Aziz," her sister scolded.

"Sorry." Lettie wandered off to take some pictures of
Nadeem and Marcel.

Margaret's cheeks flared red. "It's not like that. We're
not trying to rush justice or push a conviction for political
gain."

She might not be, but I could imagine that some within
the administration were doing just that.

We didn't get a chance to ask her more about the situation. The photographer was ready to start. The first set of
photos was going to be the First Lady with the babies.
Later, the President would join them.

Since we were in the way, the Secret Service directed us
back to the colonnade, where Manny was still talking with
Thatch.

"Listen to me," I whispered in Lorenzo's ear right before
we joined up with Manny again. "Unless you have pictures
of Lettie committing the crime, you will lose your job if
you accuse the First Lady's sister. Do you *understand* me?
You will lose your job. And if that happens, I'll be the one
in charge of the gardens."

The last part convinced him.

He straightened.

"Now, Lorenzo," Manny said when we returned, "what

was it you were saying? You said you had proof? If not Gordon, who killed the curator? And what proof do you have?"

"I . . . um . . . it wasn't me. It was Casey," Lorenzo stammered.

"I figured as much," Manny said with a nudge to my arm. "You're a bad influence on the people around you."

"I inspire people to seek justice," I said, and regretted immediately how hokey that sounded.

"She's always going off on crazy tangents." Lorenzo's voice grew louder. "Just this morning Casey told me that she knows how to find Thomas Jefferson's lost treasure."

Once again everyone, from the photographer to the interior designer, stopped what they were doing to turn and gawk. My cheeks burned with embarrassment. This wasn't the best way for my plan to unfold. Or the safest.

But we'd have to make it work.

Soon, Frida's killer would hear—if they hadn't already heard—that someone else had joined them in the race to find Jefferson's treasure. And, I suspected, that person would feel compelled to act.

"That's right," I said. "I know how to find the treasure."

"WHAT HAVE YOU DONE?" **JACK BURST INTO THE** grounds office. "Everyone is talking about how you announced to half the administration that you know how to find Jefferson's mythical treasure."

"I do . . . well, I think I do," I said.

"And you made that announcement, why?" Jack asked.

I glanced at Lorenzo, hoping he'd speak up and take the blame. But what was I thinking? He never took the blame for anything. "I didn't—" I started to say.

"It is part of our larger plan," Lorenzo pointed out. "Find the treasure, find the killer, remember? How will we flush out the killer if no one knows Casey is on the verge of digging up Jefferson's legacy?"

"Have the two of you lost your minds?" Jack planted his

fists on the drafting table, where I was seated, and leaned dangerously close to me. So close, I could feel his heat and smell his tangy aftershave. "You've put yourself in a very dangerous place, Casey. Do I have to remind you that Frida is dead?"

"Things didn't happen exactly like I'd envisioned," I admitted. If I turned my head, our lips would almost be touching. I resisted the temptation and instead pointed to the schematic on Lorenzo's drafting table in front of me. "Look here."

The schematic was the new one Lorenzo had recently finished re-creating. I'd initially pulled it out to work on relocating the President's commemorative trees for Seth but had gotten sidetracked by sketching in pencil all the places where Milo had dug.

"In Dolley Madison's letter, the one that fell out of Gordon's archived files, the former First Lady mentioned how the gardener had taken the treasure for safekeeping. And then later, on the article that Nadeem found, Frida had written, 'It's still here.' I think Frida meant the treasure was still on White House grounds." With my pencil, I drew a circle on the schematic that encompassed everywhere we'd found Milo's holes.

"We've been busy having to fill in all the holes that Milo has dug in the lawn."

"It's a pretty large area," Jack noted.

I nodded, and then drew a tighter circle on the schematic that encompassed the holes Milo had dug after Frida's death. "See here. It's a pretty specific area now. I think the killer has been looking for the treasure all along, but didn't really know where to start until he—or she—got ahold of Frida's research."

Jack leaned over the schematic to study it. "Sounds as if the two of you might be onto something, but—"

"We need to be smarter than our treasure hunter. So we still need to figure out what this part of the South Lawn was being used for in 1814. Was it a garden? Was it part of

Jefferson's arbor? Or was there a structure here? We need to find a clue that will give us an edge."

"I'm going through the archives to see what old plans from that time period show," Lorenzo said from the other side of the room.

Jack nodded. "Other than Gordon, I suspect the two of you are the best equipped for puzzling it out. But I'm worried you'll be making yourselves prime targets. Don't forget that your treasure thief is also a killer."

"Exactly!" I said. "We get that edge, and we'll force the killer out into the open. We'll make him—"

"*Or her*," Lorenzo corrected.

"We'll force *whoever* killed Frida into making a mistake," I finished.

"I don't like how that sounds," Jack said.

"We're running out of time," I reminded him. "The DA is getting pressure from the administration to make a move. That's why they're going to press charges tomorrow, isn't it? Once Gordon is charged, the skittish Lev Aziz will return."

"I don't know why anyone bothers trying to keep secrets around here," Jack grumbled.

"You already knew Aziz wouldn't return until the killer was caught?" I pushed away from the drafting table, away from Jack, and stomped over to my desk. "Of course you knew." I flipped open the set of Dolley Madison letters Dr. Wadsin had sent over this morning. These were letters from the 1840s. Dolley Madison had been in her eighties at the time. After mounting debt had forced her to sell her property, including her husband's beloved Montpelier, she moved back to Washington, D.C.

I doubted the former First Lady would still be thinking about Jefferson's lost treasure at this point in her life, but copies of these letters were part of the research Nadeem had reported as missing from Frida's office, so I couldn't ignore them.

"I received another death threat from Simone this

morning," I said, hoping to sound as if her threats didn't bother me. But they did. Not because I was scared of her. But because it seriously ticked me off that Jack hadn't told me earlier about his crazy ex-girlfriend. What if she had tried to hurt me? He shouldn't have held back such an important part of his life.

But then again, I'd been keeping secret the information about my father from him . . . not that he didn't already know all about my dad. So it really wasn't the same thing, was it?

"I know you're angry with me, Casey, and I'm sorry. But you don't have to worry about Simone. I spoke with both her parents and Manny this afternoon. She won't be bothering you again."

I crossed my arms over my chest and refused to look at him. No wonder jealousy was one of the deadly sins. Just thinking about beautiful, model-thin Simone kissing Jack made my insides burn as if they were on fire.

"You'd better watch out, Jack-o," Lorenzo said. "If Casey ever ends up in the same room as Simone, you're going to have one wicked catfight on your hands."

Tired of hearing Simone's name uttered in my presence, I said a little too loudly, "What are we going to do about Lettie?"

"Lettie?" Jack sighed. "What's she up to now?"

"What has Lettie done in the past to make you ask that?" I demanded at the same time Lorenzo said, "I overheard her on the phone. She's set up a meeting with a reporter. I think she's so anxious to prove Gordon is guilty that she wants to make sure it's the only conclusion anyone will make. She crowed about the impending DA action less than an hour ago. She's out to destroy Gordon's reputation."

Jack scratched his chin. "Are you sure that's what she's planning?"

Lorenzo nodded. "There was no mistaking her meaning. I overheard her say she couldn't wait to meet with the reporter and that she'd bring the goods. Casey doesn't want me to say anything, but I know Lettie killed Frida."

"Hm," Jack grunted.

My jaw dropped open. If I'd accused Lettie of murder like Lorenzo just had, even if it was only between us, Jack would have blistered my ears from now until sundown.

"Do you know when Lettie has set up this meeting of hers?" Jack said instead.

"No, that's why we need to keep a close eye on her," Lorenzo said, getting more excited and chummier with Jack than he'd ever been with me. "Perhaps you and I could team up."

"We could invite Lettie to help me with tracking down seed savers," I suggested. "It'd kill two birds with one stone. I'm having a devil of a time finding anyone who knows anything about many of the historic plant varieties we need to grow this spring."

"And then when she leaves?" Lorenzo asked. "What do we do? Follow her?"

Jack cleared his throat. "I might have a solution."

He started to lay out his plan, but he hadn't gotten very far when my cell phone sang the first few lines of Kelly Clarkson's hit.

"It's Deloris," I said and swallowed hard before answering.

Deloris didn't let me say more than hello before she started talking so quickly—her voice garbled with loud sobs—I couldn't understand a word she was saying.

"Slow down." My heart pounded out of control while Lorenzo shouted, "What's going on?" I pressed a finger against my free ear so I could better hear Deloris. "Please say that again."

I prayed we weren't about to hear the worst.

Deloris drew a shaky breath. "It's Gordon," she said.

My legs turned all watery.

"He's not—"

"He is," she cried.

No. I'd feared this could happen. But it had only been an abstract fear. While the doctors had remained cautious, warning that the worst might yet happen, I had refused to face the pain of losing Gordon.

I loved him. And he'd loved me.

How was I going continue working here day after day without him?

My knees started to buckle and I would have fallen in a heap on the hard concrete if Jack hadn't caught me. He wrapped his arms around me and held on tight.

"I'm so sorry," I rasped into the phone.

Tears dripped from my cheeks as the world fell apart beneath me.

Chapter Twenty-eight

Clouds and darkness surround us, yet Heaven is just,
and the day of triumph will surely come, when
justice and truth will be vindicated.

—MARY TODD LINCOLN, FIRST LADY OF
THE UNITED STATES (1861–1865)

"**S**ORRY?" Deloris shouted into the phone. "Why on earth are you sorry? Gordon is awake!"

"*Awake?*" I whispered, afraid to believe that it could be true. "He's awake?"

"Yes, honey. And he's asking for both you and Lorenzo."

LESS THAN A HALF HOUR LATER, LORENZO AND I arrived at the hospital. Jack was still on duty, so he agreed to stay behind and keep an eye on Lettie.

In the hospital lobby, Deloris and I hugged tightly.

"He's still weak," Deloris warned. "But the doctor said he's turned the corner. He should continue to get stronger."

"Thank God," I said. "Thank God."

While we were anxious to get into the room and see Gordon for ourselves, Deloris still remained curiously hesitant to let anyone other than his immediate family enter his room. "He needs to rest. He needs his family," she insisted as she blocked the door.

"You need a break, Momma." Junior, the older of her two sons, hooked his arm with hers. "While Dad's two favorite gardeners cheer him up, I'm taking you down to the cafeteria. No, don't argue. You're going to eat."

He flashed us a smile. "I'm glad you're here. She has refused to leave. She barely eats. She needs this break."

"Go, then," I said. "We'll keep your dad entertained."

"But he shouldn't be alone," Deloris protested. "He doesn't know what—"

"We're going. Kevin's staying." Junior dragged his exhausted mother down the hallway. "We'll be back in a half hour."

Once they were gone, Kevin pushed open the hospital room's swinging door. "He's been asking for the two of you ever since he woke up."

I rushed through the door, while Lorenzo remained in the hallway. When I glanced back to see what he was waiting for, I saw that he was wiping his damp eyes with a linen handkerchief. He snarled when he noticed I'd seen his tears and marched into the room as if nothing in this world could touch his prickly heart.

Behind a draped partition in the large, wood-paneled hospital room, we found Gordon looking like a sultan draped in sheets and surrounded by pillows in his elevated hospital bed. A blue monitor beside the bed beeped softly.

"Hel-lo." His voice sounded muffled as if he had cotton stuffed in his mouth. He looked pale. His skin sagged as if it was too loose for his face. But his blue eyes sparked with life when he spotted Lorenzo and me. "Ca-sey," he rasped.

"I'm here, Gordon." I rushed to his side. "Do you need anything? Water?"

"No, no water. The allée of little-leaf lindens, Casey."

"Yes, Gordon." I patted his hand. His skin felt as fragile as dried leaves. "We're rescheduling the President's commemorative tree planting."

"No. No." He thrashed around in the bed. "Not there."

"You don't have to worry. I've relocated it. And Lorenzo

has re-created the lost schematic for the South Lawn. There won't be any problems this next time. I promise."

He nodded and swallowed several times. "You're a good girl. Both you and Lorenzo . . . you two are like the children I never had."

That was an odd thing for him to say.

"Your boys are here. Kevin is by the window," I said gently, in case he was confused about the identity of the young man standing by the window. "Junior took your wife to an early dinner."

Gordon tightened his grip on my hand. "They hate gardening."

"We do," Kevin agreed. "I'm glad he has the two of you."

"It doesn't upset you?" I asked.

"Why should it?" Kevin said. "He's happy. And we're not constantly being pestered about raking leaves or mucking around in his backyard. It's a win-win."

"I see." I smiled and shook my head.

"They're good lawyers." A weak smile tugged at Gordon's dry lips. "Always could talk their way out of their chores."

"Don't listen to him. He never let us get away with anything," Kevin protested as he laughed.

We laughed with him. It felt good to laugh.

"Gordon," Lorenzo said, "do you remember anything about Monday? We've been trying to piece together what happened in the Children's Garden, but we've hit one dead end after another."

Gordon closed his eyes. "No." His breathing sped up. He started to pant as his head thrashed side to side. "She's dead," he said.

Kevin shot to his feet. "I should get the doctor," he said and left the room.

"Gordon, it's okay. You're safe now." I held on to his hand. "Take a deep breath. You're safe."

"Did you see anyone in the garden? Anyone other than Frida?" Lorenzo pressed.

"Frida," he growled. "Stupid, stupid woman. The treasure. It's not there. It's not there. Frida. She started shouting. But the treasure. Her damned treasure. It wasn't there. The hole. It was empty. Of course it was empty. Frida didn't know."

Was it me, or had the room suddenly turned to ice?

"Gordon, what . . . are . . . you saying?" I whispered.

"She needed to be silenced." Gordon's voice grew weak. I lowered my ear to his mouth and even then could barely hear him as he repeated over and over. "She needed to be silenced."

The doctor and a couple of nurses rushed into the room with Kevin following. The nurses nudged Lorenzo and me out of the way as the doctor checked on Gordon's vital signs.

The medical staff talked in steady, hushed voices. They reminded me of the buzzing of honeybees back in the kitchen garden.

Or was that my head that was buzzing?

I looked over at Lorenzo. He'd backed into the corner by the window. His fingers were digging deeply into the arms of his sleeves. All of the color had drained from his face.

"*Gordon?*" he mouthed to me.

LORENZO AND I LEFT THE HOSPITAL WITHOUT discussing what we'd heard or what either of us planned to do about it. I didn't know where Lorenzo was headed. Nor did I know where I was going until I ended up wandering through a gap in a large granite stone mountain jutting out from the eastern end of the tidal basin known as the Mountain of Despair.

The clouds had cleared. The sun hung like a bright beacon in the early November sky. A herd of schoolchildren ran past. A little girl squealed with delight as she pointed to the large structure beyond the mountain.

I hugged myself as I surveyed the tidal basin's ancient cherry trees intermixed with a new planting of crepe myrtles, liriope, English yew, and jasmine. The jasmine reminded me of my home in the Lowcountry of South Carolina.

I walked around the granite boulder that had been pushed out of the Mountain of Despair and found an empty bench to contemplate what had happened at the hospital. The police and Secret Service both felt as if they had enough evidence to prove Gordon had killed Frida. What if they were right? What if Gordon did do the awful deed?

After Frida's death the strange thefts had stopped. Neither Lorenzo nor I had been especially secretive as we searched through Dolley Madison's files for clues to the treasure's location and no one had threatened us.

Only Milo continued to dig holes in the lawn. And all in one general spot, too. I'd thought the killer had been digging the holes, and having Milo cover the tracks with his digging. But what if I'd been wrong? What if Milo had continued to dig the holes after Frida's death as a learned behavior on the overgrown puppy's part?

Had the thefts and odd happenings stopped because Gordon had been in a coma and was unable to cause any more trouble?

My phone started to sing, indicating an incoming text message. I checked its readout. Seth was looking for my site plan for Monday's commemorative tree planting. He needed it on his desk ASAP. Just as I hit Ignore, another text came in. Again, from Seth. *FLOTUS asking for full list of seeds procured for the founding fathers' garden. Wants project to move forward ASAP.*

I'd been able to find a few seeds. *Too few.*

My shoulders dropped in defeat. I'd contacted seed savers, plant historians at obscure arboretums, and seed banks searching for the seeds I needed, to no avail. Most of the plants simply no longer existed, at least not in the form that the founding fathers would have served at their dinner table.

I hadn't wanted to believe Dr. Wadsin, but her dire prediction that I'd run into trouble had been spot on. I'd learned from the last seed saver I'd contacted that a staggering ninety-seven percent of the vegetable crops being grown at the turn of the twentieth century were now extinct.

I was going to have to tell the First Lady that I'd failed. There'd be no founding fathers' vegetable garden this spring. At least not like the one we'd envisioned.

I'd failed with the President's commemorative tree planting—when had a tree planting ever blown up in anyone's face? I'd failed to find the vegetable seeds. And now I'd failed to save Gordon.

What was it about the father figures in my life? Was I doomed to cling to men with murderous streaks? Or had Gordon been able to get through my iron-clad emotional defenses because he was too much like my father?

But my father wasn't a murderer.

The schoolchildren had moved on to another site, leaving me alone in the Martin Luther King Jr. Memorial to contemplate what, if anything, I was going to do with this new piece of information.

"She needed to be silenced," Gordon had said about Frida. Not exactly a confession. But . . .

Kelly Clarkson started to sing about being stronger on my cell phone. Even though I didn't recognize the number on the caller ID, I answered.

"Casey? Where have you been?" It was Jack. He must have picked up a new phone since Simone had smashed his. "I've been trying to reach you all afternoon."

"I—I, um . . ." I stared at the massive granite stone that had been pushed out from the Mountain of Despair. A larger-than-life figure of Martin Luther King Jr. was carved into the rock as if he was emerging from the mountain. The memorial designer called the sculpture the Stone of Hope.

I could use a healthy dose of hope right now.

"Talk to me, Casey. Lorenzo wouldn't tell me what's going on or where'd you'd gone. He's being nice. I mean, he . . . he complimented your gardening skills. Why would he do that? What's happening? How's Gordon?"

"He's . . ." What could I say? Did I tell Jack that I heard our beloved head gardener confess to murder? He'd feel duty-bound to report it to Manny, which would only strengthen the DA's case. I respected Jack too much to put him in that kind of difficult position.

"Casey? Where are you? I'm coming over."

"No, don't do that. I need some time alone."

There was a long pause. "What aren't you telling me?"

"Gordon's still weak. So weak. And confused." That must be it. He must have been confused. "I just need time."

There was another long stretch of uncomfortable silence. Jack did that sometimes when trying to get more information. The interrogation technique wasn't going to work this time. I wasn't going to be the one to condemn Gordon.

"Okay," Jack said with a resigned sigh. After assuring me Lorenzo was keeping a close eye on Lettie and setting up a dinner date for tonight where we could have a mini-council of war, Jack reluctantly disconnected the call.

I stared at the Stone of Hope, wondering what the heck I was going to do. Things were looking blacker than a devil's heart. At times like these, my grandmother would tell me to keep my chin up because that would be the only way I could see the good things coming down the road.

My father wanted back in my life. That was something I needed to tell Grandmother Faye. Though she tried to hide her feelings from the rest of us, I could tell she fiercely missed and worried every day about her fugitive son. She deserved to know he was alive.

I reluctantly pulled my phone from my pocket again. But instead of dialing the number for Rosebrook, I punched in the number for someone I never thought I'd call.

"Hello, Nadeem?" I said.

"Casey! Have you spoken with Jack? He's been trying to get in touch with you."

"I've talked with him."

"What's going on? Where have you been? You've had us all worried."

"I needed some time to think."

"I can understand that." He tried the long silence technique on me as well.

I closed my eyes.

"Casey? Are you still there?"

"Yes. I just . . ."

I don't know why it was so difficult to say the words. I tapped my foot on the pavement. The Calhoun women might be eccentric and even the tiniest bit foolhardy, but we weren't cowards.

My foot kept tapping a quick beat on the pavement. "I think it's time I met my father."

NADEEM WASTED NO TIME IN SETTING THINGS up. Less than an hour after my phone call to him I walked up to the red brick row houses on O Street in Dupont Circle. Three of the houses had been joined together to create the Mansion on O Street, a hotel and restaurant known for its theme rooms, fancy events, and Sunday teas. In recent decades every President had stayed in the hotel's special presidential suite at least once prior to his inauguration.

A tall, attractive woman dressed all in black greeted me at the door. She lit up like a halogen lightbulb at the mention of James Calhoun. Before she left to check on whether he was in residence, she directed me into a sitting room just off the front foyer. I perched nervously on the edge of a flowered sofa that was at the center of a room crammed with artwork and collectible knickknacks available for sale, and I waited. A friendly member of the waitstaff carried in a pot of chamomile tea and a delicate bone China teacup.

I took a sip of the flavorful tea. Even it couldn't ease the tension coiled around my throat. The clock hanging on the wall looked like an orange tabby cat, with great big eyes that moved from side to side and a tail that swished with each passing second.

Ten minutes passed.

Fifteen minutes.

I finished most of the tea. Tired of waiting, I rose from the sofa and swung my backpack over my shoulder. A loud creak stopped me in my tracks as one of the room's bookcases swung out to reveal a secret passage.

Startled, I jumped back. My backpack knocked over a small figurine of a shepherdess that had been sitting on one of the sofa's end tables. The poor shepherdess tumbled off the table to smash into a thousand pieces on the hardwood floor.

I glanced at shattered porcelain and then back at the opening in the wall. The man who emerged from the other room wasn't the towering hero everyone had been telling me about, but the unfriendly guy who protested in front of the White House.

He leaned heavily on his cane as he hobbled into the room. "Let me help you with that," he said, wagging a crooked finger at the smashed figurine.

"It's okay. I've got it." My hands trembled as I scooped up the broken pieces and set them on the table. "I suppose I've bought it." I turned the broken piece with the price tag around in my hand. "It won't break the bank."

"Glad to hear it. Do you mind if I sit with you a bit? It's been a long day." He settled on the sofa where I'd been seated.

"I was supposed to meet someone," I said. It was twenty-five minutes past the hour. "I don't think he's coming."

The old man thumped his cane on the floor. "You were stood up? Impossible!"

I smiled at his burst of anger on my behalf. "It's okay. I think I'd much rather talk with you." I glanced at the shattered shepherdess on the end table. "I don't think I was ready to meet the man who was supposed to come. I doubt I ever will be."

"That sounds ominous. Who were you waiting for?"

I thought about how I should answer that before saying, "No one important."

"Hm . . . Should I call you on that lie or change the

subject? No, don't worry," he swiftly added. "I know who
you're meeting is none of my business, so I'll change the
subject. How is Gordon doing?" His voice was gentle and
nearly as soothing as the chamomile tea.

"He's finally awake."

"But that troubles you?" He tapped the sofa cushion,
inviting me to sit next to him.

"The murder investigation troubles me," I said after
joining him on the sofa. "What if Gordon isn't the man I
think he is? What if—"

"No one ever is truly who they appear to be on the outside," the old man said. "We all wear masks of some form
or another."

"But—"

He clutched my hand in his. "Listen to me, Casey. Forget the evidence that has been thrust upon you. Trust what
you feel in your heart. If your heart tells you that Gordon
Sims is innocent, then you have to believe it. You have to
fight to make others believe it."

"But he practically confessed to the crime when I visited him." I don't know why I'd said that, and to a man who
was a stranger to me. But once I'd started, it was as if a dam
had broken. The words I had been too afraid to tell Jack or
anyone else poured out of me. "Gordon knew all about the
treasure. He said that Frida knew too much and had to be
silenced. I don't want to believe it, but he confessed to the
crime."

"Did he?" the old protestor asked.

"I think so."

"What exactly did he say?" When I hesitated, he added,
"You can trust this old protestor. I won't say anything to
help the fuzz."

I had to smile. "That's what my aunt Willow calls the
police."

I then related what I could remember about the conversation Lorenzo and I had with Gordon. His frown deepened with each new detail.

"Listen to me going on and on. You're so easy to talk to.

I appreciate your company," I said, realizing I'd taken up too much of this nice man's time.

"What about the thefts you were telling me about? How are they connected to Gordon killing Frida?" he asked, tapping his finger to his chin.

"The killer needed the papers to help him find the treasure. Wait a minute. Why would Gordon steal the schematic to the South Lawn when he could have access to it at all times?"

"Good point." He leaned heavily on his cane as he rose to leave. "I've only met one other woman as clever as you are. Lord, I miss that girl more than a flower misses the sun."

He started to walk away.

"Wait. You've never told me your name," I said.

He extended his hand. "I'm James." He hesitated. "James Calhoun."

Chapter Twenty-nine

*You gain strength, courage, and confidence by every
experience in which you really stop to look fear in the face.
You are able to say to yourself, "I lived through this horror.
I can take the next thing that comes along."*

—ELEANOR ROOSEVELT, FIRST LADY OF
THE UNITED STATES (1933–1945)

"**Y**OU?" I shot up from the sofa. "You're my—"
He nodded.

"*Why?*"

My emotions erupted in a blinding flash. I suddenly
couldn't catch my breath. I sank back to the sofa and buried
my face in my hands.

"Why? Why did you abandon us? How could you? She
died. Because of you, she died."

"I didn't mean for it to happen that way."

I lifted my head. The old protestor . . . um . . . my *father*
started to pace. It was a slow, uneven gait as he leaned
heavily on his cane.

"I left because your mom and I thought that if I ran, the
Yurkov brothers would follow me. They were hunting us
because of the information we'd found."

"But it didn't happen that way," I said.

He shook his head. "No . . . It didn't. We were set up."

"Who were they, these Yurkov brothers?"

"KGB." His icy gaze made goose bumps run up my

arms. "They were part of a large sleeper cell in the U.S. You don't have to worry about them, though. Justice was served."

"So if they were gone, why didn't you come back for me? For two years I was lost in the foster system. No one knew my identity. Or if they did, they ignored it. They sure as heck knew who you were. Your name was plastered in the newspapers, even. How could you have let that happen? How could you have let me suffer alone?"

"I had no other choice," he said, sounding defeated. "Someone within the agency had sold our identities to the KGB. After your mother died, I couldn't risk losing you. So I made sure your paperwork—and your identity—was lost. Your life was still in danger. I'm sorry, Casey."

"And after you found the leak in the agency? Why didn't you come back then?"

"I sent you to your grandmother. She knew how to care for you."

I clung to my anger. Without it, I'd have completely fallen apart. "And that's supposed to explain why you never came back? Why you never visited? Why you abandoned your only daughter?"

"Don't you see? I did what was best for you. I kept you safe. If I had been able to choose, *I* would have died that night! But I didn't. So I had to continue the work your mom and I were doing. And I couldn't do it with a child to worry about."

"*How dare you.*" I couldn't stay here and listen to this. I jumped up from the sofa and started for the exit. "You didn't die. I don't know what I'm doing here. You should have never gotten Mom mixed up in your dangerous world in the first place."

"It didn't happen that way." He thumped his cane on the floor several times. "Emma, she recruited me. Espionage and counterintelligence was her life, and she was damn good at it, too. I would have never asked her to quit."

"So you're blameless. Is that what you're saying?" I slashed my hand through the air as I hurried toward the exit. "No, don't try and defend yourself. Don't tell me how hard it was for you. You weren't there for us. You didn't have to watch her die. And as far as I'm concerned, you're not here, either."

THE DYING SUN'S ANGRY RED STREAKS JUTTING across the late afternoon sky matched my mood. My nails dug so deeply into the palms of my hands as I emerged from the Metro station and marched across McPherson Square, I wondered if I'd drawn blood.

Boy, oh boy, that man and his empty explanations could make even a preacher cuss. The nerve of him. He hadn't even bothered to apologize. If he'd had, I would have thrown it back in his face. No apology could absolve him of his sins. Even if he hadn't killed my mom, by running away from his responsibilities and abandoning his only child, he had destroyed his family just as effectively as those murderers who had stolen my mom from me. There was no forgiving that.

I darted across the street against the light and followed Vermont Avenue to Lafayette Square. Unlike my father, I didn't shirk my responsibilities. Despite everything that had happened today, I was determined to get Seth those plans for the rescheduled tree planting.

I crossed the seven-acre Lafayette Square, and even though I knew he wouldn't be there, I deliberately kept my gaze turned away from the empty spot where my father, for months, had set up his lawn chair and had held his protest sign directly across the street from the White House.

Some men spent their retirement years golfing. Others honed their woodworking skills in the garage. My father apparently chose to spend his golden years spying on his estranged daughter. Lucky me.

I'd been so wrapped up in my own maelstrom of emotions I almost didn't notice Lorenzo leaning against a rake next to a large oak tree. The first thing wrong about this picture was that Lorenzo was dressed in one of the grounds office's dark blue windbreakers. He rarely wore his. And while both Gordon and I occasionally pitched in and helped the grounds crew with the lawn work, Lorenzo nearly always found an excuse.

Not that he was actually doing any work now.

I crossed the park to find out what he was up to.

"Lettie." He drummed his fingers on the rake's handle. He gestured with his chin in the direction of a bench a few hundred yards away. The First Lady's sister, dressed in old jeans and a sweatshirt and with an oversized hobo bag slung over her shoulder, paced back and forth in front of the bench.

Unlike immediate members of the First Family, extended family members could come and go without Secret Service protection. For the most part they remained anonymous. Just last week, I'd bumped into Lettie at the nearby convenience store and was the only one in the shop that knew she was related to the First Family.

"What is she doing?" I asked as I watched Lettie continue to pace, taking the same path over and over in front of the bench.

"Don't know," Lorenzo answered without taking his eyes off her.

"If she keeps that up, she's going to kill the grass."

Lettie abruptly stopped pacing as if she'd heard my complaint. I held my breath, afraid she'd caught us watching her. Her gaze passed over us and then shifted to her watch. She said something and then started pacing again.

"She's waiting for someone. Perhaps the journalist you'd heard her talking with this morning?" I wondered aloud as I scanned the park's seven acres.

"Probably." Lorenzo slumped against the rake's handle. "Not that it matters anymore. Once Manny talks with Gordon, it'll be all over for him."

"Maybe not," I said. "Gordon didn't exactly say he killed Frida."

"It sure sounded that way to me."

"He was coming out of a medically induced coma. He was groggy and confused." My father had been right about

one thing. If I believed in my heart that Gordon was innocent, it was my duty to stand up for him. Gordon would do
no less for me. "We need to protect him."

"How? We need to face the facts, Casey. He was alone
in the garden with Frida. She had needled and needled him
all day. On top of that, she'd destroyed his wife's career and
now it looked as if she was out to destroy his. He cracked."

Lorenzo thrust the shovel's handle at me. "I can't stand
here and try to prove a lie. I can't. Milo dug those damned
holes in the lawn. They don't coincide with any garden
structures that would have been there in 1814 when the British invaded. I've looked and looked through our historic
documents. And there's nothing there. There's no treasure.
No treasure hunter. No killer." Tears brightened his eyes.
He lifted his hand when I tried to speak and swiftly turned
away. "I love that man. But . . . I can't defend a lie."

"Lorenzo, wait."

"Sorry, Casey." Lorenzo headed back toward the White
House. "I can't do this anymore. I'm simply a gardener."

I glanced over at Lettie to see if she'd noticed our argument. She continued to pace and seemed to be in an agi-
tated world of her own.

Since I was standing in the grass with a rake in my hand
and doing nothing but watching Lettie, I decided to keep
myself occupied and rake up some of the leaves that had
dropped from the park's forest of towering trees.

After several minutes, Lettie brushed off the bench
she'd been pacing in front of and sat down. She fished
around in her oversized hobo bag and pulled out a file
folder stuffed with papers and marked with the presidential
seal. That looked official. Using my raking as a cover, I
inched closer.

She opened the folder and started flipping through the
pages. I needed to get closer to see what was in the file.
Gripping the rake handle tightly in my hand, I crossed the
distance between us.

"It is you," I said with a great big smile plastered on my
lips.

She slammed the file folder closed before I could see any of the papers it contained. "Oh, I didn't see you there, Cathy."

"Casey," I corrected. "Do you mind if I join you?" I asked, and then without waiting for an invitation, sat down on the bench next to her. I pointed to a wall of dark clouds. "Looks like another storm will be rolling in."

"Right," she said, not following the direction of my gaze. "A storm."

"I like to come out here when I need to think things through." I tapped the rake. "Luckily for me, there's never any shortage of gardening tasks. You should see me in the spring. I can get a whole mess of thinking done then."

"I see," Lettie said as she scanned the park as if searching for someone.

"So I've been raking leaves just now and thinking. And do you know what I can't seem to figure out?"

"How should I know?" She kicked a pebble with her boot.

"Well, I've been thinking about Frida's murder and how Frida was looking for Jefferson's lost treasure. Those two events must be connected, don't you agree?"

"I don't know." Lettie scanned the park again. I got the distinct impression that she wanted to push me off the bench and tell me to go away.

"You don't have any ideas? I just thought you could help make things clear in my head since you have a mind as sharp as the fictional Miss Marple's."

Lettie's mood brightened in response to my praise. "I am rather clever when it comes to mysteries. I never reach the end of a novel without already guessing the who, what, when, and where of the crime."

"So do you think the killer is searching for the treasure?" I asked.

"Seems like the most reasonable assumption. Who knows, maybe Gordon needed money. Or perhaps it was as Frida had claimed—professional jealousy."

"Yes. Yes, I suppose that could be it." I rubbed my chin

thoughtfully. "But why would he need to steal Frida's notes when he knew just as much, if not more, about the gardens than anyone else at the White House? Why not just dig up the treasure before Frida could?"

"Maybe he didn't know as much as he led everyone to believe. People do that, you know. People hide behind all kinds of lies and masks." She turned and looked me in the eye. "It's hard sometimes, you know? There's so much pressure to be the perfect sister, the perfect wife. But I'm just me. And I'm far from perfect. Maybe Gordon felt that way."

"Or perhaps someone else killed Frida? Someone with a background in history but only a basic knowledge of White House lore." I drew a deep breath and forged forward. "Someone who is being pressured to pay a large sum of money and has to do whatever she can to get whoever she owes off her back. You know what I mean?"

"I have no idea what you're talking about," she answered and pretended to wave me off. But I could tell by the way she'd jerked as I'd laid out my scenario that I'd hit too close to the truth. "I don't mean to be rude, but I'm meeting someone. I have to go." She stood up without bothering to zip up her hobo bag. Her quick movements caused the bag to tip to one side, spilling its contents.

The camera she'd been using earlier in the day to capture pictures of her sister and nephews landed hard with a thud on the hard-packed soil beneath the bench, which was nearly as hard as steel. The file folder slid to the ground next to it.

"What have you done?" Lettie dropped to her knees and grabbed the camera. "Please, don't be broken."

I picked up the file folder but watched over her shoulder as she flipped through a few of the pictures. In the file folder I found printouts of the amateur shots she'd taken of her sister and the babies.

It dawned on me that Lettie wasn't meeting a reporter to pin Frida's murder on Gordon. "You're planning on selling these pictures. What news organization agreed to meet with you?" I demanded.

She mumbled the name of one of the most notorious newspapers out there. Their reputation had dropped so low that the White House Correspondents' Organization had banned their journalists from attending any White House press events.

I reached out my hand to help Lettie back to her feet. "You're going to sell pictures of your own sister and new-born nephews to *a tabloid?*"

Lettie tossed her arms around my neck and burst out sobbing. "They were the only ones who agreed to pay me."

Chapter Thirty

No news at 4:30 a.m. is good.
—CLAUDIA "LADY BIRD" JOHNSON, FIRST LADY OF
THE UNITED STATES (1963–1969)

LETTIE clung to me with her arms wrapped around my shoulders like an exhausted child as I guided her back to the White House. "I'm such a failure, Cathy," she wailed as we entered through the North Portico.

Chief Usher Ambrose Jones stepped out of his office, located next to the front door, to see what the commotion was about. When he spotted Lettie in hysterics, he made haste backtracking to his office and closed the door behind him.

"How can I ever face Mags again?" Lettie released me and turned around and around in the large entrance hall. "She's so perfect. Look at this place. She's the freaking First Lady of the United States. She's never made any mistakes in her life. Not one." Sobbing with renewed vigor, she collapsed against me again.

"That's not true, Lettie. Just this summer Margaret realized she'd been neglecting some of the most important power players in Washington. Her oversight threatened to collapse President Bradley's political support structure from the inside out."

She lifted her head from my damp shoulder. "Really? She did that?"

I nodded. "We all make mistakes. It's the owning up to our mistakes and doing what needs to be done to make it right that defines us, that gives us grace. Are you willing to do that?"

"What has happened?" President Bradley demanded, giving Lettie the perfect opportunity to do the right thing. Dressed in a suit with his tie loosened and his coat draped over his arm, he had a strained expression that made me wonder if this was one more crisis than he was prepared to handle today. Even so, his gait increased in length as he closed the distance between us in the grand entrance hall. "Lettie? What's wrong?"

When his personal secretary surged forward to intercept his sobbing sister-in-law, he waved her off. "I'll take care of this."

"Oh, John, I am so sorry!" Lettie cried.

"Not here," he said and looked genuinely concerned for his wife's sister as he led us into the adjacent Green Room. He took the time to close each of its many doors.

Thomas Jefferson once used the Green Room as a dining room with a green floor covering. James Madison converted the room to a sitting room, which was its use today. In this very room in 1812, Madison signed the nation's first declaration of war. Two years later the British, in retaliation, burned the White House to the ground. And had—apparently—been the reason a priceless treasure had been buried and lost somewhere in the South Lawn.

President Bradley didn't look as if he was thinking about the history of the room with its green silk-covered walls, or how the events that had happened in this very spot two hundred years ago may have led to a very modern murder. He closed his eyes and drew a deep breath. "I've been patient with you," he said to Lettie.

This was a private family moment I had no business witnessing. I tried to quietly move toward the door, but Lettie refused to loosen her grip on my arm.

"I didn't mean to hurt anyone," she whispered, squeezing my arm with bruising strength. "It's just—just that—"

"You've been drinking again," Bradley said not unkindly. Lettie nodded.

"Did it start before or after your troubles at the college and with your marriage?"

"Before." Her voice sounded small, distant. "I—I met . . ."

"Another man, Lettie? Again?" Bradley walked over to gaze into a round gilded mirror hanging on the far wall. "And I suppose you liked to go out drinking with him?"

She pressed her face to my shoulder and started sobbing again. "I didn't mean to. I didn't mean for him to . . . He loaned me money. I don't even remember what I spent it on. But when it was gone, he loaned me more money."

"Not again, Lettie," Bradley said, still gazing into the mirror as if he could wish his problems away. "How much this time?"

"He said that he loved me and didn't need it back right away. But then things changed. He's been threatening to go to the press. I thought that maybe I could use . . ."

Bradley turned away from the mirror. "I don't understand."

Lettie looked to me for help. I nodded encouragingly. This was something she needed to own up to. In halting sentences, she explained to her brother-in-law her money troubles and how she'd planned to sell pictures of his wife and two young babies.

"Do you have the pictures?" He held out his hand.

"Cathy has them," Lettie said.

Without bothering to correct Lettie, I handed the President the folder. He nodded as he looked through the pile of pictures. "These are all very similar to the shots we're going to release to the press tomorrow morning."

Lettie sniffled. "I know. Although I needed the money I didn't want to hurt Mags and her boys. But it seems I've hurt her. And I don't have the money. I've gotten myself into a real pickle, John."

"Yes, you have." He pulled her into his arms and held her

as she cried some more. "But you're family, Lettie. We'll take care of this together. And we'll get you help. I promise. We won't let you face this alone."

Smiling to myself, I started quietly for the door.

"Casey," Bradley whispered over Lettie's shoulder. "Thank you."

I nodded.

NOT TEN FEET OUTSIDE THE GREEN ROOM I RAN into Marcel Beauchamp. His round belly bounced as he followed me across the colonnade in the entrance hall. "Casey, the President, is he in that room? I have a desperate need to speak with him."

"He's busy right now. Perhaps his secretary is still waiting somewhere near here?" I looked around, but the entrance hall was now curiously empty.

"It is most urgent that I get an extension. Monday is impossible. Creativity cannot be rushed," Marcel explained.

"I doubt he'll have time to talk with you," I warned. But he looked so upset, with his round flushed cheeks and quivering brow, I wanted to help him. "Have you spoken with the First Lady's secretary?"

"*Mais oui*, I have. No one in the East Wing understands the artistic process. I'm sure President Bradley, he is a smart man, will give me the additional time. You understand the need for time, do you not? With Gordon, he is to be charged with the murder tomorrow. It must be most troubling to you, with your work to clear his name. Have you found your proof? I overheard you tell the gendarmes that you know how to find the treasure Lettie has been so intent on uncovering. Have you done so? Do you know where the treasure is hidden?"

"Not yet. But I'm close. I hope to have this all resolved tomorrow morning before the DA can bring charges against Gordon."

"Is there anything I may do to help? I could scour the gardens with you for this treasure of yours."

"Thank you, but no. I have—"

"You have your Secret Service lover to help you," he said, apparently not at all concerned I might be embarrassed to discuss my love life (or potential for a love life) with anyone, especially someone I didn't know very well. "No, don't deny it. I see the way he looks at you. And the way you look at him. He will help you unearth this missing treasure of yours, *n'est-ce pas?*"

"You!" Special Agent Steve Sallis shouted as he charged up the stairs and into the entrance hall. "You're in big trouble!"

"Me? I haven't done anything. Not lately," I said.

"Not you, Casey. Him!" Steve grabbed Marcel's arm. "You were supposed to be meeting with the florist."

"Yes, yes. I was with the florist. She and I, we discuss—"

"I don't care if you were solving world hunger. You aren't there now. You can't roam the residence without a proper escort."

"I—I don't . . ." Marcel threw up his hands. "I must do my job. I don't understand why you try to stop me. And you speak too fast. I—I can't understand your—"

"Cut the crap. You understand well enough." Steve waved over a uniformed agent. "Please, see that Mr. Beauchamp finds his way to the gatehouse. Thank you."

Steve was still bristling with anger as he charged back down the stairs to the ground floor.

I followed. The scent of spices and fresh vegetables cooking grew stronger with each step. I inhaled deeply, savoring the symphony of flavors floating in the air. Thanks to the talents of the White House chef, the ground floor smelled like heaven at about this time every evening. "Why are you so mean to Marcel?"

"Because I hate phonies," Steve answered.

"I don't understand. He seems sincere. And a little frightened."

Steve snorted. "He's not even French."

"He isn't?" I asked. "How do you know?"

"It was in the security check, of course. He's Mac Baker

from New Jersey. Not Marcel Beauchamp from Paris. He legally changed his name, but he can't change his past. Everyone in the Secret Service knows he's a fake. A fake who breaks the rules, goes where he's not supposed to be, and then pretends he barely understands a word of English. It's infuriating."

And very, very interesting.

Chapter Thirty-one

*I must make believe very hard now that I am
a different kind of woman,—in some respects,—
not all, thank Heaven.*

—ELLEN WILSON, FIRST LADY OF
THE UNITED STATES (1913–1914)

"**M**Y desk!" I exclaimed when I returned to the grounds office. I don't know why it surprised me to find it like this anymore. Once again every inch of my desk was covered with stacks of file folders and rolled-up schematics.

"Lorenzo, what happened out here? And why just my desk?" I stuck my head into Gordon's office, where Lorenzo had taken up residence. The office was empty. Lorenzo was gone. He must have left for the day.

"What's happened?" Jack rushed into the grounds office only a few seconds behind me. "I heard there was a commotion in the entrance hall involving you and Lettie. Are you okay?"

"I'm okay. My desk isn't." Lorenzo had clearly packed up and left, but not before he'd dumped all of his research on my desk. My poor desk. It was doomed to be in a perpetual state of disorder. I picked up one of the files and recognized it as part of the research Lorenzo had been doing to help us

find the treasure . . . and the real killer. "I can't believe
Lorenzo gave up on Gordon."

"Why would he do that? And what's going on with you
and Lettie? Don't hold out on me, Casey," Jack said.
"What's happening?"

"Hold out on you? What about you? Why didn't you tell
me about Marcel . . . or should I say Mac?"

Jack retreated until he realized what he was doing. He
then pulled me to him and planted his hands on my hips.
"You know I can't talk about what we find in the security
reports. And we're not talking about random visitors to the
White House. You're the one who disappeared after visiting Gordon at the hospital. And then returned with the
First Lady's sister sobbing all over your shoulder." He
caressed my face with his rough thumb. "I'm worried about
you, Casey. What's going on?"

"I got a confession, but not the one I was expecting." I
explained to him what had happened with Lettie. "Although
she might be guilty of many things, murder probably isn't
one of them. But I think I know who killed Frida."

He raised his brows at that. "You do?"

I smiled and nodded.

He stood back and crossed his arms over his chest as he
watched me. "And?"

"Perhaps I shouldn't say anything more until I have
proof. I don't want to—"

"It's Nadeem, isn't it? He knows how to circumvent
security systems. He's shifty. And too interested in getting
cozy with you. I don't like it."

"That's unfair. You don't like it that I'm friendly with
Nadeem, but it's okay for you to have secret meet-ups with
your ex-girlfriend?" The angry words popped out of my
mouth before I could stop them.

"No. It's not fair, but it's how I feel." Jack wrapped his
arms around me. Our bodies fit together like two puzzle
pieces. It would be so easy to sink into his embrace. I lifted
my head. Our lips were just a whisper's distance from

touching. So close I could already taste his tantalizing heat.

I wanted to hold on to this moment and forget all about murder and betrayal and vengeful ex-girlfriends. But Gordon needed me. I had to find the killer before tomorrow afternoon when the DA was going to charge Gordon with the crime.

"We'll talk more about fairness later." I turned away from his tempting lips. And pressed my fingers to his mouth when he tried to follow me. "And no, I don't think Nadeem is involved. But he did give us an important clue. A clue I would have had days ago if you'd told me about Marcel."

I wiggled out of Jack's embrace and started scooping up random file folders from my desk, dropping them on the floor, until I found my computer's keyboard. I typed *HMS Fantome* in the computer's search browser and scanned newspaper headlines until I found the one that matched the article Nadeem had showed us last night. "Here it is," I said and clicked on the link that brought up the full article. "Cowboy Baker." I read the name of the treasure hunter aloud. "I wonder what happened to him. Did he ever get his hands on the treasure he'd found at the bottom of the sea?"

My next web search led me to Cowboy Baker's obituary. I read the article aloud to Jack. Tragically, Cowboy had died with the court case still unresolved. The short obituary spoke of how he'd dedicated his life to finding lost treasures, and that he'd considered the discovery of the *HMS Fantome* to be both his greatest success and most disappointing failure. In his last days he'd become convinced he'd made a mistake and that the most important treasure lost during the British's 1814 march on Washington had never made it onto his sunken ship.

While interesting, that wasn't the reason I'd pulled up the obituary. "Here it is." I tapped the screen. "He is survived by . . ." I scanned the list until I reached the last name. It was tacked on almost as if it was a last-minute addition. ". . . and a son from Cowboy's first marriage, Mac Baker."

"AKA Marcel Beauchamp?" Jack said as he leaned over my shoulder to read the obituary for himself. "You might be onto something here."

I tamped down the excitement that started to bubble in my chest. "It's still too early to contact Manny. Just because he's the treasure hunter's son, perhaps even an estranged son, it doesn't mean he killed Frida."

"It doesn't even mean he jumped on the treasure-hunting crazy wagon," Jack added. "If we have any hope of changing the DA's mind, we need to get proof that Marcel is our guy."

"Which means I still need to force his hand and search for the treasure tomorrow morning. Only, I don't know where to look." I started to dig through the research on my desk. "Why has the treasure remained lost for so many years?"

"Because it doesn't exist? Even if a gardener buried treasure in the lawn before the British attacked, why would he leave it there? Why wouldn't he dig it up as soon as it was safe to do so?"

"Dolley Madison mentioned in her letters that in the confusion following that time, with the rebuilding of the White House and the need to calm the nation, the treasure had been overlooked, forgotten. Dr. Wadsin had sent over some copies of Dolley Madison's letters written in the years right before her death that she thought might help. Where is that folder?"

Jack reached into one of the piles and handed me the file he'd grabbed. "This file?"

My mouth dropped open. "How did you do that?"

He gave me one of his infuriating wouldn't-you-like-to-know looks before admitting, "I remember seeing it on your desk yesterday and just happened to recognize the label."

Jack and I spent the next hour reading the many letters

Dolley Madison had written to friends and family starting in 1844, when Dolley Madison moved back to Washington, D.C. A sad melancholy filled her letters as Dolley reminisced about her life at the White House. She occasionally alluded to searching for a missing item from that time, but never to a treasure.

"Given how deeply in debt she was at the time, barely having enough money for provisions," Jack said, "you'd think she'd be as obsessed with finding lost treasures as you seem to be."

"I agree." As interesting as the letters were, they weren't really helping us. I was about to call it quits when I reached a series of letters written in 1844 between Dolley Madison and Julia Tyler, President John Tyler's new First Lady.

Julia, at twenty-four years old, married John Tyler barely more than a year after his first wife's death and found herself suddenly thrust into the social obligations of First Lady. Dolley Madison provided advice and guidance to the young First Lady. And that's where I found a most unusual request.

In one of the letters, sandwiched between optimal seating arrangements and suggestions for conversation topics, Dolly Madison asked Julia to look for "an item of immeasurable value" that had been lost when the British had destroyed the White House. She noted that she'd recently discovered from someone who knew someone who once knew Thomas McGraw, the White House gardener during Dolley Madison's time, that this "item" might have been buried next to the third tree in Thomas Jefferson's allée of little-leaf linden trees.

"This is it! The clue Frida and our mysterious treasure hunter had used to search for the treasure," I announced as I dug through the rolled-up schematics on my desk for the old South Lawn schematic. I'd marked on the schematic where the allée of lindens had originally been planted.

"But Casey," Jack said as he read through the reply Julia Tyler had sent several weeks later. "She had the gardeners dig up the area, and nothing was found."

"She did?" I chewed the inside of my mouth. It looked as if we'd hit yet another dead end. Perhaps Thomas McGraw stole the treasure. Or perhaps some treasure hunter had found it decades ago. Or perhaps . . .

"Gordon was trying to tell me what happened to the treasure, Jack." My heart pounded like a drum in my chest. "He wasn't confessing. He said the treasure wasn't there. Of course it wasn't there. Many things changed after the White House had been rebuilt. I bet the allée of lindens was relocated."

I dug through the archived schematics Lorenzo had dumped on my desk. He'd been reviewing them to see what, if anything, matched where the most recent holes in the South Lawn had been appearing.

And Lorenzo was right—in 1814 when the treasure would have been buried, that part of the lawn had been . . . just lawn. But when I reviewed a rendering of the South Lawn that showed the location of the gardens and plantings shortly after the White House had been rebuilt, I discovered that Jefferson's allée of little-leaf lindens had been moved.

This new location perfectly matched where we'd found the holes in the lawn . . . and it was nowhere near where Jefferson had planted the original allée.

"No one has found the treasure because everyone has been searching in the wrong place," I said.

"That may be true, but it's flimsy evidence and still won't prove to Manny that Gordon is innocent," Jack warned.

"Which brings us back to my original plan: I need to dig up the treasure. That'll force the killer to act."

"No, Casey. It's too risky."

"Not necessarily. Not if I'm smart about this."

Jack grabbed my hands and pulled me out of my desk chair and into his arms again. "I don't like how you keep talking as if you're on your own. We're in this together."

When I started to protest, he pressed his finger against my lips. "I know you have doubts about my feelings toward you, but you're wrong. I care for you, Casey. More than you can ever know. I die a hundred torturous deaths every time you put your life in danger. Please—"

I kissed him. It seemed to be the only way to get him to stop talking.

Once I caught my breath—Jack was an expert when it came to seducing me with his lips—I explained my plan.

Jack listened and helped refine certain points. And once we were done, even he agreed that nothing could possibly go wrong.

Chapter Thirty-two

*A woman is like a tea bag—you can't tell how
strong she is until you put her in hot water.*
—ELEANOR ROOSEVELT, FIRST LADY OF
THE UNITED STATES (1933–1945)

THE next morning, I arrived at the White House
before sunrise. Save for the distant clank of pots and
pans in the kitchen, the hallways were silent. The quiet
seemed to amplify my jangling nerves as I flipped on the
lights in the grounds office. The fluorescent lights flickered
on, bathing the room in a light that felt too bright for the
predawn hour. Soon the White House would be bursting
with life, but now it felt as if I were in the belly of a sleeping dragon. Waiting.

I finished up my most pressing projects, such as sending
Seth the plans for the rescheduled tree planting, and started
searching again for plants to grow in the founding fathers'
kitchen garden. A depressing task. Much of the rich diver-
sity available to our forefathers to grow in their gardens
was forever lost to us.

According to the large industrial clock hanging over the
office door, Jack should have arrived for duty by now. I
pushed back my desk chair and went searching for him.

I found him in the Palm Room. He was entering the

room from the West Colonnade, and I was entering from the main residence.

Thatch was with him. Both men were dressed in solid black battle dress uniform complete with assault rifles.

"Um, Jack, I was wondering if you had a moment," I said. They looked as if they were getting ready to go on patrol. "I, um, wanted to discuss that project the grounds office is working on."

Of course, Jack, a member of the CAT, would never be the agent to consult with on gardening projects, but I didn't know what else to say.

"You don't have to pretend around me," Thatch said. "I know what you're up to."

"You do?" I cringed, fully expecting him to explode with raging fury.

"I briefed him on our plan this morning," Jack said in the awkward silence that followed. "I had to."

My shoulders dropped. "I understand." I turned around and started back toward the grounds office.

"Where are you going?" Thatch demanded.

"Back to my office."

"Why?" Thatch snapped. "We need to get this started."

"Really?" I whirled back around. "Now?"

"In a minute," Jack said. "Marcel has arrived. He's in the florist shop, but . . ." Both Jack and Thatch listened to their earpieces while I bounced anxiously on the balls of my feet.

"Okay, now we can go. Nadeem has just gone into his office," Thatch said.

"Nadeem?" I said.

"We're simply covering all our bases," Jack said with an easy smile. "Now don't frown like that. You won't be in any danger out there."

"I know." And I also knew there wasn't any way on God's green earth that Nadeem was a killer. But I kept that part to myself.

In advance of when the President or the First Lady visits the South Lawn, the Counter Assault Team moves into position in the bushes with their assault rifles ready for any contingency. That's what Thatch and Jack were doing now.

I waited ten minutes and then headed out to the grounds shed to fetch a shovel. The sky was a dark predawn gray. A light scent of dried leaves hung in the cool air.

A car honked in the distance as I crossed the lawn with the same red-handled shovel the President had used for last Monday's tree planting. I scanned the shadowy bushes, searching for Jack or Thatch. I couldn't find either of them.

I passed the kitchen garden with its empty rows of bare earth. Gordon's friends from the USDA were scheduled to arrive in a few hours to install the hoop houses. I passed the South Fountain, its water making a soothing shushing sound in the still air.

I then pulled out the schematic and paced out where the third tree in the original allée would have been planted.

"This must be the spot," I said aloud, sure that Jack and Thatch were listening.

I thrust my shovel into the ground. As I dug, the leaves on the nearby trees trembled as if someone was moving through them. I glanced up, but saw only long predawn shadows. My heart thudded heavily in my chest as I waited for Marcel to make his presence known.

I took comfort knowing Jack and Thatch were hidden somewhere out there, ready to spring to action at the first sign of danger.

The digging was slow going. I had to break through several thick roots. But then, when I thrust the shovel in the ground again, there was a thud.

Not the thunk of a water line. But a wooden thud.

I put the shovel down and, kneeling, reached into the hole. I used a trowel to dig around the dirt-encased wooden box in order to break it free from the two hundred years of packed earth and roots. I had to lie flat on my stomach to get a good grip on the box in the hole. It wasn't small. About two feet across and about a foot wide. And firmly wedged under a fat root.

I felt rather than saw the shadowy figure emerge from

the underbrush to stand behind me. I pretended not to notice him and continued to pull and tug at the stubborn box. The shadow knelt beside me, reached into the hole, and helped me lift the wooden casket from the earth. "It's heavy," he said. "And larger than I'd expected."

I pushed up from the ground to crouch next to the box and the man holding it. "Nadeem! What are you doing out here?" I demanded, but his eyes were glued to the treasure chest.

"It's not so heavy that it could be packed with gold, though," he said as he caressed the dirt-encrusted box's rough surface. "Do you think we'll find diamonds?"

"I don't know," I said. "What are you doing out here?"

He fingered the corroded latch. "Frida would have killed to be here right now, to take the glory." He paused. "It's ironic and a little sad that she was killed because of this, don't you agree?" He finally lifted his gaze to meet mine.

"What are you doing here?" I asked for a third time.

"You didn't think you could keep me away, Casey? Not after everything I did for you, everything I went through." He struggled with the corroded latch again. "Now let's crack this box open and see what's inside."

"You need to leave," I said quietly. Marcel wouldn't make an appearance with Nadeem practically sitting on top of the treasure chest. "You need to leave now. I'm—"

That had been the wrong thing to say to the assistant curator.

He dropped the wooden casket and swung toward me. "*I have to leave?*" He grabbed my shoulders. His voice tightened. "I put up with that damn woman as she belittled my work, and then as soon as I'd turned my back, she stole my notes. *My* notes. Sure, she was brilliant. She was a *brilliant* thief. I was the one who started to wonder about those letters Dolley Madison had written. They'd been in the archives for centuries. And no one cared to look at them. Not until I arrived. And the moment I find something interesting, Frida locks up the filing cabinet and tells me to mind my own business." In his frustration, he shook me. "And now you're telling me that I have no business being here?"

Jack burst from the bushes with his gun drawn. "Let go of Casey. Now!"

Instead of doing as he was told, Nadeem's fingers tightened on my arms.

Mike Thatch burst out of the bushes from the other side, his finger on the trigger of his gun. "Put your hands in the air."

Nadeem glared at me. "You set me up?" His fingers dug painfully into my arms.

"You're bruising me," I said just as Jack swung the butt of his assault rifle and knocked Nadeem unconscious.

I jumped to my feet. "Why'd you hit him?"

"Because you'd never forgive me if I shot him," Jack said as he secured Nadeem's wrists with plastic zip ties.

"But he didn't confess." The treasure forgotten, I started to pace. "He didn't even give us any clues to what happened on Monday. You should have waited."

"He was about to hurt you," Jack said.

"He was a threat," Thatch agreed as he helped haul Nadeem, who was already semi-awake, to his feet.

"I'm not a threat. Casey, tell them." Nadeem slurred his words. "I'm not a threat."

"Tell that to Manny," Jack said as he unceremoniously marched Nadeem up the hill toward the White House. "You have a lot to answer for, including Frida's murder. You have one hell of a motive there, buddy."

The sun was just starting to lighten the sky as Thatch and I stood side by side staring at the wooden casket I'd unearthed.

"Because of a box, Nadeem killed Frida?" Thatch nudged the wooden box with his toe. "Do you even know what's inside it?"

I shook my head. None of this made any sense.

Where was Marcel?

"Come on, I have work to do." Thatch bent down and

picked up the box. "Not too heavy. Can't be gold," he said, echoing Nadeem's earlier comment.

Thatch carried the casket to the grounds office and dropped the filthy piece of history on my desk. He then put a hand on my shoulder. "Don't worry so much. I'm sure Manny will be able to get this sorted out. What we saw this morning should, if nothing else, delay the DA's action against Gordon. And it should convince the envoy from Turbekistan that it's safe to meet with the President. Heck, we can show Aziz that we have not one, but two suspects in custody. Gordon and Nadeem. Not only that, your dad has been wining and dining Aziz for several days now. Apparently, the two men worked together years ago on bringing down the Berlin Wall. He's an amazing man, your father. And the only guy Aziz would talk with. So don't worry, everything is working out."

So that was the Calhoun whom Aziz had wanted to talk with? I was starting to wonder if I was the only one in D.C. who didn't know about my dad or that he was in town.

And none of that mattered. Not really. I paced the length of my office. What mattered was Gordon. Whoever killed Frida—*Nadeem?*—had made sure all the evidence pointed to Gordon. And nothing we'd done this morning counteracted that.

We needed a confession. I dropped into my desk chair. My stomach clenched as I stared at the box. Because of this hunk of dirt and wood, Gordon may go to jail for a crime he didn't commit.

Everything about this morning just felt . . . wrong.

I dug around in the desk's top drawer until I found a digital camera. The curator's office should be in charge of opening the box, but since Frida was dead and Nadeem was in custody, I supposed it wouldn't hurt if I pried the lid open. But before I did that, I thought I should take some pictures to document the outside of the box. And the opening process.

Once I'd finished taking pictures from every angle, I rattled the old brass lock. It was encrusted with two hundred years of dirt and corrosion. Even if I had a key, I doubted it would work. I dug around in my desk drawer again, searching for something I could use to pry the lock open.

"Do you need a knife?"

I whirled my desk chair around just as Marcel—or should I say Mac, since he no longer feigned a French accent—stepped into the room. The large messenger bag slung over his shoulder bounced off his hip.

"You!" I lunged for the phone. I managed to get my hand on the receiver and off the hook, but Marcel moved with amazing speed for the amount of weight he carried on his body. He used that weight to slam me back into my desk chair. His leather-gloved hand slapped across my mouth before I could scream.

From his jacket pocket he produced that dirty handkerchief I had seen several days earlier and stuffed it into my mouth and slapped a pre-cut piece of tape on it. Before I had a chance to react, he had pulled out a roll of duct tape and had taped my wrists to the desk chair's armrests and my ankles to the rolling chair's center support, wrapping the duct tape layer upon layer to keep me from being able to pull free. I twisted and turned, kicked and wiggled to no avail while he locked the office door.

"Now, let's see what we have here." Marcel stuck his knife in the casket's corroded latch. "Don't look so surprised, Casey. I know you and your lover planned this morning's outing to trap me. But everyone underestimates poor, bumbling Marcel, *n'est-ce pas?*" He played up his false French accent for only a moment. "Who do you think tipped off Nadeem about the treasure? I did! I sent the lovesick fool running to your side. Pretty clever of me, don't you think?"

Marcel twisted the knife's blade against the lock. With a *crack*, the old brass latch broke. He set his messenger bag on the desk next to the box and opened it. Clearly, he meant to walk out of the White House with the treasure in that bag. His mouth twisted into an odd grin as he pried loose the wood lid, swollen from the rains, and opened the box.

"I have your treasure, Dad," he said, beaming up at the ceiling with a look of triumph. "I didn't let anyone get it. Mom was wrong. She should have never let you leave us. Because here it is. It's yours. It's all—"

He froze as he stared into the box.

I leaned forward, straining against the tape holding my arms in place, trying to look inside the box.

"What's this?" he picked up the box and tossed its muddy contents at me. What landed on my lap and spilled over onto the floor wasn't gold or diamonds or pearls . . . but parchment sleeves.

"What have you done?" He moved with lightning speed as he swung out his thick arm and slapped me across my face. "Is this a joke?"

I blinked furiously, trying to tell him that it was no joke. Knowing how much Thomas Jefferson loved his gardens, I should have known envelopes of seeds would be his treasure. And oh, what a treasure it was! Not that the seeds were viable anymore. But the packets holding them were elegantly illustrated with color renderings of each plant along with written descriptions and their Latin names. And all of this had been done by Thomas Jefferson's own hand? It was a treasure more wonderful than anything I could ever have imagined, truly priceless.

Clearly, Marcel didn't agree. He pressed the steak knife to my throat. Its razor-sharp blade bit into my skin. "Where is the treasure?"

I don't know how he expected me to answer with this sour-tasting gag in my mouth. He seemed to realize the problem. "If you scream, I'll slice open your throat. Do you understand?"

I nodded.

He removed the tape and dirty handkerchief. And stared at me.

"Why?" I whispered. "You have a successful career. Why are you doing this?"

"It's my father's legacy. His dream. He abandoned his

family and ultimately died in search of this treasure. This *worthless* treasure. I had to do something, something to prove to him that he shouldn't have left me. If he had stayed, I would have found his treasure. You wouldn't understand."

Wouldn't I? I'd lived most of my life without a father, and still his presence haunted me. What if I had done something differently? What if I'd been a better daughter? Perhaps then he wouldn't have run away. Perhaps then my mother would still be alive.

Those ghosts turned round and round in our heads. Never letting up. Never letting go.

I suppose my penchant for sticking my nose into trouble could be considered a kind of madness.

But I never felt the pull to kill anyone.

"Is that why you pretended to be someone else?" I asked. "So no one would suspect you?"

He looked confused by my question. "Oh, you mean Marcel." He put on his French accent like some people don a hat. "*Mon Dieu*. That fool, he was my ticket into the designer world. No one would hire *Mac from New Jersey*. But Marcel from the fashionable *Paris* is a natural, *non?* Where is the treasure most magnificent? Tell me before I am forced to kill you."

I glanced at the clock on the wall. Lorenzo should be arriving any minute.

"It's—" I started to say when the doorknob shook.

"Casey?" Lorenzo called out. The door shook. "What's wrong with the door?"

"Don't answer him," Marcel rasped.

"What are you going to do?" I whispered back. "That's Lorenzo. This is his office, too. He's not going away."

"Casey!" Lorenzo pounded on the door.

Marcel seemed to hold his breath, waiting. I discovered I was holding my breath, too.

Much to my disappointment, Lorenzo did give up. Silence seemed to press against my ears. Marcel whirled back toward me. He pressed the knife to my throat again.

"I have to get out of here. And sorry, Casey, but you know too much." The blade dug deeper into my neck. I felt a hot trail of blood as it dripped down my neck.

"Wait!" I needed to stop him. "The treasure. You're right. It was gold. We dug it up last night. Right after you left. This old box, it's just a decoy. The real treasure is in Gordon's office. It's under his desk. You can fill your bag and get out before anyone is the wiser."

His gold-flecked eyes glittered with madness. "In Gordon's office."

"Under his desk," I said, careful not to move my head with that knife too close to my neck's important arteries.

"Thanks, but unfortunately, I'm still going to have to kill you."

Oh, no he wasn't. As soon as he lifted the blade from my neck in order to make a slashing motion, I gave a hard jerk to the left side on the chair. It tipped up onto two wheels and then dropped again. I jerked hard to the left again.

This time the desk chair toppled over. Marcel's blade nicked my neck right before I landed hard on the concrete floor.

I shouted at the top of my lungs while wiggling like mad, desperate to break free from my restraints. My foot popped out of its shoe and sock and was suddenly loose. I used the opening to kick Marcel hard in the knee.

He cried out in pain. As I kicked him again, the door splintered open.

Jack and the rest of the Counter Assault Team came pouring into the grounds office. They moved like a tidal wave, washing over Marcel, disarming him, and pulling him to the ground.

"Oh God, Casey! Her neck's been cut." Jack dropped to his knees beside me, his face going pale. "Get the doctors in here. Now!" He pressed his hands against my neck.

"Jack, I'm fine. It's a scratch." He didn't listen. "I'm not bleeding to death, but the arm of my chair is digging into my side. Can you cut me loose?"

He tentatively lifted his hand. "The bleeding is slowing. Are you sure you're okay?"

I nodded. "I will be as soon as I'm no longer taped to this chair."

He used the same steak knife Marcel had used to threaten me and sliced through the layers of duct tape. As soon as I was freed from the desk chair, Jack pulled me into his arms and hugged me so tightly I heard my ribs creak. "I love you, Casey. I love you so much it hurts."

I drew a long breath. This was the Jack I knew . . . and trusted. He never lied. He would never try and hurt me. I wanted Jack in my life. I drew in another deep breath.

He was waiting for me to tell him how I felt. "Uh, Jack, there is something I've been wanting to tell you."

"Yes?" he said.

Like removing a bandage, I told myself and took a deep breath. "I, um—" I screwed my eyes closed and said with a rush, "I love you, too, Jack. I do. I really do."

When I opened my eyes, I found Jack smiling at me. "See, that wasn't so hard to say," Jack said. And then with all his buddies watching, he kissed me silly.

THE SUREST WAY TO SCARE YOUR RELATIVES IS to have your face show up on the evening news. Since I dearly loved my grandmother and aunts and had no desire to frighten them, as soon as Dr. Stan had stitched up my neck and Manny had finished taking my statement, I dialed the number to Rosebrook.

While Grandmother Faye listened and my aunts babbled questions in the background, I told her all about the excitement we'd faced at the White House and she in turn relayed what I'd told her to Aunt Willow and Aunt Alba.

"Goodness gracious, child, trouble has always beat a path to your doorstep. You weren't terribly hurt?" she asked when I'd finished.

"Of course not."

Jack, who had stayed by my side the entire time, squeezed my hand.

"Um, there is something else I need to tell you." I took a deep breath. "It's about James Calhoun."

"What about him?" Grandmother Faye's voice grew tight with worry. I could picture her timeworn fingers closing around the plain golden cross necklace she always wore.

"He's living in D.C. He contacted me the other day." I told her about his service to the nation, about why my mother had died, and the secret life my father had lived. "Even today, he made sure the President's meeting with an oil-rich country went forward. I—I thought you should know."

Grandmother Faye fell silent.

"What's happening?" Aunt Willow shouted onto the line. "Mama dropped the phone. And she's crying. I've only ever seen her cry one other time. And that was when she'd learned about you."

"I told her about my dad, that he's—"

"Oh Lordy, he's dead, isn't he?" Aunt Willow cried. "I knew it. He's been dead for years. He would have called Mama if he could. But he's dead. Poor Jimmy. Poor Mama, she never gave up on that boy."

"He's not dead," I said. "He's living in D.C. And he contacted me."

"He did? Did you see him? You'll bring him home," Aunt Willow implored. "You must bring him home."

"You mean to Rosebrook?"

"For Thanksgiving. It would be such a relief to see that little squirt again."

I'd been so wrapped up in my grief that I'd forgotten how deeply my two aunts missed their younger brother. A younger brother no one ever talked about. The only picture of him in the house was a black-and-white snapshot of a roly-poly toddler, which Grandmother Faye kept hidden in a bedside table drawer.

I don't know when or why he left home or what they

thought had happened to him. That was a mystery still waiting to be uncovered.

"Please, Casey. It would mean the world to Mama." How could I say no to my family? But at the same time how could I commit to facing him again?

"I'll see what I can do," was the best I could promise. Even so, my stomach twisted into a knot.

"And Jack?" Willow added. "You'll bring your hunky Secret Service agent home as well?"

"I don't know. If he's not working, he'll probably want to spend the holiday with his brothers. They could use the together time to disinfect their house."

"My brothers are on their own with that house," Jack whispered in my ear. He twined his fingers with mine. "Wherever you go, I want to go, too. If you'll have me."

Chapter Thirty-three

"**G**ORDON! What are you doing here?" I exclaimed as our beloved head gardener ambled into the grounds office.

Although he was using a cane and walking much slower than usual, his cheeks had a ruddy glow and his eyes sparkled with mischief. "I work here," he answered.

It had only been three weeks since we caught Frida's killer and two weeks since Gordon was released from the hospital. With Marcel's confession and subsequent arrest, Gordon had been completely cleared of the crime. Since he didn't have a murder charge to worry about, Gordon was supposed to focus on rehab and on his recovery, and nothing else, for at least another month.

I jumped up from my chair with such speed the pile of Jefferson seed packets I'd been studying scattered onto the floor. I didn't care. I rushed across the room and wrapped my arms around our beloved head gardener. "Of course you work here."

"Does Deloris know where you've gone?" Lorenzo

asked as he joined us at the door. He patted Gordon on the shoulder as a broad smile transformed his usual gloomy expression.

"Bah! Deloris! That old woman is a nag. I can't breathe in that house. I had to get out. So I talked with Ambrose. He and I agreed that I should come in for a few hours two or three days a week. I'm calling it my sanity breaks."

"I'm thrilled to see you. But the holiday . . ." It was a few days before Thanksgiving. My bags were packed and stashed in the corner. Jack and I were planning to drive straight to the airport after work.

"I'll still be here when you come back," Gordon assured me with a chuckle. "How's Nadeem doing? He's not still angry that you dug up a historical artifact without him, is he?"

"Being appointed head curator seems to have cheered him up," I said. "He's been keeping to himself, though, spending most of his time cataloging and organizing documents."

"Turns out Frida's filing skills were even worse than Casey's," Lorenzo added. "But he seems to be a good guy to work with."

Neither Lorenzo nor Gordon knew about Nadeem's clandestine background. The ex-spy still lived in the basement apartment of my building and, I was sure, was still keeping watch of my comings and goings for my dad. But on the whole, I agreed with Lorenzo's assessment. It seemed like Nadeem was one of the good guys.

"Sorry to interrupt the happy reunion," Jack said as he joined us in the grounds office. After shaking Gordon's hand and telling him how good he looked, Jack turned to me. "There's a woman at the gate insisting that she needs to speak with you, Casey. The guards were going to send her away, but I happened to see that she wanted to give you this."

He handed me a velum envelope that looked identical to the ones found in Jefferson's treasure chest. Only this one didn't contain any seeds. A beautiful rendering of a purple pepper had been drawn on the envelope along with a variety name I didn't recognize.

"She had this?" I asked. "I need to talk with her. Is she still out there?"

The days were gradually turning colder. The morning air smelled of winter. Jack and I crossed the North Lawn to the large white hut that stood at the northwest gate.

"She's over there." The uniformed guard pointed to an elderly woman dressed in a blue gingham dress and an oversized tan barn jacket. Her short silver hair and pinched face made her look like a pixie masquerading in human clothes.

As soon as I passed through the gate, she hurried over to meet up with me. "You're the lady from the TV," she said.

"I'm Casey Calhoun. An assistant gardener here." I held out the seed packet that Jack had given me. "Where did you get this?"

"That packet of seeds has been in my family for countless years." She drew a deep breath as if giving herself time to gather her thoughts. "I'm Katie McGraw, and where those came from has been a mystery that has been handed down from generation to generation. It started with my ancestor, Thomas McGraw. He died of natural causes in 1814. Family lore says he died of a broken heart after seeing the White House's burnt shell. I don't know if that's true. But the story of how he came to have that"—she pointed to the velum envelope—"if it was ever really known, has been lost. All my father knew was that one day *it would be time*. I never understood what he had meant by that, but I stayed faithful. I cared for my family's legacy exactly as I'd been instructed. And then I saw the article in the newspaper. I saw the picture of the seeds in their envelopes that you found buried on these grounds. And I finally knew what old Thomas had meant for us to do."

"What did he want you to do?" I asked.

"He wanted us to return the treasure."

"T-Treasure?" I stumbled on my words. Thomas McGraw had been in charge of hiding Jefferson's treasure for Dolley

Madison when the British had invaded D.C. He'd buried the casket of seeds . . . seeds that had sadly been forgotten. Forgotten, because he had tragically died? Was there more to the treasure than the seeds? Was there also the gold that Marcel had been so desperate to find?

"I was mighty glad when I saw the article, ma'am." The corners of Katie's eyes crinkled as she gave me a wan smile. "I have no children to carry on after me. And I'm old and tired. The task of caring for the treasure grows more difficult with the passing of every year. Now the treasure can finally be returned to its rightful home."

KATIE MCGRAW GAVE ME THE DIRECTIONS TO her home. She'd written them down. So I knew we were in the right place.

"This can't be right," Lorenzo said as the White House van bounced down·a badly pitted gravel drive with small trees growing up through the stones.

When Lorenzo and Gordon had heard about Katie and her mysterious treasure, they both insisted on coming along with me. The three of us were crowded in the van's front bench seat, but it felt good—right, even—to have Gordon with us, like we were a team again.

Even Lorenzo smiled as he continued to find fault with everything I did.

The overgrown drive took us up to a modest and dilapidated house. Paint was peeling off the siding. A large crack bisected a front bay window. "No one lives here," Lorenzo said just as old Katie McGraw emerged from around the back of the house.

"All the McGraws have lived here," Katie explained as she led us to the backyard. "It's just me now. And the upkeep of the home and the gardens has become too much for me to handle. I'm afraid I'm letting old Thomas down."

"You won't have to worry about that any longer," Gordon said as he made slow progress around the side of the house. "We'll help you with the maintenance."

We all followed Katie into a large backyard that gently sloped down to the Potomac River. A cool wind blew off the water. Geese called out to one another in the distance.

Katie spread her skinny arms wide. "I give you the treasure."

Tears filled my eyes when I saw it.

It wasn't gold or pearls, but plants. Wonderful, wonderful vegetable plants that everyone had believed forever lost. I wandered up and down the rows and rows of plants, finding variety after variety that had long been thought extinct. Everywhere I looked, I found the plants that Thomas Jefferson had so painstakingly illustrated on the envelopes he'd used to store his treasure trove of seeds.

Not knowing or questioning why their ancestor had made them promise to keep this living treasure alive, the McGraws had carefully cultivated and saved the seeds from Thomas Jefferson's treasure for nearly two hundred years. It was truly a wondrous sight to behold.

"Thomas McGraw must have taken a few seeds out of each envelope and carried them home with him in the envelope you have," I told Katie.

"I was told old Thomas believed these plants were special and that we needed to keep growing them and saving the seeds until the time came to return them to their rightful owners. I'm starting to think he was waiting for the White House to be rebuilt, but he died before that could happen." She led us inside the house and into a small kitchen. She opened the refrigerator door to reveal Mason jar after Mason jar of carefully harvested and packed seeds.

"Oh, he was right," I said, clutching my hands to my chest. "These seeds *are* special."

"This is indeed a priceless treasure," Gordon said with awe, his face lit in the dim light of the refrigerator. "Priceless."

"THERE'S JUST ONE MORE THING I NEED TO do," I told Jack when I returned to the White House that afternoon. I think he understood what I meant to do since he didn't ask any questions when I asked if he could drive me to the Mansion on O Street. He'd also offered to come inside with me, but I figured this was something I had to face on my own.

Once again the friendly woman at the door led me to the parlor while she went to find her favorite lodger, James Calhoun. Not long afterward, the floor-to-ceiling bookcase slid open. And the harmless protestor limped out from behind the wall.

"I feared I'd never see you again," he said and suddenly looked away. "I'm glad I was wrong. I heard you captured Frida's killer, recovered Thomas Jefferson's treasure, and helped save the President's oil deal with Turbekistan."

"I heard *you* might have had a hand in that last part," I said.

One of his gray bushy brows quivered. "I'm just an old man."

"We both know that's not true." And I wasn't there to pick an argument. "I told Grandmother Faye and your sisters about you."

"You did?" He hobbled toward the door as if he feared he'd need a quick escape route.

I crossed my arms over my chest. "They want you to come home for Thanksgiving."

"Is that what *you* want?" He tilted his head to the side as if trying to read my expression.

"Those women mean the world to me. I want them to be happy."

The corner of his mouth twitched as he seemed to consider my request. Finally he drew a long breath. "I suppose I want that, too."

"Then you'd better pack your bags. The plane leaves in two hours."

I CLIMBED INTO THE FRONT PASSENGER SEAT of Jack's beat-up, gas-guzzling Jeep while Jack plotted on a map the fastest route to the airport. My heart hammered in my chest just as wildly as it had when I'd dug up the South Lawn in search of Jefferson's treasure.

I was going home.

My father took the seat directly behind me and pulled the door closed with the stealth of a master spy. I had no idea where the relationship with my father was going to lead. But whether I liked it or not, he was back in my life. He was family. And I supposed I owed him a second chance. If not for myself, for Grandmother Faye's sake.

After Jack stashed the map, he took my hand and brushed a kiss burning with promises against my knuckles. "Ready?" he asked.

With Jack sitting by my side, and my dad in the back-seat, we were all headed home to Rosebrook . . . and to a world of new possibilities.

"I'm ready," I said.

Tips from Casey's
Fall Gardener's Notebook

Grow the Tops of Your Carrots

This is a quick and fun gardening project that anyone can do. When you are preparing your fresh carrots, cut off the top of the carrot (about a half inch will do). Remove all but a few small leaves from the top.

Fill a glass or bowl with water. Set the carrot in the water so that it is partially submerged.

Place the glass or bowl in a sunny window. Change the water every few days. In a few weeks the carrot will sprout roots and new leaves will grow.

Plant the rooted carrot in a pot or in your garden.

You won't grow new carrots from the plants, but swallowtail butterflies will enjoy feeding off the nectar from the flowers.

Grow the Bottoms of Your Onions

Did you know you can grow a new onion from just the bottom part with the roots? Well, you can! Here's a fun gardening project to try.

Cut off the bottom of your onion, the part with the dried roots. Leave about an inch to an inch and a half of onion with the roots.

Dry for a couple of days in a well-ventilated area. This will allow it to form a callus and help prevent it from rotting.

You can get the roots started by soaking them in water for a few days. (It's fun to watch.) Or plant the onion root-side-down in a pot or directly in the ground, burying it about a half-inch deep. Within a few weeks the onion will sprout.

About the Author

A lover of puzzles and perhaps a bit too nosy about other people's lives, Dorothy St. James lives a charmed life at the beach just outside Charleston, South Carolina, with her sexy sculptor husband.

She earned her bachelor of science degree in aquaculture, fisheries, and wildlife biology from Clemson University's School of Agriculture and her master's degree in public administration from the University of Charleston with an emphasis on environmental urban planning. Most recently, she gained entrance into the highly competitive Master Gardener program run by Clemson University.

Dorothy has put her educational experience to use, having worked in all branches and all levels of government including local, regional, state, and federal. She even spent time during college working for a nonprofit environmental watchdog organization. She's a tried-and-true career bureaucrat who intimately witnessed the democratic process at work. And she hasn't gone screaming into the marshes . . . yet.